ONE WINTER

ONE WINTER

Tom Davies

Foreword by Don Dale-Jones
Cover painting by Chris Griffin

Published with the financial support
of the Welsh Books Council.

ISBN: 0-86381-947-8

Cover design: Sian Parri
Cover images: 'Welsh Chapel 1', Chris Griffin

New edition published in 2004
by Gwasg Carreg Gwalch, Llanrwst.

This book is for my three boys,
Julian, Steffan and Nathan
to remind them who they are,
where they came from
and what they should be proud of.

FOREWORD
by Don Dale-Jones

Almost exactly one hundred years ago a young blacksmith, Evan Roberts, took a group of people into the back room of a small chapel in West Wales. He locked the door and called on the Holy Spirit to come and work in their midst. Next morning the first converts of a great religious revival stumbled out, red-eyed, into a new dawn.

What followed in that winter of 1904 has been described as the greatest event in the history of twentieth century Wales. As Roberts travelled around with his small group of lady-singers, crime ceased, prisons emptied, drunkards sobered up and long-standing debts were repaid. In the mines, services were conducted underground with lamps held aloft as hymns of love went gusting down the roadways.

That Christmas strange flashing lights were reported, a chapel-cleaner at Ynysybwl saw a vision, apparitions hovered over Bala Lake and meteors flashed above Ynys Môn. A small, insecure, imaginative nation was renewing its love-affair with its Maker.

Roberts told his packed congregations of God's love, as a tide of evil threatened, for a nation whose time had come. Wounds would be healed, Wales would march forward to a brilliant destiny.

How wrong he was.

This novel, first published twenty years ago as *One Winter of the Holy Spirit* and now republished to celebrate the centenary of that turbulent winter of 1904, is the tragedy of two lovers fatally at odds: the socialist cockle-picker and the beautiful young chapel-singer seeking redemption for past mistakes.

It dramatises how Wales and the world have changed. The Revival is long past; the shame of bearing an illegitimate child long gone; Wales no longer dominates rugby as in the Edwardian era (when they took six and tied one of the thirteen championship titles and were the only side to defeat the All Blacks in 1905). Yet the Welsh character remains rich and the running of true love is no less important and certainly no smoother than it was then. Socialism, rival of the Revival, divider of the book's main protagonists and on the way up in 1904, however, is down and out now, albeit somewhat less in Wales than in the rest of the Kingdom.

Tom Davies gives a memorable impression of Wales, from the slate-quarries of the north:

> The 2,000 foot high work face pocked and terraced by a century of quarrying; the slashed rocks cut sheer by saws and drills, the gaping black galleries burrowed into the sides of the cliffs, the giant yellow gantries . . .

to the 'colourless, brutalizing world' of the Valleys

> with zinc baths hanging on nails in gardens strewn with dead marigolds; outside wooden lavatories too cold to sit on by night and too hot and smelly by day . . . ;

from the violence of the rugby field:

> Another penalty followed another foul and the ball was kicked straight into touch. In the ensuing line-out elbows went jabbing into ribs and, as the winger hoisted the ball into the air . . . a hand was stamped on, a wrist bent in a direction it was not built to move in and a rogue elbow smashed into a nose.

to the free market slavery of Tiger Bay:

> a flourishing slum teeming with rag-pickers, maimed miners, skittle sharks, ticket-of-leave men and child beggars. Chinese sat on steps in the billowing steam of their laundries. Arab tribesmen were playing pitch and toss with ruffians from Los Angeles . . . A mangy dog was sniffing around the heels of a sailor long gone mad and, straight through these milling hordes walked a tall African man, naked from the waist up and carrying a plank on his head.

The story begins on the sands of Pen-clawdd, where Michael Evans scratches a living as a cockle-picker. He loves 'the flatness of the marsh and the sheer emptiness of the sands . . . space, and high winds which flung their dangerous passions around his home village of Pen-clawdd'. Here he meets and falls in love with the beautiful, vulnerable nurse, Beth Williams, whose illegitimate daughter has been disposed of to a childless couple in Cardiff.

When Evan Roberts begins his Revival, Beth, with her fine singing-voice, joins his choir. Michael, whose panacea is Socialism, is in the congregation, arms folded, immune to religious enthusiasm. The story which unfolds is a kind of roller-coaster revival itself – we laugh almost as often as we weep, are raised up only to be cast down.

There is a strong cast of supporting characters: Dan Roberts, cured of blindness by his brother to become the detached, efficient manager of the Revival, whose resemblance to a troupe of travelling players is in no sense accidental; Annie Davies, heart-stopping contralto and merciless mimic; W.T.Stead, the original muck-raking journalist whose overheated reports were largely responsible for much of the hysteria Evan Roberts generated.

Most striking of the lesser characters is 'A stumpy man wearing a large black felt hat with a floppy brim . . . He had dark bulbous eyes and a lantern jaw which he occasionally moved around pugnaciously. The front of his cape was streaked with cigarette ash, and, in his fat hand, he was carrying a battered leather bag.' This is Dr Enoch Jenkins, the articulate and humorous local G.P., known as Jenko. His consulting-room is the bar, his fees are paid by the pint. He becomes an indispensable part of the plot, a kind of Chorus. Tom Davies says that the character was given to him by the writer and broadcaster, Gwyn Thomas, a neighbour when he was writing the book: 'Jenko is my memorial to a fine man,' he says. 'I wanted to make dear Gwyn live again.'

This compulsively readable story moves inevitably to a dramatic conclusion which the reader finds as hard to bear as it is inevitable. A national literary critic who read it on a beach in Sweden declared that it quite ruined his holiday.

Married, with three sons, Tom Davies lives in a former coastguard tower at Penarth. His sixteen books, all with spiritual themes, include accounts of pilgrimages to the major shrines of Europe, theology, biography and three more novels set in Wales: 'Fire in the Bay' (Cardiff between the Wars), 'Black Sunlight' (the Rhondda miners' struggle to save their pit) and 'The Secret Sex Life of Polly Garter' based on Caitlin and Dylan Thomas's life at New Quay during World War Two when 'Under Milk Wood' was forming itself in Dylan's mind.

Tom's 'Merlyn the Magician and the Pacific Coast Highway', shortlisted for the Thomas Cook Travel Award, was said by 'Bono', front-man of U2, to have transformed his life by converting him to cycling as both exercise and an aid to spirituality. 'Stained Glass Hours' won the Winifred Mary Stanford Prize for best book on a spiritual theme.

Tom is working on a long memoir, 'Mirror Man', the story of his philosophy and its origins. 'We are nothing more than the personal genealogy of our ideas,' he maintains, 'and I'm trying to work out which films, books and plays mine came from. We are created in the image and ideas of others, and those who read my story will, I hope, discover more of themselves than of me. I believe this to be a revolution in the art of memoir and a complete explanation of our predicament today.'

But 'One Winter' remains his favourite: not only was it his first novel, but its love-story mirrors a relationship which caused him severe pain: 'I fell for a girl who'd had an illegitimate child and, perhaps in the shadow of the Chapel, couldn't get her life back. Writing it into a novel is a great way of handling pain because then the anguish doesn't seem to have been for nothing.' He was so moved by the story of Evan Roberts that he lived in the area for more than a year, interviewed people who remembered him and often sat quietly in deserted chapels while his imagination recreated the flame and flood of those passionate meetings at which Wales was, if only briefly, re-born.

'I've had my own tussles with God. I was dramatically and painfully converted myself, in Malaya when I was teaching there,' he says. 'I was working on a violent and perverted book when God threw me against a wall and said he was getting fed up with people like me undermining his world. In a way I've always looked on Evan Roberts as my Godfather: when a college-friend, Elfryn Lewis, told me his story, I knew I had to write it. However doubtful his sanity, Evan Roberts turned me from a journalist into a writer and made me whatever it is that I am.

'Today, torn apart in so many insidious ways by an evil and corrupt media, we need another period of spiritual renewal. That Welsh winter of 1904 shows that God is always prepared to give us another chance. Is there, at this centenary of our last Revival, another prophet in Wales who can channel the Holy Spirit and save us again?'

D.M. Dale-Jones

What they said about it . . .

'Socialism, revivalism and rugby bounce off one another throughout this fascinating novel set in the Gower. The chapels are packed, homes divided and passions running high. Descriptions are vivid and the same raw power permeates the whole story. The old Welsh blend of poetry and brutality, tenderness and tragedy, flesh and spirit, cries out as much in the local Ebenezer chapel as it does in the Pen-clawdd bedroom, or the terraces at Cardiff Arms Park.'

Radio Four

'Opposites attract but the love of a happy-go-lucky cockle-picker Michael Evans for the devout and beautiful Beth Williams is fated to prove a torment for both. Beth is the most fervent revivalist in all preacher Evan Roberts' flock, touring Wales in search of converts, while Michael is a true cynic, whose mockery of religious hysteria cuts Beth to the heart. A sense of impending disaster hangs over this compelling – and often funny – story by an author with a wonderful ear for the rhythms of Welsh speech.'

Sunday Telegraph

'One Winter is an absorbing story of a young woman who is first to join the worshippers of a revival and the man who is the first to condemn them, two people in love, but tragically at odds. A well-told tale against an authentic background, impeccably researched, pounding with the atmosphere of the mass hysteria that prevailed until the movement's final breakdown.'

Llandudno Advertiser

'One of the most talked-about novels of the year set in the 1904 revival when Evan Roberts summoned people away from their pubs and beer to hymn-singing and the chapels. Since its original publication Tom Davies has been sent letters and cuttings from people whose parents were at those stormy meetings including a set of marked cards which one card sharp renounced after seeing the light. Most of the letters were complaints about the sad ending which was to make Tom Davies even sadder (and poorer) since two American publishers made substantial offers to publish it in America if he would tack on a happy end. Which he would not.'

Western Mail

'One Winter is a fiction set against a factual background in and around Pen-clawdd, its village life, marsh scenery and seascape being memorably portrayed. The spread of the Revival, however, and the involvement of local characters enables the writer to evoke the wider world and the problems of South Wales valleys in an exploration of the conflicting (revivalist) religious and revolutionary (socialist) to the many miseries of industrial Wales. There is a memorable picture of the Blaenau Ffestiniog of the time. Readers will be reminded of the work and preoccupations of Alexander Cordell although it is by no means clear where Mr Davies' sympathies lie.'

Book News from Wales

'This novel is well-written, warm and witty with a compassionate understanding of life in a small Welsh village at the turn of the century. Tom Davies does not presume to judge, restricting himself to the role of an observer which he manages brilliantly. There is so much detail from a blow-by-blow account (literally) of the local rugby derby matches to the cockle-pickers on the Pen-clawdd sands. The characters include Jenko, the alcoholic village doctor; Megan Evans, the nymphomaniac sister of the cockle-picker and Vera, the neighbour, who is kept awake at night by the noise of prancing slugs.

Only a Welshman could have written it; in terms of observation, if not poetry, it is worthy of Dylan Thomas.'

South Wales Argus

'All the natural melody of the Welsh is in this vivid romance which blends the great beliefs of socialism and religion in a powerful drama. Torn apart by conflicting demands are Michael Evans and his girl, Beth; he looking to socialism and she to the chapel. There are memorable scenes of the quarrymen's revolt in Dinorwic and the gathering of miners in Bethesda as preacher Roberts takes his message through Wales. A brilliant, enchanting book.'

The Daily Post

'The writer keeps you juggling with moral dilemmas of an abstract nature until the last section of this finely-crafted novel, which focuses on the trauma of Beth Williams' life. Her story sucks the reader into this moral debate and the shocking ending to this tale acts like a cold flannel on the face, a reminder that her dilemmas are much like our own. Poignant and provocative and occasionally explicit *One Winter* is a welcome book from an increasingly gifted Christian writer.'

Strait

'This book, which is a Book Club choice and may well take Britain by storm, is about how a blacksmith offered people salvation and thousands turned up to listen to him. Tom Davies – or Tom the Book, as he is known in the Valleys – has woven the momentous events of the time into a hauntingly tragic love story describing how two people got caught up in the revival and were ultimately doomed by it. Tom's period and atmospheric detail is absolutely authentic as he relates how, for one winter, the whole nation turned to God because of one man and his evangelistic tradition.'

South Wales Evening Post

'The best novel to come out of Wales. Ever.'

Red Dragon Radio

Chapter One

The tide was ebbing fast with some sixty people, with their horses and carts, moving out towards the cockle beds on the sands of Pen-clawdd. Late for the tide as usual, Michael Evans was travelling along one of the marsh gullies, quietly cursing his horse. Glorying in the name of Lightning, the beast moved as if he had chronic arthritis in every joint.

'Let's have a bit of effort now is it? *Duw*, there's more life in a bottle of pop.'

At the end of the gulley the horse ambled to a halt and Michael stood up on his cart, trying to decide which part of the sands to work in. He had plenty of choice. When the tide had fully ebbed, there was a belt of two miles of sand between the green mounds of the marsh and the sea. This belt was seven and a half miles long and even those working the sands often could not see one another. Those who did not know the sands could easily get lost on them, or get caught by the tide, or even – as had happened the previous year – get swallowed up by the quicksands near Llanrhidian.

But he loved the flatness of the marsh and the sheer emptiness of the sands. The sands were space and high winds, which flung their dangerous passions around his home village of Pen-clawdd on the Gower.

The problem in choosing a likely patch to work in that long, wet summer of 1904, was that the cockles had been moving around fast. Only old Lizzy Harry ever seemed to find a rich patch with any accuracy, but there was no sign of her red and green flannels that afternoon. Doubtless she was hanging back behind one of the marsh pills, waiting for the rest of the cocklers to commit themselves before she travelled out, a beflanneled Boadicea triumphant, to pull her rake through a patch which would yield more bags in an hour than most could dig all tide.

Michael decided to head away from the other cocklers – they spent more time watching one another jealous than digging for their own – and, with the help of a few cracks at his horse's ribs with a stick, abandoned his usual route and headed out towards Llanrhidian. He had been lucky out there a few times that summer. The horse, as usual, took no notice of the new directions at first and only acceded when he received a few firmer kicks in the rump.

A mile further on, he reined the animal to a halt on a sloping bank with seawater running out of it. He always preferred to work near running water – it made the cockles easier to sieve.

The sun still hung high and bright over the sands and, after tethering the horse, Michael walked around in large circles looking for the cockles' air-holes, sometimes getting down on one knee to brush away seaweed as the gulls wheeled and screeched overhead. A brisk south-westerly was moving in over the estuary and, on no evidence at all, he decided that he was going to have a fine productive afternoon.

A young woman came walking across the sands, strands of dark hair being blown across her face and a hand steadying the sides of her billowing dress and petticoat. She spotted Michael crouching down in the shimmering sand and smiled to herself as she walked towards him. He was clearly one of the local bumpkins, she decided, what with his baggy trousers tied up with a bit of rope and a large tear down the left arm of his shirt.

'How are the cockles this year?' she asked.

Michael's eyes widened a shade on hearing the voice behind him. It sounded playful, pumped full of laughter and he looked up, guilty, like some dog being caught in the act of burying his favourite bone. He had never seen this one before.

'They've been better,' he said, standing up. 'And they've been a lot worse. Trouble is, the little devils seem to have been sleepwalking all summer. One tide you can dig them out by the bucket and the next tide you go back to the same spot and they've all vanished like ghosts at dawn.'

She just stood there, silent, for a few seconds, amused by his words while picking the strands of hair off her face and tilting her chin up into the sighing wind. A ragamuffin he might be, but he had a way with words for definite. And he was that attractive, too, with sharp angular features, whipped brown by the wind and sun, with a large nose, full of character, as well as a tiny white scar on the side of his chin. But it was his eyes that were so arresting, pale blue, like those of a dead fish.

'I didn't know cockles move around,' she said, final.

'I wouldn't say they just moved,' he explained. 'Most tides they sprint around as if they're on a hundred yard dash. Run faster than light those cockles do.'

'I don't believe you,' she snorted. 'You're from Pen-clawdd, aren't you?' They always say 'they tell nothing but lies in Pen-clawdd.'

'It's true, girl. If you track down a bed, that's fine, but never expect them to be there the following tide. They come up on top of the sand to feed when the tide is in, but where they decide to feed when the tide is out, that's anyone guess.'

He looked at her hard, unable to understand why she was so interested since she was a real looker, a rare beauty indeed. It was all there in the high, sculptured cheekbones and the long-lashed brown eyes but, most of all, it was in her smile – unforced and without flaw, a perfect match for the warmth of the sun. He had to look away to stop himself gawping.

'These cockles of yours,' she said, 'Next thing you'll be saying they're all dashing about under the sand wearing running shorts. I'm not so stupid as I may look, you know.'

She didn't look at all stupid to him. She was anything but stupid, but he decided to egg her on a bit. He pointed at some holes in the sand. 'These are the breathing holes, see. Sometimes you can put your ears close to them and hear them all snoring.'

'Rubbish. Tell me. Do they teach you how to tell lies in the school in Pen-clawdd, or do you just tell them natural?'

'Listen, will you, and you'll learn something. Now we'll follow the holes along here.' He crawled and she followed. 'There's a few more snoozing here.' He crawled another few feet. 'They've been moving around a lot there and eureka! There they all be, just waiting to leap into my sieve. Stand back and watch this, oh ye of little faith.'

He strode over to the cart hoping that all those holes had not been caused by ragworm – it was only his second year out on the sands and he had all but starved the previous year after his father, a cockler also, had died leaving him nothing but his debts, his cart and a near-defunct horse. He returned with his rake, shovel and sieve and raked near the holes when, happy day, up came the thickest clump of cockleshells he had seen for some weeks. He shovelled them into the sieve, shook off the sand and she actually clapped her hands by way of applause.

'Easy when you know how,' he smirked.

'You must be very rich I would think,' she said and once again he heard the compacted laughter in her voice, as if she was coming to the end of a joke. 'You must be very rich indeed, digging up all these cockles.'

He missed the edge of her irony and leaned on his shovel. 'I make a penny or two, but if you want to see someone who is really clever at this game, go and find Lizzy Harry. A master of the sands she is – or should I say mistress? The cockles jump up out of the sand and call out her name when she rides past.'

17

She just stood there for a moment, again admiring that weather-worn face. His eyes were clearly those of a heart breaker and there were hard muscles in those leathery arms.

'I don't believe that,' she said, deadpan.

'Neither do I.' He shrugged and smiled. 'But that's the way the others explain why she usually digs out twice as many cockles as anyone else.'

'Jealousy I expect.'

'Aye. Jealousy. There's a lot of it about.'

His voice had taken on a dry, nervous edge. They stared at one another for several seconds, she shifting her weight from one foot to the other. She was about twenty-five, he guessed, the same as him. Her white blouse had frilled, leg o' mutton arms, and a bright golden brooch was pinned just at the bottom of her throat.

'I'd better leave you,' she said, final.

'No rest for the wicked,' he said, far too hasty. 'Look, you were here when I found these, so it's only fair you take some back with you. You'll have to boil them, of course, or come up to my boiler later . . . ' He could hear himself gabbling and bit his lip.

'It doesn't matter. I haven't got a basket with me anyway.'

'I'll loan you. You can bring it back when you like. Or I could pick it up sometime?'

'No, really.' She took half a step backwards – polite but firm in the face of a too-persistent salesman. 'Perhaps I can bring my own basket down sometime though?' The wind was shaking the conversation, picking out some words and blowing them clean away.

'Come when you like,' he replied, less avidly he hoped this time. 'You'll always find me down here when the tide is out. That's what they mean, in Pen-clawdd, when they say the men have gone with the tide though, truth to tell, it's usual for the women to do the work. Most of the men are even lazier than my horse here and, most of the time, he's too lazy to yawn.'

Her cheeks were flushing up by now and he saw that he had better let her go or, any second, she was going to make a bolt for it. Living with a horse had taught him a lot about people. 'But what's your name? Stranger here are you?'

Even in the wind he could have warmed his hands on that blush.

'Beth. Beth Williams. I live over the water in Loughor.'

'Oh Crazy Town. I know it.' A certain angry sharpness in her glance told him that she did not like that remark. They called the place Crazy Town because of its jumbled houses – not because of the people in them – but explaining all that seemed pointless. 'I sometimes sell cockles over there. Perhaps I'll see you again?'

'Perhaps.' Now she was even more anxious to leave and half-turned to walk away, but still he did not want to let her go.

'Look girl, if you won't take a basket then take a cockle here and now.'

She turned back, puzzled, and he reached down into her sieve to pick out one sandy cockle and offer it to her. She looked at the gift in his hand and up into his eyes, almost holding up her hand to shade out their brilliant penetration. He clearly had a funny, generous nature too. She did hope that they would meet again.

'Let's call it a souvenir of the sands, shall we? Go on, girl. It's not too heavy.'

Her laughter returned with that remark and she accepted the cockle, turning to leave. A girl like you deserves a million oysters, not one little cockle, he thought as he watched her stroll away with the wind whipping tiny whirlpools of sand around her shoes. His mouth had gone bone dry and he swallowed hard. Ah, if only he had told her about his cats. If only he had told her about the way his chicken was always bullying the cats. If only . . . He continued watching her until she disappeared behind a mound on the marsh – gone as sudden as she had arrived. She had not looked back once, either. Oh well, there were the cockles to get out. There was a living to be raked.

Beth had not looked back as she walked away because she had not dared to do since there was something strange and crumbling going on inside her and, had she looked back, she was certain that she would somehow have made a fool of herself. She kept walking slow until she came to the ash path at the top of the marsh, when she stopped still. A wasp flew past her and landed on a blade of grass. Probably one of the last wasps of the summer. She was always happy to see the back of them.

What was really surprising was how that cockle-picker had managed to singe something tender inside her; how, in just a few minutes, he had brought something to life that she had long considered dead. And that was surprising, wasn't it? She clutched one of her wrists with her hand and squeezed it. But he was probably married or had a girl already. Men who immediately declare their difference from other men like that are rarely alone for long.

Michael worked on that patch of cockles swift, while his horse sat busy doing nothing and gazing out over the peaceful sweep of the Burry estuary on the North Gower coast. The cockles came up thick, but even the satisfaction of seeing bag after bag filling up did nothing to soften the keening sense of disappointment hanging deep inside him. The very music of her hung on him – invisible but vital – all afternoon. Those eyes.

That smile. The laughing voice.

The untidy strings of cocklers returning to their boiling sheds told of the reclaiming tide and the end of the working day. His back stiff with effort, he was careful to cover most of his eight bags on the cart with some sacking. Jealousy was a hard fact of life out on the sands and he did not want half the cocklers in the estuary following him out the next day. Some of them would have sold their granny's knickers for an extra bag of cockles and were never so happy as when locked in argument or violent feuds, passed faithfully down from one generation to the next. He kept his distance from all such disputes and only took a stand when absolutely necessary.

The tide was moving in fast now – the sands were so flat it often came in faster than walking pace, especially when helped by a south-westerly – so he had to get his horse up on his legs. 'Come on now,' he shouted at the horse, who continued gazing out over the estuary as if immersed in a dream where time had no meaning. Yet the horse knew as well as anyone else that the time had come to move, for already the disturbed waders were circling above them.

Michael walked over to deliver a sharp boot in the flank and the horse hauled himself up, wide-eyed and *hurumphing* at the effrontery of the assault. Michael could see that he was in one of his especially awkward moods; he resolved not to boot him again or he would go into a flat sulk all week. 'Come on, Lightning,' he said, his manner getting softer. 'Let's have a bit of effort, is it? All you seem good for these days is sleep.'

He put both arms around the horse's neck and gave him one of his long chuckles in his ear. These chuckles almost always managed to cheer up the horse and he went into the shafts as willing as putty after that. Michael gave him his head on the way home so that he could find the best way through the marsh gulleys, while his own mind was caught again by that girl.

She was, he supposed, what the Welsh would call *crachach*. From some sort of posh family who were big in the chapel and lived in a huge house, he shouldn't wonder. She wouldn't have much time for his socialism, he was pretty certain. Too far back for that kind of thing. He wondered what *she* cared about.

He trundled past a pack of wild horses grazing on the marsh and they bolted abrupt, manes flowing and hooves hurrying over the muddy banks. It only took one to start running, when, as if responding to some code, they all took off. That year there were more than two hundred wild horses on the marsh, all descended from retired pit ponies and the amorous wanderings of the cocklers' own horses. Every conceivable feature they had stitched into some of them – from Arab to palomino to Welsh Cob.

Michael loved to watch the wild horses run together, struggling across deep ravines and bounding over the great grass pills, but even seeing them now, all in full flight and with *his* full load as well, he plunged into an edgy, black mood. By the time he returned to his own cottage, even while he poured his cockles into the large Dutch boiler in the yard, his mind was again besieged by pictures of that girl. She had not even asked his name.

Steam clouds came hissing and piling out of the boiler as he wondered what kind of house she lived in. It might, of course, be some sort of fairy castle with its gables and turrets obscured by lazing clouds. There might be a moat stretching under its drawbridge and, on the still black waters, many swans.

By contrast, there was nothing his imagination could do to invest his own home with any glamour. It was a three-up, two-down terraced cottage on the Pen-clawdd seafront. There were fungus patches on the kitchen walls; the dominant feature was dust and, lurking in many corners were many strange smells, since he lived alone with an eccentric, aggressive bantam chicken which spent much of its time bullying the two cats, Pitch and Toss. Some days, if it was very cold or raining, he even let the horse come indoors as well.

He was carrying a bucket into the garden shed when a face appeared over the fence with its chin resting between two hands. The eyes were small and ferociously beady, the nose resembled a medieval axe head, while her voice reminded him of a collection of rustling dried senna pods. 'Michael Evans, are you going to pull my potatoes this year or not?'

He looked around at Vera Owen and sighed. He would have loved to have pulled the old crone's tongue. 'Vera, girl, don't I pull your potatoes every year?'

'Are you going to or not? It's time, it is.'

'I'll pull them, Vera.' Then I'll plant you in their place, he added under his breath.

Vera Owen's nagging had become one of the greatest legends of the Gower Peninsula. Even when her husband died, some said she had leaned over his coffin and bleated about his bad timing and thoughtless selfishness. As usual he said nothing in reply but, when Michael paid his last respects, he could have sworn that there was a faint yet triumphant smile on the old man's lips. He certainly looked the happiest that Michael had ever known him.

'And when are you going to tell that chicken of yours to stay out of my turnips?'

'I'll tell her, Vera. I'll have a quiet word with her before she goes to bed tonight. But she's not a well chicken, you know. There's a draught in her hutch. Think she may have a cold coming on.'

'Those cats of yours have been after my tortoise again, they have.'

There was no point trying to reason with her and he returned to the business of boiling cockles, aware that her chin was still resting on the fence, her beady eyes still watching him and her brain still trying to dredge up new complaints. Lately she had been going on about the slugs prancing in the garden and, as if that had not been bad enough, blaming him for all the noise they were making.

You really had to keep the peace where you could in Pen-clawdd.

As Beth followed the metalled road down into Loughor she saw that the signs of the coming winter were everywhere. In the outlying fields, in the small rolling hills and blackberry dales, the chill fingers of autumn were turning the leaves brown. Swarms of chattering house martins were gathering on the telegraph wires, preparing for their flight to the warmth of Africa. Soon, too, the oystercatchers would return from Greenland to the Pen-clawdd sands and winter proper would begin.

She hoped – no, prayed – that it would be a gentle winter. She did not want to live through another of those hard cold winters when life was reduced to a miserable struggle to keep warm. She wanted it to be warm right through to next spring when it would become a good deal warmer. That's what she wanted. And she wanted to see that cockle-picker again. She wanted to find out how he would hold her in his arms – to see, perhaps, if he could keep her really warm after all these long years of cold.

Chapter Two

Saturday morning in the forge in Pontarddulais and Evan Roberts was pounding a red-hot horseshoe, banging it one way and another on the blacksmith's anvil. It was particularly hard iron they had been using this week – even, somehow, when it was red-hot – and it seemed to him that he might have had to pound it twice as hard as, say, those bars they had worked with the week before.

He did not mind the muscular precision needed for this slow work of the hammer and the anvil though; in fact, he rather enjoyed tough, hot work such as this. The shaping of those shoes was much the same as the shaping of a man's soul. His hammer blows gave the soul authority, strength, character. It prepared them for another ordeal by fire to come. Fiery sparks exploded angry with each beat of the hammer, sending tiny glowing stars dancing over his ragged leather apron.

His body was as tall and thick as an oak tree and every joint might have been forged in that fire. You could see the strength in his hands and the enormous fingers. Most of all, you could see it in the powerful set of his jaw and those deep-set hazel eyes. The coals' light flickered in the sweat on his forearms, which he occasionally ran across his damp, heated forehead. Sometimes, when he looked direct into the fire, he would smile faint since, these days, his thoughts were much concerned with the triumph over fire.

He lifted the red-hot horseshoe with his tongs and doused it in a bucket of cold water, standing and watching the explosive bubbling hisses. All this was but a raindrop exploding on a saucepan compared with the fires of hell. In fact, if you took the whole of the Bristol Channel and flung it on to a red-hot saucepan it would still be but a raindrop exploding when compared to the fiery vistas of hell.

Evan was the first to admit that he was afraid of hell. Even if he had decided that he did not believe in God, he still would have gone to chapel since he was that afraid of hell he did not want to take any chances. His life was dedicated to avoiding it – and helping other people to avoid it too.

Samuel Morse, the blacksmith owner of the forge, walked in through the door, taking out his fob watch and, as was his unfailing habit,

23

rubbing his thumb over the glass dial before checking the time. 'Time for home then, Evan,' he said. 'We'll not be having any more in here today.'

'Isn't Leighton Jones bringing in his horse, then?'

'He said he might. He *might*. If I spent my time sitting around waiting for Leighton Jones when he said he might I wouldn't have done much in this life, I can tell you.'

'Have you done much in this life, Sam?'

Sam's eyes darted away sharp. He knew Evan and his taste for those serious questions intended to make you look at yourself. However, he wasn't going to be drawn. 'I mustn't forget to get them some more milk,' he said, walking to the backyard where seven fox cubs were tied up on a long piece of rope. 'Those cubs are growing so fast I'm going to have to let them go soon.'

He leant down and played with one, his leathery, torn fingers impervious to the sharp little nips on the cub's teeth. He had taken in these cubs after the mother had been snared and, on some afternoons, the local children came over to take them out on walks, wearing leads.

'There's much love in you, Sam,' said Evan, his manner more jaunty now as he took off his leather apron and hung it up behind the door. 'You should be careful to give your love to people, too. The good book says much about how a man is weighed by the size of his love for people, but I can't say it says much about love for foxes. One day you should let me tell you about St. Paul's views on love, too.'

'Yes. Well . . . some other time perhaps.' Sam was not worried overmuch about the state of his soul.

* * *

Summer was still hanging on the fields, with a few gunmetal clouds chasing one another lazy across a blue sky, as Evan walked the three miles from the forge in Pontarddulais to his home in Loughor. Clouds of midges tingled around his face, bees buzzed in the cow parsley, flies zoomed around the rich pats of cow dung. All around him he saw the same story of Mother Nature at her busiest, and he just loved the sense of activity and creation in the air as he strode through it with long, purposeful strides.

He was all of six foot three inches tall, a blacksmith these days, though the two tiny blue scars on his face told of the time when had worked the coalface in nearby Broadoak Colliery, where the black coal-dust had congealed with red blood to create the tell-tale miners' blue scar.

He crossed over a crag and came down towards Loughor, the small town straddling the mouth of a muddy tidal river of the same name. Just nearby, the gas inside a coal tip had been ignited by the heat of the summer sun with drifting tunnels of grey smoke escaping from deep within its belly. Over at the other end of the town, a Roman castle towered like a sentinel over a police station, three chapels, a Church of England, four public houses and a railway station on the main line between London and Milford Haven.

The three collieries on the outskirts of the town had managed to drain the colour and symmetry out of the crouching terraces. Pit subsidence had caused some of the houses to sway and sag drunken. Cracks zigzagged across the roads while, in certain streets, houses leaned forwards or backwards, their supporting walls bulging as if pregnant.

The opulent warmth of the late afternoon corresponded well with Evan's mood. He felt as tall as the very sky on such days, able to reach out across oceans and over mountain ranges to bring the good news of Christ's love to every corner of the world. That's what he was going to do soon, though he had not told anyone about it yet. Each hour now the Lord was preparing him for the beginning of The Great Work.

A herring gull went lolly lagging over his head and he shaded his eyes as he looked up at it flying free. Yes, soon, he too, would be flying free.

Next to the town boundary Evan passed Will Williams, an old miner standing with one hand against a telegraph pole and the other kneading his chest to get the blood moving as his dust-raddled lungs gasped for oxygen.

A woman in a green cardigan was gossiping so furious with a neighbour she blew her nose twice and still managed not to lose a single syllable. Another woman, out with a shopping bag, waved at Evan as he went by, but many others pretended not to see him or even ducked back into their doorways. Mrs Probert took three steps out of her front door, caught sight of Evan and, in four quick strides, had reversed back into the safety of her hallway.

The word was out in the town that Evan was a bit *twp* and the traditional Welsh way of dealing with the unconventional was either to classify it as a genius or ignore it. A few thought Evan a genius, but many others believed he was becoming a touch daft. To be thought slightly eccentric, and to be so young as well, led to social isolation in Wales, so Evan managed as best he could, identifying himself with the loneliness and suffering of the prophets of old. He had to put up with the suspicious mutterings and cautious greetings just as those stoic prophets had done. It forged him, for the fire of the coming work.

He stopped on the bridge and looked down over the parapet at the waltzing brown waters of the river. Just upstream, the blackened pit ponies dashed pell-mell into the same water on being brought up from Broadoak Colliery at the end of the shift. On those leafy banks over there, bags of kittens were drowned in the secrecy of darkness and lovers held one another tight on warm summer evenings.

A stumpy man wearing a large black felt hat with a floppy brim came walking across the bridge. He had dark bulbous eyes and a lantern jaw, which he occasionally moved around pugnaciously. The front of his cape was streaked with cigarette ash and, in his fat hand, he was carrying a battered leather bag.

'Well, well. If it isn't *the* Dr. Enoch Jenkins,' said Evan with a smile. 'So tell me now. How many have you managed to kill off today?'

'They don't need any help from me,' said the doctor, his thick black eyebrows knitting into one long furry caterpillar. 'They're past masters at doing it themselves. I've just been down to the café to have a look at that Bracchi woman.' He coughed and put his bag down, arranging his fat fingers in the air like some magician about to do the impossible. Dr. Enoch Jenkins – or Jenko as everyone called him – did not so much converse as make big speeches. There was nothing he loved more than the sonorous boom of his own voice though, it had to be said, the beer did run a close second.

'This Bracchi woman. She's got Angier's Petroleum Emulsion for her lungs, bile beans for her biliousness, Carter's Little Liver Pills for her liver, Eade's pills for gout and Dr. Schuffman's cure for asthma.' He had counted them all out on the fingers of his left hand and began on his right. 'She's got phosferine for her neuralgia, Gloria Tonic for gouty fingers, Gwilym Evans' quinine bitters for furred tongue, Doan's kidney pills for a bad back and Coleman's Wincarnies for dropsy.'

He had run out of fingers and began waving his hands around as if conducting the wind. ''Mrs Bracchi,' 'I said, 'I don't know why you bother with this café. You could run a chemist's shop from your bedside here. What do you want from me?''

Jenko paused and took a step sideways, fixing Evan with a steady gaze and determined, as ever, to extract the full dramatic flavour of the story. ''Dr. Jenkins,' she said, 'I'm suffering from brain fag and I can't get any pills for that.' Brain fag! I ask you now. Gout in the brain, more like.' He took a step forward.

'I told her. I said, ''Mrs Bracchi you've got every known pill in the history of the British Empire right there on that bedside table of yours. There might be a few pills the Chinese have got that you haven't but I doubt it. If I shook you it would sound like castanets. So what's the point of giving you any pills for this . . . this brain fag?" ' He sighed and looked down at his bag, his big speech far from over. 'You know what she said then?'

Evan shook his head.

'She said she did not want any more pills. She was fed up with pills, she said. They only gave her headaches. Headaches! The combined might of every quack and trickster known to mankind and they just gave her headaches. No. No more pills. All she wanted me to do was to go down and tell her husband that she was very sick and couldn't serve any more coffee *or* ice cream in the café. She was going to die – *kaput*, gone, die right there – if she had to go into that café just once more. And they say the Welsh dramatise everything!'

'So what did you do?'

'I told Mr Bracchi. I told him my fee for the visit was a guinea and next time I called it would be three guineas. Double that if it was opening time in the pub!'

'He loved that, no doubt. These ice cream parlours only open all hours to make money.'

'You're right there, Evan. He was eating a plate of spaghetti at the time and worms went flying out of his mouth in all directions. He went rampaging up the stairs, shouting something about he didna care ifa she hadda terminal thrombosis. She hadda to getta out of beda and serva da coffee and da ice cream or he couldna afforda to havea me back.' He wiped his mouth with the back of his sleeve. 'So how is the great Evan Roberts?'

Evan chuckled. In their different ways they were both unconventional people; they felt at ease with one another, almost as if they came together with the same sense of shared menace. 'The great Evan Roberts is just great. I am off to Bible School next week, you'll be sorry to hear.'

'I had heard. Newcastle Emlyn, isn't it? What they'll teach you there that you don't already know I haven't a clue. You must have been reading that Bible of yours in the womb. Most babies cry when they came out but you were reciting bits of Genesis. Tell me. How are you going to manage for money?'

'God provides.'

Jenko shook his head in disbelief. Whenever he had treated the Roberts family they had always said that. He had once treated Evan after an explosion in the colliery and his patient had put his hands on the old doctor's head and blessed him. Jenko had thanked him in return and then asked about the shilling for treatment.

Jenko never did get his shilling. The truth of the matter was that the Roberts family – all twelve of them – were rarely ill and, even had any of them been at death's door, were highly reluctant to put their ailment in Jenko's shaking hands since he ran his surgery, during opening hours, in the Lewis Arms. He picked up his bag. 'Oh well, time to get along.'

'Opening time, is it?'

'It just might be. Pray for me, Evan. Pray especially that they stop watering down the beer in the Lewis Arms. It's got that they're even watering down the lemonade now.'

'Well, they're doing something right.'

Evan walked on down past the police station and came to the rugby pitch, when he stopped still and felt the good humour of the day drain out of his body like oil out of a sump. Two rugby sides were out facing one another and Evan realised it was the first match of the season at which Loughor met Pen-clawdd for the needle game of the year when, for long periods, the ball would be irrelevant to the fighting. This rugby violence had become a national scandal and made Evan practically speechless with rage. Friends were wiping out friends. Necks were being broken regular, and no game was a game unless at least a dozen bones were broken. Even chapel members were joining in.

Last year, the Pen-clawdd team had left their clothes along the line on the pitch when the match had started and, when the final whistle blew, those who could still walk scooped up their clothes and escaped along the marsh road as fast as their torn and bruised legs would carry them. This year the tone was set when the Pen-clawdd team came walking down the marsh road with no clothes at all to change into and just wearing their rugby kits.

Of course, there had been cautions. There had also been sendings-off, and even suspensions, but the bitterness between Pen-clawdd and Loughor had gone too deep to be healed by mere rules. Even a general discussion about tactics in the days before the match was seen as a waste of time; winning or losing would largely depend on how many players were left standing at the end.

Evan was about to walk on when he decided that he had better stop and watch for a while. After all, he could not condemn something he had never seen, though the Press reports were enough to convince him of the terrifying shame such matches were bringing to the land. He also recognised a member of the Pen-clawdd team, Michael Evans, one of those socialists who had been friendly with Evan's brother, Dan, before that explosion down the pit when Dan had gone blind. To be a socialist and a rugby player – now there was a great yoke of sin for you if ever there was one.

Michael was rubbing his legs down with embrocation and his belly was rolled into a solid knot of nerves as he waited for the kick-off. He played centre three-quarter and, for this particular game, followed one rule for survival: if the ball was ever passed to him he passed it straight out again. If there was no one to pass the ball to he kicked it into touch. It was that simple. The most he ever hoped for was a couple of golden moments when he would get the ball, far from hacking or strangling distance, and then run it hard since, when he so chose, he could beat the very wind.

He took small comfort in the size and strength of his Pen-clawdd forwards who, animal-like, were lumbering around passing large brown jugs of beer to one another and smoking cigarettes to get themselves warmed up. Their chests were full of muscle and menace, their shirts seeming to shrink on them by the minute. None of them had shaved that morning, in the hope of getting a soft tract of skin in the scrum and giving it a good scrape. They belched like thunder and spat like camels and picked their noses as if they were turning over their gardens.

The famous New Zealand All Black rugby team had their *haka*, the Maori war cry designed to put fear into the enemy. The Pen-clawdd forwards frightened their opposition into surrender merely by acting in character. Their very appearance was worth ten points.

Five minutes and as many scrums into the match, with the referee already lecturing both hookers, Marnie Prees, the tiny, toothless, Pen-clawdd fly-half, strode towards the largest forward in the Loughor pack and kicked him straight in the knee-cap. 'Let's get it straight from the beginning is it?' Marnie hissed as the forward danced around on one leg while nursing his attacked knee with both hands. 'I may be small but I am not to be interfered with.'

Another Loughor forward immediately punched Marnie. Ernie Thomas punched the Loughor forward and four others went motoring into the fray, including a spectator bearing an umbrella. Bobbing around in the middle of it all was the referee, blowing his whistle frantically. A gallon of adrenalin surged through Michael's veins. So it was going to be one of those games again, he thought. Not for the first time he asked himself why he bothered with rugby at all.

When order had been restored the referee brought both sides together, reminding them that this was not the Zulu War and that he had the right to send men off. He invited them all to try again.

Marnie's eye had swollen into a thick red bulge, while the forward with the kicked knee was still limping about showing Marnie the business end of his fist.

'You're going to look awful funny *mun* when your tongue is pulled out as well.'

Another penalty followed another foul and the ball was kicked straight into touch. In the ensuing line-out elbows went jabbing into ribs and, as the winger hoisted the ball into the air, the forwards really got down to it. Even as the ball still hung, tantalising, in the air a hand was stamped on, a wrist bent in a direction it was not built to move in and a rogue elbow smashed into a nose.

It was usual for the game to settle down a bit after their early ritual posturing and breast-beating – but not just yet. Loughor missed a penalty kick and, after a relatively bloodless maul, one of Pen-clawdd's flank forwards, Dai Llewelyn, a tin miner as broad as he was tall, found himself free, the ball in his hands and steaming for the line. Three Loughor forwards caught him after he had travelled a mere five yards. Dai fell into the tackle with two perfectly good ears on either side of his head but, when he stood up, blood was pouring down his neck, since the lobe of the left ear had been bitten clean off.

Michael wondered what an ear tasted like as Dai trudged off the field, avoiding a fight, which had broken out between two groups of rival supporters. A bit like salty bacon, he decided. Tough, salty bacon, which took an age to chew. It was then that he resolved that, should the ball ever get to him, he really was going to kick it straight into touch. He was rather fond of his ears.

So when the ball approached him Michael hoisted it into the air with the wildest of kicks, making it travel some hundred yards off the pitch where, from a safe vantage point, Evan was standing watching the game with his emotions running hot and cold at such barbarism. It was usual for a spectator to punt it back on to the field, but Evan was having none of that. As it rolled towards him he almost ran away, as if the ball was some bomb hurled by an assassin in the dark. Indeed he ran for almost fifty yards before stopping still and watching the game again. This savagery had to be stopped. When he became a leading figure in the chapel he was going to be the first to try and put a stop to it.

Pen-clawdd nearly had a try towards the end of the first half, after the toothless Marnie had worked the ball loose on the blind side just ten yards from the line and with no other player near him. Then a Loughor supporter stuck out his leg and hooked Marnie flat on his face. It was difficult to tell who had the prettier face by the time Marnie had finished with his reprisals. The referee did not try to interfere either, since there was nothing in his book of laws to cover what to do with a player who beat up a supporter. Mindful of the supporters' wrath, however, he blew for a scrum offence soon afterwards and gave Pen-clawdd an easy kick at goal.

When the whistle went for half-time Pen-clawdd were still leading by that penalty goal and were also doing that much better for players since they had only lost one to Loughor's three.

'Right lads,' said the Pen-clawdd captain, Dai Clements, as they sucked on their half-time oranges. 'Let's try some rugby, shall we?'

The referee, sitting on the ball nearby, rolled up his eyes. 'Cows may do cartwheels,' he muttered, picking himself up and nipping the end of his cigarette. 'The North Pole might melt.'

By the time the whistle had gone for the second half Evan had gone home in disgust, hands thrust down deep in pockets and shoulders hunched in anger. Some would say that it was a pity that he had chosen to go then since soon afterwards the game showed an unexpected flash of poetry, which was both its justification and delight – when Michael scored a try, diamond-like in its brilliance.

Marnie fed out a long sweeping pass from the scrum to the other centre, Howard Morgan, who sold his opposing player a perfect dummy and jinked inside him. The remnants of the Loughor pack were bearing down on him when he caught Michael's eye as he ran past, giving him a quick backflip of a pass, which left Michael in space and barely twenty yards from the line. It was a moment of the purest exhilaration as he took off with the speed of a penny rocket, running and jinking off his left foot until he dived and touched down, wrapping his arms around his head to protect it from Loughor reprisals. The try was not converted.

Michael was not at all clear what happened after that little moment of glory. A few minutes later, the ball bounced out of a ruck. Standing nearby, lost in a daydream and with absolutely no intention of touching the ball again for the rest of the game, a Roman phalanx of legs, arms and studs just ran over him. His arm was stamped on and he was kicked in the head and chest. He did manage to stand up, his head staging a wondrous extravaganza of lights, when what looked like the same phalanx – and certainly felt like the same phalanx – reversed back over him. Just making sure that he had got the point of their displeasure at his try, he supposed, as he curled himself into a foetal ball. Something hit him very hard indeed on the back of his head and the world flooded up with a great sea of darkness.

Water came hissing out of a sponge and seemed to burn. He stood up with the trainer's assistance and looked at the figure H of the rugby posts only to find that there were now three of them: H H H. Then the pitch began swaying and dipping so much he had to place his legs apart to stop himself falling off it.

'Say what you like,' he told the Pen-clawdd trainer. 'That Lewis always dilutes his milk with water.'

A few seconds later the whole of the pitch did turn upside down, and he flung himself downwards to keep himself upright. There was a lot of whistling and then there was nothing.

Voices were chattering and he opened his eyes to see a boy sucking a liquorice sherbet looking down at him. 'Dead, is he?' the boy asked a man next to him. 'Dead?'

'Just having a little nap,' the man replied.

'He looks dead for certain,' said the boy.

'I'm dead all right,' said Michael. 'Dead as that dodo.'

'I told you he was dead,' said the boy. 'They teach us all about that in school, they do.'

When Evan got home two children were playing with a small wheelbarrow in the garden and his mother was pegging out the washing on the line. Home was a grey bungalow built out of Pennant grit, Island House, on the edge of the marsh with a high wooden fence all around the garden to keep out marauding sheep and wild horses. It was barely big enough for the large family that lived in it, though they all got on surprisingly well despite the cramped conditions.

Evan washed his hands in a bowl in the scullery and went straight to his bedroom to say his daily prayers. Early evening was the best time for this since he shared a bedroom with two of his brothers, Nathan and Dan, and found it difficult to concentrate when, come bedtime, they were in the room too. He placed his Bible on the bed before kneeling in front of it, kissing the black cover, clasping his hands together and closing his eyes.

He regarded prayers as neither a duty nor a chore, but as the highlight of his day when he journeyed to distant places, tending the sick, freeing the captive and raising the dead from their graves. Prayer, he believed, was the one activity of man in which God took a great delight and, because of that delight, God, in turn, rewarded men with gifts of the Holy Spirit.

At first he just knelt there, clearing his mind of images while waiting on the Spirit; watchful, awake and listening for the distant thunder of the hound of heaven. The thunder soon came and his mind unlocked and wandered in it, still listening and not speaking, still watchful but not active, turning and turning again as he raised his hands in supplication.

When he had finished listening Evan Roberts, spiritual sorcerer, began rolling a fireball of love around and around Island House, warming the roof and walls, bringing peace and comfort to all the family. After the warming he erected a Tent of Meeting over the house, that it might be protected from all evil spirits, those creatures of dominion and darkness who were abroad and active in a fallen world.

Next he took an angel in his hands, lustrous and dazzling in its purity, before anointing the head of each of his family with it and finally moving to Dan. Dan was very much at the centre of Evan's prayers these days, since he was blind and Evan had determined to pray for the gift of sight to return Dan's vision to him.

Come Dan, bach, and I will lead you out of the thin drizzle of your life and into the glory of God's universe.

His last prayer was for the rugby players and the injured: that their violent hearts would be warmed by love and a way found to stop all this savagery.

He remained praying with his eyes closed for more than three hours until he was disturbed by the faint sound of a melodeon scratching out of the darkness. He opened his eyes and looked around him at the billowing lace curtains, the huge china washing bowl, the truckle bed for Nathan and the Bible on the bed in front of him, open at Revelation.

All at once he began sweating and was gripped, vice-like, by fear. His breathing became jagged and the sweat began pouring out of every part of him. Dogs can smell fear, he knew. His father had also once told him that there were twenty-four reasons for fear, ranging from ghosts to the dark to loneliness. Now, in this room, there was a new fear for a new reason, and it hung over him like an eternal curse from which there was no escape in this life or the next.

He stood up and stumbled over to the window where he stood shaking from head to toe. Through the curtains he saw that the moon had thrown a bright sheen over the black, jumbled shapes of the marsh. The distant wheel of the pit was spinning fast. Beneath the window a few scraggy sheep moved around in a yellow splash of a gas lamp, which was hissing, quiet, like a small threatening snake. His right eye became caught by the moon while his left was caught, from inside his head, by the gaudy heart of the gas lamp. Both lights began moving towards one another, fast, while his whole body vibrated and he held both his ears tight with the hams of his fists.

The two lights exploded together on the mystic nerve in some hidden part of his mind and he reeled backwards with his insides falling away in echoes. All his past prayers came bubbling up out of him: the pleas, the assurances, the regrets – all whirling around and around in a confused, shimmering circle. Shafts of sunshine plunged through black storm clouds. Winds bundled flocks of frightened birds before them and bent the thick trunks of trees very low. He flung himself down on his knees, forehead to the floor, to take shelter.

A woman was bending on a bank next to a chapel graveyard, digging a deep hole with a trowel. Her sobbing was audible even in the howling storm, and when she had finished digging, she took the small dead baby, wrapped in a shawl, and placed it down the hole. The child was a bastard and, as the chapel would not allow the child to be buried proper, the mother had taken advantage of the cover of the storm to bury her baby as near to consecrated ground as possible.

He turned back, and now an old bow-legged man, holding himself up with a crook, approached him from out of a storm. He had large bushy eyebrows with grey thinning hair and his back serrated from frequent stoning and whippings. 'Every soul is sacred,' he told Evan. 'Pray without ceasing. Believe, that's all, and always remember that the mind of the flesh is death.'

Evan held out his hand but the old man disappeared along with the storm and there was the moon hanging over Loughor again with its face breaking up and dripping with blood. Evan's mouth was dreadful parched. He was at the breaking point, he knew, entering into the arena of the last things while moving through a Mass of the World.

A bright silver figure in a black cloak and with jagged bloody teeth came near on horseback. Rebel angels and the hobgoblins of nightmares were wheeling around his head as he began laughing blasphemies at Evan; startling, serious blasphemies against the Holy Spirit, the source of all life. 'The Holy Spirit is dead but I am here to serve you.'

Rage overcame Evan's fear and he picked himself up and began to run against the Prince of Darkness with a sword when the blasphemies suddenly stopped and The Great Blasphemer disappeared within a sigh and into the air.

He stopped still and looked around him. At the truckle bed. At the china basin. At the lace curtains. Oddly, in the circumstances, he let out a small laugh. The Lord was calling on him again. Soon the work would start proper.

Chapter Three

Michael woke that night hearing voices and with a strange smell in his nose. His body was undulating gently, as if floating on moving water, but there was nothing gentle about his headache.

'Lewis always dilutes his milk,' he said. 'Mam always said he did and now I'm positive.'

'You must lie back and take it easy.'

'He gives you bad eggs as well. Never buy eggs off Lewis.'

He tried to lift his head but shooting pains went searing through his body, neither was there any strength in his neck.

'Lie still. Rest. That's all you need now. Lots of rest.'

Everything was swimming around but, even in the delirium, he recognised the voice immediately. 'Is it you Beth?' he asked, opening an eye and seeing three square starched hats, then two, then one, then those big brown eyes, unsmiling. What was she doing here? How had she found him? 'Is this a nightmare, girl, I'm dying then am I? You can tell me. I'll take it like a man.'

'Just mild concussion, I'm afraid,' she answered. 'Nothing more serious than that but you *are* in hospital.'

'Hospital? So I'm on my way to the pearly gates at last? You think I'll be let in?' He stared intently at her.

She stared back and smiled. 'You haven't been too much of a naughty boy, have you?'

'A bit of a naughty boy I suppose. Haven't murdered anyone or anything like that. Look after my horse, will you?'

There was that laughter again; pure, rich and so infectious he felt a dart of happiness pierce his sickness.

'Hold my hand, girl.' She took it and he felt the warmth and fullness of a large mushroom in her palm. 'About this horse of mine. There's no harm in him as long as you give him hay and the odd raw egg. There's two cats as well. And a chicken. Give the chicken carrots.'

'And the cats?'

'Milk. Give them milk . . . but don't buy it from Lewis. And one more thing.' His hand shot out and gripped her arm tight as he lifted his head sideways and was sick all over her white apron. She held his heaving head while he was sick a second time and still did not move when he brought up yet more frothing bile.

'Sorry about that,' he said.

'Don't worry about it,' she murmured, calm, and settled him back on to his floating stream.

'I'm sorry, girl,' he repeated with streaks of darkness spreading across the swelling chambers of his mind.

'You must rest now.'

'Promise me one thing.'

'What's that then?'

'If I ever recover . . . if . . . you'll come out with me on to the sands one day.'

'We'll see,' she said. 'Now you just lie back and rest.'

He sank below his stream and the blackness rushed to greet him again.

It was the middle of the night when he woke again, surprised to find his mind lucid but his back giving him hell. At the far end of the ward a man was groaning amidst a symphony of snores. The fat snores seemed to take it in turns to serenade the thin ones. A doctor in a white coat walked up to the end of the bed and looked down at him. 'Come around, have we?' he asked as if he somehow found Michael's continuing existence a matter of the deepest regret.

'Something like that.'

He left the ward and returned a minute later with a stethoscope to listen to Michael's heart, before checking the pulse and feeling various parts of the body. 'It's my back that's playing me up,' Michael said.

'You just think it's your back,' the doctor said, deadpan. 'Actually it's your neck.'

'Oh is it now? Let me tell you my neck feels fine.'

'That's just what you think.'

'That's what my bloody back thinks as well,' he moaned, tired of medical riddles. 'Well, what's the verdict?'

'Your heart rate is up and the blood pressure is still high but you'll be out in the morning and back to work on Monday.'

'Not a terminal case then?'

'You almost sound disappointed.'

'Well, it was one of your nurses, see. She was going to look after all my animals. Beth. Beth Williams. Send her in to me will you.'

'She's gone home. Even nurses have to sleep.'

Gone home! Had the girl no feelings about her? No human

36

compassion? Come the morning he might well have left this world forever and she had gone home to sleep. Well, he hoped she had terrible nightmares. You never get your own way, he decided. Not even when you're dying you don't.

* * *

But he did not die and, on the contrary, woke up in the morning with more bounce than a handful of grasshoppers, pulling on a shirt and a pair of trousers from out of a bag that the rugby club had left for him.

'About this bill,' someone said to him as he was folding up his muddied rugby shirt. 'There's this matter of six shillings.'

'The club will pay it,' he said without looking around and stuffed the shirt into the bag.

'The club will pay it,' she mimicked. 'The club will pay it. They always say that. Every Saturday they come in here torn to pieces and half-dead. We stitch them together and what do we hear? The club will pay it. The club will pay it. We've sent the club hundreds of bills and all we get from them is silence.'

He turned to face the ward sister, a hard-faced woman with grey hair so straight it must have been ironed. He fancied all the starch in her cap had trickled into her face too. 'I was sick all over one of your nurses last night,' he said. Her eyebrows rose towards her cap. 'I would like to apologise to her.'

'Why not pay the bill instead?'

'Have you got wax in your ears, woman? The club will pay. Now about this nurse.'

'If they work on nights they don't come in until late afternoon. Let's talk about this six shillings shall we?'

'Send the bill to the club.'

He picked up the bag and strode out through the ward with her chirruping-angry in his wake. 'You can tell that rugby club of yours they can send their dead and dying somewhere else in future. In two years they've paid just one bill. Anywhere else and they have to pay in advance.'

'What right have you to charge people for being sick?'

'Oh I get it now. Another of those socialists, are you? Well, that's no surprise is it? All socialists are suffering from concussion, permanent – not just after a rugby match. Got nothing and want to share it with everyone. That's the socialist way, isn't it?'

'No, it's not the socialist way, woman. The socialist way is for the

37

strong to help the weak. For free. It's our way for the state to help the sick. For free. Socialists want to take starving children and stuff them full of good food. For free. That's the socialist way.'

'Well, that's all very fancy, I'm sure. Now about this six shillings for the bill.'

'Woman, you're beginning to sound like a bad hiccup. Give it here.' She handed him the bill and he folded it up, putting it in his pocket and patting it. 'Right. *I* will get the club to pay. Correction. I will *try* to get the club to pay but, if they don't, I will send you a plate of cockles every week for a year. How about that?'

A smile flickered, faint, in the starch of her features. 'I can't put cockles through the accounts,' she pointed out.

'Well, try eating them, woman. Good for the bones cockles are. Put hairs on the chest they do.'

'Hairs on my chest I can do without,' she said, sharp. 'Now about . . .'

'Could you tell me one thing,' he interrupted. 'This is serious now.'

'What's that?'

'Have you any idea what the final score was in that rugby match?'

* * *

Sunday morning sat on Pen-clawdd like a fat man munching an apple, content. A bunch of children played hide and seek among the moored fishing boats on the shingle off the foreshore. Faint wisps of sea mists moved slow down the main street. Most people were sleeping off the fatigue of the week's work; the faithful few were already in the Tabernacle Chapel singing hymns.

When Michael returned home he found his cats so hungry they all but attacked his hand when he put their food down. He also fed the chicken and the horse before putting on his jacket and walking out onto the marsh to look for flowers.

He loved the desolation of the marsh and knew its dark, secretive patches where waders and warblers gathered for conferences; the bulging deltas where a flock of Brent geese would soon be wintering and attracting the attention of guns; those twisting tidal gullies, crooked like the ways of deception and which once so confused a porpoise Michael had to spend a good hour dragging it back to the sea.

This morning he had some rather special flowers in mind and, down on the main pill, sought out the fragrant lousewort only to find that its blooms had shrivelled since the autumn was foreclosing fast.

But the marsh is full of colour and unexpected life for those who know where to look and, following the main pill, he jumped down on to one of the boggy deltas where, hardly able to believe his luck, he took off his cap and went down on one knee in front of them . . . four clumps of yellow and purple marsh orchids, their twirling flowers mingling with graceful leaves. They were ravishing to look at – even if nothing to smell – and he took out a knife to cut them with care.

Flowers were the best words he knew for speaking of love, affection and thanks.

Later that afternoon he was back outside the small yellow-painted hospital in Loughor, sitting on a wall and trying to affect a studied nonchalance when Beth arrived for duty. His heart did handstands when he saw her coming down the road with her eyes squinting in the sunlight. She did not spot him there until she was almost on top of him, whereupon she smiled with genuine warmth. 'Fit and well then are we?' she asked. 'Not going to get buried just yet?'

'Aye.'

'That's good. I don't think I could have managed feeding all those animals. Are you always so morbid when you're feeling bad? I mean, are you always going around thinking you are going to die?'

'Truth to tell, girl, I've never thought about death much before. It's this here brain. It surprises even me with what it comes up with sometimes.'

'Yes, I'd believe that too.'

She smiled at him, admiring his surprising choice of words and ideas. With most men you could tell what they were going to say about half an hour before they said it, but with this one you could not even make a guess. It was entirely typical that he also surprised himself when he spoke out loud. There was so much honesty about him, she thought. He would never tell you a lie – not like some men she could name.

'Actually I've come to apologise for being sick over you.'

She laughed that magical laugh and, for a terrifying second, he thought he was going to be sick over her again. 'So what I've done,' he said jumping down off the wall, 'is pick you some marsh orchids. They can make their own apologies.' He held out the bunch of flowers and she took them with both hands, without hesitation and with joy, like a child receiving a long-coveted present.

'But Michael, they're so beautiful. Beautiful, I call these.'

'Well another job done. Apologies were never my strong point.'

There was a short silence. 'I bet you didn't pay the hospital bill,' she said, as if sensing his embarrassment and seeking to change the subject.

'Um. Er. No. I'm afraid I didn't.'

'Rugby players never do. They always say . . . '

'Send the bill to the club.'

She threw back her head and laughed again. 'Mm. That's exactly what they all say. Well, I'd better get back on duty. Another twelve hours coming up.' She touched him on the shoulder, light. 'Many, many thanks for the flowers and don't you go worrying about being sick over me. I'd prefer you to have done that than have you dying on me.'

There seemed a genuine affection in her words and, as she seemed in no hurry to get away from him, he decided to seize the moment. 'Do you ever get days off?' he asked.

'Oh yes. Hospitals are not prisons, you know. Even hospitals give you a day off. It moves around. The next one is next Monday – a week tomorrow.'

'How about coming out with me? On your day off, I mean.'

She gave him a long searching look and quite what was in that look he could not tell, but, he fancied he saw a definite tinge of suspicion. Suddenly as if coming to a hard-won decision, she brushed her hair off her forehead and, with no trace of laugh let alone a smile, said, 'Why not?'

A flame of pure pleasure lit inside him. Why not? Why not indeed?

'I'll meet you at the cross at Loughor at two then,' he said, making to leave quick lest she began to reconsider. 'We could go over to Gowerton Fair. You'll be there, will you?'

'I'll be there,' she said with a firmness that told him she would be. Oh yes, she would be there all right. She wanted to know a lot, lot more about this one. Her only real problem was waiting that long.

He winked at her and walked away. She wouldn't come, he knew it. She had far too much style to go out with a man like him. In fact, she would most probably forget all about him by the time she turned into the hospital gates.

Chapter Four

'Greek!' Evan exclaimed, disbelieving. 'The Greek the Greeks spoke you mean? But Principal, I've not time to learn Greek.'

'You've got three years, Evan. You can learn a lot of Greek in three years.'

'But there is no time, Principal. Time is short. Man who is born of woman and who has but a short time to live. A short time to live, Principal.'

Evan stared out through the window at a row of chestnut trees at the other end of the playing field. The autumn was turning the edges of the leaves a ruddy brown and, on occasion, one drifted down slow to the damp green grass. The room smelled of polish and old theological books. It also smelled, Evan had already noted with some distaste, of cigar smoke.

The Principal, Rev. Dr Glanmor Williams, stooped forward in his chair and sighed as he steepled his fingers on the desk in front of him. He had the well-fed features of a bullfrog with thinning grey hair and a gold pince-nez perched, like a cliff diver, a the very end of his nose. 'You must remember now that there is nothing hurried about the divine,' he said, 'and nothing divine about the hurried.'

'But there is every hurry, Principal. God is bearing down on me daily now to begin my work. You see, the times are right and I must be ready with them. This urgency is weighing down on me like a great burden . . . there is this . . . the other night . . . like a great shout.'

Evan began scratching the side of his nose with his forefinger and stopped speaking. His thoughts were all banging into one another, reflecting the urgency and fire inside him. The Holy Spirit had prepared him all his life for this work and now he was ready. He was one of the young people who were seeing visions while the old men were dreaming dreams. But how could he explain all this to The Rev. Dr. Glanmor Williams, Principal of the Bible College, Newcastle Emlyn, who was sixty-five if he was a day? When did those with degrees and doctorates understand anything about anything? All these theological books must have made him muddled and dull. He simply could not understand what it was like to have a blazing fire in your belly.

'Is it, perhaps, that you do not like the other students here, Evan?'

'No. The other students are fine. But they are not for me. They do not care about what I care about.' He raised his right hand and let it fall again. 'Maybe they will enjoy learning Greek. Who knows? Someone must have enjoyed learning Greek. But I have no time for such things.'

'But Greek is the basis of all scriptural truth, Evan. When you understand Greek you can go straight to the very heart of scripture. That's why we teach Greek here – so that you can learn of the word of God from the very source.'

'You do not understand, Principal,' Evan said as he raised a bunched fist, his knuckles white. 'I understand all too well the word of God because he is speaking to me daily. He is calling me to revive his people and prepare them for the day of the locust. He is weeping for them. He wants his children ready and prepared for the fire to come. He wants his children back in his arms. You can see that, can't you?'

'I understand that a father wants his children back, yes.' The Principal moved his body back a bit, as if unable to bear the full heat of Evan's prophetic anger. He took off his pince-nez and held it up to the light as if looking for dirt, before taking out a snuff handkerchief and giving the lens a good wipe.

He had seen plenty of young men with a mission to save the world in his time. They usually ended up in some rural parish with six children and a fondness for sherry.

'The first lesson of the Old Testament is that God always warns his people of the evil tides to come,' Evan went on. 'And that is my mission – my purpose, if you will. He wants me to make a proclamation. He wants a revival. He wants me to spread the word about the coming pain. That's what my visions are telling me. That's what I have to go out and do.'

'That is all very well but arm yourself with learning first. Prepare yourself first. That's why you've come here.'

Evan brought his fist down hard on the desk and his voice took on a harsh angry edge. 'I *am* prepared. I *am* ready.'

* * *

Later that afternoon Evan and his friend Sydney Jones were sitting in the back of a pony trap as it clattered up the Cardiganshire coast road. They both held Bibles on their laps and were silent as the bumps of the iron-clad wheels shook their bodies around.

The broad-shouldered breakers of the Atlantic collapsed, lazy, over the rocks at the foot of the cliff. On occasion they spotted the big, brown eyes of seals, startling in their tearful melancholy, bobbing around in the waves.

'I just can't help it,' Evan said, final. 'The place is full of devils and I can't stay there any longer. I cannot explain these feelings. I just know them to be true. I know when there is sin in the hearts of the men around me. I feel it as you feel fire or a prick of a needle. I feel it and therefore I know it to be true.'

Sydney gazed out on to a hillside where a sheepdog was darting around a flock of alarmed sheep. 'Just give it some time then, Evan. You've only been there five minutes, after all. You've not given the college a chance.'

Evan closed his eyes. 'I have no time. I have but one short life and God is calling on me by the hour.' He stopped and listened to the groaning of the waves. 'All the Principal wants me to do is learn Greek. Does he expect me to convert the miners in Greek?'

'Well why not just wait until the call then, Evan? A month or two's not going to make much difference, is it? Not much difference in a whole lifetime.'

'Maybe not, but a month or two is a month or two longer than I want to be in that college. There is nothing they can teach me there, Sydney. They know nothing that I want to learn. The place is full of devils, I tell you.'

They came to Blaenannerch, a small market town in south Cardiganshire where the men began working at dawn and stopped at dusk. When they were hungry they ate and when they were tired they slept. The grey stone walls of the cottages and slate roofs spoke of the simplicity of the ordinary. As their trap rattled up the main road, nothing moved and all appeared abandoned – even the milk cart with its tin measuring jugs hanging on their hooks and jingling together in the breeze.

Yet, just outside the chapel in the main square there was plenty of movement. The crowds milling around had come, together with Evan and Sydney, to see and listen to the itinerant preacher Seth Joshua, who had been travelling the land for the past few years, recounting his own vision of that man from Nazareth nailed to the cross of shame.

His following was sizeable, his collected sermons bought avidly and there was no one anywhere in a pulpit – or out of it – who could match the fervour of his oratory as he urged immediate repentance and promised sudden destruction. Evan knew some of his sermons on the fire and the fall practically by heart. His favourite passage was Seth's description of the valley of the avalanches with a huge precipice hanging over it. 'Walk slow and quiet brother lest the precipice fall. A curse, one swear word is enough to shake the mountain and grind you into powder. The ungodly are always walking through the valley of the avalanches.'

As official guests from the Bible College both Evan and Sydney were led up to the seats on The Big Seat – the one up the front and normally reserved for the chapel deacons. Evan lowered his head and prayed that the Lord would come among them for the service. Then he looked up at Seth Joshua.

He saw a man of inordinate bulk – six feet four with a beer barrel chest and a voice of roasting walnuts which lent itself to his Welsh stately flow of vowels and musical syllables. Even as the crowds filled up the chapel he stood ramrod erect, one hand on the Bible on the lectern, the other playing with the chain of his fob watch. Behind his watchful body there was a scroll on the chapel wall: 'Enter into His gates with thanksgiving and into His courts with praise'.

No sooner had he begun speaking than he tore into those three Roman soldiers with their unmitigated insolence and blasphemous daring in their rough handling of the Son of God.

'There is a special place for those soldiers. Oh yes, come near now and I will tell you about it. It is an infernal place of heat and flames where the thirsty will call out but no water will touch their charred lips. It is an infernal place where acid will be poured, endless, over the damned souls; where the gurgling, loaming misery will mount day after day, year after year, century after century.

'In this infernal place the dark will get progressively darker. In this infernal place, abandoned by the gentle and good, all those lost souls will stumble and fall over plateaux. Their journey will be hopeless in this infernal place. It will be a journey that will last for eternity; a journey with no prospect of release. There will be no mitigation of the penalty.'

Just then a shaft of light broke over Seth's head. As he continued talking a golden halo formed over him. The sight of the halo greatly excited the congregation and Evan sat upright, feeling ice moving hot through his veins and the old tribal passions boiling inside him as reality began dissembling before his very eyes.

A tiny red flame danced out of the air then another and another, until he found himself in a fiery pit surrounded by an impenetrable wall. Faces floated around in the flames and a voice told him: 'You, too, would be in this pit apart from God's grace.'

The mention of grace opened a solitary door and he saw a further group of chained people being driven towards the door. Evan held up his hands in horror. 'Let my people go,' he screamed out silent. 'Oh please let my people go.'

The vision lifted out of his imagination like a silken veil and he noted that the burly Seth was still speaking, finger prodding the air. 'And I am telling you here now,' he said. 'I am telling you all that God has laid it on my heart that he is going to take a lad from the collieries – just as he took Elisha from the plough. He is going to take this lad from the mine and he is going to use him to revive God's church.'

To revive God's church . . . Evan put is face in his hands, barely able to believe the evidence of his ears. Then he stood up and let out a weird, hollow call of triumph, which startled the congregation and even silenced Seth, who leaned on the lectern and looked down at the tall young man.

He is going to take a lad from the mine . . . Evan brushed the tips of his fingers over his blue mining scars. So God's call had come at last. He raised both hands up into the air and shouted out: 'So bend us now, Oh Lord. Bend us all now.'

Barely had he shouted these words when his body fell forwards into the aisle and a woman screamed as he rolled over on his back, his eyes wide open, the whole of his body stiff and his cheeks darkening with asphyxia.

'Stand back and pray my people,' Seth called out, holding his Bible aloft. 'Pray as you have never prayed before that this man be delivered from the evil one and be returned to the loving arms of the Lord.'

Muttering prayers shivered around the chapel and, a few seconds later, the stiffness broke up in Evan's body and his breathing returned and his legs thrashed around as if being touched by live electric wires. Bloodstained saliva frothed upon his lips.

The prayers became louder still and, when they had died down, an old man – magnetic and massive-browed – called direct on the Holy Spirit to pour out healing blessings. He spoke with a deathbed urgency, clenched fists held high and, as the amens and hallelujahs fluttered all around, Evan regained consciousness and stood up wiping his mouth with a handkerchief. A woman began singing *Diolch Iddo* – Thanks to Him – and Evan turned to face the congregation, lifting his arms and singing along with them.

And so the Revival of 1904 began.

* * *

Gowerton Fair was a whirl of gaudy brilliance, which attacked the peninsula once a year in the autumn. For three days the harsh bright lights and the screeching music dazzled the eyes and scraped the ears and attracted people for miles around to Gowerton. Held a few miles inland from Loughor, the fair also gave farmers and fishermen their annual opportunity to drink with and taunt one another.

Over there the big wheel dipped amidst whinnying screams and hands holding onto best bonnets; here the pig with the human hand and the sheep with five legs. There were stalls selling Bibles and baked potatoes; vendors of dumplings, sherbet suckers, toffee apples and bars of chocolate. Clowns, sweeps and threshers could all find themselves a large audience, none larger than the Punch and Judy show surrounded by a sea of jeering, helplessly laughing children as the grotesque Mr Punch bashed his wife with a stick, hurled the baby out of the booth, fought with everyone from the policeman to the crocodile and, when about to be hanged, got the hangman's head into the noose instead.

A prizefighter was flexing his muscles in the boxing booth. 'A bob for anyone who can stay five minutes with my man here.' If none of that intrigued you could always try riding a bucking donkey, have your palm read by a gypsy, see the smallest man in the world or marvel at the man who played the piano with his toes.

Beth and Michael walked through the spiralling dust and noise of the fairground and he was positively bursting with the pride of it all since, beautiful as she was, Beth was also wearing a stunning white calico dress edged with embroidered violets. Her petticoat had more layers than a large onion but, with her hair pinned back and up, it was her throat that caught the eye, unadorned yet long and full. Men's heads turned wherever she walked and Michael had to keep looking away from them looking at her. They stopped near the big wheel.

'This is what life must have been like before the chapel got at it,' he said.

'I doubt if it was ever like this.'

'There's no laughter in a chapel, girl.'

'There's not supposed to be laughter in a chapel, is there?'

Her question was underpinned with a sharpness and seriousness which he did not understand. 'Has anyone ever told you how beautiful you are?' he asked.

'No,' she said with comic surprise. 'Never.'

But she was, she was. If she had asked him to have a go at the prizefighter he would have done that; if she had asked him to play the piano with his toes he would have tried that, too.

A large crowd was gathering around the boxing booth. Michael took Beth by her elbow and led her over to find that Leighton Huyton, a kitchen worker from Crofty better known as Useless, was standing in the middle of the crowd, stripped to the waist, smoothing beer over his nipples with both hands, rolling around his tattoos and calling on the prizefighter to step down and get a good pasting.

The prizefighter also had an accomplished range of insults and the booth's proprietor – delighting in the spitting venom of the confrontation – was busy milking it for all he was worth, even raising his offer to two shillings if Useless could beat his man with no time limit on the fight.

'I'd smash him with both hands tied behind by back,' shouted Useless.

'Well, get up here and try it, little man,' the prizefighter shouted back, his thumbs pulling out the sides of his leotard.

Michael explained to Beth that although Useless was only nine stone soaking wet he had hidden strengths. 'I know he looks as though he couldn't fight his way out of a wet newspaper, but the same man would fight a brick wall if the wall looked at him the wrong way.'

'The other man seems very tough,' she said. 'Look at those muscles.'

'Tough he may be, but Useless is an animal. He's such an animal even rugby teams won't play against him. I'd put nothing on the other man's chances. You fancy watching it?'

She shook her head. 'No.'

'No what?'

'No, thank you.' They both laughed and walked over to one of the booths where he paid a penny each to go in and look at Nature's Miracles. Inside the small, dank tent the pig with a human hand turned out to be a shrivelled foetus in a bottle with a tiny shape of a hand growing out of its side; a hand so tiny Michael could not even see it until Beth pointed it out to him. The sheep with five legs was alive and fascinating enough but, for the life of them, they just could not work out what the remaining exhibits were supposed to be. 'I found something like that in my garden once,' she said pointing at some kind of centipede. 'Is that the snake with a hundred legs?'

'You tell me.'

They decided that Nature's Miracles were not very miraculous after all. When they got outside, he told the lady in the ticket booth it was all a fraud.

'We make a living where we can,' she said. He couldn't argue with that.

'Did you notice that woman's eyes?' he asked as they walked away. 'They reminded me of dead fish's eyes. Like the ones you see in Swansea fish market.'

'Funny, you know. That's just what I thought of your eyes when I saw them. There's something strange in those eyes, like a dead fish's, I thought.'

'That's charming, that is! You normally brim over with such compliments, do you?'

'Oh, now and then. Anyway I decided you probably get too many compliments. You've got a way about you so I decided to get in a few jabs and keep you down to earth. Compliments never did anyone any good. They go to your head. You fancy a drink?'

'A drink of what?'

'Beer, gin, dandelion. Whatever you fancy.'

'I don't touch alcohol, you know.' She sounded uncharacteristically prim and looked at him hard. 'You're not one of those boozers, are you?'

'Doesn't do you any harm, girl. Something to do with the chapel, is it?'

'I've seen too many go down with the drink. I had a wonderful doctor once and he went down with the drink.'

'Jesus had nothing to do with the drink, you know. He made the finest wine. And when they had drunk it all he made some more.'

'Don't talk about him like that if you please. I don't approve of that kind of talk.'

Michael frowned and Beth went silent. A shadow had fallen over their friendship that neither fully understood. He had glimpsed a flint-like seriousness that he did not entirely like. She saw levity with hints of blasphemy that worried her.

In the event no more was said and she put her arm through his and they went on the big wheel. She clung to him, too, as Gowerton rose and fell before them. Later on he won a goldfish on the darts and she took the gift with radiant warmth and thanks. She really knew how to accept gifts, he decided and, as he really liked to give them, there was promise in the air.

As they continued walking around the fairground she was already designing the tank for her fish. She would fill it with seaweed, rocks and sand, she said.

'I'm not sure how he'll get on with seaweed,' said Michael, doubtful. 'Don't goldfish come in fresh water?'

'One of Dada's friends knows all about fish. He'll know what's good for it.'

'I'll bet he doesn't know tadpoles can eat a goldfish.'

'I don't believe you,' she said.

'It's true, that. If there's enough of them, that is. Tadpoles can eat anything if there's enough of them.'

'You know the silliest of things.'

* * *

Night settled on Loughor with the single gas street lamp still hissing soft outside Island House. A few small black clouds and the odd call of a cormorant clotted the silver darkness as Evan knelt next to his bed, deep in the imaginative heart of one of his prayers. The other members of the Roberts family had long been asleep.

He had come home immediately after his call at the feet of Seth Joshua and told his family all about it. Their reaction was warm and full of thankful wonder, since fear of the Lord was strong in all of them. Even Dan, who had been having a worrying flirtation with socialism until he had gone blind in that first explosion down the pit, had muttered a little prayer of thanks and Evan had taken that as the best sign of all.

The father, Henry – a bluff, broad miner who liked stretching his braces and letting them twang against his chest – was collapsed with the honour of it all. 'Well, well,' he kept repeating, his legs stretched straight out in front of him as Evan spoke of his visionary call. 'Well, well.'

A huge lump of glowing coal fell off the fire and crackled on the hearth.

'Well, well,' Henry said again, fanning his flushed cheeks with his hand. All his life he had taken his greatest delights from the chapel and his only reading had ever been the Bible. Once, when a lot younger, he had learned a hundred and seventy-four verses in a week.

When Evan finally stopped speaking Henry gave his braces another gleeful twang and went down on his knees to give thanks that their house and family should be so honoured. A simple standard bearer, who had kept the faith all his life, he then urged that all the family should pray deep that Evan find his way and that he be guided by the great spiritual gifts of discernment and wisdom. 'The wisdom of the serpent, Lord, and the gentleness of the lamb.'

But now, late as it was, Evan was still praying and concentrating on the empty polished pews of the nearby Moriah Chapel. It was there, he sensed, that his mission must start. He heard the surging hymns of the congregation. He gave himself a tongue of prophetic fire which would scorch through the multiplying banks of prayers. He saw young children everywhere, young girls in pretty frocks and even a couple of stray sheep. There was going to be much fun and joy in this revival. Oh yes. There was going to be laughter in the tears.

Yes indeed. All heaven was going to break loose as the Holy Spirit blew the winds of Pentecostal passion throughout the land.

'I would like to be there with you when the work starts, Evan.' It was Dan, speaking in the tangled, lamp lit darkness.

'You will be, my brother, ' Evan said, his eyes still closed and head

49

bowed. 'You will be there with me. So it is written.'

There was a short silence. 'Is it also written that I shall have my sight restored?'

'Yes, Dan. Yes it is. The Lord has sworn and he will not repent. He too wants you to become a priest forever, according to the order of Melchisedec. There will be great acts of power . . . there . . . ' His eyes opened wide, as if startled by something immense, which moved deep within him. He held his hands straight out and smiled in an overwhelming sense of God's practice and presence. 'Your sight *will* be restored, Dan. And it will be restored tonight.'

He kissed his Bible and stood up to walk over to the bed, putting one hand on Dan's head, the other holding Dan's hand tight. 'Pray with me now, Dan. Come fighting in the prayer with me. He closed his eyes and gave Dan's trembling hand a reassuring squeeze. 'Dear Lord, oh you who are the great healer and with whom nothing is impossible . . . bring to us the healing spirit of the living Christ which is the very air we breathe. Come and direct your love and compassion through these hands. Open up the blood veins of intercessions that your faithful son Dan may see again.'

He stopped praying and moved behind the bedhead, now reaching down and covering Dan's milky blue eyes with both hands. 'Just as in the sacred days of old when Ananias laid his hands on Saul so now I, your humble servant Evan Roberts charge you, the holiest of holies, to come and work through these fingers, that my brother Dan may have his sight restored so that he can better serve you in the great work to come.'

Chapter Five

Michael leapt over one of the marsh gullies and turned, waiting for Beth to jump after him. Her foot slipped on some mud when she landed but he caught and steadied her by the wrist before they walked on, hand in hand. 'We lost Ben Rees out here last year,' he said. 'One of the finest fishermen on the Gower he was, too. These tides here sweep in along the gullies all around you and even the expert can get caught unawares.'

'Like love,' she said.

He turned and surveyed her with some curiosity. 'Yes. It's a bit like that.' She ducked his gaze and looked out over the muddy flatlands.

'You know, if there's anywhere I'd like to die it would be here. This must be the most beautiful and dangerous place in the world.' She held her face up to the breeze. 'I suppose anyone who has anything to do with the sea must accept danger.'

'Are you afraid of danger, girl?'

'Mmm. Always.'

'You always back away, do you?'

'Always.'

'Not good, that. You've got to fight it sometimes. You've got to stick in there and keep jabbing away or else everything gets on top of your head.'

'Not everyone is good at fighting,' she pointed out.

'Perhaps, but you could always get someone to do your fighting for you.'

The wind was whipping her hair around her neck and cheeks. 'I think I'd like to go down on to the sands,' she said. 'It's such a nice afternoon. What do you think?'

'It's your day off. Wherever you like.'

They were walking across a bank when their ears were assailed by the sound of raucous gabbling. 'What's that?' she asked.

'Shush!' He moved her forward with his hand pressing against the small of her back and, just over the bank, they found about a hundred seagulls all gossiping together in a stream. One took off when the human shadows fell over them, then another and another until they all rose in a rush, circling around their heads with furiously flapping wings.

'They must spend all day nagging one another,' he said as the birds swept away. 'You never hear a seagull sing. They just gabble and gossip and nag, endless. Not like the thrush. Now there's a real singer, full with the most enthralling rapture.'

He picked up a shell and polished it on his trouser leg. 'Did I ever tell you that I used to do a lot of singing in the chapel?' she asked. 'Have you ever done any singing?'

'Me? No. I'm the original lavatory tenor. My voice sounds like a rope under the door.' He spat on the shell and polished it again. It was green with streaks of blue. 'Sing me something, then,' he said.

'Don't be silly.'

'Go on, girl. Sing one of your hymns. If you sing any good I'll give you this priceless shell.'

She began gulping and mouthing the words, swallowing and humming for a while until they came trickling out with all the enthralling rapture of that thrush. He went completely dry inside.

When I survey the wondrous cross
On which the Prince of Glory died
My richest gain I count but loss
And pour contempt on all my pride.

Her voice was big and mellifluous and, when she had finished the verse, she looked at him and smiled. She knew she could sing but hated being seen as a show off.

'Beth Williams,' he said, important. 'In the whole history of song there has never been such a notable singer and, to mark this great occasion, I do hereby present you with this very valuable and unique shell.'

He shook her hand and presented the shell before lifting her chin towards his face with his forefinger and kissing her lips. There was the smell of sun and sea in her hair but, although he put his hand up between her shoulder blades to try and press some urgency into the matter, she did not close her eyes as she accepted the kiss. Neither did she reject it.

'One cold kiss in the sunshine,' he said.

'I'm afraid so,' she said, lowering her head and examining the shell. 'I'm sorry.'

She had, for a second, wanted to kiss him hard but extinguished the sudden flame of excitement within her almost as soon as it had flared. That sort of thing had caused enough trouble in the past. She wasn't going to get struck by lightning twice. She walked down the bank and out towards the sands, now standing quite still with her back to him and waiting for him to follow.

'Tell me girl, what does move inside you?'

She raked her fingers down through her hair and moved her head from side to side but still did not turn around.

'What goes on with you, girl?'

'There's quite a lot going on if you really want to know. But men don't understand. Men never do.'

'I might. If you told me all about it I might.'

'You couldn't.' She looked up at the sun and shaded her eyes with a hand. He thought he glimpsed something painful in her face; something unutterably sad in the sudden tightness of her mouth. She was struggling with something he did not understand. That was very clear. But what? She seemed to have the strange ability of being both warm and cold at the same time. Whenever, encouraged by her warmth, he reached out to be comforted by it, she turned as cold as ice.

Two small grey marsh horses were standing on the next bank, their necks entwined, biting off each other's fleas. They seemed content and happy enough. In the next life he wanted to come back as a marsh horse.

Later they were walking, silent, along the river bank into Loughor with his horse following at some distance behind when she suddenly stooped down to brush her dress with her hand. 'Do you think this mud will come off?' she asked.

'Let it dry first. It'll brush out easy enough.'

'Do you want to see me again?' she asked, bland, her hands still fussing around with her dress.

Just nearby there was the hovering flash of a purple kingfisher. He stopped still and took hold of an overhanging branch, his eyes narrowing in the glare of the low-slung sun. 'Of course. Why do you ask?'

Fluffy dandelion seeds caught the sun as they floated around her head. 'You have to give me time if you want to know me,' she said. She stopped speaking but he said nothing, letting her find her own way. 'I'm like that new pair of shoes,' she continued. 'It takes a lot of time to get used to me. You know. Lots of cramped toes and all that. A few blisters. You'll have to decide if I'm worth a few blisters.'

'One maybe.'

'You see, Michael, I could never rush anything. You clearly like to move at a hundred miles an hour but I'm the tortoise that travels inch by inch. With care. But you know, Michael . . . ' Such talk was clearly a great effort. 'I don't want you to leave my life because you've become impatient with me. Just wait, will you? I'll come to you, in time. I'll be there.'

He took her by the shoulders and, bending his head forward, stole a kiss from her cheek. Then he kept his lips within inches of her cheek, letting her feel the warmth of his breath and waiting for a reaction. But she merely just stood there looking at him, cold. He was about to kiss her again when she shrugged off his hands and said, 'I'd better be going now. It's getting late. But remember what I said, would you?'

'I'll remember, girl. You've got all the time you need.'

She nodded and all at once seemed pleased. 'Good,' she said and, after running the back of her hand soft down the side of his cheek, walked away quick, her emotions in mutinous disorder. Even as she walked she feared that she would burst out crying and that would never do. You should never show the colour of your tears to men. There again, Michael wasn't the sort to take advantage, was he? Was he?

She could still hardly believe that she had met someone like him, this handsome, loveable diamond with his silver tongue and his stupid horse. Might he understand it all if she told him? Might he?

Michael was asking himself his own questions when he walked back towards his horse, who gave a small delighted kick with his back leg when he saw that Michael was alone. The horse did not like Beth at all and was all sulks and tantrums whenever she was around. Horses suffered from jealousy too, Michael knew. Even horses must know the way love grabbed greedy; the way it asked for more and more, particularly when it was given less and less.

He decided that he wanted a long hard ride on the marsh and gave his horse a long chuckle in the ear. 'You and me are going for a good ride and I don't want any complaints,' he whispered.

He mounted him bareback and heeled him hard whereupon, wonder of wonders, the horse actually started galloping. As unpredictable as the weather, Michael decided, as the animal kept on galloping – without stopping or even trying to roll over in the mud and bite him. Michael had soon put a stop to that particular habit, though, by biting the horse back.

He rode down into the huge hurrying winds of the sands and felt purged and healed. He pulled the horse to a halt and just sat there, hands wrapped in the mane with sweaty steam rising out of the horse's flanks, a gaunt black shape in the sunset. But it was no use. Even then, apart from the distant hooter of the mine, all he could hear was the longing beat of her in his captured heart.

* * *

The architecture of the Moriah Chapel in Loughor reflected the peculiar passions of Welsh nonconformity. In its severe square design and absence of ornament it told of the traditional yearning for simplicity of worship: the rejection of the stately masked ball of an alien English liturgy. In its sheer size and beautiful carved pews it also told of an affluence that had come to the chapel after a century of struggle and dissent from the three perils of Anglicanism, a complacent monarchy and Tory politics.

But, that Sunday night, it was the large crowd in the usually empty building – since nonconformity had, by now, lost its visionary drive – that proclaimed a renewed contract with something godly. And there was unusual interest in the man who was doing the reading, too, since the word had swept through the town, with the power and speed of a blower down the mine, that a miracle had happened here in Loughor.

To the left of the pulpit – the central point of all chapel interiors, since the sermon was always at the very heart of the service – sat the women, their elaborate hats skewered in place by rapier-like hatpins, and the girls in their best bonnets. On the right of the pulpit were the men and boys, polished and burnished in their Sunday best, with gold fob watches and throat-choking high starched collars.

Such a division of the sexes recalled the seventeenth century chapel Puritanism which had subsequently been much influenced by Charles Wesley. Yes, he said, there could be dancing but it should be men with men; women with women; by daylight and out of doors.

As they finished singing Dr. Parry's *Dies Irae*, the unfamiliar figure of Dan Roberts stood up to do the reading from John.

'And as Jesus passed by, he saw a man which was blind from his birth. And his disciples asked him, saying, Master, who did sin, this man, or his parents, that he was born blind? Jesus answered, Neither hath this man sinned, nor his parents: but that the works of God should be manifest in him.'

Dan's face was muscular and even heavy, with the strong nose and jaw of the Roberts family. Though the skin on the left side of his face was crumpled and scarred by an old mining accident he spoke in a beautiful modulated voice. His mother, Hannah, wept throughout the reading while Evan and his father sat together, beaming with pleasure and praise.

Dan, blind for five years after that explosion down in Broadoak, had had his eyesight restored, sudden. The next day they had sent for a specialist from Swansea who had examined Dan's eyes and pronounced them completely cured. It was a miracle, pure and simple. An act of God.

Dan and Evan had agreed not to say anything about their prayer together that night. Evan believed that such healings were gifts of the

Holy Spirit, which could just as easily be withdrawn if flaunted in public. Jesus, who cured with but two hands and a compassionate heart, had been quite specific that healing came through the power of believing prayer in private. However, his family saw it as still further proof that God was showering blessings on Island House.

'Then again called they the man that was blind, and said unto him, Give God the praise: we know that this man is a sinner. He answered and said, Whether he be a sinner or no, I know not: one thing I know, that, whereas I was blind, now I see . . . '

The smiles and tears redoubled at these words. It was almost impossible to express what everyone in the family felt about the cure, though Evan had an added reason to be pleased since he was now certain that Dan would renounce all that damned socialism and devote himself to God.

Socialism had been breaking out like a plague in the South Wales valleys that year and, if that wasn't bad enough, the Merthyr colliers had sent Kier Hardie, the first socialist MP, to the Houses of Parliament. The real curse of socialism – in the chapel's eyes – was that it attempted to do for men what God alone could do. In its assumptions and practice it proclaimed that God was irrelevant. Where would all such ideas end? Those Merthyr miners had taken the first step, in Evan's view, to creating a new Gomorrah.

Later, after a windy sermon which, in itself, explained why the pews were so empty in the Moriah, the minister, in his announcements, said: 'Dan's brother, Evan, has also returned to us today from his studies in Newcastle Emlyn. You will all remember him as an outstanding Christian who is training for the cloth and who once used to play fiddle in our orchestra. He had asked if he can speak to all the young people in the vestry at the end of the service. He wants to talk about his experiences in Newcastle Emlyn and any who are interested are welcome.'

The vestry, Pisgah, was the tiny mother chapel of the Moriah and was now used just for the weekly Bible classes and Sunday School. At the end of the service twelve young people, eight boys and four girls, went in there to sit on the long wooden benches with the yellow gaslights flickering on two of the walls.

Evan stood up on a tiny dais and, in firm business-like tones, said, 'Anyone who wants to go home should go at once since I want all the doors locked, with no one entering or leaving, until the Holy Spirit has come among us.'

No one moved and, on a signal from Evans, it was Dan who closed the windows and bolted the thick wooden door.

'You may not know what the Holy Spirit is but I will explain it to you,' said Evan. 'The Holy Spirit is the mind and strength and power of an active, holy God. The Holy Spirit brings you prophecies on the wind and tells us the deep things of God, which are known to God alone. The Holy Spirit knows all the things of God and reveals only what he chooses. The Holy Spirit is a person in his own right, with his own purpose who, said the prophets, would never, ever leave you desolate. So I come unto you.' He nodded and smiled, raising both hands up in the air and far apart. 'Yes, my children. I, the Holy Spirit, come and minister unto you.'

He clenched both his hands. 'I want each of you to speak aloud in turn: Oh Lord, send the Holy Spirit for Christ's sake. Amen.'

They each said the prayer in turn but Evan shook his head. He made them repeat it again and again. Round and round went the prayer until Janie Rees burst into tears. Her sister Lizzie began crying, too. Henry Penry, a young farmer, had to hold his ears since, as he said later, they were echoing with a mighty hurricane of all his sins of old. Hugh Edwards fell to his knees as if struck on the shoulder by a mighty punch. Still Evan urged them onwards.

'Bend us in our sin, bend us in our shame, Oh Holy Spirit. Bend us, your worthless servants. Bend us until we are completely broken under the shadow of the cross, that we may be born anew.'

At 4.35 a.m. the wooden door of Pisgah was unbolted and the first converts of the Revival stumbled out, singing hymns and red-eyed, into the grey, dripping graveyard.

Chapter Six

All that summer the price of cockles had been very poor. Sometimes, if Michael had dug a real load, he took the morning train from Pen-clawdd to Swansea market. Selling them wholesale, the price could go as low as a penny a pint – and there are a great many cockles in a pint. But, set against this possibility of at least some profit, was the four pennies for the return train fare or, if he went by horse and cart, the penny each way for tolls at Waunarlwydd – and nothing but irritability from the horse.

To make matters worse the intense rains of the summer, combining with a late rally of intense autumnal sunshine, had produced a corresponding glut of cockles on the sands. Now the cocklers could not even rely on the derisory penny a pint. Whenever the cocklers met their conversations were merely endless complaints about the price of cockles, laced with wistful nostalgia for the year when they had brought in four pence a pint. Everyone conveniently forgot that it was a lucky man indeed who could dig out a pint a tide that year.

Some of the Pen-clawdd cocklers – especially the ones with large families to support – had to get out into the pubs and valley towns selling for a farthing a dish. It was a tedious business, to be sure, but the only way to secure a decent price.

Michael, too, made the rounds of the alehouses. He actually enjoyed working in the jubilant atmosphere of the pubs and, with Beth still very much on his mind, there was only one town he wanted to work in now: Crazy Town. Ever since last seeing her, he had just worked the tides and moped around the place, brooding and feeling as useless as a fungus. Sometimes he sat on the sea wall and watched the children riot in the schoolyard while the headmaster played fiddle in a locked study. Henry Thomas loved fiddles and had long abandoned supervision of the school in favour of fiddling all day alone.

Some nights Michael got drunk in the local tavern and chatted with Peter Taylor, a farmer much taken by melancholia who worried about the continual disappearance of his geese. 'There's nothing easier to steal,' he moaned. 'You just stuff their heads under their wings and they don't know if they are coming or going.'

'I know the feeling,' said Michael, burying his nose into the froth of yet another pint of beer.

But that day, 11 November it was, he had built up a sizeable stock of cockles and there were traces of an unexpected summery warmth in the grey-streaked night when he dropped off ten pints at Mrs Hooch's shop in Gorseinon, before taking the high metalled road down into Loughor. A brisk westerly wind was blowing in over the river and a dog was howling in a farmyard as the horse cantered down the road. Already the tree branches were largely bare, hanging over the road like whips with the fallen leaves crackling with brittle jokes as the wheels of his cart rolled through them.

The accident happened early that night in the very odd way in which all accidents happen. One minute he was watching the Great Western Railway's local train working up speed on its way out of Loughor towards Milford Haven – and the next the train just went missing.

He heard the jubilant steam whistle and saw the long rolling shape of the train, bright as a necklace of gold glow-worms, moving out of the station. Then it took the rolling bend parallel with the river before plummeting down into the long cutting near the colliery. Michael thought no more of it and was vaguely trying to decide which alehouse to start working in when something began turning around inside him, telling a mute but urgent story about something somewhere having just gone woefully wrong.

The train had indeed entered the cutting, but it had not come out again.

He could hear nothing since the wind was blowing quite hard away from him. He could not see anything either, but something terrible *had* happened. That was for certain. He jumped off the cart and went scrambling up a bank, which brought him out on top of the cutting. A bright explosion of flame made him shield his eyes. There was another long crunching sound and a sharp bang. He swallowed hard. It was the nearest he was ever to get to an authentic glimpse of hell.

Insofar as he could make it out in the exploding darkness, the train had slewed right off the rails with balls of fire erupting, green on black, out of the collapsed passenger carriages. The engine had tumbled over on its side, with the coal from the tender piled up high on the cab and long tongues of red fire flickering out between the wheels. He crawled closer, hearing a volley of bangs and the occasional scream with, every now and then, an erupting jet of white steam hissing bilious. He turned around the huge engine, which was lying entangled in some telephone wires like a trapped and expiring dinosaur. Just nearby a body lay near they leading coaches, illuminated in the ghostly green lights of the exploding gas from the tanks for the passenger lights.

Another green burst of incandescence revealed a number of people, their faces masked with blood, wriggling up through the broken carriage windows. One woman was crying, hysterical. Newspapers, sewing bags and portmanteaux were scattered over the nearby banks. A foot was kicking its way through one of the windows. A rag doll lay at his feet. A crumpled magazine lay near a wheel, disengaged from the track and revolving slow in the smell of burning oil. A scream died down into a spine-chilling sob.

Now people from the town were beginning to appear on the embankments; they stood there, mute and petrified by the enormity of the accident. What should be done first? Was it possible to do anything at all? Each second of staring contributed to the general paralysis. It was Martin Probert, a collier and one of the family that owned Broadoak, a man who had long learned that death should be stared square in the eye, which got Michael moving final.

Probert walked up behind Michael and, calm as you like, pushed his cap a few inches up over the back of his head as he surveyed the carnage. 'We'd better sort out that engine, boy,' he said pointing up the track. 'There might be men caught in that.'

Michael followed Probert down to the embattled engine, his belly still sucked up into his throat as he climbed up over the hot oily rails to be handed a shovel. Probert picked up the fireman's rake. 'I'll rake it out down there and you shovel it over there. Down there, look.' He raked hard as Michael tried to hold his footing on the sloping cast-iron floor thinking that it would help if he knew what he was supposed to be doing. On the other hand, he guessed Probert knew, so merely did as he was told. 'Get your back against there. Shovel, boy. Don't look at it. Shovel.'

Probert raked again and again, now pulling out such flaming bundles of coals he even burned his own trousers. 'Nothing of any use came of coal,' he spat. 'It'll kill us all in the end.'

They soon picked up a rhythm as they ripped the guts out of the mountain of coal piled up on the van but, even in his sweating, dishevelled state, Michael could not but help feel a huge uplift when he saw a gang of colliers coming to the train. Colin Pritchard, the shift foreman, was already shouting sharp, loud orders at them which the men obeyed without argument or comment.

'Right, I want four of you to rip that carriage out. Two of you keep an eye on the fire. Rees, get back to town and organise an ambulance. Peter, get those fools up there to open up their homes. Check the hospital while you're at it. The rest of you smash any windows you can find and haul them out. If they're trapped call me.'

'We've put this boiler to sleep,' Probert shouted.

'Give us a hand down here then. There's people in here.'

Pritchard picked up a rock and smashed one of the windows. 'Hold on there,' he told the dazed passengers. 'I'm going to break the rest.'

More colliers came trooping down the bank from the other pits, many carrying picks and spades which they used to tear apart the telescoped carriages ruthless. They would have dismantled a Norman castle in five minutes flat if they thought there was someone buried beneath it. There was no individual heroics either – all were busy helping one another or else keeping out of each other's way, if need be. Tactics for survival ran deep in the mining tribe.

A tall man wearing a deerstalker and a cape was one of the first to climb out of one smashed carriage. 'I've got a brace of partridges in there,' he said to one of his rescuers. Next a woman came struggling out of a broken window, holding a fur muffler to the side of her gashed face.

'I told you we should have travelled first class but you wouldn't listen, would you?' the man in the deerstalker shouted at her. 'Just look at the first class carriages back there. They're still on the rails. The Great Western only ever wrecks its second class carriages.'

Michael helped a woman down and was walking along the side of the track when he bumped into Beth, kneeling down and bandaging a man's arm with swift, absorbed care. She looked up and, even in her harassed state, surrounded by all this carnage with those gas cylinders still flickering their green flames over the scene, Michael could not help being captivated by the look of her. 'Get those stretchers over here,' she was shouting at a group of colliers. 'There's a man down there with a twisted back.'

'Anything I can do, girl?' he asked and she looked up at him curious, at first not recognising him in fiery darkness, particularly as his face was so black from all the shovelling.

'Oh, it's you,' she said final.

'Of course it's me. I asked if there's anything I can do?'

'You can . . . there's a little girl wandering around over there. Take her up . . . ' She was off guard and unusually flustered. He guessed that it might have been the sudden sight of him that had shaken her. She reached out and squeezed his hand quite hard. 'Come and see me at the hospital tonight, will you? You might have to wait around – I've no idea how long cleaning this lot up will take. But that girl. Hurry now.'

He nodded and turned, running back to where he had remembered

61

seeing the little girl wandering around, clutching a doll and calling out for her mother. He found her, unharmed, sitting on a pile of railway sleepers, talking to her doll so he took her hand and led her up to a woman on the bank. 'If you want to do something useful,' he said, giving the girl's hand to the woman, 'take this little one home and look after her. Tell the police you've got her first, though.' The woman swooped up the little girl in her arms and left immediate . . .

* * *

By now the colliers had set up dotty lamps all around the scene of the accident and Michael was threading his way back to where he had last seen Beth when he noticed a group of five come hurrying out of the darkness and kneeling together in prayer. Michael knew straight off that it was Evan Roberts, up to his chapel antics again. He had heard a lot about the preacher boy of late.

'A fat lot of good that's going to do,' Michael shouted at Evan who remained kneeling, head bowed and eyes closed. 'It's done *mun*, done. That's what your great God of mercy and love does.'

A few of the group looked up, anxious at the taunt, when a woman came stumbling by them, coughing up blood over the front of her dress. Still Evan kept praying, holding out his hands for the others to stay calm.

'Typical chapel, that,' said Michael going to the distressed woman. 'Typical, that is. The world dies and the chapel prays.'

He led the woman over to the hospital workers and, checking that Beth was nowhere around, walked up to the row of terraced houses on the other side of the cutting. 'You can wash in here if you want,' a woman in a floral pinafore said to him. What with everything swirling around him he had hardly been aware of himself – let alone his appearance – and he saw that his arms were black with coal dust; there was a blister on his elbow too where a jet of steam had got him and his trousers had been burned by the cinders.

He walked into the back kitchen of the woman's house and stared at his reflection in the mirror, his face as black as night, the coal dust clogging up his eyelashes and hair. The woman poured out a basin of hot water. 'There's plenty more of that,' she said. 'The fire's lit so take all you want. Do you want anything to eat, do you? There's apple pie in the oven. No? Some bread and cheese maybe? No? Well, give me a call if you want anything.'

He washed as best he could and walked out into the passage, noticing some people in the front parlour. He walked in and sat on the arm of a sofa next to a man sitting on a chair. He did not recognise the man, but asked how he was. There was the deepest grief in the lines of the man's face and he did not reply to Michael's question.

'You were in the crash, were you?' Michael asked. 'A bad one that.'

His head slumped down on his chest.

'Any idea what started it?' Michael went on.

The man's fists clenched and unclenched, then he just stood up and walked out of the room.

'It's his boy,' a woman said. 'His boy was killed in the train.'

'I'm sorry,' Michael said. 'I didn't know.'

'Bill always wanted him to get out of the colliery. Trains are safer, he always said. Pits are dangerous to be in, he said. Now look at it. Cut in two, he was. That's how safe trains are.'

On the other side of the room two men were trying to console the woman in the floral pinafore who had invited Michael in for a wash. She was crying pitiful now but, seeing Michael again, she said even in her tears, 'Are you sure you're not wanting anything to eat, *bach*? I only made that apple pie this morning. This morning I made it. Apple pie.'

Michael shook his head and stood up, feeling strangely shocked. The woman in the pinafore was clearly the mother of the dead boy. So what was she doing offering him apple pie and a wash? The woman had been struck by a sword stroke and she had been going out offering hospitality to strangers. It was odd to be sure but, somehow, oddly Welsh too.

He made his way back over the railway line to discover that his horse was grazing on the bank, exactly where he had left him. He rode back to Pen-clawdd to change.

* * *

It was pandemonium that night in Loughor Hospital. People hurried from ward to ward, carrying stretchers or pushing trolleys of medicine. 'I won't be getting out for hours,' said Beth walking alongside Michael and shaking her head with the fatigue and hopelessness of it all. 'How was the little girl?'

'She was fine.'

'You looked after her then?' Even with the thousand other details she had to think about there was real concern in her face. Michael felt a tiny spasm of guilt that he had merely handed the girl over to someone else.

'Of course. She was looked after fine.'

She nodded, satisfied. 'Good. Look, Michael, it's hopeless now. I'll see you on Thursday then, shall I? There's things we should talk about.'

'If you want. Same time?'

She looked behind her, anxious. 'Yes. Fine. Look, I'm in such a mess. My hair's a tip. Everything's so . . . But do something for me will you?'

'Anything, girl.'

'Come here.' She took his hand, looking back again, as if to check that no one was watching, as she pulled him into the darkness by a hedgerow. 'Just grab hold of me would you? Go on. I won't bite. That's it. Now give me a nice big kiss.'

He kissed her and her very being all but rose up and smothered him with her warmth, holding him tight with both hands, pushing her thighs into his as a faint squeal of breath came out from her mouth. 'Now give my back a good rub and kiss me again,' she added.

He complied, speechless with astonishment. Going out with this girl was a bit like gazing into that conjuror's hat – you just never knew what was going to come out next.

'Mmm, that's a lot better that is,' she said. 'Nothing like a good rub to pick me up. I feel a lot better now. I can even face that matron. See you Thursday.' She planted a damp kiss on his cold nose and hurried back into the hospital. There was nothing cold about his insides, though, which were erupting, volcano-like, with the warmth of her.

* * *

Michael walked home, slow. He heard an unusually loud volume of hymn singing coming from out of Moriah Chapel when he passed but thought nothing of it. Later he came to the wreckage of the train, where workmen were still busy clearing the line by the light of the dotty lamps. One was leaning on his shovel.

'They're sending inspectors down from London tomorrow,' he said, seeing Michael standing next to him. 'But I could tell them what done it without them coming all the way down here. There's old mine workings under here. Subsidence. That's what it was. See those metals over there?' He nodded at the twisted rails. 'They sank, they did. They've sunk before, too.'

'The whole town's sinking,' Michael replied. 'There's hardly a straight building in the place. How many died? Have you heard?'

'Ten I heard. Six from the town here. The fireman lives just up there. Only a young boy as well.'

'Six is a lot from a small place like this.'

'One is a lot,' the workman said. 'You expect it in the colliery but not on the railway.'

A group of people was standing at the top of the bank watching the clearing operations and, down near the line, Percy Rees, a local idiot, was shouting and gesticulating to the crowd. He had found a boot with a foot in it, he claimed. 'It's down here,' he repeated. 'Come and look. It's down here.'

A lone figure did break away from the group to go down and have a look but, in the event, it turned out to be yet another of Percy Rees's many delusions. Seconds later he was shouting that he had found a head with a cap on it. This time they all ignored him.

'That lot have been standing there since it happened,' the workman said, spitting for punctuation. 'Wouldn't be surprised if they hadn't taken root.'

'Vultures all,' Michael said. 'With any luck another train will come along and run them over.'

'Well, we'd better get this one cleared up first.'

The night was big and quiet as he followed the marsh road back to Pen-clawdd. Just near the dead oak an owl hooted, mysterious; the wind had all but disappeared and the branches on the hawthorn were perfectly still. He would long remember the way it was that night, precisely because everything was magical and still with no pain or commotion in the air. He would remember it because he, too, was comfortable like the night, warm with his renewed link with Beth, his body still alive with the unexpected show of her sensuality.

But even as he remembered that night – painted the colours of calm, alive with the scent of great happiness – there was a sense of imminence, the faint feeling of massing storm clouds. It was there in all the stillness, but he could not put his finger on it.

Winter was striding down on them and this terrible disaster had fallen right on their doorsteps. Prophetic senses are always vague and elusive and sometimes wrong, but it was almost as if the times were preparing for a great lament. It was gathered there in that night. A sleeping man is quiet. A graveyard is very quiet indeed. And, so too, is the eye of a storm.

* * *

The high tides of autumn began the following morning, flooding up over the marsh and lapping around the bottom of the gardens on the Pen-clawdd seafront. The marsh horses took to the roads and outlying fields on such tides and, with chilling westerlies gusting up to fifty miles an hour, the horses would often stand in immobile sodden groups behind the shelter of moored fishing boats or garden walls.

For two solid days waving sheets of rain came swirling in over the sands, scouring the rooftops of the houses, knocking the last of the leaves off the trees and sending them riding down the overflowing gutters. The railway workers, toiling to clear away the last of the wreckage and to repair the damaged track, turned up their collars and cursed.

Even in such weather the cocklers still worked the tides, but they were miserable hours with the damp seeping into the bones and telling stories of the arthritis that was to come. The one great moment everyone looked forward to was the end of the tide, when they could stretch out in front of the fire and feel their muscles thaw out one by one, for frozen joints really do creak.

Michael was out working on the sands when he first heard them. *Beep, bleep; beep, bleep.* He saw one rising into the air and then a whole flock flew through the grey weeping sky in a careless V formation. With their bright red bills and black heads they were not difficult to recognise but it was the monotonous bleeping – barren of song or melody – that told of the return of the oystercatcher.

These birds had been wintering here since 1860 and would now begin swarming around the cocklers all winter, scavenging for the leftover cockles until the summer sun drove them back to Scandinavia. Only birds as illogical as the oystercatcher would follow the cold, he decided, as a pair fluttered down on to a patch of sand he had raked earlier, breaking open some of the baby cockle shells with their long, dagger-like bills.

Oystercatchers opened shells with a plodding but murderous efficiency; if a shell refused to part, the bird would carry it high into the air and drop it on to a rock or a hard patch of ground. Bright golden patches of broken cockle shells littered the sands like frozen sunbursts.

Michael knew that the cockle beds were pillaged by crabs, flatfish and flounders; that cockles even eat their own baby young. But, with the oystercatchers eating half their own weight of cockles each day, they took more out of the beds than all the other predators put together. He could not help but feel a slight shiver of distaste whenever he looked at them. He loved birds yet always thought of oystercatchers as little more than rats on wings. So they were back, and bringing their irritating bleeping with them.

The two birds nearby were still busy slicing open the shells and sucking out the cockles. He threw a rake at them. They looked at the rake unperturbed but took off when his sieve when sailing towards their heads. *Beep, bleep; beep, bleep.*

* * *

The final count in the train crash, fourteen dead and thirty-four injured Dan wrote in his diary. *Evan says it's God's way of preparing the ground for the work here. Subsidence of rail was above the old No.3 Shaft in Broadoak. Tredegar! My old friend. Last night sixth meeting in Pisgah. Eighty-two converts so far. Moved to Moriah now. Chrysanthemums on the altar. Ordered sixteen tons of Abercarn. Nights turning very cold.*

* * *

But come Thursday the weather staged a miraculous reversal. Bright, hard sunshine streamed down over the rooftops of Pen-clawdd and the tiny streets were alive with morning dreams and children's whirling tops. It came as both a celebration and a gift. As they rode in the cart along the marsh road down to the slags, Beth stretched herself in the luxuriant warmth of it all.

'I can hardy believe it,' she said. 'I'd thought we'd seen the last of the sun for the rest of the year. Everyone is still that fed up after the train crash. You've heard, I expect, what's going on in the chapel?'

'No, what's that?' Michael asked.

'There's this young blacksmith, Evan Roberts.'

'Oh that sledgehammer. I've come across him. It adds up, of course. Big disaster – everyone down in the dumps and he comes along promising eternal joy. It adds up.'

She was surprised at how badly his remarks upset her. She had not looked at it in anything like those terms; in fact, she rather approved of it all – albeit secretly. In the event she decided to ignore what he said. 'He's been conducting services in the Moriah and more and more people are going along every night. There's talk of a big revival. Some of the services have been going on for five or six hours. Dada wants me to go along too.'

'What rubbish. You're not going, I hope?'

She had, as it happened, been planning to go along when she had a free evening but clearly saw no point in revealing her intentions to him. She had heard him blacken the air with blasphemy once before and didn't want to hear that again. 'Where did you say we were going?' she asked, changing the subject.

'You're not going to listen to that toss-pot are you?' he asked, changing it back again.

'I might. It's nothing to you, is it?'

'Stuff and nonsense. That's all the chapel ever doles up. Listen to that for long and you will go soft in the brain.'

'Yes. That's the trouble with you, isn't it? It just wouldn't do for you to listen to anyone, would it?' She was angry now, more angry than she could remember being for a long time, her tongue running renegade and malicious. 'Oh you've got it all sewn up, haven't you? You and that horse of yours. The pair of you are really going to make a great contribution out on the sands, aren't you? You're really going to build the world anew out here, aren't you? Just who do you think you are anyway?'

'Listen, girl.' There was no friendliness in his voice either. 'They rounded up two hundred children in the streets in Swansea last month for selling matches and sent them to the workhouse. There's hardly a child in Pen-clawdd with a decent pair of shoes. Children are still going down the pit at the age of twelve. Every week now starving Irish are being dumped on Mumbles beach. Now if . . . ' A lot of prodding the air to underline the *if*. 'If the chapel started doing something about all that I might, just might, go and listen to what they are saying.'

She was sitting upright, her arms folded, as cold and distant as the moon. 'You're one of them socialists then,' she said final. 'You know, I sensed you were trouble. I just knew it from the very first second I saw you.'

'I'm for life. Here and now.'

'So is the chapel. The chapel's for life too. It's not your version of life, I can see.' She was finding him arrogant to the point of insufferability. 'All you socialists do is go around pressing your version, as if no one else had a brain. But what gets to me is that you lot never do anything. No, never! I've nursed men like you. Forever lying in bed and talking about the new Utopia but never doing anything about it. Do you? What are you going to do about those starving Irish in the Mumbles?'

'Feed them.'

'Oh I see. You're going to go down there with your horse and give them a plate of cockles each when they land, are you? That's brilliant, isn't it?'

'Individuals can't do anything. It's the state that has to change.'

'I don't think I'm enjoying myself any more. Just take me home, will you?'

He did not reply since they come to the slags, a high squat jumble of rocks flung out into the estuary at the end of the sands where – or so Michael had planned before the argument – they would pick mussels which grew in encrusted, bearded clumps on the sides of the rocks in the sea. It was normal to harvest them with long rakes, but you could also pick them by hand when the tide was right out.

'Listen, Michael, just take me home first, will you?'

He ignored her and jumped down off the cart, untethering the horse

68

to let him graze before throwing a sack over his shoulder and walking down towards the sea. When she saw that he was not going to wait for her or, indeed, take any notice of her at all, she followed, her movements still stiff with anger, still smouldering inside.

He noticed that she had walked up behind him. 'There's a story attached to these slags,' he said, chirpy as a grasshopper. 'A mermaid came ashore here one day and married a local farmer. It's a true story, this. Well, they fell in love with one another deep and got married. Nine boys they had in all and, when they grew up, they all went to sea one by one. After the youngest left home the father died sudden, so the mermaid decided that she would go back to the waves and watch out for her boys. They say that on wild, stormy nights she can be spotted keeping watch on the end of the slags. If any ships get into trouble she slips into the water and guides them back to the safety of the port. That's why they never have any wrecks out here. Do you like that story?'

'Mmm. It was lovely. Tell me another.' Her good humour had returned in full blaze now. She liked the way he could pull her out of herself. It was good for her, that. 'Go on. Tell me another.'

He wagged a finger at her. 'Only if you're a good girl and stop arguing with your superiors.'

'Oh foof to that,' she said, stamping her foot in comic anger. 'I want to hear another story.'

'First there's this cask to fill before the tide turns. All you've got to do is pick the largest ones, swish them around in a pool and put them in a sack, like this.' He tore a clump of mussels off the side of the rock and plucked off three of the largest ones. 'Try to leave the little ones because they've got more growing to do yet. If you can find them growing in any mud, they come away easier.'

'It's as easy as that, is it?'

'Just as easy as that. When you've filled the sack I'll tell you another story.'

'As good as the last one?'

'Better. Much better.'

They worked for half an hour and the sack was filling up well. She stepped from rock to rock and at one point he caught himself admiring her silhouette as she stooped, with one hand holding the bottom of her dress, in a pool iridescent with sunshine. An exotic fawn, perhaps, come down out of the jungle to drink at twilight. 'How are you getting on?' he asked.

'My back's a bit sore,' she said. 'I hope this story's going to be worth it.'

69

'It'll be worth it.'

'What's it about?'

'Jungle creatures.'

'What sort of jungle creatures?'

'Beautiful ones that drink at twilight. Now fill that sack.'

'Oh foof.'

She felt a smile stretching right through her as she continued picking the mussels. She wondered what it would be like to have him lying on her, licking the side of his neck and tasting the sun and sand in it, having him bury himself in her hard . . . but Beth, no girl . . . that wouldn't do at all. She looked sideways at him, guilty and even fearful that he might have guessed at her thoughts. Must be all this sun having a strange effect on her. She thought about her Mam making scones in the kitchen. That was safe, that was.

She stood up, kneading the small of her back with her right hand. 'What are we going to do with all these mussels anyway?'

It is said on the Gower that if a swallow flies near to the ground or cows hold up their tails to the wind or cats begin to jump around for no reason at all then it's a definite sign of a coming storm. Michael was not sure about any of that but he did know that he felt a twinge in his elbow and looked up to see a thin wisp of blackness curling around and inside itself over the outlying waves. It swirled and grew fatter; there was a darting flash of white electricity and it became very cold.

'Girl, we're in dead trouble,' was about all he could say. There was a blinding sheet of lightning and the blue sky turned dark around the edges with fat drops of rain spitting spasmodic like a faulty machine gun. He took off his jacket and flung it over her head and shoulders, already wincing as the first of the hailstones stung his skin. 'We've got to run for it. And I mean *run*.'

They dashed back along the side of the slags as the hailstones and rain got caught up with the thunder. Lightning drove through the sky in luminous gashes. When they reached the marsh road she stopped, uncertain, her hands forming a cowl with his jacket. He pushed her forward again towards the small cliff.

'Up here. That's it. See the hole? Make for that.' She ran again, bending into the wind and stumbling over the rocks as he followed and bundled her forward. At the entrance of the cave he took her hand and pulled her into it. 'Plenty of room inside,' he said. 'It just looks small.'

He flopped on to the ground inside the mouth of the cave and stretched out his arms, sore and faintly bruised from the battering by the hailstones. She sat on a rock, body bowed and arms encircling her waist.

'What was that?' she panted.

'An electric storm. I've been caught in a few but none that sudden. It won't last long but it makes up for its shortness by its savagery.'

'You can say that again. It was like being punched all over.' She sniffed a sort of smile.

'It's a good job we weren't out cockling. Lightning goes for rakes and spades. You've got to fling them as far as you can when they start.'

'What then?'

'You run as fast as you can.'

'What about the horse?'

'That's about the only time he will run fast.'

'Now, I mean. What about him now?'

'If I know him he'll be hiding under the cart – if he hasn't bolted straight home. He's not very keen on suffering, is that horse.'

'Who is?'

'Aye. Who is?'

The storm raged on outside the darkness of the cave. Lightning flashes lit Beth like a slide on a magic lantern. Her damp dress clung to her full form and, just sitting there half in darkness and half in jagged brilliance, he found her unutterably beautiful. Perhaps she caught what was in his look, he thought. Perhaps she did not. But, not for the first time, he had to turn his head away.

'Here's another place thick with legend,' he said, staring into the darkness of the cave. 'If you can get your father to borrow some miners' helmets I'll take you down it one day.'

'No fear. I'd cry. All that darkness would make me cry.'

'You wouldn't. You'd wonder at it. There's unbelievable limestone formations in some of those caverns. Coloured beauty petrified over the centuries. Anyway, the story is that a monk once lived here . . . '

'Who tells you all these stories?' she interrupted. 'Or do you just make them all up?'

'Certainly not. All my stories are true. Look, do you want to hear this story or not?'

'Sorry I spoke.'

'Well this monk had fallen madly in love with a woman over in Crofty but, being a monk with his vows and whatever, he could never touch or go near her . . . '

A shadow fell over him and he turned his head to find that she was standing astride him, now sitting down on his knees, her hair dripping over his face and hands fondling his chest. 'Kiss me,' she said.

He swallowed. 'This monk. He'd really got it bad.'

71

'Kiss me.'

'Well, this woman died and still the monk could not get over her.'

'Finish the story later. Kiss me, will you?'

She stretched out her body on his and the universe shrank to that small space between their lips. They kissed and he held her firm as her hips moved, gentle, with his before he rolled on top of her, pouring kisses down on those full parted lips, the harsh jubilation of the storm playing on the edges of his mind. His imagination had put him in this situation often enough and a voice told him to keep calm.

But self-control had never been one of his strong points and, with her becoming more fevered by the second, he put his hand up between her legs, all the time ready and prepared for her to call a halt to it.

Yet she did not want to call a halt to it, her juices running thick and warm as boiling metal scorched through her veins and her hands reached out wanting more, more, more. Every inch of her was stiff with passion as she moaned with a fury which shook him to the core and her legs moved compliant.

He was certain that at that moment they were of the same thought and desire. He was determined to possess her, not so much for physical satisfaction as for the fact that the absence of physical love seemed to get in the way somehow, to stop everything growing between them.

He was engaged in some awkward movements with his trousers when a baby, whirling in a coracle, screamed out on the sea of her passion. It was a scream of desolation and pain with the mite's forehead rumpled red and angry. Whole parts of Beth fell away to the ground and her eyes opened, wide and startled, as if she had just seen something horrific. Letting out a mewl of anger, she shoved her palms up against his shoulders and pushed him off with such a force that he fell sideways and cracked the side of his head against the wall of the cave.

She rolled over on to her stomach, head lowered with thin, silent sobs making her shoulders heave and tremble. He wanted to smooth her hair or give her a piggyback or one of his chuckles into her ear . . . anything to brighten her up. But he knew that it would all be inappropriate, that there was a lake of sorrow here that he would never drain, even if he smoothed her hair and gave her piggybacks and chuckles in her ear for the rest of her life.

'I think the storm has settled,' he said.

She stood up, snuffling and wiping the tears off her flushed cheeks with her fingers, now turning to bow out of the entrance of the cave. She stopped and her head turned towards him, her face cold now, the tears stopped.

'I'm going to walk home on my own,' she said, evenly and without emotion. 'What is more, I don't want to see you ever again. Not ever.' The word 'ever' was spoken with the harsh finality of a death sentence and he did not doubt that she meant it.

She ducked out of the cave, leaving him feeling like a small boy who had been offered an ice cream and then had it snatched away. It was all this emptiness in him that was so hard to take: a great canyon of emptiness echoing with empty sounds.

He was still lying there, staring up from the bottom of his canyon, when he heard the noise of moving rocks outside the cave. He looked up at a familiar silhouette. It was Beth, back again.

'The storm's over so are you coming or what?' she asked. 'We've still got that sack to fill, haven't we?'

He said nothing, emerging from the cave and walking down to the sea with her. The sun was glowing ferocious again, sitting on the blue sky like a fiery coin. She slipped her arm through his though, curiously, he still felt that empty gulf.

'I'm going to make you a mussel pie,' she said. 'If you can spare enough mussels, that is.'

'Take all you want. They're free like the wind.'

'I'll make a pie for Dada, too. He likes mussel pies. Trouble is I'm not very good at pastry. Sometimes it goes messy like tar. You wouldn't mind, would you?'

'Well, to be honest with you, I was never that mad about eating tar.'

Chapter Seven

Beth woke early on Sunday morning to discover that Jack Frost had been out with his ladder during the night, busy making silver patterns on the window; kaleidoscopic starbursts and fanciful cobwebs which all glinted in the sunshine, like priceless treasure.

She threw one foot out after the other, each with two socks on and, as had been her daily habit since childhood, first wound up her tiny fretwork clock before pushing up the window and looking out over the glistening grey slate roofs towards the estuary. The texture of a Welsh town's Sunday morning was always unmistakable: nothing moved and the mahogany aroma of the weekly joint, being cooked slow and to perfection, was already seeping out of some kitchens. Quite soon, the church bells would join in the Sunday celebration, nudging people out of their slumbers as the peals romped down the roads and bounded around the corner, reminding people of their duty to pray.

During the rest of the week at this time, men were going noisily to work, carrying their snap tins and scuffing the cleats on their boots against the flagstones. The women would already be on their knees, their backsides wobbling as they stoned their doorsteps. But not today, since today was the Sabbath, the day of rest.

Geraint Jones was walking along the road pushing a cart overflowing with turnips. It was his queer way of walking that always made Beth laugh, since he seemed to bob from side to side as if he had taken one drink too many. She smiled and leaned further out of the window; they usually exchanged good-natured abuse whenever they met. It was a sort of private game.

'Good morning, Mr Jones,' she called out, her breath turning into great tongues of vapour. 'Been busy digging, have we?'

He stopped and looked up at her, his cap falling off the back of his head as he did so. 'Where were women when sense was handed out?' he yelled, before bending down to pick up his cap. 'How can you dig turnips in frost like this? Frost makes the ground hard – like your brain, Beth Williams. Beautiful you may be, but you're about as clever as these turnips here.'

'The frost hasn't got your tongue then, Mr Jones?'

'It'll get you pneumonia if you stand there much longer in your nightie, milady.'

'Time for the flannels you'd say would you, Mr Jones?'

'Your what?'

'The flannels, Mr Jones. I always get them out when the weather turns.'

'You get them on, girl. They go with your flannel brain. Where's that father of yours anyway? Ask him if he wants any of these turnips.'

'There's a door down there Mr Jones and, if you look hard enough, you'll find a knocker on it. Why don't you ask him yourself?'

She pulled the window down and lifted the lid of her huge wooden *gist.* Clearly it was flannel drawers weather and she could never take them out and look at them without a little chuckle. They were a light grey; baggy enough to hold a dozen cabbages and reaching down past the knees. It was a very chilly wind indeed that managed to raise a single goosepimple on her legs when she wore them, and putting them on was much like meeting up with an old friend who would now stay with her for the rest of the winter until the spring came around again.

She pinned her hair back and up, stopping as she noticed that the sun had already wiped down all Jack Frost's hard work, making the window wet with hazy driblets before they too dried up. She looked over the estuary to the sands of Pen-clawdd, wondering what Michael was doing at the moment. Probably cussing his horse, she guessed.

She still found something about him that made her go all funny in the joints but she could never trust herself with him again after that business in the cave. She kept brooding about that one, was both hurt beyond words and uneasy. She had shown him the dark side of herself and he had taken advantage of it. It was a shame, really, since she had hoped that she might even have to come to love him – until he had taken it too far. Men always tried to take it too far. They were all the same. Even the different ones were all the same when you got down to it. Men were only ever interested in one thing. She quickly remembered and then dismissed her own passionate responses to Michael, refusing to grapple with the memories.

At breakfast her Dada was so excited he barely touched his boiled egg. He was one of the under-managers at Broadoak and for the last few days had been spluttering with all manner of different stories – part fact and part fantasy – about the effect of Evan Roberts' Revival on the mine.

'You know Beth,' he told her, incredulous. 'I normally hear hundreds of swear words and every known blasphemy in that colliery but, yesterday, not one. There was singing in the Number Four shaft and the only problem with all this Christianity down in the pit is that the pit ponies can't understand what's happening. They only move for swear words and kicks and now they're just standing around bamboozled by all these quiet, gentle phrases.'

He buttered some toast, picked it up to put in his mouth and put it down again. 'Absenteeism has gone down too, and there's talk that the feuds between the unionists and non-unionists might come to an end. The last month there's been some terrible fights over the union. Oh and I forgot to tell you about Glyn Jones. He used to take beer down in his teapot, to drink in the break, but now he's going around saying that the good Lord has converted him, converted his wife and converted his teapot too.'

Mr Williams was a balding, precise man who used his hands a great deal for emphasis when he spoke. Beth laughed out loud at his stories, noticing that her Mam was not laughing at all. Quite the contrary she was in one of her worried-to-death moods, looking at her daughter out of the corner of her eye from time to time.

Unlike her husband, Mrs Williams had never been keen on the church or the chapel or, for that matter, people such as Evan Roberts. When Beth was a child her Dada had always insisted that she went to Sunday School, but her Mam would have much preferred it if Beth had spent all Sunday sitting in a stream or playing with mud. Mrs Williams blamed the chapel for all the mishaps and failures which had befallen her life and saw nothing but trouble coming from this latest eruption.

But she kept her thoughts to herself as she poured the tea. She was a private woman like her Beth. She would have kept the whole of her face from the world if it were feasible.

'You're not coming with me to the Moriah then, Mam?' Beth asked.

'No, cariad. Uncle Jimmy wants to go too, so I'll go and sit with Betty. She's getting too old to be left on her own.'

That was typical of her Mam, Beth decided. Wild horses would not have got her to chapel but, rather than say so, she had found an excuse, which upset no one and let her off the hook without any fuss.

Beth and her father left home in plenty of time for the morning service, but soon discovered many others had had same idea. Even this early, massing sounds of hymnody were coming from the Moriah, choruses louder and longer than she had ever heard before. Banks of bodies, five and even ten deep, were standing around the muddy, rutted entrance to the nearby farm while packed traps were still pulling up. A contagious and hypnotic noise was coming from deep within the belly of the chapel. 'Look,' said her father. 'Here comes the man who has done all this.'

Evan was walking down the centre of the road, accompanied by his brother Dan, three ladies in black broad-brimmed hats and a policeman. It was Evan alone who caught Beth's eye.

Despite his youth he had an unusual and almost holy air about him. It was in his statuesque slimness and the determined lines in his features. Perhaps most of all it was his great height which gave him such an imposing air: tall and strong like the lighthouse. Now *there* was a man who would never let you down, Beth decided. In his confidence and great sense of inner calm; in the maturity of his conviction and the ramrod straightness of his back, he told you that he was a man of power and trust and strength. You can always rely on me, he stated without so much as even a trace, say, of Michael's arrogance.

Evan's suit was pressed immaculate, too, with a long unbuttoned topcoat beloved of deacons, a high starched collar and the leather-bound Bible he held, high and proud, to his chest. When he neared Beth his sparkling hazel eyes caught hers and she had the feeling of being lifted a full inch off the ground. As he moved on, she was left with the equally puzzling feeling of total calm.

What she could not know was that Evan's mind was blazing with prayers; he was trying to warm everyone he met with love. It had little or no effect on the majority but, on a few, it went straight to their hearts and brought them an immediate inner joy. Evan always noticed when this happened – just as he had noticed the small but marked change in Beth when he had faced her.

The chapel vestry was crowded and the three ladies gathered around him. Hands reached out to touch his topcoat. In all the excitement Beth and her Dada managed to follow the small group through the parting crowds and, turning again in the vestry, her eyes once more met Evan's. He unleashed a bolt of hot prayer, which, once again, washed over her with a renewed feeling of serenity.

One of the ladies took Evan's Bible as he slipped out of his topcoat and handed it back to him. He smiled and winked at her and then, with a sharp spring off his right foot, he walked into the crowded chapel where a lusty hymn was riding the back of battling organ notes. Once into the pulpit he put his Bible on the lectern, clasped his hands together and watched, smiling, as the hymn continued. 'Happy day when Jesus washed my sins away . . . Ever praise him for remembering the dust of the earth . . . '

As the congregation sang he examined them face-by-face and pew-by-pew. As his eyes moved from face to face he saw expectation, trust, eagerness, hostility, love, admiration, suspicion, hate – *yes, hate.* Every face, in its own way, told Evan all about the individual's dispositions: each one unique, each with a different story, except for the one abiding quality that was peculiar to all – their sin. The mark of Satan was on every face.

More than a few eyes were bloodshot and sunk in black rings since they'd had no sleep for nearly a week now. A few were vacant and dazed; others fresh and impudent. He saw it all in their faces and it was from this preliminary study that he would decide how the meeting was to go.

He lingered when he came to Beth's face. There was another curious quality here, apart from her clear beauty. Twice that morning she had responded immediately to his prayers, suggesting to him that she would make a wonderful new lieutenant for The Work. Even now, at the third time of looking, he could not be absolutely certain quite what that quality was or, indeed, make out her stance. The hymn ended as he continued studying the faces for a further full five minutes, evoking curiosity, establishing uncertainty, breaking up the congregation's former mood so that the unpredictable could take control. Meetings, he believed, were only really successful when unpredictability was in the saddle. He gazed at Beth again.

He pointed a finger at the rafters final and said, 'God's promise is that where the shadow of the cross falls over people gathered in love and prayer . . . '

He swallowed and paused. His public voice was quite different to his private voice since, in the pulpit, it was deep and loud with a rich core, jubilant with power and resonance. It also seemed to spring from somewhere way back in his throat; given the sharp acoustics of the small, square chapel, everyone heard every syllable.

'God's promise is that where there is holy obedience which leads to purity of heart; where people bow their heads, broken-hearted in their shame and sin, to listen for the distant barks of the Hound of Heaven; when people do all this then so, too, will they be given a blazing vision of the truth of God and be guided through the danger of their days by the radical power of the Holy Spirit.'

Amens and hallelujahs fluttered around, bat-like, when the three ladies stood up to lead the singing of yet another hymn. They had sung but two stanzas when a male voice in the gallery shouted, 'I see God on high confessing the man – even as the man is now confessing the God.'

Evan lifted his Bible high with his right hand and pointed at it with his left forefinger. His smile had such breadth it pushed back his ears a fraction. Then the smile dimmed and hardened into a glare and he put

78

the Bible down again. 'Where do you wish to spend eternity?' he shouted, his long arms moving around ceaselessly as he spoke, hands one second smoothing the Bible and the next grabbing hold of the sides of the lectern as if about to wrench it from its supports. 'Into whose arms are you going to run when you die? Into the arms of Satan, the father of lies and the foundation of all sin? Or into the loving and enfolding arms of Jesus who will wrap you in a greatcoat of love and take away your sorrow forever?'

He swallowed in the urgency of his anguish. 'Take very great care, you sinners. Repent, convert, confess, bend. Take very great care lest you fall too low and you find your arms locked in the flaming embrace of Satan's forever. Ask the Lord to bend you that you may repent.'

The directness of his commands provoked a muttering chorus of prayers in which a beautiful hymn burst out, like a dove out of a thick wood; a hymn so loud and compelling it was taken up by the crowd outside. In the duelling between those inside and those out, Evan strode up and down the aisles, one second kneeling alongside a praying collier and speaking into his ear, the next putting a comforting hand on a woman's shoulder. He sprang down the aisle announcing that there had been another conversion, shouted a few words and laughed out loud. Then he strode back to the pulpit, read a verse from the Bible and hung over the lectern, as silent and still as the figurehead on the prow of a ship, gazing at Beth again, his brain firing fast hot prayers straight at her. He wanted her on his side. He was quite sure of that now.

* * *

That same Sunday Michael was sitting, as he had been for most of the day, on the back step of his cottage, gazing out into the yard where his chicken was foraging around in the dust, when there was a knock on the front door. He knew that it must be her; that she had to come back. He dashed through the living room so fast he knocked over a chair. When he opened the front door, though, all the day's expectations went cold and tumbling down inside him; he saw the grotesque Vera Owen standing there. 'What do you want now?' he asked, wondering if expectation and reality could possibly be further apart.

'The slugs were prancing again last night,' she bleated. 'I had to go out and deal with them myself, I did.'

'What do you want me to do?'

'Come and sweep them up. The snails were at it too. All of them jumping and dancing about. Your mother would have done it for me, she would.'

79

'Let me know the next time they start. I'll come and sort them out for you.'

'And what about my potatoes? I'd pull them myself but there's this arthritis, see?' She held out her two gnarled, knobbly claws of hands. 'No strength in these any more.'

'Vera girl, I'll pull them tomorrow. There's no hurry.'

'Oh yes there is. There was a frost last night. Potatoes don't live in frost. Frost kills.'

He fended off a few more requests with a few more vague promises and, after closing the door, decided that he just had to walk over to Loughor, if only to be in the vicinity of the lovely Beth and out of the vicinity of the ugly Vera.

It was getting dark when he crossed the town boundary and came to the great crowds still massing outside the Moriah. So that was what all the gossip had been about. Then there came a triumphant roar and he could not resist the urge to go over and investigate.

He pushed his way into the crowd, surprised at the ease with which the bodies parted for him. He got as far as the chapel graveyard where people were moving around and over the gravestones as if uncertain what to do. Some were listening to the sounds from inside, a few were down on their knees praying in the torn-up grass. Four shawled women were cowering together near the railings in the manner of trapped sheep; when he asked one if there was any way inside she moaned, as if she was going to be sick, and slumped to her knees. The others followed her lead and he just stood there feeling foolish.

He moved down the side of the chapel. A man was pressing his forehead against the wall, laughing and crying alternately, muttering, 'Thank you, Lord. Praise you, Jesus. Oh thank you, Jesus.' Michael walked past him and, seeing one of the windows open, shinned up a drainpipe to get a look inside.

The service had been rolling along on a wave of hymns, prayer and *hwyl* – as the Welsh describe the driving engines of their tribal passions – for just over four hours. For long periods Evan took no part in the proceedings and it was almost as if the meeting had developed a wild and wilful intelligence of its own, splitting into fragments and coming together again, only to break up into eddying pools of further commotion. Groups had formed, each praying for their own unconverted with the prayers, in their turn, being drowned by hymns. Rambling autobiographical confessions were interrupted by the announcement of another conversion; occasionally the three lady singers stepped forward, as if on some invisible cue, to sing in short thrilling bursts before sitting down again.

'Sinners,' Evan bellowed so loud and sudden it even made Michael jump. 'Sinners, some day time will present you with a panoramic replica of your sins. The mother who died of a broken heart years too soon. The father you drove out of the home. The girl you used and deceived. The poor man you stole from. The child in need you turned your back on. All these people will be presented to you on the day you die. All your sins will be there in full length and full height, with your blood dripping like the drum of eternity on the endless torment of your damned soul.'

His finger was wagging, the eyes manic and the voice full. 'So put us under The Blood. Wash away ours sins in The Blood.' He began wrestling with the lectern as if he was holding the horns of an enraged bull. 'Place us all under The Blood and bend us Lord. Bend us now.'

The outcry which followed this outburst was such that it was as if the hot coals were already being shovelled onto the congregation's heads. Even hanging outside on the window-ledge, Michael sensed a dreadful and almost obscene power swirling around him. He saw grown men standing up with tears running down their faces, grandmothers with their bunched fists held aloft. Spurting spasms of emotion were chasing one another around like flames following rivulets of paraffin, with some women clutching themselves and crying out as if on the rack.

When the outcry subsided the three ladies sang again, their voices shocking in their clarity as they soared and plummeted.

Here is love as vast as the ocean
Loving kindness as the flood
When the Prince of Life our ransom
Shed for us his precious blood.

The congregation rose to its feet for the next verse, the three ladies' voices setting the pitch of the hymn with many carrying the descant as the tenors and basses moved in to give the hard texture. Several times now Michael had involuntarily found himself touched by the sheer power of the meeting. Perhaps he too had become slightly enfeebled by the hysteria and heat but, in the next hymn, his ears teased out just one voice from the hundreds of others.

It was a familiar soprano voice; something of a fragile and mesmeric delicacy which told of sunshine and the sands. Michael pulled himself further in through the window and saw Beth standing several rows from the front. Evan had put his arm around her and was whispering something into her ear. She nodded and smiled as he spoke; then, still singing, she walked up to join the other three ladies. An axe of anxiety slashed down inside Michael. Oh, Beth girl! Oh Beth, what have you gone and done?

Up to that moment Beth had heard no thunder nor seen a flash of lightning. In one way it had been as simple as peeling potatoes or pegging out the washing; she just stood there with a great, strange warmth suffusing every muscle and bone. Yes, she kept hearing the words inside her. Yes. Come to me. This is the path you've been looking for. Come and find me, the light and the life. Yield to your doubts and learn to love only me. Yes, yes, yes.

She felt secure, unafraid but, most of all, *forgiven*. That was really all that she had always been looking for. She understood that now, so when Evan had asked her to step forward while she was singing she had forgotten her normal reserve, thinking that it was right to go up and sing with the other ladies. Her self-consciousness had been overcome by her joy. She had learned to say yes.

Michael had seen and heard enough. He dropped off the window ledge and shouldered his way back through the crowds outside, all seemingly unaware of the chilliness of the night as they joined in the hymns and prayers. He walked up the cobbled street, brisk, his mind still reeling with it all, and sat down in a shop doorway and tried to arrange the facts. It was freezing cold. He would be far better off back home, tucked up in bed. He needed a pint of beer but had no money. He wanted – oh he so much wanted – to be with her.

A cat walked near him and looked up, its saucer eyes a brilliant green in the darkness. The cat brushed its body up against his shoe before stepping over the other one and sauntering off into the darkness again. The clear black sky was encrusted with stars and, with continuing crescendos of noise coming from the chapel, he decided to walk home. But even as he walked down the hill to the marsh road, he felt the tug of her calling him back to the chapel. He turned around again and walked back up the hill.

He stopped near a group of people gathered around a storm lantern, about fifty yards away from the main crowd of the chapel. The group was circling, slow, around the lantern's incandescence, not talking to one another, just repeatedly threading and re-threading, their cloaks brushing up against each other's as quiet as clashing butterfly wings. Sometimes the lantern's glow caught crooked or blackened teeth, faces dusted over with white chalk. Their cheeks were deep hollows and the sockets around the eyes were but black craters highlighting the protruding whites of their eyes.

The women wore small black poke bonnets while the men had close-cropped hair and carried elaborately carved walking sticks. They could easily have been taken for a pack of mummers or strolling players except there was no evidence of merriment nor hint of a song as their heads jerked around, their arms rising and falling, saying nothing and smiling nothing as they continued to circle the lantern, almost as if immersed in a plot of diabolical proportions.

Few chose to stare for long at the Taibach wailers, a group of professional mourners from an area of Port Talbot. Those in that area had suffered from a strange family mutation – something to do with the practice of incest, they said – but, transforming a punishing deformity into a profitable virtue, they had now become the best-known and most active group of mourners in Wales, prepared to wail and gnash their teeth at funerals anywhere in the land. Some found them funny and others frightening. Michael would happily have poured petrol over them and set fire to the lot.

There was a fat cry of pain from inside the chapel followed by a rising babble of prayers. One of the wailers pointed at the chapel and they all ran towards it as one, worming through the crowds and barging in through the vestry door. Michael had followed them as far as the edge of the crowd when one of the women flung her poke bonnet into the air and dashed, screaming, inside. She was followed by the others, all war cries and piercing shrieks. The screams of the strangers were met by even louder screams inside; the one set of screams jumping on the heads of the others and on and up again – and yet again – almost as if they were intent on lifting the very roof. The corridors of Bedlam could never have heard such decibels of madness and pain. They spoke of an innocent people being herded to slaughter in their prime; of the cutting down of youth in the full flower of their manhood; of screaming babies being pitchforked into the fire.

Michael left immediate. He had no machinery to cope with such matters. He became aware of himself wandering outside the town and sitting on a dead tree trunk, looking out at the curling mists of the marsh. Even after a full half hour of gulping on that fresh sea air, the sounds of those tormented shrieks were still flapping around inside his mind.

He stood up final and walked along the marsh road, barely conscious of the wind chattering in the hawthorn hedgerows or the extreme cold of the night. He stopped near an oak, holding his hands against the thick bark and trying to get a feel of its great strength. He put his hot flushed cheek against the bark, trying to draw solace from the old tree's wisdom and great age, when he heard some noises on the road behind.

A group of people were walking towards him, carrying lanterns and singing a Sankey hymn.

He pulled back behind the tree as the lanterns bobbed around in the darkness, listening to the jaunty melody riding the night winds when, for no reason, a kind of violence broke out in the group. No one person seemed to start it and he was not even sure if it was violence he was watching since, in the flurry of shadows and tumbling lanterns, there were no cries of pain or even any shouts.

The group had fallen down together, as if pouncing on a luckless frog or a gold sovereign though, after a minute or so, when he could see all by the light of two blazing paraffin puddles, the scene which met his eyes held him mesmerised.

The group – three men and three women – had not jumped on a frog or sovereign but on top of one another, their hands ripping soundless at one another's clothes. One woman was laying on her back, her legs apart, a man's hands pulling and tugging at her draws. 'Oh my dear sweet Jesus,' she called out into the flickering paraffin night. 'Oh dearest Jesus.'

The second couple were rolling over and over one another while the other two were so engrossed in some sort of animal-like coupling that they had rolled into one of the blazing puddles. The woman's hair was scorched but still they kept doing whatever it was that they were doing, with the man heaving his legs about in some strange carnal rite.

Just then the couplings ended almost as soon as they had begun and four of the people stood up, not looking at one another and hands re-arranging their dress, while another lifted a lantern and proceeded to walk along the road. Michael drew back into the shadow of the oak as they went past, as if on marching parade, silent now – though the woman they had left behind was sobbing, piteous, like a bear robbed of her whelps. Her man had dashed back the way they had come.

When they had all gone Michael left too and began running as fast as he could, down to the parapet on the foreshore and out on to the marsh, leaping the gulleys and sprinting across the flat mounds, his breath coming in breast-tearing bursts until he reached the edge of the sands. A curlew called; the huge silvery hands of the sun beginning to lift the edges of the night. He stopped and wrapped his arms around his trembling body.

A flock of oystercatchers flew bleeping over his head. The tide had turned too but, even with it trickling around his shoes, bubbling and curling around as dangerous as gas; even with it gathering a deep foaming momentum as it coursed silent into the gulleys all around he did not turn and run for it. For in that breaking dawn, with the sounds of a great and frightening madness in his mind, Michael did not care whether the tide caught him or not . . .

Chapter Eight

Long after the Taibach wailers had gone home to Port Talbot and the marathon service had come to a climax, a few impromptu, lantern-lit meetings were still being held on the street corners. Out on the rooftops the cockerels were leading the dawn chorus. For a change the birds, accustomed to having the dawn all to themselves, found themselves duelling with scratch choirs singing hymns.

'I'm not feeling at all tired,' said Beth as she walked home, her arm linked with her Dada's. A pink flush of exultation glowed in her cheeks. 'You know, I think I could go through it all over again.'

'He's a wonderful man, to be sure,' said her Dada. 'Pleased with you getting up to sing as well, I should think. What did he say to you?'

'You know, I just don't remember.'

They were turning down their lane when they were caught by Tudwal Jones, a deacon at the Moriah, who had run after them and was panting with breathlessness and excitement. 'Beth! Beth! I've a message for you from Evan Roberts,' he gasped.

'Come on, Tudwal. Get it out mun,' said Williams as Jones struggled to regain his puff.

'He says,' Jones continued gasping. 'He says he wants you to join his singers. You, Beth! An honour indeed! He says he wants to take the Revival out into the streets and the valleys. If you want to join in God's work then go over to Island House at noon.'

It was Beth's turn to be too excited to speak. Her first worry was for her job as a nurse; her second that her voice was not good enough.

'She'll be there,' said her Dada.

'But what of the hospital?'

'There'll always be work in the hospital, but this is work for today, Beth. Work for the souls of men. This is God's work. I'll settle it with the hospital. Have no fear about that.'

'I'll tell him that you'll accept then, shall I?' asked Jones, his shoulders bobbing up and down with an eagerness to return and, indeed, already walking away from them.

'You can tell Mr Roberts that my daughter is very honoured and that she will be at Island House at noon.'

Beth nodded, uncertain. Her Dada often believed that she did not have a mind to make up; often treated her still as if she was still the age of six.

'I will tell him that, Mr Williams. I will go and tell him that right away.'

They continued walking the last few yards back home. 'Do you really think I'm good enough?' she asked. 'My singing, I mean.'

'Of course you're good enough,' he retorted, affectionate. 'It's a great honour you've been granted and perhaps you'll find yourself a page in history. If Evan Roberts can do all this in a week what can he do in a lifetime? Think about that. He'll change the world, that's what he'll do, and my daughter will be right there by his side. It'll be a great honour for me too. And your mother.'

Events had happened that sudden Beth did not seem to be able to collect her thoughts on the matter at all. Once inside the house she saw that her Mam was in bed and, realising that her Dada was in no mood for sleep, she made a pot of tea as he settled down for his customary bedtime pipe in front of the banked-up fire. He seemed so content with his own thoughts she did not speak as she poured out the tea.

They both sat looking at the flames for a few minutes. There was a small red fiery canyon in the coal, across which tiny blue flames flickered, light and fast, like the tongues of snakes.

'Your mother will be very proud of you about all this,' he said eventually, nodding his head in agreement with his own statement. 'She's not very strong on the chapel, is your mother, but this will bring her around for sure.' He re-lit his pipe with a taper from the fire. 'Your mother always said you had the best voice in the family. Your uncle Billy fancied he had a voice – he was always singing down the pub – but it was never a patch on yours. No. Not a patch. It would be good to hear it again. Wasted, it was. Do you think Evan Roberts will let you do solos?'

She did not reply and held the cup to her lips, blowing on the hot tea. Her goldfish, kept in a tank on the dresser, was swimming around and around; she wondered if he ever stopped for anything or if had to keep going around and around just to stay alive. Oh, to be sure, her voice might be good enough – it *was* good enough, let's face it – but there was another consideration and she really had better get it all out now.

'I never did understand why you didn't keep up your singing lessons. Maggie Rhys always maintained that you could have gone to Covent Garden if you'd applied yourself.'

'Oh Dada, I wasn't *that* good!'

'That wasn't what Maggie Rhys said. She said that you had the fullest . . .'

'Look Dada, there's one thing I'm worried about and I want to have it out now.' She sipped her tea and her hand gave a small tremor. 'You've been very good about it, never once mentioned it but, if I join this great crusade . . . if . . . ' She could feel the colour rising, red and warm, around the bottom of her neck. 'If I join up with Mr Roberts I will get in the public eye. I might even have a page in history as you put it. But do you . . . is it possible that, you know, that matter will ever come out?'

'What matter?'

'You know. *That* matter. What other matter has there ever been in my life?'

He regarded her with his eyebrows raised in surprise, as if she were some stranger who had accosted him in the street and demanded that he take off all his clothes. His mouth opened and closed but, sitting back in his armchair, he said nothing, putting yet another taper to his pipe. 'I suppose I'll have to give this up now,' he said, taking his pipe out of his mouth and studying it. 'The chapel never did approve of tobacco.'

'Dada, I'm talking to you! I mean, if it all came out, it might harm Mr Roberts' work. Mightn't it?'

He looked at her in genuine astonishment before gazing back at the fire. He was, for once, stuck for words. The grandfather clock seemed to be ticking very loud, Beth thought. You only ever notice the ticking of a clock at night in an empty house, she decided, ticking away the seconds of your life. You never ever noticed the ticking of a clock in a house full of people.

He leaned forward and tapped his pipe out on the inside of the black-leaded grate with four sharp knocks. The thick dottle hissed on the glowing coals as he settled back in his armchair again, letting a long low sigh of exasperation.

'Mightn't it?'

'That matter, Beth. That matter, as you call it, is dead and forgotten.'

'Not by me, Dada. Maybe by everyone else, but not by me.'

'Beth. Dead and forgotten. We've all of us got skeletons in our cupboards but God's way is forgiveness. Where there is true repentance then there is always forgiveness. That, Beth, is the Way of The Cross.'

'But what if it all came out, Dada?'

His body rose a good inch out of the armchair and his voice took on a firm, almost harsh, edge. 'I don't want you to mention that matter – to me or your mother or to anyone – in this house ever again. You've suffered. We've suffered. Now it's dead and forgotten.' He stood up and took out his fob watch to check the time. 'You remember that now, my little lady,' he added, his voice softer. 'Where there is repentance then so too there is always forgiveness. It was to forgive us our sins that Jesus died for us. Forgiveness is the way of the Lord. So my girl . . . it really is time for the wooden hill.'

There he was treating her like a six-year-old again. She picked up the teacups and carried them out into the scullery. It was not dead and anything but forgotten, she thought as she rinsed the cups under the tap. Barely an hour went by when she did not dwell on it and reflect that it could all have been different.

But, there again, maybe God really had given her a chance to restore the balance, to atone for her past.

* * *

She set off for Island House just before noon, as nervous and fearful as a child on her first day at school. She had been careful to slip a hymnal into her pocket since she had forgotten the words to almost all the hymns. She could not even remember the first line of *Calon Lân* and every rugby supporter in the land knew that backwards. Neither had she time to wash her hair properly and there was a lock at the back which insisted on poking out no matter how hard she tried to pin it in. Her confidence often ebbed and flowed like the tides, and it ebbed total when she saw a policeman standing outside Island House with groups of sightseers milling around in the road.

She knocked on the door; there was no immediate reply and, hearing the gales of laughter erupting from inside, she was on the verge of making a run for it. Then Evan himself opened the door and thrust out a welcoming hand. She took her own hand out of her muffler and hoped that he would not realise that it was shaking; even if he did, he did not show it. He just smiled, captivating. It was always that smile, a smile like some beacon in a storm, she thought. His hazel eyes were surrounded by the most loveable laugh lines, his whole face overwhelming her like a marvellous and unexpected gift. She detected something angelic in his face; something which was both bright and holy.

'Beth,' he said, soft. 'Beth Williams. Welcome.'

'Mr Roberts. You may remember . . . '

'Come inside please. Come. Your hand is cold. I will take your coat. There is a nice big fire in the parlour. That will warm your hands up. Sunny it may be but warm it is not.'

Still smiling, he opened the parlour door and beckoned her inside. She was not familiar with such easy charm and good manners, nor was she much at ease when she walked into the parlour. Five people turned to look at her.

'Ladies and gentlemen,' Evan said, crossing the room to pick up a chair, which he placed just next to the fire. 'This is Beth Williams, a Loughor girl whom I've asked to join our mission. You may have heard her singing last night. Sit yourself down, Beth. Beth, this is my father and this is my brother Dan.' He moved around the back of each person and put his hands down on their shoulders as he introduced them. 'Some of us you've met Beth. Here are our three singers, of course. Priscilla Watkins from Gorseinon; Lavinia Hooker from Gorseinon too and Pat Jones from Nantymoel. It certainly is good to have a Loughor girl working with us.'

The three ladies all had Bibles on their laps and nodded at her with smiles, which were formal but nonetheless friendly. Priscilla had a wide, open face with a *retroussé* nose and an amused, scampish sparkle in eyes brimming over with mischievous plots. Lavinia had a large, slightly crooked mouth with a deep line along her upper lip and the chicken sinews of age beginning to show on her neck. Pat's face had a darkness in it and seemed to lower, a bit like a ruined mansion on a rainy day. This darkness was in her excessively bushy eyebrows, the crowded palimpsest of lines around her eyes and thick tangle of raven-black hair.

Beth felt totally inadequate in such company; her fingers played, nervous, with her gilded cameo brooch on the lace ruffles of her blouse. When Priscilla offered her a cup of tea she had to refuse, certain that she would drop the cup. Her flannel drawers had made it a mistake to sit so near the fire as well, but she did not dare to move just yet.

'We will be meeting here every morning about this time,' Evan said, pacing about the room but speaking directly at her. 'We will meet here for prayers, to set up plans and sort out any problems. For example, we have been discussing the Taibach wailers who joined our meeting for a very noisy period last night. What do you think about them, Beth?'

She went into a flat panic wondering what she was *supposed* to think about them, looking around at the ladies before deciding to say what she really did think. 'I thought they were comical and of little importance,' she said straight out. 'Noisy yes, but not relevant to the meeting. They left quick enough, after all.'

Evan stared at her, intent, then smiled. 'I agree with you, Beth,' he said, 'They are not important, it is true, but they are a part of the noise of the throng – a piece of the weave. For you see that God will even bless the noise. The throng can be a sermon in itself.' He stopped speaking and chuckled out loud, as if recalling a private joke. 'Why should I control the meetings and say who must come and who must stay away? The meetings must control themselves or, rather, the Holy Spirit must control them. Wherever there is the Spirit of the Lord there is liberty; to love God means we are free and not slaves. Wherever you see freedom then so, too, you see the workings of the Holy Spirit.'

He sat down on a chair and locked his hands together, thumbs circling one another for some twenty seconds. Beth noticed that no one spoke or interrupted his meditative silences. He chuckled again. She thought how pleasantly informal he was, but she remained conscious of an underlying gravity about his bearing. Responsibility seemed to sit heavy on his shoulders.

'After all we are not running a prison or a bank. There is no reason at all why our services should have any order. It is all up to the people to join in. There will be no clock. The clock does not control the workings of the Holy Spirit. You will see that I never carry a watch or a clock. There will be no hymn books, no collections, no advertising and absolutely no long sermons.'

Beth remembered the hymnal in her coat pocket and hoped that he had not noticed it. She also hoped that no one had noticed the way she was wriggling around on her chair, trying to get away from the heat of the fire. These flannels were not acting like her old friends at all and, if they did not behave, they would find themselves locked up in that chest again. You could have fried eggs on her knees.

Once again, Evan had fallen silent for a while. 'I never prepare a sermon and certainly do not believe in long sermons. There are those who say I do not know enough words to make a long sermon, but let me tell you ladies I can be as boring and long-winded as any of those valley preachers.' He smiled and threw back his head, squinting at the wall as if trying to focus on something. 'Remember ladies, never fear what people will say of you. Heed not the world's opinion. Do each one of your own portion. When you are moved to do so you must open your hearts and mouths to sing – even if I am speaking. The disorder has its own logic and you ladies will become the key to it. Whatever the Holy Spirit tells you to do you must do.'

The three ladies, Beth noticed, hung on his every word and, what was even more impressive than his own self-confidence, was his confidence in them. *You ladies are the key to it.*

'But we should remember that this Revival is deeper than its tears, its singing and its noise,' he was saying when a big-hipped woman in a floral pinafore walked into the room, knelt down in front of him and proceeded to polish his shoes. 'What we are witnessing now,' he continued without looking down at her, 'is a summons from God to revive his church, the beginning of a rising revival throughout the West when all . . . '

He stopped speaking, waiting for the woman to finish polishing his shoes. Then he put an arm around her waist as she stood up and examined his jacket for bits of fluff before moving on to his neck and collar. Beth was reminded of a monkey searching a mate for fleas; she had to put her hand over her mouth. Priscilla turned away, too, finding something interesting on the floor on the other side of her chair while her left shoulder shook with mirth.

'If you haven't already guessed,' Evan said, 'this is my mother.' His gravity had vanished and he was in a light, playful mood.

'You ladies may all be fancy singers,' Mrs Hannah Roberts, said, looking around at them. 'But if my Evan is going to lead this Revival he's going to do it smart. If I catch any dirt on him I'm going to box his ears. You see if I don't. Even if he's talking to King Edward himself I will.'

Beth had been that absorbed in Evan she had not so much as noticed the other two men in the room, she realised with something of a shock. In the case of Evan's father, Henry, this was not surprising since he had all but buried himself in the corner, saying nothing and even looking a bit uneasy whenever he spotted anyone looking at him. He had clearly also been subjected to a once over by Mrs Roberts, since the carbolic soap had given his features bright red blotches while the thick muscles on his neck were bulging and bloated as if in some odd tug-of-war with his starched white collar. His arms were folded peaceable enough, though, and when he caught Beth studying him, he rolled his eyes up into his eyelids as if asking what was an old miner like him doing caught up in all this?

Evan's brother, Dan, on the other hand, did not look in the least tense. He did not have Evan's fine, youthful features – he was in fact eight years older than Evan – but it was the Roberts face for sure, with the heavy nose and determined clip of the jaw. He always seemed to have a faint smile on his lips, his hand forever rummaging in his pockets with his head lifted slightly in the general air of happy distraction of someone smitten to the depths by a great aria.

Beth had heard the story of Dan's miracle cure and studied his eyes – greenish with yellow flecks. She noticed the way he always moved his head – rather than just his eyes – when he wanted to look in a particular direction. She decided there and then that Dan would be an ally.

Evan stood up and kissed his mother on the top of her head. 'Never mind about that nonsense,' she said, brushing him away with the backs of her hands. 'Let's have a look at those fingernails now. *Ach y fi*. When did anyone ever get converted by someone with dirty fingernails? ' She turned to speak to the ladies again. 'He was always the same, this one, too busy reading the Bible to wash. A lick and a promise. That's what he called a wash.'

Evan bustled his mother out of the room and began pacing around again. Beth had relaxed well enough by now and felt she could move her chair away from the fire. Somehow his mother's fussing had given Evan a touch of true humanity. A proud man would have found it all embarrassing in the extreme, but Evan had taken it all, good-natured, made no apologies for her and was even now speaking as if nothing had happened.

It was his way of swinging from silver-tongued demagogue to ordinary boy just given a lollipop that intrigued Beth. She had never seen an act like it and was utterly charmed. Utterly.

'This afternoon we are going to Broadoak for a short meeting at the end of the shift,' Evan said, his demeanour serious again. 'Later we will be going back to the town square for another service and, tonight, back to the Moriah. Remember, it is the colliers that God wants – and we want – in our mission. Colliers have always found theology entrancing and, if we get to the hearts of these rough, magnificent men, then we get to the bedrock of the Revival.

'Also, as I have told you before, it is the singing, not the preaching, that stirs the hearts of men. So I want you ladies to get inside those hymns and sing them as they have never been sung before. Oh, and another matter. I have decided that, in future, we must all walk into the chapel together during the first hymn. I have told the deacons that I always want the singing to have begun before we arrive. It's the singing that helps me judge how strongly the Holy Spirit is present in the service. Well, before we break for food, let us pray.'

Beth closed her eyes but her heart was pounding so much she could hardly hear what was being said. *I want you lades to get inside those hymns and sing them as they have never been sung before.* Oh dear. She could not sing a note, she was sure, and had forgotten every hymn she had ever learned. Could she really have got herself caught up in the great work of this great man? Even sitting there, with her eyes closed and her heart pounding, she could feel the glow of his stirring idealism and she prayed fervent that she would not let him down. There were movements around her, familiar smells too, and she opened her eyes.

Dinner, just that minute brought in by Mrs Roberts, turned out to be bowls of steaming *cawl*, a vegetable hotpot. When they had finished she brought in the pan with what was left of the stew. Beth was certain that there was nothing left in the larder, but it was traditional to stuff your guests and starve your family. She was sitting next to Priscilla who, Beth learned, had an enormous appetite and was also something of a chatterbox.

'He's an expert in shorthand you know, Beth,' she whispered. 'He even has his own shorthand Bible. He plays harmonium and fiddle and has read Hodge, Bunyan *and* the Welsh encyclopaedia.' She wiped a piece of bread around inside her bowl. 'What else? Yes. He hates being photographed, always refuses to be recorded and often only needs an hour's sleep at night. True, that is. Not always but often.'

Clearly all the ladies were fascinated by Evan. Beth gazed down the table at him. It was that proud, angular jaw that made him look the fighter he was. Sometimes, he passed the back of his hand under his chin as if something was itching there. She noticed that, on occasion, he also reached out to touch Dan's arm as he spoke to him and that, in fact, his hands were rarely still.

Evan glanced up and noticed that Beth was gazing at him when he smiled. She flushed and looked down at her empty bowl; nerves or no, she had finished the lot.

* * *

Ever since Beth had come to Island House that morning Evan had been studying her. He had spotted her nervousness and the way she wanted to move away from the fire but stuck it out rather than cause any fuss. He noted the way she blushed from the bottom of her neck. He was very taken by her beauty and long-lashed eyes, the spruceness of her clothes and the rich sheen of her black hair. But, even in this great and most satisfactory picture of a woman enjoying the prime of her loveliness, there was something that he could not see, but was there nevertheless. This insight worried him since he always liked to think that he saw people clearly; that he could absorb the whole of their nature with a long, soft look of his hazel eyes.

She seemed, somehow, to have a great melancholy running out of her. Yes, that was it. Even when she smiled that heavenly smile there was a sadness there. It was almost the sadness of the prophet in the wilderness: the prophet's pain that he is proclaiming the truth but knows that no one is going to take any notice. Well, he wanted to purge that sadness. He wanted to make her well again.

When all the meal plates had been cleared away he stood up and walked over to her. 'Can we have a word in private, Beth?' he asked, touching her, light, on the shoulder with his hand and once again noting that blush and the uneasiness in her fingers.

She glanced, worried, at Priscilla then followed him out into the passage and into a smaller, colder room, normally used for family Bible readings and prayers. He made her sit down but remained standing himself just in front of a framed piece of embroidery which said that the Lord was with you in everything that you do. He turned his back on her for a few seconds then turned to her again and chuckled. 'Tell me, Beth. You are a nurse. I have this wart on my hand and wonder if you know how to get rid of it.'

She looked up at him in some surprise as he held out his hand to show the small, orange excrescence. 'Well you just cut it off and paint the skin with iodine,' she said, holding his hand and looking at it. 'But warts are not my subject, I'm afraid. Now, if you had a boil I could do something about that. Boils, yes: warts no, I fear.'

He laughed at that remark and she joined in the laughter, uncertain. 'You could always go down to the hospital,' she said. 'I'm sure they'd fix you up.' She took his hand and looked at it again. 'But it's no use me telling you. I just don't know enough about warts.'

He enjoyed her genuine concern. 'Well I will tell you now,' he said. 'If it means the knife Evan Roberts will not be going near any hospital not if . . . '

'They do spread, you understand. They do spread if you don't treat them. I do know that.'

'Oh it was not about this I wanted to talk to you.' He paced up to the window and looked out at the bank of people still watching the house. 'I just wanted to say, Beth, that I hope, no, I pray, that you will find a great place in our work. I have been watching you today. I saw the way you wanted to move away from the fire because it was too hot for you but you did not. Forbearance. I saw the way your eyes were weighing us all up. Analysis. I saw the way you are good at boils but not warts. Humour. I always see things about people you see. Always. I want you to know that. I want you to know that and trust me.' He turned away from the window and looked down on her – surprisingly calm as he lifted veil after veil.

'Please do not say anything for the moment, Beth, but I also see a great sadness in you. I may be wrong but that is what I see. No, please, please, do not say anything. Just say nothing at all.' He lifted his hand, looked at his wart and smiled.

'All I wanted to say, Beth, is that I can make you happy and well. Come with us into the work and we will all become happy and well. The joy is going to be boundless. You just wait and see. So what I want you to do is this. Whenever you are sad, whenever you are in pain, whenever you are in fear . . . then reach out and take hold of God's hand. Just like this, look.' He reached out into the air with his palm upturned, then closed the top of his thumb slow on to the tips of his fingers, as if making a silhouette of an animal against a candle flame. 'If ever you are walking down the road and you are worried then just reach out, like that, and take God's hand and say "God I am worried. Please help me in my worry". The strange thing is, Beth, it always works. God is always there when you reach out for his hand. He will never let you down. He has never let anyone down and he will not start with you. Just reach out. "God I am worried." That is it. As simple as that. "God I am worried." Then you,' he reached out into the air and closed thumb on fingers.

Beth reached out too. 'God I am worried,' she said and smiled. She was utterly charmed again. Utterly.

* * *

Later that afternoon the whole group of them set out from Island House to walk down through Loughor to Broadoak Colliery. Word seemed to travel through the very walls of the terraces as they followed the road down past the Post Office where Percy Rees was sitting on a wall, kicking his boots against it and cackling to himself. People appeared in doorways and some even applauded.

Children scooted around the group too and, on occasion, Evan would reach into his topcoat pocket and offer one a sweet. A few shrank back from the proffered gift, but the cheekier urchins snatched, confident, and ran.

'His pockets are always full of sweets,' Priscilla told Beth. 'He won't move out of the house without his sweets.'

'There's nothing like starting them young, I suppose.' Beth replied. 'If you can't get them one way you might as well get them in another.'

'He's got you, hasn't he Beth? How did he get you?'

The town was bright with thin autumnal sunshine, which burnished everything like some angelic table polish. A chicken jerked its way across the road in front of them and a couple of sheep regarded them all with black-eyed stupidity. Just past the crossroads the milkman's horse relieved himself in large brown steaming lumps which slapped down on the cobbles and, while polite society pretended that nothing had happened, this was the signal for Stan Jones and Peter Rees to come dashing out of their homes, wielding shovel and pan, and racing for the steaming heap with, today, Stan Jones the clear winner as he scooped the lot up in triumph before transporting it back to his vegetable patch.

The group walked up the path to Broadoak alongside the river and fanned out behind Evan at the entrance to the pithead. The cage wheel was spinning silent above them, with a few black-faced colliers standing around the lamp room watching the proceedings. Just next to the lamp room a few rusty drams lay on their sides, redundant and useless now, after many years of carting slag off to the tip.

Some of the townsfolk had followed them out to the colliery too, the men standing around with their flat caps and shonny scarves, hands in pockets, all grateful, perhaps, to the Revival for providing a diversion from the grim business of being unemployed in a town where one out of every three men, that winter, was without any work.

'Remember now, I want to greet the men with a rapture of song,' Evan said. 'We'll start with *Great God of Countless Wonders.*'

'That's his favourite hymn,' Priscilla said to Beth. 'You'd better get cracking and learn the words of that for a start.'

'I don't suppose you know what page it's on?' Beth asked flicking though the pages of her hymnal.

'Mime it for now,' Priscilla said putting her hand on the hymnal. 'And put that away. Evan likes hymn books about as much as he likes drunks. If I don't know the words I always sing bits of Latin.'

'But I don't know any Latin.'

Priscilla pitched the hymn with Lavinia and Pat joining in with her immediately. Beth sang soft, not altogether certain of the words and quite content, for the moment anyway, to feel her way into the small choir. But, small though they were, the range and clarity of the ladies' voices was astonishing; although her voice tended to creak a bit on the top notes, Beth knew that was only a matter of practice and that she would fit in.

After *Great God of Countless Wonders* they began *Love Comes in Copious Torrents*; Beth becoming more confident because she knew this one, singing it with her head back and eyes half-closed to concentrate on the right notes.

The wooden doors of the two wheelhouses were open wide and, when the pit cages clanked open, the ladies turned up the sweet volume of their song. There followed a faint rumbling in the ground, reminiscent of some kind of earthquake. The rumbling came again and Beth frowned and looked at Lavinia when, out of both wheelhouses, about fourteen blackened pit ponies came charging down the path, snorting and stamping demented, as they headed straight for them.

The words dried up in the ladies' mouths complete as they looked one way and another for an escape from this unruly stampede; all of a

96

sudden, Lavinia and Pat bounded one way while Beth and Priscilla scampered in the other with Evan but inches behind them.

Beth could never remember moving so fast and the watching crowds behind them had parted too, since they knew the ponies were running straight into the river, to clean themselves up and cool off after their statutory ten days working in the heat and dust of the coal face.

The ponies pranced around in the muddy water and exchanged faint whinnies of glee with one another, as joyous as little children on a day out on the sands in Barry Island.

'Well, someone might have told me it was the time the ponies came up,' Evan said, huffing a bit and straightening his topcoat. 'Someone might have said. Where is Dan anyway?'

'I don't think we got any converts there, do you?' Priscilla asked, dangerous.

Evan looked at her hard, then a radiant smile broke up his seriousness. 'Ponies were always the stupidest of animals,' he said with a dismissive wave of the hand. 'They never did appreciate good singing.'

A black-faced collier with a lamp dangling from his belt came and stood near Evan, plainly admiring the ladies. 'I don't suppose you're looking for any men to join in this choir of yours, Mr Roberts?'

'Men are no good at making tea. Just ladies in the choir for the moment.'

'I'd be making the tea all day long if I could be with ladies like these.'

Evan looked away, his good humour vanished again. 'We had better get on over to the town square now,' he said.

* * *

There were no stampeding pit ponies to interrupt the meeting around the Celtic stone cross in the square where, beneath advertisement hoardings sporting the red triangle of Bass Beer and another for Emulsion Pills, Evan spelled out the burning, urgent need for repentance which, in its turn, would lead to redemption.

His voice carried strong and well in the open air, penetrating the shops and the dairy and even carrying into the tap room of the Lewis Arms where card players were playing nine-card Don as unrepentant drinkers sat, beer glasses in unrepentant hands, in sullen, unrepentant silence.

When he had finished speaking the ladies took over, lifting up their hymns on waves of triumph as odd groups of townsfolk joined in too, one group of men in particular providing some extremely cunning harmonies while the ladies held the whole vocal spectrum together.

It was then that Beth saw Michael. He was leaning against a lamp post, his arms folded and legs crossed like some snooker hall oaf. He was gazing at her with those piercing eyes of his and she stopped singing. Even though she would have died rather than admit it, he did exercise a most curious power over her. It was those eyes of his, twinkling with ancient Celtic magic. She would have spotted them in a crowd of thousands; she would never forget the time she first saw him out on the sands and his eyes had loomed up at her and all but drowned her. His eyes changed moods too, much like a river changes from dawn to dusk; sometimes mysterious, sometimes sardonic, sometimes quivering with affection . . .

But today those eyes were cold and accusing. There was no expression on his face and, when Evan approached him and held out his hand, Michael did not unfold his arms; he merely looked down at the proffered hand as if it was too dirty to touch. Then he looked back at her again. She could have died with the shame of it; she turned her head away.

Evan seemed nonplussed by Michael's deliberate snub; he stood in front of the ladies and read a few verses from his Bible. On closing it, though, his manner was dour. 'There is so much unbelief around,' he said, without a trace of a smile. 'And such a great fight lying ahead. But tonight we will have several important visitors and it must be our greatest meeting yet.' He smiled again, cheered up by his own words. 'Tonight then.'

He turned to walk away. 'Oh, Beth,' he called out, turning again. 'You sang very well today. Welcome to our work and remember . . . ' He reached out into the air closing thumb on fingers, slow. She turned her head to one side, her eyes sparkling with amusement, reaching out in turn and making the same sign back to him. It was to become *their* sign, the first step in the making of a strong bond.

She was walking home, still warm with the pleasure of knowing Evan, and did not need to be told whose footsteps were following her.

'Taken the pledge at last have we, girl?' Michael asked, his voice thick with sarcasm.

'I took the pledge when I was fourteen. You may remember that I don't drink or swear. Not like some we could name.'

'To each his own,' he said, catching up with her. 'That's what I've always thought it's about. Everyone doing as they want, when they want.'

'That's just the kind of remark I'd expect from a socialist. Licence to do anything they want. That's what you lot believe isn't it?'

'Something like that.'

'Well I don't,' she said, prim. 'So let's leave it at that, shall we?' She was still seething at the way he had snubbed Evan.

'You know, girl, sometimes you're as stubborn as that horse of mine and that tosser has a brain of solid bone.'

'Look, Michael, I'm in no mood for your insults. If you've got something to say, then say it out plain.'

'I've got lots of things to say but it would take a few days to say them.'

'I need to rest before the service tonight..'

'What's going on then? Are you signing up with this madman permanent, or what?'

'I am. From now on I want to work for God. I've been invited to join Mr Roberts, you know. A great honour which I've accepted. But you wouldn't appreciate that, would you?'

'Great honour?' he spat, apoplectic. 'What possible honour can there be in all this? You've got a few problems, that's very clear, but this is no way out. Life is there to be faced and worn like a badge. You can't escape from it into the chapel of all places.'

She quickened her pace. Sometimes his words hurt her more than he could possibly have guessed. He moved in front of her, bullying her again. 'Explain, then, where this leaves us.'

She felt weary and oppressed. She did not like hurting him but it had to be spelt out. 'Well no more and no less than we ever were.'

'So what do you mean by that?'

'What do I mean? I don't know what I mean. I was never that sure where we were. We couldn't have come together, Michael. We might have once. Once, many years ago. Not now.'

He put his arm around her shoulder, but she sprang away from him. She so wished he did not need to touch her all the time.

'But there were days when we got on well,' he said. 'Not great but well. Didn't we at least have a start, something to build on? Now you've gone and got yourself tied up in all this madness.'

'Look, if you're going to be so insulting about it all, why don't you either just go away or try understanding something for once?'

'Understanding this nonsense! What's there to understand? One great crowd of sledgehammers in search of a dead God.'

'Oh, Michael! Don't.'

'Read history, girl. That's what we socialists believe in. Read history and you'll learn about daft movements like this, breaking out in Wales, every fifty years or so. Vicar Pritchard's revival. Howell Harris'. The Baptist revival in 1740. Christmas Evans'. The Beddgelert revival in 1817.

The cholera revival in 1849 – noted for its fierceness and the torrent of backsliders when the disease lifted. I've read about these revivals. They're just distractions from the real issues – that's all they are. Just mushrooms in history.'

'Not this one, Michael.'

'Mushrooms in history, girl. But the real trouble with this one is that the girl I love is right there in the middle of it.'

She stopped walking and turned to look at him in the face. 'Love,' she mimed silent. He had never told her that he loved her before and, in the circumstances, the very word seemed funny on his lips. Unforgivable, but she laughed.

'It's a joke then, is it?' He was visibly hurt. As he put his hand up against his cheek, as if it had been wounded, she saw that his fingers were shaking.

'I'm sorry,' she said, and meant it.

'Beth, girl.' He put his hands on her shoulders and, in spite of herself and her new resolve, something moved deep inside her. He had a way of stoking up feelings that she did not like or understand; feelings that seemed to have a mind of their own. Her fingers played with the buttons of his jacket as he spoke. 'Please don't do this. No good will come of it. None at all. Come away with me now. We could go away somewhere and find a new life. There's nothing in the world we couldn't work out together.'

She shook her head. 'I'm sorry, *cariad*.' She found the primitive strength of his emotions so difficult to cope with; they came in waves and, at times, she felt swamped by them. She did not share their strength, nor, for that matter, did she appreciate the need for such intensity. He demanded too much, more than she was prepared to offer. She wished he would take his hands off her shoulders. She could feel the trembling in his fingers.

'Let's make this the last goodbye, then,' he said. 'I love you too much to watch you get carried away by all this. I had already decided to go away, with or without you. My old mate Huw Davies has started a building business over in England and he says I can have a job anytime. But, if you decide you want me, just put your head out of the nearest window and shout my name.'

'I'm going to have to shout very loud if you're working in England,' she said, hating the finality of the meeting and hating herself for caring.

'I'll hear you. I'll hear you if you just whisper it.'

Then he strode off, wondering what had prompted his spur of the moment statement. She walked home alone, biting on the inside of her mouth, thinking that part of the promise of the day had been snatched away. She reached into her pocket and felt the cockle shell he had given her on the day they had first met on the sands. She had never told him that she took her shell with her everywhere she went; when she changed her clothes, she found a new pocket for the shell.

She stopped walking. Maybe she *did* love him. There were sides to him that she positively adored – that mixture of dreamer, poet, teller of tall stories and little boy lost. There had been moments when she had looked at him with naked longing. She had to admit to all of that. She had never told him about this, of course, had never told him about a lot of things. She had always managed to bottle up her private self away from the world.

But that was behind her now, wasn't it? She had met a man of greatness and vision and was about to start on a wonderful new work. Evan Roberts knew things about her and, what is more, knew things without having to be told. He was offering her renewal and she wanted all of that; she wanted to be whole again.

Yet, there again, Michael had touched a part of her that had never been touched before. As she walked on she was overcome by a strange sense of loss. Men always took a bit out of you. They were never content unless they were hacking off whole parts. They were only really happy if they captured and ran off with your soul. *That* was men for you.

'God I am so worried,' she said, holding out her hand by her side and closing her thumb on her fingers. 'Take my hand and tell me what I should do.'

Invitations to speak in eighteen towns, Dan wrote in his diary. *Estimated 4,032 conversions in Loughor and district. Evan asked for a free pew for the Press. Thirteen newspaper men last night. Six fainted in meeting last night: one serious, went to Bridgend hospital. £84. 4s. in donations so far. Marigolds from Mrs Annie Pierce. Soon we travel out.*

Chapter Nine

Nothing was predictable in the early, disordered days of the Revival. One of its first effects was to provide the four public houses in Loughor with a boom in trade – for it was there that the sceptics and doubters, for so long left alone, ran for peace and refuge.

Some went for other reasons, like William Gelly of George Street, who had been a lifelong attender of chapel yet felt he had to announce that, if the chapel had surrendered to a man like Evan Roberts, then he had no choice but to surrender to the pub.

Take the tap room in the *Lewis Arms* the following Wednesday night; heaving it was, with the romping smell of beer and the chink of many glasses; with the Don players screaming at one another about how the opposing partnership's hands should have been foreseen with more care; with chattering groups standing around the bar swapping the latest horror stories and, just over there, Billy Morris, an old shepherd with big knobbly hands the size of shovels, occasionally back-heeling the air with his left boot, a habit picked up from a lifetime of having a sheepdog at his heels.

'It'll fade out. A flash in the pan. Mark my words,' said Ray Wright.

'That's not what my old girl says,' was the response of William Gelly from the bar. 'She says he's going to take over the whole world. That's what *he's* saying, too.'

'Aye. That's what they're all saying.'

Jenko was sitting in a group in the far corner, surgery long over, his bag between his feet, a pint in one hand, cigarette in the other. 'It's the full moon, that's what,' he said, coughing a small gale of cigarette ash over the front of his cape. 'The moon is high, the spirits are low. A train crashes, Wales lose at rugby and along comes this theological gnome and we've got all this. If the sun shines it's the golden blessings of God. If it rains it's the warm tears of God crying for his wicked children. Anything that sparkles, anything at all is a bloody vision. I'll tell you something. I've never had a vision that I couldn't explain by what I'd drunk the night before.' He paused and took a long guzzle from his pint. 'Beriberi of the brain. That's what this Revival is all about.'

'You think it'll last long, Jenko?'

'According to this newspaper here it's going to last forever and a day.' He unfolded a copy of *The Western Mail*, the national newspaper of Wales. 'Here. Listen to this lot. Evan Roberts says that we are on the eve of a grand revival, which is going to overtake the world. It is going to be the greatest ever seen. Some clown reporter on *The Western Mail* has swallowed it, anyway. Those reporters drink even more than I do, which might explain why the reports are getting more extravagant by the day. There were three of them sniffing around here yesterday. Between modern reporting and Shakespeare there is a very wide gulf indeed. The illiterate publicising the insane, that's what this Revival is all about.' He folded the newspaper into a roll and banged it on the table. 'These newspapers have decided there's money in it, see? There's always been money in Welsh sentiment.'

Ben Thomas put a pint down on the table, dragged up a wooden stool, sat down on it and let out an endless sigh as if suffering from a terminal puncture. 'I've had it,' he moaned. 'My wife is reading the Bible all day long. My two girls are singing hymns when they're not reading the Bible. Even my boy is on his knees praying all the time, and I had great hopes for him. And you know what this is all for, Jenko?'

'More housekeeping money, is it?'

'Would that it were that simple. No. There's all this babble going on because they want me to give up the drink. The brew of the devil they're calling it and, what's more, my wife is saying that if I don't listen to reason – not to mention all those prayers – I'll have to go and live elsewhere. Where's the Christian charity in all that? You're something of a philosopher, Jenko. Explain to me why they want to throw a man out of his own home because he likes his pint. Beer is the only thing that makes me happy. Why should I give up the one thing that makes me happy?'

Jenko's eyelids began to flap, as if dangling on a piece of elastic, a sure sign that his back teeth would soon be floating and that he would be happier than a small baby. Yet, oddly enough, a tiny biological miracle seemed to happen then since alcohol never seemed to immobilise his tongue. 'The way to look at it all is this,' he said, bubbling rings of foam on his lips. 'The Greeks worshipped the body; the Romans the mind and the English just adore commerce. But the Welsh – hah! – with the Welsh the only thing that gets their kidneys glowing is melancholy and what they've started here is a sort of national *eisteddfod* of grief. This lot know that beer makes you happy and that's why they want it stopped. They don't accept happiness. The sound of laughter confuses them. But now they've got wave after wave of melancholy collapsing all over the place they think it's wonderful. They glory in the glamour of pain and just love contemplating their imminent destruction. Why are all the chapel hymns in a minor key? Why are the best-received sermons about The Blood? When did you last hear a good joke in the pulpit? There *must* be a Himalayan range of melancholy, that's why, with not so much as a pebble of happiness in sight.'

He paused for breath and lit another cigarette. But no one attempted to pick up the conversation; when he was in one of these moods, Jenko was considered as good entertainment as the great Lillie Langtry herself.

'The problem is that the Welsh were the last in the queue when analysis was handed out,' he continued. 'By the time it was the turn of the Welsh the Lord was clean out of analysis so he gave them an extra helping of emotion instead. It's forever emotion, emotion, emotion and now our Evan Roberts is busy stoking it all up and selling them fire insurance; a hollow protection clause against being roasted in the pit. I could weep for them all. Thank God we only get these revivals once a lifetime, that's all I can say. Life would be difficult to the point of tuberculosis if we had them all the time.'

'You can say that again,' said Ben Thomas. 'But I'll tell you something. I will go and live elsewhere if it gets any worse; somewhere they're sure *not* to have Grace at meals, Bible readings before going to bed and hymns first thing in the morning.'

'If I'm going to put up with it, you can be certain that I'm going to have plenty of this inside me,' said Ray Wright. 'With a bit of luck and a fair wind I'll be able to stay drunk until it all dies away.'

'Correct. We'll all become born-again drunks,' said Jenko, holding out an empty glass in front of him. 'Just a pint for me.'

William Gelly came over to join them. 'You know what my wife's saying now?' he asked.

'Don't tell us. She wants you to give up the booze.'

'She hasn't started that yet. She's saying we must count all the chicken eggs that are laid on Sunday and give all the proceeds to the chapel.'

'You could always stuff the chicken with cement on Saturday nights,' Jenko suggested amidst merry laughter. 'Then scrape it out on Sunday nights.'

'It's cement in the mouth my wife could do with.'

The card school erupted in heated argument with dark accusation of secret signals. 'Hang about now,' one was shouting. 'You pitched the two of trumps yet you were strong in spades. Your partner has got all the trumps . . . '

'Are you calling me . . . ' One of the players stood up and a chair toppled backwards.

There were three sharp raps on the taproom door, and then it opened with a resounding crack. A tall, burly stranger wafted up to the bar like a windjammer running before the wind. The card players stopped arguing, Jenko dried up in mid-sentence, conversations tinkled into silence as a few pints hovered, indecisive, an inch away from the lips with all heads ratcheting around, as if turned by the strings of the same puppeteer in the rafters, to gaze at this stranger, the likes of whom they had never seen before.

He was carrying a silver-topped cane in one hand and wearing a broad-brimmed Panama hat on his head. A giant green dickey-bow with white spots was tied around his high starched collar, a check-patterned cape dangled from his shoulders and baggy, brown worsted trousers hung off his waist.

'A gin and hot water,' he said to the barmaid in a loud voice, amplified by the stunned silence he had created.

'A gin and hot water,' the barmaid shouted into the scullery, a bright blush gathering in the hollows of her cheeks as she turned to face the stranger. He was appraising her pneumatic bosom, unashamed, even taking off his monocle and polishing it with a snuff handkerchief before slipping it back into his eye again. A boy brought out the gin and hot water and the barmaid asked for a groat.

The stranger flipped a coin on to the bar, took off his Panama and, steaming mug in hand, looked over one shoulder with his body swivelling around slow on his hips. He took in the crowd gazing at him. His face was as extraordinary as his dress. Great bushy eyebrows squatted on top of the tiniest brown eyes, a greenish-brown moustache had been waxed at the twirled-up tips, several jaw-lines rolled into one another with patches of hair missed by the razor and, smack in the middle of it all, sat one enormous nose with tufts of hair poking out of the nostrils and its whole surface patterned with tiny red veins, pockmarks and burst blood vessels. The nose put Jenko in mind of a very small, rotting, exploding beetroot.

'Stead. William Thomas Stead, at your service, gentlemen,' he said. 'Chief reporter of the *Daily Chronicle* and editor of the *Review of Reviews*, come all the way down here from London to make you famous and see to it that your names will be written in silver and gold across the top of the parchments of the great book of the world.'

The only thing that moved was the back-heeling boot of Billy Morris. Everyone continued to gaze at Stead in slack-jawed silence. 'Are you quite sure you've got the right place?' one of the card-players asked, final.

'Yes, quite sure, sir. Great golden clouds of glory are going to rise up out of this town, float across Offa's Dyke and bear the good news of all your names throughout the drawing rooms of the world. Evan Roberts, your most famous son, is the ambassador of eternity in the court of time. This court is made of the greatest palaces of all the greatest kings, from the wise Solomon to our own beloved Edward.' He raised his steaming mug to toast his audience. 'And you are to be its costumed courtiers.'

There was another extended and puzzled silence when the same card-player said, 'You know the chapel is up the road, do you? You know this is a pub here where they sell beer. Up the road is the chapel where they sing hymns.'

Stead sipped his drink until the laughter had subsided. 'I know that, sir. I *do* know the difference between the home of the Lord and a tavern of the ungodly but it is only amidst the fallen that the true work of God can be seen and felt. Jesus told us to bring him the weak, the crippled and the fallen. While others go to the chapel, I come here for you to help me find my vision of the fallen and suffering. I've come here for you to help me in my vision. You must understand that the visionary writer needs the lowest vantage point, so that he can lift his eyes to the highest.'

The next silence was a good deal shorter. 'Kick the silly bugger out,' said William Gelly.

'Never heard such a load of old cock in all my life,' Ray Wright amplified.

'You may laugh, gentlemen,' Stead shouted into the teeth of a gale of laughter. 'You may laugh and I take the greatest comfort in your laughter but I want you to be assured what a great honour it is for me to be here with the majestic hard poetry of men like you. Be sure that I am here to be of any service that I can.'

'You can buy us all a drink, if you like.'

'Certainly.' He turned and banged the ham of his fist down on the bar. 'Give all these gentlemen a drink.'

'That's put the tin hat on it,' said Jenko as a surge like a loose scrum moved towards the bar. 'If that fat old windbag has moved in you can be sure we've all had it. The fallen will fall a great deal more.'

'Know of him, do you, Jenko?'

'I know of him all right. Not long out of prison, as I remember, for writing about child slavery in London. That blunderbuss is more full of wind that Evan Roberts himself.'

'Even more than you, Jenko?'

'Even more than me, too. The move to canonize Evan has begun in earnest now. Soon he'll be surrounded by the greatest marvels and miracles the Gower has ever seen. There's just no telling where it will end now.'

Chapter Ten

Loughor railway station, just after seven that November morning was deserted; a grey rain, so thin you could barely see it, hissed soft over the wooden canopy above the waiting room, around the intricate timber valancing on the awnings and against the gas lamps, bent like question marks. The rain washed the advertisement hoardings and enamel signs extolling Hudson's Soap, Epps' Cocoa and Mazawattee Tea.

The drizzle even rinsed away the rancid smell of oil that usually hung over the lines, making the air sweet and fresh to the taste as it kept tumbling down, distributing its damp favours over all, dribbling down the sides of the red buckets full of sand on either side of the stationmaster's door, spreading in widening puddles over the paved platforms and making the silver rails glisten as if newly polished.

At the end of the platform Beth stood alone, gazing out past the brown clapperboard signal box and along the lines that curved away to places she had never heard of. Today marked the beginning of the group's first mission out into the valleys of South Wales. She had always enjoyed making journeys but now, after all the astonishing meetings of the past month – most conducted in the glare of the national newspapers with almost as many reporters in attendance as people – they were going out to meet the world head-on. Last night, she had barely been able to sleep a wink, thinking and worrying about it all.

She walked back along the platform to where her Dada had left her trunk, past the waiting room where a man wearing a black silk hat with a red band on it was sitting next to a fire. Beth had been half surprised that Lavinia and Pat had not slept in the waiting room overnight. The pair of them practically raced one another up the path to Island House when they got off the pony and trap each morning. As far as they were concerned, Evan was the only star in the firmament. Priscilla, a more independent spirit, did not seem as badly smitten as the other two. But Beth had noticed often enough that even Priscilla was more than ready to sheepdog Evan into a corner and get him all to herself whenever she could.

Indeed, they all had their own little ways for capturing his attention, and he was pleased enough to respond to this, though Beth tried to stay a little more detached, ready to serve but needing to retain her independence.

Perhaps no one was going to turn up after all. She checked the station clock and the knot of nervousness inside her tightened. Even with two pairs of socks on, her feet were still cold. She looked at her trunk and sniffed a smile at her hopelessness at leaving anything behind. 'You're not going away for a year little lady,' her Dada had pointed out but, nevertheless, she had managed to pack away just about everything she valued, including her tiny fretwork clock.

There was a sudden babble of voices outside the gate. Here at last was Evan, flanked by Lavinia and Pat. They must have gone to meet him as he was leaving Island House; she should have guessed. She noted that Lavinia was carrying his Gladstone bag. Three reporters were with them, too. She could always pick out their bright tweeds and brogues, their cocky airs and faint, but definite, stink of the drink. Slurring his words, one had even had the nerve to come to Island House one night, but he had been sent packing soon enough.

Beth had developed a particular aversion to Stead, who kept bobbing up everywhere, unexpected, these days. Try as she might, she could not find a single virtue in him, nor any excuse for the crushing boredom of his behaviour. She found him boisterous and self-important, just like her old music teacher. There was no keen edge to his verbosity either and, although she had never been much of a one for words herself, she did appreciate fine language when she heard it.

But, even more irritating than Stead's butchery of the language was his habit of giving his own interviews to reporters after Evan had finished. Worse than that even, the reporters jotted down all his words as though they were gospel, oblivious to Stead's nasty habit of putting his arms around the ladies whenever he spoke to them.

She moved closer to the group. The reporters, with their eager questions, showed no sign of leaving and Evan greeted her without even looking around. Perhaps he had spotted her earlier on the platform, she thought, yet he had often enough greeted her without seeming to see her first.

'We're a bit puzzled about this business of your denomination Mr Roberts,' one of them was saying to him.

'Oh I am a bit puzzled, too. The short answer is that I do not know. People say that I am a Methodist but I just do not know. What I do know is that we have got a church which is failing to come together and dying apart. I further know that this narrow sectarianism melts in the fire of the Holy Spirit and, while sect fights sect, Satan claps his hands with the greatest glee.'

'Is it true that you never wear a watch?'

'Quite true. A watch is not the way of the Holy Spirit who reaches through all the world and all time. The Holy Spirit does not need to be told the time. The Holy Spirit sustains time in the palm of his hand. The Spirit is time. Right, gentlemen. We have a train to catch and you have your deadlines.'

Evan put his hand on one of the reporter's heads and laughed when the reporter winced as if in great pain. 'Perhaps one of you Press people will stand up one night and announce his own conversion instead of just sitting there taking notes. There are too few faithful Mr Steads in your business.'

'Dogs may sing and cows may fly,' said one.

The reporters moved away. 'I don't know why you bother with them,' said Beth. 'They're always rude and get it wrong more often than they get it right.'

'One day they're going to learn how to spell my name as well,' Lavinia added. '*The Western Mail* got it wrong three ways last week.'

Evan smiled and put his arm around Beth's shoulders as they walked out on to the platform. 'You should not be too hard on them,' he said. 'They have their shortcomings, I know, but there are plenty of people who take their ideas from the morning papers. I have been told that some have even confessed after reading newspaper accounts of our meetings, so we must always be careful in looking after them.' He chuckled and nodded at Beth's trunk. 'You have brought your sandwich box along, I see.'

'It won't be any trouble, will it?'

'Certainly not.' He gave her a reassuring squeeze. 'A lady needs to travel with whatever makes her comfortable. Did you have a good breakfast? That is the important matter. The Lord's work needs a full stomach.'

Just then the train came clanking into the station, all wheels turning slow and flashing rods, the brakes groaning in squealing entreaty and the locomotive spurting with such eruptions of steam the ladies had to stand back as their dresses ballooned up. Their driver looked back at them, leering as their hands sought to control the billowing hemlines and petticoats. Beth was certain he had done that on purpose.

Evan was opening a carriage door when Priscilla came running along the platform one hand on awry poke bonnet, late as usual and gasping for air.

'There are some who would be late for their own funeral,' Evan said as he held open the door for her, but smiled reassuringly at her in his usual manner.

Priscilla looked up, nervous, as the porter worked Beth's trunk into the rack above her head. 'I bet that's yours, Beth,' she said, fanning her face with her hand. 'What have you got in it?'

'Oh things,' Beth said vague. 'I like having my things with me.' She noticed that Priscilla had acquired a fur muffler very like her own. 'What things have you brought with you?'

Priscilla looked over at Evan. He had already settled down next to the window with a Bible open on his lap. 'I've got one Bible and plenty of knickers,' she whispered.

They both turned to look at Evan. He did not seem to have heard anything. They giggled, soft, to one another like two children, up to no good at the back of the class. Beth liked Priscilla, a great antidote to pomposity was she; honest to the point of pain; incapable of recognising what Edwardian society would call sophistication even if it punched her in the nose.

The train picked up speed with the wheels tick-tacking over the lines and the rain sheeting wild against the window. Houses chased fields, mines chased rivers, with every now and then a huge tip squatting and looking at them like a monstrous black toad. Swansea came and went, a haphazard jumble of grey and red houses flung down around a dock, where men in working clothes and flat caps were already walking along the pavements, past a smoking tar machine and into the lightening morning. Tongues of red fire spurted out of Port Talbot ironworks as if seeking to set alight the wet day.

Beth was already feeling more relaxed as she watched the unwinding scenery. Priscilla was admiring Lavinia's anthracite jet brooch with Pat sitting, her eyes closed and head swaying gently from side to side, when Evan finished his morning Bible reading and put the book to one side. 'I have brought something to show you ladies,' he said.

He opened his Gladstone bag and took out a worn, leather-bound book. 'This is the first edition of Vicar Pritchard's *Canwyll y Cymry* – the first cheap edition of the Welsh Bible.'

'It's very beautiful,' Lavinia said. 'Old, is it?'

'Very old. This book, no more and no less, saved the Welsh language from repeated and savage Westminster assaults. The worst was a report by barristers in 1847, which attacked Welsh as the language of slavery. The report killed Welsh in the schools. The infamous treason of the blue books, that was.'

As Evan spoke of his Bible, Beth ran the tip of her index finger along the side of her cheekbone and smiled. In the pulpit he became a figure of wrath, with startling insights into the destructive powers of sin or the healing bonds of the family. But now he was a child, guarding his most coveted treasure so close he would not even let the ladies hold it, almost as if he feared that they would steal it from him or tear the pages.

'People were urged to do anything to raise the five shillings for the *Beibl Bach*,' said Evan as he turned over the fragile, wafer-thin pages. 'Every house was expected to have one and it saved our precious language.' He chuckled. 'Of course it would take more than a couple of English barristers to destroy the Welsh tongue. The English have been trying to kill it off for ever.'

Beth looked out at the sea lapping lazy against the rocks of Aberthaw. Two seagulls rode the drizzling winds above. There were many ways in which Michael was similar to Evan, she decided, even though, on almost every single issue, they were on opposite sides of the fence. They both exhibited violent mood changes, they were both sometimes sad and sometimes happy; one minute as angry as a lion and the next as meek as a lamb. And, despite their humble backgrounds, they were both forever surprising her with what they knew. These special men also needed a special woman, she guessed: someone who would never be quite sure if she was wanted as a mother, lover or for target practice.

She smiled at her rain-sodden reflection in the window and reached into her pocket to feel his cockleshell. She wondered if he had gone off to England. Him and all his plans. Him and that horse – forever abusing it when he clearly loved it dear. He would never go to England and leave his horse. Not him. She was surprised to find that the idea of never seeing Michael again sent a cold bolt of despair through her.

* * *

The rain kept up unceasing all that day. The clouds – giant black butts overflowing with thousands of gallons of water – were shunted by the winds over the roof of Wales, across the bald peaks of the Brecon Beacons and down into the valleys of South Wales.

The rain raced down the sides of these valleys, tumbling and dancing over the crags and smoking tips, waltzing over the roads and down the gutters of the mining towns before bouncing off banks sideways and down into drains, where it joined up with yet more waters from the underground springs. As one, they surged along with the coal-black rivers at the bottoms of the valleys for their overwhelmingly urgent appointment with the huge tidal surges of the Bristol Channel.

A massive belch of thunder heralded yet more rain. It drove down on to the curving terraces of the town of Trecynon in the chapel-sentinelled Aberdare valley. Even today, the impact of the new doctrine of socialism – its revolutionary and radical talk of a fair day's pay for a fair day's work – could be seen at the mine: there had been yet another labour stoppage, with the pithead silent and the shaft wheel motionless. Rain rinsed the winding machinery and the small brick house of the lamp room where canaries bobbed and chirped in their cages. Rain hissed over the long centipedes of the terraces with their weeping chortling gutterings. Rain soaked the dirty scraggy sheep to the bone.

Nothing escaped the rain – not even the manse just down the hill from the Ebenezer Congregational Chapel where, in one of the bedrooms, Evan was down on his knees, deep in the passionate grip of fervent, secret prayer; beseeching God to reveal the thrust of his mind, that he should come to understand it better and, in so doing, be better able to serve his Holy Spirit.

He had been praying for a full two hours now, releasing his own mind to float around in God's spacious love, letting it roam where it willed that it might come to rest on a mystic point of communion where he would be charged by the pulse and direction of Divine intention. He spoke to God, asking that, this night, the Holy Spirit would perform a great act of devastating power and that this meeting might be seen as the first instalment of a massive repayment by his people for the ever-rising mountain of grief they were causing God.

The rain was still rattling against the bedroom window as he drew together the concluding strands of his prayer. He took up the subject of the four ladies, for whom he prayed at least twice a day. He was convinced that, through the ladies, he had been given weapons of great power. He believed that they, almost alone, were going to be responsible for the destruction of the world's sinful pride.

Downstairs he found them sitting around the drawing room, clearly nervous and off-colour, with only Priscilla eating the sandwiches that had been left out for all of them. Beth was wondering what had happened to Dan, who had been sent down the day before as advance man and planner. She took great comfort in Dan's practical wisdom; she would really like to have him here now, with this lions' den of a meeting they were about to face.

It was not until they were all in a cloaked group and struggling up the hill, the ladies' cowls up and heads down in the driving wind and rain, that Dan came hurrying down towards them, arms flapping around and legs seeming to run away from his body. Neither was he wearing any topcoat. 'Evan,' he shouted, excited. 'Just *listen* to that. You've never seen anything like it.'

All of a sudden Evan was transported by a great and strange warmth. The sound of song was louder than anything he had ever heard in the Moriah, indeed louder than anything that he had ever heard before. The chapel was crowded inside but there were even greater numbers outside, sending the hymn, *Diolch Iddo*, marching through the dripping twilight and straight to war.

'Do you hear the throng, ladies?' Evan asked turning towards them and walking backwards up the hill. 'The sermon has started already. The throng is always mightier than the sermon. This is going to be a great meeting. The Spirit is there, and mightily too. I can feel it already. I prayed for it and, with your ears, you can now hear it.'

The damp warmth inside the chapel was as suffocating as an oven. There were pent-up bolts of lightning in the body of the congregation, waiting for a conductor to unleash it into a flashing and dazzling force. The very walls were soon going to shake with thunder – and a mightier thunder than that which had been crashing around the skies all day. Evan knew all this within seconds of mounting the pulpit, looking up at the lines of singing faces peering down from the gallery; at all the young boys and men sitting on the window sills and hanging off the pillars. The Press had clearly spread word of his work throughout the land and they had come to see for themselves, with their own eyes, come with such spine-tingling excitement three had already fainted, even before the service had begun.

In his customary search of their faces, he saw a trusting expectancy, which he could exploit and explore. In the singing, he heard a tremendous spiritual tension channelling with which he could work magic. Even in the smell of the damp clothing and the polish that hangs thick on every chapel pew he sensed the rich, musky veneer beneath which the small miracles of conversion could be fashioned. He was Noah who had just been given all the right tools with which to build his Ark.

When the hymn had finished he pointed at the gallery and shouted out loud: 'Who are you appealing to?'

There was no reply. He asked again and the tremulous voice of an old man called back: 'We are appealing to God.'

'Good enough!' Evan shouted. 'But there is not enough love and prayer in the singing. There is a need to sing more powerfully. Take these lovely words and sing them with a gentle power. Sing as if standing in the life-giving breeze of Calvary. Feel the breeze of Calvary on your face and sing, deep in your grief, for your Saviour who suffered so much for you. *Yes*, for you.'

It was Priscilla who stepped up and pitched the hymn in that alto voice of hers, as pure and delicate as Nantgarw china, with the other three ladies moving around her, singing straight and clear – as they had planned in advance – so that the congregation could follow easily and find the vocal level which best suited them. Evan clapped his hands and sang along with them, soaring on the wings of his own pleasure, since the minor-key hymn surged with Calvary's breeze, eddying with love one way and gusting with angels' wings in the other, all underpinned with feelings which were as passionate as they were powerful.

The tenor voices of the men attacked the notes and burnished the melody with the finest flourishes; many were holding a cupped hand over one ear to prevent the person next to them upsetting their pitch. Outside in the rain the crowd took up each verse and made it their own, making the words echo and echo again down the sides of the dark, damp valley.

Some found the hymn so moving they were openly weeping. One man, who was clearly having trouble with his singing, took out his false teeth, wrapped them in a handkerchief and placed them in his top pocket.

Evan urged them to sing the last verse not once but five times and, when they had finished, he leaned over the pulpit, his fingers outstretched into the muttering prayers, seeking to set light to the fire.

'Of all the treasures that God gave us the soul is the greatest, more valuable even than all Solomon's treasures. A soul is not something to gamble with. You cannot redeem your soul after losing it. When you have lost your soul in the sea of sin then so too you have lost yourself for ever. It is your passport and only with it intact will you, one day, rise again and be returned, in heaven, to the arms of all those you once loved and lost. That is God's solemn promise to us. So who will now repent and save his soul?'

The tone of his voice was measured and calm; the pitch of a salesman whose goods enjoy fine reputation and quality. There was no need for the ringing cadences, which he sometimes used to overwhelm the reluctant will.

A man stood up, announced simply that he had become a Christian and then sat down again. A woman said a few words no one could understand and another man, with badly shaking hands bunching and pulling on his cap, said, in a voice which kept cracking and swallowing: 'I left my wife three years ago, the two children as well. I went to live with another woman, let her down too and returned to live with my mother. I stole from her today to buy whisky and have some in my pocket now. Last month, between the cards and whisky, I lost twenty-six shillings. There is nothing in me but the taste for whisky and the love of gambling. It has . . . '

'Shush!' said a voice.

'Never say 'shush' to a confessing voice,' Evan interrupted, pounding the lectern angry. 'A drunken man has come to this meeting and been sobered up in half an hour by the Holy Spirit. Carry on, sir. Your words are golden shower in my heart. We will stay here all week to listen, if necessary.'

The man had remained standing, head slumped forward and shoulders heaving with sobs; suddenly he lifted up his head and held it in an almost military manner. 'I would like to say here and now that God has shown me my folly. I want to say here and now that I want my wife and children back. I want you to pray that she will have me back. I want to say here and now that I will take the Lord Jesus into my life and heart.'

> 'Praise the Lord. Praise the Lord.'
> 'Christ be praised.'
> 'Thank you Jesus.'
> 'Praise your name Lord. Praise your name.'
> 'Hallelujah.'
> 'The Lord be praised.'

It was Beth who stepped up at that point to lead a chorus of *Diolch Iddo* – Thanks be to Him for remembering the dust of the earth – which was to become, after that night, the great love song of the Revival. Beth's voice chased down the beauty of the song hard, and even she found it difficult to sing the first verse without her eyes misting over and a great choking lump rising in her throat. After each conversion she led the singing of *Diolch Iddo* which became an anthem of triumph, with everyone clapping their hands or waving their handkerchiefs so that the whole building appeared to run amok with a storm of cabbage white butterflies.

'Anyone else to confess?' Evan called out when the singing had stopped. 'Anyone else wanting his life renewed and returned?'

An old man with short grey hair stood up, holding his Bible to himself. 'This Book of Books is my chief and only guide through the brief journey of the world,' he said. 'I am now on the edge of the old river and sing in rapture at the prospect. Only the other day I had a vision of a beautiful land with the friendliest people in it. Between me and this golden country was a shining river to be crossed only by a plank. I was anxious about the crossing, fearing that the plank would not support me. But, at that moment, I gave myself to God and, on a great wave of faith, crossed to safety.'

A silence trawled through the chapel as everyone pondered on the simplicity and dignity of the man's words until Priscilla stood up and led the singing of *Abide With Me*.

Abide with me; fast falls the eventide;
The darkness deepens; Lord with me abide
When other helpers fail and comforts flee
Help of the helpless, O abide with me.

They were just about to begin the second verse when Evan called out for them to stop, adding that he saw amongst them a man in distress. 'This man is in the struggle and ready to make a decision. He is hovering on the very brink of eternal life. Step up, brother. Step up into the sunlight. Receive His grace that you may avoid His wrath. He is coming there now.'

A voice shouted that he had given in and the congregation began waving their handkerchiefs and singing *Diolch Iddo*.

'Another is in dire straits and about to make a decision. His situation is too terrible for us to sing. I have never experienced such a thing before. A soul is in torment and the Lord is calling out for it. Come to the sunlight, brothers and sisters. Come riding in on a wave of love.'

Further isolated cries of surrender went up when Evan began speaking again. 'In the last days, we are told, certain things will happen. I read my Bible to mean that we are coming to the last days when the old men will dream dreams and the young men see visions. There will be bloodshed on the moon, a great darkness over the land and signs writ large in the sky. The moon . . . '

His lips kept moving but the words dried up in his mouth. He swallowed hard. 'The moon will bleed . . . ' The words went away again and, staring out at the sea of faces, his vision began tunnelling, becoming darker and murkier around the edges and brighter and more incandescent at the centre. Something big and black heaved in the white light like a whale breaking the surface of the waves, and disappeared again. Then a massive hand of hard, solid shadow passed across the face of the world. The face cried out in the greatest fear while the hand now dangled over Evan's head like an eternal curse.

'He is coming and will engulf the world,' his lips said with the purest fire. 'Satan and all his dark angels have finally escaped from their dungeon in hell and are even now gathering for the last desperate rebellion against God. Beware, my people, arm yourselves with holiness, for this hurricane of destruction is coming down on you with a terrible force. This hurricane will tear your lives apart in ways you do not understand. It will come offering money which destroys charity; offering power which blights love; telling of the triumph of carnal knowledge which attacks fidelity; insisting that right is wrong and that wrong is right.

'This force will come scattering illusions at your feet. It will come bloated with gluttony and malodorous with the stink of its own corruption. Its walk will be slow since it will be burdened with grudges and resentments, trailing ahead of the slime of its hatred. This invading force of evil will come as an organised intelligence. Never underestimate it, since it is so clever it will come dressed up as men of respectability, anxious to serve you and even able to convince you that Satan does not exist. But he does, my people, and he is going to throw a cloak of violent perversion all over the world.'

His head moved around, trance-like, hands fastened on to the pulpit, arms ramrod straight but with the whole of his body vibrating like a single flower in a breeze. The words came gentler now, smilingly jubilant rather than savagely apocalyptic. 'But this move to drive God from His throne will fail. Oh yes, it will fail. This mighty struggle between God and Satan to mount the horse of the human choice must fail in Satan's destruction. This ultimate blasphemy will end where it began, in that dungeon in hell. But it will only fail when the powers of darkness seem to reign over the whole world since only then, when we are weeping in the ruins, will that bruised and torn Galilean arise again and deliver the world in The Second Coming. Yes, my people, that great day when the blessed will be separated from the damned and love will rule every heart and the dead be resurrected in joy. Repent and prepare for that hour when the Son of Man will come again in all His glory. Yes, he is coming like the sun, striding down the land, but will you be ready for Him? Are you ready if He comes tonight?' He stopped speaking and his accusing finger traced a wide arc all around him. 'Well are you? Are you ready if He comes this minute? Be ready.'

The effect of his words on the congregation was immediate. In just one vivid burst Evan Roberts had revived, in the minds of an insecure and imaginative people, a vision of the Puritanism of their forefathers. With flaming clumps of words – wrenched up from some dark and dangerous abyss – he had suborned ordinary thought with poetic emblems of something ancient and precious to the tribe. They stood up and declared themselves ready in prayers and shouts of praise. They rose in salute to the spirit of a man who had come before them and struggled somewhere in the imperial destiny of old Cambria; the line that went back to the reign of Hywel Dda and took in such mythic spellbinders as Owain Glyndŵr, William Williams, Christmas Evans and Howell Harris. Here was another mind-possessor, come with withering thunder.

The Doxology was chanted over and over again as Evan leaned on the pulpit, sweating and as exhausted as a marathon runner crossing the finishing line. Every ecstasy and every vision punished him deep and sometimes enfeebled him for days. He pressed his two bunched fists against his forehead and prayed to the Lord for strength.

A crowd outside began singing *Abide With Me*, some even kneeling in the rainy puddles. The only ones who had not surrendered and been converted inside the chapel had fainted first. A breeze from Calvary indeed. A gale!

Chapter Eleven

After that first tempestuous meeting in Trecynon, the evangelical group crossed and recrossed the valleys, packing out chapels in Tylorstown, Abercynon, Ferndale and Pontypridd.

It was a colourless, brutalising world with zinc baths hanging on nails in gardens strewn with dead marigolds; outside wooden lavatories too cold to sit on by night and too hot and smelly by day; everywhere, the sorrowing bleating of black-faced sheep. Whole towns had been scattered over brambled slopes, around flaming ironworks or newly sunk pits, the canals slithering with coal barges and ghosts of the old Chartist leaders come to pray that their people would one day be delivered from all this.

That winter one third of the world's total export of coal was coming out through the ports of Newport, Cardiff and Swansea. The valleys were supplying the needs of an Age of Steam and had become the single great artery of the British Empire.

Wherever Evan Roberts spoke, and his ladies sang, the colliers – excited by news of this newcomer with his searing visions – left their pubs, shuffleboard and dice; they abandoned their whippet-training, pitch and toss, mountain fights to the finish, the dog and cock fights. They left off browsing great literature in the first of the miners' libraries and stopped listening to the first foreign teachers of socialism – all to return to the empty chapels to listen to a man tell of a holy God's requirement that his people be holy too.

The group went to windy, cold squares by day and hot, stuffy chapels by night. They ate the food that was given to them and slept in whatever homes they could be accommodated. Looking back on the emotional turmoil and long, intense meetings, Beth later decided that it must have been as tiring as working those narrow coal seams, a few miles below ground. She kept going as best she could – calling on her training and stamina as a nurse – but there were moments when even she wept with exhaustion, her voice hoarse with the singing, her body battered by these vicious valley winds which struck out from behind the ends of grey terraces and knifed the kidneys hard.

In all this stress and commotion she was thankful that they had one great marshal and ally – Dan. Everywhere they went a smiling Dan would be just ahead of them, meeting with the ministers and deacons of the various chapels, listening to what they wanted and explaining what they might get. It was Dan who always checked that there was jug of water in the pulpit and plenty of smelling salts in the vestry. It was Dan who arranged where each of the ladies was going to stay the night. It was Dan who kept a detailed diary of the Revival on a blue, cloth-bound pad covered in tea stains. It was in there that he recorded the daily number of converts and letters received, the types of coal each chapel used in their boilers or the start times and ends of the services.

Any fact or figure fascinated Dan – he even noted the flowers on the dais and the numbers of hymns. This arsenal of facts also made Dan something of a miracle worker, who could reel off just about every time of every train in Wales, whistle up a pot of tea in the middle of a field and even lend you money for a bag of chips.

When anything at all went wrong the ladies sent up a general cry for Dan. Whenever possible, Beth enjoyed going along with him on his planning forays. Amongst many other odd subjects, for example, he was an expert on those chapel boilers which seemed to work either spasmodically, not at all or fry everyone within ten yards. He could find a blockage in a pipe in a flash, while his usual diagnosis of why a boiler was faulty was that the caretaker was using the wrong coal.

'There are two hundred varieties of coal in this country, ranging from Smethwick Black to Wyndham Red Ash,' he explained to Beth on one occasion. 'Some are better suited than others for individual boilers, but these caretakers always manage to pick the wrong one. Quite how they manage it, I don't know, but they always get it wrong. It's all down to the ash content. If the coal gives out a lot of ash then the ash needs somewhere to fall. They don't seem to understand that simple fact.'

Dan loved his work. The warts and knobs of reality entranced him; he admitted that he preferred looking at chapel boilers to talking to the ministers who journeyed across the land to beg Evan to come to their parish and wake up their flocks. 'It's them that need to be woken up first,' he argued. 'I had one around the other night, telling me that his problem was that he no longer believed in the Bible. I ask you.'

He told Beth one night that they had now accumulated enough invitations to keep them going every night for ten years. 'They've been coming in from all over the world, too. We even had one from the Welsh church in Patagonia this morning.'

He began humming to himself merry while staring out of a window. Beth noticed he hummed a lot when Evan was not around – usually a sign that he was going to say something slightly off-colour. 'But I'm not at all convinced,' he began, 'about this business of converting yet more Welsh – particularly in Patagonia. There's frequent reports about St. Peter getting really browned off with all the Welsh already in heaven. Everywhere, they are. There's this story that St. Peter was that fed up one day, with all the Welsh singing or playing their harps or composing hymns all the time, he ordered one of his angels to stand outside the heavenly gates and shout *caws pobi*: toasted cheese – *caws pobi:* toasted cheese. The Welsh, mouths slavering for their favourite dish, all rushed out in a cavalry charge and the angels slammed the gates shut and locked them all out. For a bit, this made heaven an agreeable place to be in again.'

It was the humorous cynicism of such stories that made Beth wonder why Dan gave so much of himself to the Revival. He did not seem a particularly religious type and never once had she seen him lower his head in prayer. Perhaps he was such an active worker because he was thankful for the restoration of his sight? But thankful to whom? God, or his brother Evan? She had once tried to get Dan to talk about his blindness but he merely changed the subject and she never raised it again.

Yet, while Dan organised, Evan continued speaking of the coming apocalypse with a furious power, arraigning sin, rousing the conscience and brainstorming his way through one service after the next as his imagination took him leaping into territories no preacher had ever been before.

Yet, on some nights, he said almost nothing at all, insisting that silence could deliver a great sermon, too. No two meetings were ever the same and, even when he forewarned the ladies that he was going to try something different in the service that night, he never did so. He was content to let each meeting find an intelligence and will of its own, with him standing apart, distant but always alert to those who were ill-at-ease; those who were on the brink of surrendering; foretelling convert after convert and, on occasion, becoming angry when he spotted a cynic who had clearly come along for a laugh.

The sheer unpredictability of the meetings, with the ladies dancing an intricate gavotte around the vocal outbursts and random silences, ensured constant and continuing Press attention. Beth noticed with some distaste that W.T. Stead turned up at the end of almost every meeting, spouting his views to Evan. Stead even advised Evan on the conduct of the meetings, suggesting that the ladies should sing more on their own: a suggestion, as it happened, which Evan resisted. He did not believe in giving anyone any instructions about anything, insisting that spontaneity was all.

Stead would then come to the ladies, dribbling with gratuitous advice, insensitive to their distaste, often putting his arm around them and sickening Beth whenever he managed to catch up with her. Why couldn't he keep his hands to himself? His breath stank, too – even worse than his prose, it was.

There is nothing wild or hysterical about the meetings, he wrote in The Daily Chronicle. *Unless it be wild or hysterical for the labouring breast to heave with sobbing that cannot be repressed and the throat choke with emotion as a sense of this awful horror and shame of a wasted life suddenly bursts on the soul.*

And then there was the gutter Press:

The boy preacher continued travelling the valleys with his four beautiful women yesterday. Last night they all stayed in the same hotel in Ferndale and some of the group said that Evan Roberts looked more tired when he got up than when he went to bed.

Just what were they driving at? Why did they write these things?

But that was the Press for you, wasn't it? She tried – oh how she tried – to be polite to them but Christian charity was difficult where they were concerned. One stripling from the *Western Mail* even asked her to go out with him one night. The nerve of the man! Priscilla said she quite fancied him – she just loved his wild hair, she added.

'You shouldn't be with us here,' Beth told her. 'You should be like one of those idle ladies, just laying on a drawing room couch all day reading bad novels and having the vapours.'

Priscilla laughed at that, of course, just as she laughed at everything. Everywhere she went she created noise and sometimes being alone with her was much like being in the middle of a disorderly mob. Yet Beth was drawn to this riotous gaiety and they spent a lot of time together.

Their other great bond was chips – which, Priscilla believed as an article of faith, had been designed special in heaven to look after the singing voice. Priscilla could smell a chip shop a mile away and it was a rare day indeed when the pair or them did not dispose of a bag of greasy chips, often so soggy and badly cooked they came in one dripping ball, which had to be disentangled with some skill and care.

Chips, Beth discovered, really did wonders for the hoarse voice. On emerging from a railway station, say, Priscilla's head would revolve in the air, with her nose sniffing dog-like for evidence of frying tonight. 'It's down there, Beth,' she might say. 'About three hundred yards away.'

Off they would trot and, sure enough, down there, about three hundred yards away, some melancholy Italian with flabby, hairy arms or small unsmiling Welsh woman, built out of billiard ball muscles, would be sweating, profuse, behind a counter as they joggled the hissing chip pans around. Beth and Priscilla invariably brought amusement to the chip shop owner's life, though, since they were always surprised, and even amused, to see two ladies in their Sunday finery come in and ask for a pennorth of chips – and even more surprised to see the pair sharing them as they walked back down the street.

The other two ladies, Lavinia and Pat, stayed together for much of the time, reading sections of the Bible aloud to one another or testing a new hymn. Their adoration of Evan was total and without reservation.

'The ladies must go with me wherever I go,' Evan told Stead. 'I can never part from them without feeling that something is absent if they are not there. Their singing is the most important key to this Revival.'

After each service he always managed to compliment each of them on their singing – even Beth one night in Pontarddulais when her voice had been so hoarse she had not sung a single note. Evan was clearly fonder of Beth than any of the others, sometimes catching her eye and exchanging glances of warmth and, somehow, complicity.

* * *

It was odd, in a way, that when Michael turned up at a meeting in the Libanus Chapel in Treherbert, on a rainy night in December, Beth had been expecting him. She often caught herself thinking of him, especially when she was tired, and suddenly there he was just sitting there in the front row of the packed gallery. It was those eyes that made him stand out from the rest.

She had fancied that she had spotted him from time to time in the street crowds too, but she could never be sure.

Now here he was again.

Something inside her knotted up; she was not sure whether to acknowledge him or not. For the first few minutes at the start of the service she just sat looking at her hands, while stealing odd glances at him – her head facing one way and her eyes squinting in the other.

But could it be, perhaps, that he had become a convert like the rest? Oh foof! Him on his knees praying! She could not picture it – unless he was praying for a pint of beer. That one was too full of his socialism to go down on his knees before anyone – least of all the Lord. So why had he come? She stole another glance at him. He seemed calm enough, just sitting there with his arms folded and looking, well, lovely. He always looked lovely, him. That was his trouble.

Any idea that he had become a convert, though, was dispelled immediately when Evan began leading the prayers and everyone bowed their heads except Michael, who sat upright in his seat, eyes still open and with his arms still folded. Beth looked up at him with flickering, nearly-closed eyes. Neither had he sung any of the hymns. Her knuckles bunched white in anger. She was going to kill him when she got hold of him, she was.

It was after the prayers had finished that Evan, for the first time ever, lost control of a meeting. There was no authority in his words. His hands kept fumbling with the pages of his Bible. When he did speak he just unreeled complaint after complaint.

He complained about the singing, the prayers and the disorder. 'Stop, stop, stop. Some persons are getting up to do certain things when they have been told to sit down. Others are sitting down when they should be standing up.' Beth did not dare look up at Michael in the gallery.

'I used to allow free expression in these meetings, but that must come to an end. I know when anyone acts and yet is unmoved by the Holy Spirit. I even know when there is a single person here not praying that we should all embrace the Spirit. There is such a person here tonight. We must all work in prayer together. *All of us.*'

Priscilla started up a hymn but he stopped that straight away. 'Do you believe in what you are singing? If not, it would be better if you did not sing at all. It would be better if the singing was confined to those who believe. This singing is too formal. There is no unity in it. How did the Spirit descend on the day of Pentecost? The people were all of one accord. If you do not love there is no unity or accord. Sing then, and pray for a wave of love.'

Beth eyed Michael, cold. Perhaps it was him who was upsetting Evan. He was certainly upsetting her and she resolved, there and then, that she would never forgive him for coming here and embarrassing her like this. This was a house of God, not one of his fairgrounds.

Evan ended the meeting, abrupt, and they all crowded into the hall at the rear of the chapel for tea and ham sandwiches. A group of long-faced deacons had gathered around Evan, who was still complaining of the poverty of faith in the chapel. The ladies had gathered around the piano where another group asked them a flood of questions which, for the most part, Priscilla alone answered.

Beth was chewing a ham sandwich when her mouth gaped and she noticed right there on the other side of the room, Michael chatting with Dan of all people. The knot of anxiety inside her tightened. Dan! What was he up to now? Was Michael telling Dan all about her? What was he saying about her? Why had he come here if not just to cause trouble again? A blush broke out on her neck and she looked straight at the wall. Well *she* wasn't going to speak to Michael that was for certain.

More tea was poured and a fresh plate of ham sandwiches appeared on top of the piano. She took a quick glance at Michael again. He was still talking to Dan and they were actually laughing and joking together, as if they had been friends for years. She picked up a sandwich and put it straight back down again. But what could she do?

When the tea had finished and one of the deacons had thanked Evan for coming to share their great work with them – even if it had not been entirely satisfactory that night – Evan called on the ladies and they all left with him.

Beth kept her eyes down, careful in case Michael caught her looking at him. He was going to have some explaining to do about all this.

Once outside, the group was swallowed up by the normal large crowd except that, this time, there was none of the usual salvationist pandemonium but, rather, following word of Evan's odd behaviour, lots of curious, silent faces moving around them in the rain. Beth found herself a little frightened by this unfamiliar silence in such a large crowd and her eyes turned and turned again, looking for Michael in the bobbing, dripping light of the lanterns.

Even the Taibach wailers, on the other side of the road, were silent as they stood together like soaked, dispirited scarecrows. Beth looked around again, anxious, the light rain hanging on her eyelashes like tears, but still she could see no sign of him. A dog was snapping at ankles. One man was wearing a raincoat and a soggy pair of carpet slippers.

There was a surge of bodies just behind her and she felt a hand grip her arm. The grip was relentless and she all but shouted out with the pain of it. 'Beware lest you fall, harlot,' a man's voice said into her ear. She could feel warmth of his breath against her neck. 'Evan Roberts and his harlots will all be broken after the fall. The wrath of the lamb is warning you now.'

She saw that it was a small old man with short, grey hair and dark spectacles. His grip tightened. 'You're hurting my arm,' she said.

'Beware of the fall, harlot.'

'Let go of my arm, will you?'

She managed to wrench her arm away from the painful grip but it felt mighty bruised. Those gazing faces whirled around her again and her lungs seemed to be fighting for air. She slipped her arm into Priscilla's for support. Oh how fed up she was with all this madness . . . all the Pressmen . . . all this singing . . . all the hysteria . . . all these strange people looking at her as if she was in a zoo.

She so wanted to be free of it all, out on the sands with her Michael. But where was he? Why was he teasing her like this? Why didn't he just come up to her and take her home?

* * *

The next day Beth was standing in the parlour of the manse, looking out through the curtained windows at the town of Caerphilly with its moated castle sitting beneath shifting continents of black rain clouds. Just over the road two sheep were scratching themselves, contented, against a wire fence.

'It's all right for those sheep,' said Dan, coming to stand next to her. 'All they seem to do is wander about the place, eating up vegetables and having a good scratch now and then. They say some of these valley sheep even climb on one another's backs to get into the gardens.'

'I don't believe you.'

'I've never seen it myself, but that's what they say. Terrible they are, eating the flowers in the cemeteries almost as soon as they're put there, even butting down garden doors with their heads. Sheep are not as stupid as they look. When they smell food they can get very crafty indeed.'

'Who was that young man you were talking with after the service, last night?' Beth asked, evenly, still watching the sheep.

'Which young man was that?'

'The one you were talking with when we had tea after the service.'

'Oh, Michael Evans, you mean? Is that who you mean?'

'Is it?' she asked, vague.

'He's a good boy, that one. Bright as a button, too. We used to be in a socialist group together. Met every week in Gorseinon, we did. You know how it is when you are young. I hadn't seen him for ages until last night. Why do you ask about him?'

'Oh nothing really. He just caught my eye. He's unusual.'

'He's unusual all right. Knows a lot, too, and never had any proper education either. Wastes his time picking cockles but he'll get himself moving one day. I like his fury.'

'Is he coming around again, did he say?'

'He didn't say. Come to that, I wasn't sure why he turned up last night. I don't see him as a possible convert. I don't really see him as one of us.'

'How can you say that, Dan? We're all the same, aren't we? In the eyes of God, I mean? We're all one of the same, aren't we?'

Dan jingled some money in his pocket and glanced at her, uncomfortable, before rocking back on his pelvis. 'I suppose so. If you put it like that, I suppose so.'

Beth looked at him. She recognised doubt in a sentence when she heard it, for it wasn't just Evan Roberts who could sense a failure of conviction. She certainly could not carry on if Dan withdrew from the work. He was her private pit prop. 'Let's go and find a cup of tea,' she said.

Outside the sheep had moved on and the rain continents were still shifting around in the sky, huge and dark and ominous.

* * *

'I'm thinking of giving up the work,' she told Priscilla late that night as they walked together up a shale track to the farmhouse where they were staying.

'Don't say that, Beth. I know what you're thinking, but we all know that Evan has his ups and downs. I know tonight was another poor service but you shouldn't leave now. Not if it's because things aren't going too well. It would be cowardly.'

She wished she could talk about Michael. She did have a deep feeling for Evan and for what he was doing, but it was Michael who kept invading her thoughts and, ever since his reappearance the night before, he was there with her all the time, just like some kind of permanent headache. Yes, that's exactly what he was. A permanent headache.

The night wind made the branches of a huge oak rattle like a ghost playing with a big bag of bones. The odd star winked between the black drifting clouds and several sheep moved away from them, making Priscilla jump with their sudden shadowy movements.

'All I want is a simple home life,' said Beth. 'I'm not a performer. I'm just an ordinary girl with ordinary desires. Do you know what I really want? Lots and lots of children. Silly, isn't it? Just lots and lots of children.'

Priscilla was quiet for a moment. 'Well you'd better get yourself a man for a start. If you want lots and lots of children a man does help. But you're not bothered, are you? With men?'

The warmth of the welcome from the farmer and his wife and the comfort of their farmhouse did little to dispel Beth's gloom. She was jealously irritated rather than cheered by the real sense of love in the living room, with its gleaming brass warming pan on the wall, the embroidered antimacassars on the armchairs, the flowered curtains on the windows and the dog stretched out on the flagstone floor, snorting and spluttering to himself in front of a log fire. Family photographs stood on the old oak dresser and small sprays of flowers on the mantelpiece. It was, Beth decided, exactly her type of room. If only she could become a milkmaid, with a bucket and three-legged stool, and live here for the rest of her days.

The couple were newly married, busy trying to make a mixed smallholding work. Beth envied their happiness: the way the young wife laughed at all her husband's tall stories, despite having heard them a hundred times before. She admired the way he even went out and refilled the kettle in the backyard pump himself; rare it was to meet a man prepared to do anything around the house. All the men she knew finished their day's work and expected to put their feet up and be waited on. This couple appeared to do everything together.

Later, alone upstairs in her bedroom, Beth undressed by the light of a bull-rush candle and stood naked in front of her mirror, examining her body limb by limb, running her hands over her legs and smoothing down her hips. The light was just dim enough for her not to have to look at any of the bruises on her arm or, indeed, her breasts – which she hated. They were, she always thought, all swollen and lumpy. She could never bring herself to touch or smooth them.

Once in bed she smiled – almost for the first time that evening – when she heard the couple in the next bedroom laughing and joking together. She turned over; then her euphoria suddenly vanished and a fierce tension pulled at every part of her, as if with many hands. Oh no! Not that! Anything but that. Soft grunts mingled with the steady squeal of the bedsprings. She turned over and bit into the pillow. She pulled the covers over her head but still that dreadful, hideous noise continued and, what's more, it was going on and on and on. She sat upright with her hands fluttering around her like demented butterflies. She wanted to hammer on the wall or else go in and throw a bucket of water over them. Pigsties were the place for that. But would it never end?

She lay down again, piling the pillows up on top of her head. It only seemed to make those infernal noises louder. The thrashing and moaning got worse, and she would have done anything to have got out of that room: yes, maimed, even murdered, or sung for the very devil himself, if only she could have got away from those noises.

It did end final. Exhausted by the intensity of her terror, she lay back, half fearful that it might start again, with streams of sweat pouring from every inch of her body. When she did fall asleep her rest was fitful and she wandered in endless tormenting nightmares, thick with violation and the pain of desertion. Huge heartbeats pounded inside her and babies, screamed, angry, at Baptismal fonts.

Chapter Twelve

It was nine o'clock in the morning and Dr. Enoch Jenkins lay collapsed in the foam of his tub, the coloured suds running and dripping over his arms and legs. On winter mornings his tub was the only place he felt warm and he wailed for his housekeeper to come in with a replenishing jug of hot water. He lifted a foot out of the foam, studied the three hammer-toes and let it fall. That was about as near as he ever got to any real exercise these days, unless he counted lifting heavy pints in the pub. He believed that all effective exercise involved doing nothing.

And if that housekeeper of his did not come soon his tub was going to freeze over and they would have to chip him out of an iceberg. He turned over on one side and got bubbles up his nose.

'Are you decent, Dr. Jenkins?'

Ah, so the old bag had not forgotten! His housekeeper was one Gaynor Jones, a tiny, terrified old lady from Carmarthen who, since the Revival had started, prayed her way through every minute of the day. 'I'm decent, Mrs Jones, but this water is going to freeze solid unless you get a move on.'

Her tiny, pinafored figure came shuffling into the room backwards. 'Where do you want it, doctor? Up top or down below?'

'Down below.'

She proceeded to pour the scalding water over his kneecaps. 'Yaaaaaaaaaaaaaah!' he bellowed. 'Yoweeeeeeeeeeeeee,' he continued. 'If you opened your eyes, Mrs Jones. If you just opened your eyes for a second you'd be able to see what you're doing. I *have* got my underpants on if that's what you're worried about. Look, will you? One pair of bloody standard underpants.'

'I'm sorry, doctor,' she said, still not opening her eyes. 'It's your bad language, it is. Makes me nervous, it does.'

'Not half as nervous as you're making me, Mrs Jones. This is an old man sitting in this tub not some lobster up for the pot.'

'I think I had better leave the jug here, doctor. You put it where you want.'

She crabbed out of the room, knocking a chair sideways as she went and he stood up in a rage with the water dripping off his underpants.

That's what the Revival had done for him. Robbed him of his morning tub! She had insisted on it – even threatened to go and live with her sister back in Carmarthen – so he was now the only man in Wales who had to dress up to take a bath. He stepped out and dried himself before taking a shave. It was all so unfair. There was him, a doctor who had done his time in the hypocrisy and cant of the Victorian Age, and now it had to come to this. Soon his housekeeper would doubtless be trying to fit knickers on the bare legs of tables and he would make a stand there for certain. He cut himself and ripped off a bit of newspaper to stick on the cut. For him the only bonus that had come out of the Revival was that his patients, instead of pestering him for pills or a good bottle, were now in the chapel praying away their wretched ailments. They never caught anything interesting around here anyway, though there was a man in Crofty who'd caught foot and mouth a few years back. Jenko always thought he was too strong to die, but die he did. There were some complaints his poultices and bad jokes just could not cure.

He only cut himself twice more before finishing shaving, turning his head from side to side and noticing that his hairline was receding, definite. He once believed he had found a good cure for baldness from a travelling gypsy: powdered toadstools and the legs of field mice, all whipped up into a paste. He tried it on a collier who had a fair head of hair at the beginning of the treatment and not one strand at all at the end. 'We all make mistakes,' he told the collier. 'Baldness is a sign of virility and anyway you look good in a cap.' He still bore the scar on his cheek where the collier had hit him.

He spent a good five minutes trying to wrestle his twanging starched collar into place. The problem was that the collar had an enlarged buttonhole and therefore needed a larger stud. Why couldn't someone find a way of reducing an enlarged buttonhole? Why couldn't housekeepers housekeep? He only ever managed to get his shirt front into place by pinning it to his vest, though the days of painting out the holes in his socks with black enamel or keeping his trousers straight by filling up the turn-ups with buckshot were over. Elegant scruffiness for him from now on; he had no choice really. He had showed his housekeeper his frayed shirt cuffs the other day and her only solution was to tidy up the frayed ends with a pair of scissors. Now he had to go everywhere with his sleeves rolled up. The whole world was coming apart, like this collar here.

His housekeeper was still busy saying Grace when he sat down at the breakfast table. He let her get on with it. Taking a teaspoon, he knocked the top of his hardboiled egg; it was as hardboiled as last year's lettuce and collapsed into a small ocean of yellow mucus and bits of shell all over his plate. He pushed away the plate and checked his watch. The pub would be open soon. Drink was the only logical alternative to work and, in these bad days of the Revival, the only bearable way of life was to do both at the same time.

His housekeeper was still saying Grace. He would be far better off, he decided, if he just emigrated. He would be far better off if he did a lot of things. He could always go to the Klondyke and instruct the miners there on the subtle bathos of dreaming of home. Any Welsh in the Klondyke? They would be far better off there even if they only prospected up a single lump of chalk in a lifetime of hard digging. Wales was no place for the Welsh any longer – it was only fit for those Italian organ-grinders from Dublin and there were enough of those vermin around.

He buttered a slice of toast and wondered what his housekeeper found to talk about in those hour-long Graces of hers. She muttered into her steepled fingers, went silent for a minute, and began muttering again. Ask for advice on how to boil an egg, why don't you? Ask if it's fair he had to wear his underpants in the tub. Better still, find out how to fix an enlarged buttonhole or how to stitch up a frayed shirt cuff. He shook his head and munched his cold toast. She did, at one stage, open her eyes and lift her spoon, but clearly remembered something else since she put the spoon down again and began muttering about that. Typical Welsh this one, he thought. They lie by the yard and pray by the mile.

He put on his cape, picked up his bag and took off for his morning constitutional hobble to the newspaper shop which, happily for him, was in the same direction as the pub. There was a definite whiff of poison in the air with black, frothy clouds curdling together in some dark conspiracy and a chilling south-westerly shrieking around corners.

At the end of Bridge Street his foot went into a soft patch before taking off on a short skid. Holy shithouse. Soon everyone would need their own coracle to ride over the mounting dog messes on the cobbles. He scraped his shoe on the kerb, its stink punching him on the nose and bringing his biliousness to boiling point. He had the perfect solution to all these dogs running about the place. It was called a double-barrelled shotgun. Whenever he saw a dog having a shit he saw a dozen funerals. He had calculated that there were more mad, incontinent dogs per square mile in Loughor than any similar part of the Indian sub-continent. If Evan Roberts had started from the pulpit a campaign against dogshit he might have sat up and taken notice. As it was, he took none.

The newspaper billboard outside the shop – with its usual flair for detailed exactness – announced TERRIBLE DISASTER. Cripes, some blaggard had decided to dig up the cricket pitch at Lord's or, even worse, the rugby pitch in Cardiff. He stood inside the shop opening up the newspaper, anxious. But the TERRIBLE DISASTER was nothing more than a troop of English yeomanry being shot up by the good old Boers. He did not think that was disastrous at all. The war had officially been over for six months, but those Boers were still at it. Well, what did the English expect, after herding those poor Boers into blockhouses all the time? Medals? Champagne weekends in Paris?

It's a shame the Boers hadn't nobbled Kitchener or that old hack Kipling. He would have given what was left of his back teeth to see those two in a blockhouse. Had he been any younger, he would have doubtless fought the Boers himself, whereupon they would certainly have been decimated far sooner than had been the case. The Boers should have got the Welsh on their side; Jenko believed that the one activity in which the Welsh excelled was war. The South Wales Borderers had found a natural outlet for their murderous talents slaughtering Zulus at Rourke's Drift. They had been busy practising war ever since those days of slinging arrows and boiling oil at the English over Offa's Dyke.

As usual, he was first into the taproom, which meant that he could take up his normal seat in the corner. Setting up his practice in the pub had been one of his better moves since his patients could queue up with pints for consultations; no pints, no consultations, was Jenko's rule. With any luck, he could get through around ten pints before the place closed at four, roll home for a quick nap and then back to the pub again.

He never worked in the evenings – unless it was an emergency – and then he tried to send them to the new doctor in the town. He's a very nice man you know, they always told him – as if he cared. That may be so, he would reply, but very nice men usually have very nasty ideas.

He lit a Woodbine and was busy coughing his guts up when young Ambrose Rees, a farm labourer, bought a pint and walked over to put it in front of him. 'So what's the matter this week?' Jenko asked.

'My eye's swelling up,' Ambrose said pointing to a cataract the size of a small banana. 'It started as an itch and now . . . '

'Looks like an operation job,' Jenko said putting the wind straight up him. If you could not cure them Jenko always believed in putting the wind up them so that they would then run out and find a cure for themselves. 'But let's try an eyebath first. Seaweed is best.'

'Seaweed?'

'Crush up some seaweed and make sure it's got plenty of bulbs in it. Put the juice in an eyebath and bathe the eye three times a day. Come back in a week and, if it's not cleared up, it'll have to be the knife.'

'The knife?' Ambrose echoed again, doubtful, squinting at Jenko's flapping fingers.

'Well, let's see what the seaweed does first.'

Ambrose left, a good deal faster than he had come in, and Jenko was lighting his second cigarette of the session when Michael Evans came shuffling into the taproom, calling two pints then wandering towards Jenko with all the verve of a stunned slug. Jenko had known the Evans family for virtually his entire life and all but exclaimed out loud at the state of him. This cockle-picker was an authentic scrambled egg, but usually cheeky with it, and now here he was sighing as if he had lost a sovereign and found a penny. Raindrops hung in his curls.

'Rain ought to be banned,' Michael said, placing the two foaming pints on the table and sitting down. 'This is the twenty-fourth day of rain and I don't even remember what the sun looks like. When the sun's out I'm fine, but this weather . . . ' He sighed again and examined his hands. 'You got the sun locked up somewhere have you, Jenko?'

'You realise, I hope, that you are talking about the warm tears of God?'

'You feeling all right, Jenko?'

'Me? Never felt better, but you've got to watch for the blasphemy, see, boy. Raindrops are the warm tears of God while the sun is his golden eye.'

Michael let out a long puncturing hiss. 'Jenko, if you're going to tell me you've got converted too I think I'll just go outside and shoot myself. You were the one lost soul I was banking on staying lost. You've not taken the pledge, have you?'

'Of course. Hasn't everyone?'

'Well I'll have that pint back for a start,' Michael said, reaching out for the drink he had just bought.

'No, you won't,' Jenko said grabbing Michael's wrist. 'I've written a few exclusion clauses into my chapel contract. The pledge I've signed is to drink myself into a coma every day and all day, Sundays included. So what brings you here, then?'

'I'm not well, Jenko. In fact, I'm as weak as a robin.'

'Rubbish boy. Robins are the busiest birds in the garden. They're on the go all the year round.'

'It's true, Jenko. You need strength for those sands, particularly at this time of the year but, after I've finished working the tide, I haven't got the strength to sink my teeth into a plum. I used to love plums, too.'

'What's the trouble?'

'I was hoping you would tell me. Bits of me keep falling asleep.'

'What bits are those?'

'Well, some days, it's my arm then it's a leg. They just go useless and numb. Other days I get the twinges something awful. You ever heard of anything like that, Jenko?'

'How long have you had this . . . this rotating rigor mortis?'

'On and off about two months. Sometimes it goes away and then it comes back worse. Just give me some of your magic pills, will you, before the whole lot goes to sleep? Arsenic will do. Or some sleeping pills that'll put me out for a couple of years.'

Jenko finished his pint and smacked his lips. Cynical doctor or no, he had never ceased to marvel at the way family traits were passed on through one tiny, invisible sperm since, many years ago, Michael's father had sat in his surgery and complained of exactly the same ailment. Michael's sister, Megan, went down with it once too. The problem with the Evans family was they had all been great lovers; this emotional zeal ran in the blood like hereditary syphilis and Jenko had long suspected that it must be something to do with all the cockles they had eaten. When they fell, they fell with the certainty and force of a sack of potatoes thrown off the top of a cliff.

Michael's mother had died when he was a baby and then his father had seemed to embark on a one-man war against women – almost as if bent on revenge against them for some mysterious hurt. He was also a big, beautiful man who, when he had finished with his women, more or less finished them off, too. He not so much loved them as laid siege to their happiness and took it away forever. All they could be certain of getting from him was a broken heart. None ever recovered. Yet not only did he lust after every pretty face he saw he also lusted after a fair few ugly ones too. Jenko had often stated that Michael's father would put his dick where Jenko wouldn't risk the end of his umbrella. There were a lot of jubilant husbands at his funeral.

Yet, in all fairness, the father did believe that he had fallen in love for a while – he wasn't that good an actor – usually each year, at the end of the summer, when he too got the twinges and this rotating rigor mortis. Now Michael was sitting there suffering from the same ailment. This icing up of different parts of the body was the familiar Evans curse, brought on by excessive and concentrated attention on some wanton woman and compounded by the family's unusually greedy emotions.

'Who've you been shagging lately?' Jenko asked.

Michael sighed and shook his head. 'No one.'

'Well, if not shagging, who've you been going out with?'

'It's a long story, Jenko. Just give me some of your pills, will you?'

'Look at this lot,' Jenko said, taking a handful of coloured pills out of his waistcoat pocket. 'I keep pills for everything in this pocket. If they complain of earache, cramps, ulcers, shell shock or senility I just give them a couple of these. But they're useless. They wouldn't dry up a wet fart. You really would be better off eating plums than swallowing these things. Tell me what you've been up to and I might be able to do something.'

'It's Beth Williams. A beauty. Lives around here.'

The end of Jenko's nose went numb. He knew her well. 'You've been having it off with her, have you?'

'Jenko, I can't eat. Can't sleep. Bits of my body keep falling dead. I can't help it. It's the effect she has on me.' He took a long draught from his drink and dusted the arm of his jacket with the back of his hand. 'You know her, do you?'

'Yes, I do and seeing her getting tied up with old Bobo has been more depressing than pub closing times.'

'I've been to a few of the meetings. You know. Just to see her.'

'Do you know there's more chances of my playing a banjo in a balalaika band than there is of me going to one of those meetings,' Jenko said. 'But you've got to leave this one alone, boy. I've seen what you've done to some women. You should have married that Marie Edwards. I've never seen a torch as big as the one she carried for you.'

'She didn't sparkle my fancy.'

'Well you've got to leave this one alone. This one's not for you. This one's not for anyone.'

'Why do you say that, Jenko? Tell me about her, will you?'

'Forget her, boy. Fight it off.'

'You think I haven't tried?'

'It goes away in time. All complaints like yours go away in time. Did I ever tell you I was an army doctor in the Crimea? Every morning I had this vast queue outside my tent with the whole lot of them complaining of ulcers. It was so bad they were willing to submit to the knife. And you know what it was? They were just missing their women back home. And do you know who the worst offenders were? The Welsh, who else? Imagine all those Joneses and Davieses all holding their bellies and complaining of ulcers the size of rugby balls. You know how bloody dramatic the Welsh are when they get going: they've only got to get a headache and they start ordering a tombstone for the graveyard. I told them straight. I said "Stop wasting my time with your bleeding hearts. Get out and shag a few women but, if you do, don't come running back here with VD". Everyone had VD in the Crimea – even the regimental mascot. It's true, that. Even the goat had the pox. Anyway I told them "If you don't fancy VD then munch plenty of apples". Anyone who is desperate for a woman should munch apples.'

Michael shook his head, amazed. 'Tell me, Jenko. It must have been one of the wonders of the world if you managed to cure anyone of anything. Have you?'

'Here and there. I'm good at 'flu and abscesses. Foot and mouth very poor, and not too bright at rigor mortis either.'

'I just don't believe it. Here I am dying and you're saying I should munch plenty of apples. It's no wonder we lost so many troops in the Crimea. I bet you had most of them running around the country looking for orchards. Have they got any orchards in the Crimea?'

'Buggered if I know.'

'All those Welsh, suffering from ulcers and prancing about the place looking for orchards. Are you sure you weren't paid by the Russians?'

'No Moscow gold soiled this doctor's hands, I fear.'

'What's this new doctor in town like? They say *he* knows a thing or two.'

'He knows nothing. Probably end up sticking a daffodil up your nose or one of those new vacuum cleaners. Listen boy, you're just going to have to live with it. Drink a lot if you can't stand apples.'

'Drink makes me worse.'

'Tell me. What happened to that sister of yours? Megan the Measles they called her, didn't they? Infected everyone she came across. Now there was a real specialist in pain and torment for you.'

'Last I heard she was out in the Far East.'

'Ah, dear Megan. Caught them all, she did. She never chased a man. She would just go over to him and tell him he was coming with her. I always swore there was something in those cockles.' He stopped talking and looked up at two men who just entered the taproom. 'Fred Thomas,' he boomed. 'Where's that salmon?'

Both men's heads swivelled around on their shoulders, their faces studies in alarm. Even the card school looked up. 'You promised it for me last week,' Jenko boomed on. 'You said it would be there on the doorstep, so where is it?'

Fred Thomas, a small man with a flat cap and a long thrust of a nose, walked over. 'You want us to get locked up, doctor?' he squeaked, quiet, the muscles on his nose twitching like those of an investigating rat.

'It took me a good half an hour to pick all those shotgun pellets out of your arse, Fred Thomas,' Jenko continued in his normal boom. 'So where's that salmon you promised me?'

'It's not easy, doctor,' Fred said, sitting down next to Jenko while his partner shuffled around nervously in front of the table. 'They've got six bailiffs down on the river now. Even got our net the other night.'

'Since when did Fred Thomas need a net?' Jenko snorted. 'You're supposed to be *the* artist with a snatch tackle, aren't you, Fred?'

The corners of Fred's lips curled at the edges in self-congratulation. 'Look, doctor,' he said, 'We're out tonight. We've got some great jam – just great – and the first to show its nose in the water is yours. That's a promise. That's a solemn promise, now.'

'Right then,' Jenko said. 'Here's the penalty clause for late delivery. It's a pint for me . . . ' He handed Fred the empty glass. 'And a pint for my friend Michael.'

Fred stood up and walked towards the bar, only to turn on one foot in the middle of the taproom and walk back again. 'This is my butty Percy Gordon,' he said, cocking his thumb at his friend who was still standing in front of the table, like some schoolboy, waiting anxious for permission to go to the lavatory. 'Have a look at his leg will you, Jenko? Some dog has gone and taken a bite out of it.'

'It will be done,' Jenko said with a magnanimous wave of his hand. Michael moved around on his seat as Jenko nudged him; any further discussions of rotating rigor mortis was clearly going to have to wait for another day. 'So then, Percy Gordon. Pull your trousers down and we'll have a look, shall we?'

'Here doctor?'

'Here *mun*. Where else? Sudden death lurks in the bite of a dog.' He winked at Michael. 'And in a kiss and watercress and a cockle too.'

'Where do you get all this nonsense from?' Michael asked. 'Did someone teach it to you or did you make it all up?'

Just then the head of Michael's horse appeared around the door of the taproom, causing great excitement in the card school. It was only because the horse was attached to his cart that he didn't trundle up to the bar.

'Hey, Fred,' Jenko shouted. 'Get one in for the horse as well.'

* * *

Three Scottish men sang a Gaelic hymn in the meeting tonight, Dan wrote in his diary. *A Frenchman prayed for a revival in France. Lady Cadbury came wearing a black dress with grey frogging. The ladies' hats becoming very strange: Lady Cadbury's bee-keeper construction, four hats piled high with imitation fruit, an early Victorian picture hat, a Capeline Ombrelle. We are worried the Revival might turn into a fashion parade.*

139

The lady singers are all becoming very tired, Beth in particular. Nor is their singing what it was. One hundred and four converts, well down on the converts for meetings of same size last month. Holden boiler working well on anthracite from Swansea Valley.

Our biggest worry is Evan. His silences are becoming longer and are not what they appear – or what the Press say that they are. The silences come from simple exhaustion. He is becoming withdrawn, too, staying in his room more and more. Owe 2s. to Rees for tonics. Trying it on all of them. Donations now £1,028 3s.

* * *

Jenko did have one patient whom he visited regular at her home. It so happened that he had been making a weekly check-up on Mrs Gloria Edwards' varicose veins for the past ten years and, when the pub closed that afternoon, he swayed his way along Loughor's main road to see her. She lived in a small red brick house near the Post Office and a landau passed, carrying an elderly couple, when Jenko knocked on the door.

'Good morning, Mrs Edwards or, perhaps, I should say good afternoon. Just passing, so I thought I would come and have a look at your veins.'

She nodded, impassive, giving the sort of expressionless look of resignation with which a housewife might greet an official come to cut off the gas. 'Better come in then, Dr. Jenkins.'

Mrs Edwards was now in her mid-fifties but there was still a lot of poetry in her face, with its marvellous swooping lines and a full bubble-blowing mouth. Her figure had held up well over the years too, with two of everything and the right curves in the right places. She had eschewed the fashionable Victorian lace stay in her youth, for though it did produce an hourglass figure and an eighteen inch waist it also ensured that the figure collapsed into an incoherent rubble when the stay was not worn.

'Would you be liking a cup of tea, Dr. Jenkins?'

'No thank you, Mrs Edwards. In a bit of a hurry today I am. Got a few patients to see and just thought I had better check your legs while I was passing. You can never be too careful with a condition like that.'

'I see, doctor. Well do you want to examine me down here or . . . ' She took a deep gulp. 'Upstairs?'

'Upstairs I think, Mrs Edwards. Examinations are always better in the bedroom. Bedrooms are more relaxing than the parlour.'

'I see. Would you like to go first, doctor?'

'You go first, Mrs Edwards. Tell me, how is your sister keeping?'

'Ooooh not too bad, you know. Still got trouble with the gout but she's moving about the house all right.'

'Good to hear it. I had better get over to see her sometime. You can never tell with that gout.'

They walked into the bedroom and she sat on the side of the bed, back erect and staring straight ahead of her. He drew the curtains, took off his cape, hat and jacket then rolled up his sleeves. He lifted up her skirt and, after some careful tugging, with no co-operation from her, managed to loosen her bombazine bloomers, which billowed around his arms like giant jellyfish. He ran his hands over the fat blue varicose veins which criss-crossed her legs like a map of the world. That one looked as wide and fat and crooked as the River Ganges itself.

'These veins, Mrs Edwards. Giving you any pain, are they?'

Jenko had a very soft spot for Mrs Edwards, a great dreamer who once used to write him pathetic poems about dawns and sunsets. But, now she had gone and got religion along with the rest of the town, all that had changed and hypocrisy had again become the order of the day. She still allowed him to call for the weekly servicing except that he had now got the clear message that, while doing one thing, he should be pretending to do something else.

'The veins have not been too bad this week, Dr. Jenkins. That bottle you gave me last week helped a lot. I still get the pains when I get up first thing and, sometimes, they pain awful in the middle of the night.'

He was on one knee and smoothing his hand around between her legs, parting her knees further and smoothing around some more. He supposed Evan Roberts would call this treatment a laying on of hands. The flesh around the tops of her legs had not gone flabby at all. There was still plenty of solid muscle there, and she stiffened a little as he stroked the back of his knuckles up and down her pudenda.

'Sometimes when I'm bending the pains come on bad, Dr. Jenkins. You know. Doing the housework and that. It's not very good when I bring in the coal either.'

'Stand up, Mrs Edwards, and we'll have a better look. Hold up your skirt now. That's it. Step out of your bloomers there. That's it. Let's see here. Your sister's better you say?'

'Just the gout you know. Comes on surprising some days. I go over to help but what with these veins and her gout . . . you know how it is, Dr. Jenkins.'

She was standing up, holding out her dress like a matador's cape while he, the bull, proceeded to poke his fingers into her vegetable patch, working it around and inside out as he tickled away with the tips of his fingers. 'Well these veins certainly look a lot better,' he said as he tickled away. 'I'll leave you some more pills before I go.'

'That would be nice, Dr. Jenkins. That bottle last week was ah . . . it was oh . . . um . . . '

Now she was vibrating like someone nose to nose with a ghost. He looked up to see that her eyes were still wide open, though with her lower jaw juddering up and down, so he just kept on tickling until down they came – those juice-powered torrents, running all sticky and warm, smelling of bowls of mackerel. Sex and religion were two deep-running rivers in the Welsh psyche, he decided. There was that handy definition of a Welsh woman: thrifty in the market, regular in chapel and absolutely frantic in bed.

'I'm feeling a bit faint, Dr. Jenkins.'

'It's very close in here, Mrs Edwards. I think you had better lie down on the bed. Keep your legs open now. That's it. Keep looking up at the ceiling. That's it. I'll just be a few seconds. Better make it a proper examination.'

He dropped his trousers and ran into her. 'You can let go of your dress, Mrs Edwards. Just put your arms to one side. That's it. Just relax now, Mrs Edwards. Breathe deep now.'

He went riding away, in no particular hurry to finish the examination, and she just lay there in a detached coma, eyes open and gazing upwards. He wondered what she thought about these days while he was at work. Wales? Her pension? Her varicose veins? He could never ask her what was on her mind, since the question might involve recognition of what they were both doing. If it was not mentioned, then obviously it had not happened. For a devout convert like Mrs Gloria Edwards, sex was acceptable providing she never spoke about it, enjoyed it or, indeed, took part in it at all. The chapel was quite firm that enjoyment of sex was a certain sign of insanity; in fact the chapel did not recognise the existence of the sexual drive at all, and could only surmise how women ended up in an 'interesting condition' – which was the chapel's term for pregnancy. Only poor people in slums went in for any frantic sexual activity and they in turn became poor through getting too much of it. Babies still came in the beaks of storks and were to be found under gooseberry bushes. There wasn't a dictionary of diseases big enough to detail the horrors of masturbation. He knew all about this Revival, though. He had heard of a fair bit of bundling going on in the graveyards after the services and it was his guess that there was going to be a fair few 'interesting conditions' around by the time the Revival had got a bit older. He could just see all those mothers turning round and putting the blame on the fairies.

He could feel an orgasm welling up out of Mrs Edwards' valley but, apart from blinking, she still stared at the ceiling. Perhaps she had managed to divorce her mind from her body, letting her body enjoy itself while her mind chewed on the sin of it all. He kept ramming away until another orgasm came exploding up out of her loins. He never knew where she got them all – one once went on for a full minute – the others rising up and exploding like tempest-driven waves. He remembered that her husband had suddenly dropped dead with exhaustion and, come to think of it, there never had been much life in him. He just sat in the same chair all day long drinking tea – happy enough but knackered.

He took a few more speculative jabs but could feel that the massing hormones were not quite ready to stampede just yet. Tribalism. That's what this Revival was all about. Owain Glyndŵr rides again. The Welsh have always been opposed to any ideas other than their own. A typical Welshman only ever thinks in terms of his own town or village; he never troubles about continents or empires and is always moved by the call of the tribe. I carry this spear, therefore I am.

He went cantering on and could feel her stiffening for another orgasm. He had better get a move on or else, if she didn't watch it, she was going to end up with a dead doctor between her legs. And with his boots on, too. 'How did this doctor die with his shirt and boots on?' the coroner would ask. 'Oh he just liked sleeping with his boots on, m'lord.' The cattle began their stampeding run. His behind went flapping around when vibrations went erupting up out of him like the ghosts of a flock of starlings. And he was done.

He extricated himself and sat on the side of the bed, heart hammering against the inside of his chest, demented. Much more of that, Dr. Jenkins, and you'll be falling to bits and pushing up the daisies sooner than even you expected. You're not a young blade any more. But not a bad way to go. Better than cancer or tuberculosis. Mrs Edwards got up too, pulled on her bloomers and began dusting the sideboard. He just could not understand it. There she was, dusting the sideboard and not a hair out of place. She was that casual you would think she was out in the street trimming the hedge. 'So you don't think there's much to worry about, Dr. Jenkins?'

'Nothing at all, Mrs Edwards. You're as fit as a flea.'

'Are you sure you wouldn't like a cup of tea?'

'Positive, Mrs Edwards. I really am in a bit of a hurry. But I'll leave you a couple of pills.' He fished a few pills out of his waistcoat pocket, put them on the sideboard, dressed, tidied himself up and was seen to the door.

'Good day, Dr. Jenkins.'

'Good day, Mrs Edwards. See you this time next week.'

Chapter Thirteen

It was early in the afternoon and just twelve days before Christmas. Evan was walking along the sheep paths of the slopes of the Garw Valley, alone. Down below him were the slate roofs of the mining town of Pontycymmer, the smoke curling and drifting up out of the chimney pots into the rain. All around him the winter had made the hills bald with vast tracts of sheep-trodden mud and dead patches of brown bracken.

Above his head a flock of crows flapped around, shrieking black against weeping grey.

A depression had come and settled on him so heavy he could barely stand up let alone walk. Everything was going wrong. He knew that he was no longer speaking with total conviction and power. He knew that his long silences were losing sections of the congregation. Most of the Press had now gone, too. The crowds were still coming, but he saw only unbelief, curiosity and sin in every face he surveyed. He was not taking much comfort from his ladies either. They seemed to be drifting away from him, no longer singing with the same urgency or passion. Even Beth was being cold and distant – which was hard to accept.

In the midst of this looming depression – in which even what was right was perceived as being wrong – it was dawning on him, with increasing force, that God had deserted him, too. He could put up with almost anything but that; nothing in his life would have any meaning at all if he was to be left marooned on an island of doubt. There would be no more chapel meetings; no more rousing hymns; no more voyaging prayers; perhaps, worst of all, no more readings of those precious and well-known verses in the Bible. 'Cras, cras,' the crows called out to him, mocking.

So, in the time of his troubles, he had taken to the hills, seeking the liberating weapons of solitude and silence to help him fight his way out of this dark night of his soul. Jesus, he knew, frequently looked to solitude for comfort and help. He spent forty days alone in the desert before the start of his ministry. After the feeding of the five thousand he went to the hills on his own. After the healing of a leper he went into the wilderness and prayed.

So now, in the hurrying winds and spattering rain, it was the turn of

Evan Roberts to come to himself, in silence and without words, to implore the Lord for a fresh outpouring of his redeeming love. He could not live without him. Did not want to live without him. Oh Lord, touch me in my being and restore me the faith of my forefathers. Give me back the love that loved so much it died for me.

The winds kept hurrying around him and the rains kept spattering on his face. The hollow calls of the crows roamed the slopes and the depression thickened in him still further, as if a stake had been hammered into him which was being turned, again and again.

He took.yet another dung-dotted sheep track which brought him down to the bank of a stream. The clear water gurgled and danced over the pebbles, which kept changing colour from grey to green to brown. The pebbles knew. The pebbles remembered things.

He saw the weeds waving with the current and looked up when the grey sky all around him began sparkling with astonishing clusters of diamonds, all coming together, exploding and breaking apart with such a ferocious dazzle he had to shield his eyes. Love angels darted and dashed through the air, singing the great lines of the scriptures, waltzing around and around one another, some even doing reels hand in hand. He lowered his hands and smiled as he looked all about. Just then the spirits of the saints and prophets of old rose up out of the water to greet him, pulling at his arms, shoving him gently, encouraging and telling him to rejoice. Amidst all the words and singing he also received a binding promise of something new.

All at once his fear was blown away by the valley winds. His grief was melted by a great and strange warmth which surged through his every bone and every single hair of his head. He let out a great jubilant whoop and jumped into the stream, dancing around, knee-deep in water, laughing loud and shouting his praises to the Lord. Now he began running up the stream like a demented salmon that had lost its sense of direction. He slipped and fell, fully clothed, into the freezing water, but he did not care. As long as God loved him he could not have cared less if he had to live on the ocean beds for ever.

He danced around in the stream some more, whirling around and around until his head was dizzy with the vibrance of his ecstasy. 'Oh thank you, dear Jesus,' he shouted through cupped hands, his words echoing and re-echoing down the valley but only heard by the leafless trees and the sheep who did not even look up from their endless foraging. 'Praise you my dear, sweet holy Jesus.'

The sun bolted out from behind the black clouds to join in the celebration too, its rays lancing down on the small black figure dancing around in the stream and making the water shimmer and shake like a golden flying magic carpet. He was rinsed of all melancholy now, rapturous in his total surrender to God. 'God is great and I shall sing His praises to the winds forever,' he shouted, putting his hands down in the water and flinging romping fountains of it into the air. 'I will love the Lord my God until the day I die. Yes. Until I die.'

* * *

That night in the packed Tabernacle Chapel in Pontycymmer Evan stood in the pulpit, feeling armed with all the powers of the Holy Spirit. He dragged the service along by the scruff of its neck, stoking it with fire and rhythm while speaking with all the authority of the slopes of Sinai, the sentences cracking down on the congregation's head like whips.

'Though he may send thunder or locusts we will still love God. Though we be thrown into thorn bushes or pierced with swords we will still love God. Though misery and darkness and the slime of Satan overtake us we will still love God. Even though we have lost our eyes and ears; even though every bone in our bodies be broken; even though blood pours from every vein and we have fallen as low as it is possible to fall . . . we will still love God. Always love God, my people, and be certain that he adores every second of our loving praise. Know that the world is round and day follows night so that the sound of our prayer and praise will always be in his ears. The only command is to love him and, through him, each other.'

Several fainted in the excitement generated by his words and, when he had finished speaking, a man stood up and declared his conversion. His words had even uplifted Beth and she stepped forward to lead the singing of *Diolch Iddo* with something of her old power to the accompaniment of the flutterings of many handkerchiefs.

It was then that Evan first heard it and understood immediately the nature of God's promise of something new in that stream earlier that afternoon. What he heard was a voice like no other. Indeed it had such presence it began silencing all the other voices around it. Beth just turned to look at Priscilla, the hymn drying up in both their mouths. After the next verse Lavinia and Pat stopped singing, too.

It was the biggest voice that any of them had ever heard: a highly ecstatic instrument which had been fashioned in the purest perfection. Angels fluttered in that voice, which could soar majestic like an eagle riding the winds then fall and fall again like some sinner's last screaming descent into Hades. It was a contralto which embraced so many octaves

147

and stretched to so many harmonies it – and it alone – could have been put forward as the sole representative of all the choirs in Wales.

Evan's back was still with a strange, crumbling sensation as, hands on hips, he stood staring down at this tiny slip of a woman. She was dressed in a mauve bolero over a white lace blouse with a billowing, tiered skirt trimmed with cream lace. She was also wearing a plumed tulle hat but, even more fetching than all that, was her face with its fiercely chiselled cheekbones and bird-like coal-black eyes, the kind of face into which you could gaze all day and still keep finding something different.

Another handsome woman was standing next to her, possibly her sister and, when the hymn had finished, Evan walked down to the woman in the tulle hat, took her by the hand and led her up to the dais with the other ladies. 'Sing a hymn, my dear,' he invited.

She cleared her throat, turned to face the congregation and began singing *Love Divine:*

Love divine, all loves excelling,
Joy of heaven, to earth come down,
Fix us in thy humble dwelling,
All thy faithful mercies crown.

There was not detectable fault at all in this woman's voice. It burned the heart with its sheer glory – so pure that, on the one hand, it could have been the voice of a young girl and yet, on the other hand, so burly it could have been that of a barrel-chested opera singer. Priscilla kept her head bowed as the hymn continued: Pat and Lavinia held freezing-polite smiles, while Beth stared into the middle distance at nothing in particular.

It was agreed immediate that night in Pontycymmer – almost without any words – that this tiny slip of a woman, Annie Davies, and her sister, Maggie, should join the other four ladies. Now they were six.

Maggie was likeable enough but a trifle dull; she had a workmanlike voice and she spent most of her time crocheting shawls. 'We've got enough shawls in the house to keep the Brecon Beacons warm,' Annie explained.

But it was Annie Davies who reshaped the whole character of the group because she brought to it something that had been badly missing before – a great sense of fun. Everywhere she went groups would gather around her, the gales of laughter billowing out of them. Her normal speaking voice swooped and fell like her singing, making her quips and funny little stories even funnier. She was also a merciless mimic whose speciality was the ponderous Whitehall tones of W.T. Stead. She sent up

Stead's language with delicious cruelty and even poked fun at Dan's efficient and painstaking deliberation, but she never, ever made fun of Evan.

Annie's special gift to the Revival, though, was that she freed the ladies, and because of her, they all became bigger. Lavinia and Pat became more confident in Annie's shadow and even began stepping up and taking the odd solo. Annie also broke up the two pairs that had existed before, encouraging them to sing *together* more. She bolstered Lavinia in particular, saying that she had a marvellous voice, possibly the best in the group, which just needed some training.

At first, it was Priscilla who most resented Annie. Overnight she lost her role as general comedian, becoming more thoughtful and introspective. She did not sulk, although she stopped twitting people all the time. For someone as proud as she, it could have meant the end of her work in the Revival, but Annie, who was far from insensitive, immediately saw the problem and just as quickly put an end to it. Her rich and indulgent father had given her a fabulous wardrobe which she brought in for the ladies; Priscilla benefited most of all, since she was nearest Annie's size. Priscilla had never seen anything like those billowing ornamental gowns, the lace ruffled bodices, those parasols of Parisian gaiety. Any lingering hostility to Annie was totally subverted by a strawberry skirt with a taffeta lining which rustled, sensuous, like wind-blown forest leaves.

Beth also benefited from Annie's arrival since she felt relieved of much of the pressure of holding the singing together and found she sang better too, since Annie's voice was an inspiration to them all. Even her tiredness lifted and she again became an active joy to Evan. In some meetings the six ladies went driving at the hymn which such force and conviction they could well have tumbled the walls of Jericho.

Evan was entranced with them all, going about the place forever smiling like some life-long sinner who had just been informed that he had been excused hell. He found Beth relaxed enough for him to put his arm through hers, though he never did that to Annie. On catching Beth's eye he occasionally raised his hand and brought down his thumb, slow. He had prayed to God for help, he was telling her, and his prayers had been answered.

* * *

Five days before Christmas, the largest crowd ever assembled for a religious service in Wales gathered inside and outside the Walter Road

Chapel in Swansea. The only crowd that the *Evening Post* could compare it with was the one that had come to the St. Helen's ground in the town, nearly five years before, when Wales had battered – but battered – imperial England by twenty-three points to three, ushering in, it was reported, the first great Golden Age of Welsh Rugby.

Today, after unprecedented publicity in the Press concerning the miracle of Annie Davies's voice, mounted police had been drafted in from all over Glamorgan to control the crowds. From early afternoon until late the following morning, all traffic had been blocked off from the area. Countless numbers thronged the roads; an impossible three thousand jammed themselves inside the chapel.

The Taibach wailers were conducting some sort of service of their own on one street corner. On another a Salvation Army band was playing Christmas carols; their fat brassy notes bounded over the dogs, babies in shawls and vendors of potatoes baked on fiery coke braziers. Shivering children in smocks sat in the bare branches of the trees while, down below them, groups of deacons, as severe as vultures with their huge sideboards and all-black garbs, mixed with sellers of bull's eyes, brandy snaps and nosegays.

Boys on bicycles rode in and out of the various groups as policemen smiled, indulgent, at the odd lonely drunk determined to stay out of the Revival's sobering clutches. The men were in their bowlers and ulsters; the women in their yards of coloured ribbon; the colliers in flat cloth caps, smoking a deadly mixture of shag and bus tickets – all were humming with terrific expectancy – all come for what they hoped would turn out to be Evan Roberts' coronation.

There was a great rolling roar when Evan came down the road, encircled by the six ladies. The crowds parted before him and grown men cried in the purest gratitude for what he was doing. 'God bless you, Mr Roberts,' some called out. Others found words inadequate to express what they felt.

Evan sprayed prayer over all as he walked, taking huge handfuls of flashing angels and hurling them over the people's heads. Again and again he sent out the angels, bursting in the air with brilliant fireworks and raining down on them to purge them of the infection of their sins. This evil was still everywhere he looked, but he was now feeling strong enough to attack it, ready and able, if necessary, to rip the guts out of the very devil himself.

Inside the chapel, he stood in the pulpit saying nothing and shooting silent prayers at all for a full five minutes. Person after person slumped in a faint in all the heat and excitement. 'Children pray for toys,' he said, finally. 'Parents pray for their children. Families pray for communities. Moses even prayed that God would change his mind. Tonight, knowing that God only acts in response to faithful and loving prayer, we must all pray to him who sits at the very heart of creation. We must all pray to him who is life and love. We must all pray that he will send an invading army of angels to overcome the hearts and ways of our beloved Wales.'

He paused for his customary silence when Annie turned to Beth and took her hand. Together they stepped forward on the dais and began singing a hymn they had discovered that they both loved. They made a fine duet – Beth's firmer voice holding the melody steady, with the more extrovert Annie swooping up and down around it, careless yet strong, like a skylark.

Come. Holy Spirit, come;
Let thy bright beams rise;
Dispel the darkness from our minds,
And open all our eyes.

'Angels are the foot soldiers of the Holy Spirit. It is the angels who are all joyful when a sinner repents. Angels rolled away the stone from Jesus' tomb. It was the angels who closed the lions' mouths and destroyed Sodom. All of us here tonight must pray that God will send a mighty army of angels to destroy this Mammon who rules Wales. Yes, a mighty glittering army of holy angels who will scour the valleys and hills of Wales and cleanse our beloved land.'

Revive our drooping faith;
Our doubts and fears remove;
And kindle in our breast the flame
Of never-dying love.

'So come then all you angels, and bring comfort to those oppressed by their own sin. Come, blinding in your brilliance, and put the night to the sword. Come ringing all the bells of heaven and visit sudden destruction on all God's enemies. Come with holy fire you blessed angels, who know no sin, just as you once came surrounding God on Sinai, able to drag a living life out of a dying death.'

'Tis thine to cleanse the heart,
To sanctify the soul,
To pour fresh life in every part
And new created the whole.

'Know this: those same angels who sobbed and flew around with

151

drawn swords – when Jesus hung broken on the cross – will return. See them coming, my people. Oh look, they are returning. Those holy angels are coming to do battle with the dark angels. Yes, coming to do battle with all the forces of murder, pride, war, discord, envy, hate. Look, there's the Son of Man surrounded by battalions of angels at the battle of Armageddon. Look, he's leading all his great armies to chain Satan and throw him back into the lake of fire from where he escaped.'

Beth and Annie hugged one another tearfully and sat down again. It had worked out fine – just as they had hoped, with their singing so modified in volume they had not in any way interfered with Evan's speaking voice.

The congregation had immediately understood the gift that had been given to them; were warm in the privilege of listening to three people setting out to break the power of sin in the world – and save it, too. In its turn the congregation offered itself back to those on the dais and the chapel erupted with the heat of fervent praise. They had all come together in a mystical state of one mind within a loving God.

This state of Grace showed itself in another way later. When the singing of *Diolch Iddo* had finished Evan raised a pointing finger. 'Who of you all here are going to join the angels and fight for Christ? Who will take off your jackets and fight for Christ?'

A young man stood up on a pew, took off his jacket and threw it up into the air.

'Praise the Lord.'

His finger pointed up again, moving along the rows of faces in the gallery, whereupon a bespectacled man stood up and raised his arms before chattering aloud in a strange language. It was a language like none had ever heard: the chattering incantations of an agitated African trader, perhaps, or some Chinaman making an elaborate and increasingly desperate plea for a loan of more money.

When he had finished everyone looked at Evan, who stood stock-still saying nothing. Next, a woman, known to many in the congregation, stood up and she too began chattering in a strange language – *yatter, sikka – chukka, jes, jis dutta* – a few key phrases apparently being repeated but, once again, with no understandable sense in the words.

Everyone looked at Evan again. 'Praise the Lord,' he said, soft, and he too raised his arms, closed his eyes and his lips erupted with a mellifluous burst of this strange language. *Cheea soota mea, Jesus. Chutta, suddah sok.*

When he stopped others in the congregation took up the flow of sound like isolated bursts of machine-gun fire, until it all came in bigger and wilder bursts until, all at once, the whole chapel erupted in a hullabaloo of glossolalia. Prophecies mingled with shouts; phrases from the Bible jumped on the backs of the incomprehensible chatter as the outbreak of tongues reached an astonishing pitch.

Jip dong dong heepe heepe
Yatter, sikka, chukka.
Dutta, dutta, soona pober.
Sanger, sanger, soona.
Jip dong booner, tedirer jukka, jukka, maker Jesus, soona songer
poder jis dutta . . . jip dong dong.

Just then Annie's voice came scything through the strange words with the speed and authority of an express train screaming into the night. This time she too was singing in tongues, and the chattering prayers gradually faded away, with Beth taking up the song, followed by Lavinia and Pat and Maggie and Priscilla.

No one who was there that night would ever forget that service when people all sang carolling songs of love to God and his angels in a language that none of them understood. It was the great refreshing storm of Pentecost. Here, God was building his church anew.

Evan wept through the singing and waves of tongues. When it all came to an end he said, 'The world will be swept by the Holy Spirit just as it has swept through this meeting tonight. Groping hesitant Christians will see a bright light which will lead them out of darkness in their thousands. Again they will be redeemed by the power of the cross. So bend all you that doubt. Bend and yield. Obedience to the voice of the Holy Spirit. Yes. Obedience! Obedience! Obedience!

* * *

In Treherbert, at the last meeting before the Christmas break, Evan was content to let the ladies make most of the running while encouraging the congregation to orchestrate whatever service they were in the mood for. When he did speak finally it was without once raising his voice or gesturing in any way.

'People say the Revival will soon wear out. Let them. But remember . . . when a nation loses its vision of God then that nation will perish. When the nation perishes then so too will the people in it. Violence will come to the streets and homes. This Revival stands at the centre of our beloved nation; it stands in the shadow of all our forefathers; it shouts out our fear of God and our love of Wales.'

153

Annie stood up and began singing *Calon Lân*, very soft. Evan waited for her to finish the first verse and continued speaking, with Annie's voice fluting so softly it could barely be heard. 'Let it be known that, with the help of the Holy Spirit, we are going to restore this beloved land to its holy and sacred past. The music of the streets is going to be the music of prayer. The very air of the land is going to be the air of love. Heaven makes no mistake. The promises of the Bible will all be kept.'

When he stopped speaking Annie's voice soared to full power for the final verses, searing the congregation's insides with the red-hot poker of its beauty and reducing many to helpless tears. 'We are all now ready for Christmas,' Evan said. 'We are now ready for a time to cherish the birth of the Lord and, through Him, cherish our families while looking to heal any wounds in them. This will be Wales' greatest Christmas ever. The Light of the World has entered thousands of homes in fair Cambria. Keep steadfast in the faith; be as the rock on which the Church was first found and may God bless each and every one of you.'

* * *

The six ladies, with Evan and Dan, all sat together in the back of the dray that night on their journey home. No one spoke as tiny clouds of warm breath came out from beneath poke bonnets. A whip curled in the night air lazy, snapping sharp on the two horses' foam-flecked rumps. Beth looked at Evan, an exhausted and dark shape sitting at the far end with a scarf wrapped around the bottom of his face and his shoulders jumping around with the bumps of the wagon's iron-clad wheels. In that brain, behind that forehead and nose and scarf, was the mysterious and commanding force which was changing Wales. Just the thought of it made her belly knot; her body broke out into goose pimples.

As the dray clattered along the Swansea road, other forces were at work elsewhere. Small dots of light danced over the Brecon Beacons, alternately exploding and imploding until they grew into huge revolving pillars of fire. Outside Pwllheli a hazy sheet of sparkling blue – as big and deep as the night itself – shimmered over the swamps. A huge orange tongue of flame came scorching through the haze, turning it from blue to red, after which the tongue vanished and all was blue again.

On Anglesey, the mother of Wales, white and green meteors chased one another over the Menai Straits and in Harlech, home of the magical birds of Rhiannon, a huge red blob kept revolving above a chapel. Reports of strange colours and even strange shapes came in from all parts of the land that night, while Venus and Mars also shone with an astonishing and unprecedented brilliance.

A cloaked figure emerged from the waters of Lake Bala, resting ground of ancient Welsh princes, saying: 'The hour has come but not the man.' A steel worker in Cardiff saw a large white throne suspended in the night with the word DISOBEDIENCE written in large black letters upon it. He was gripped as if by a vice and only a promise to obey made the vision disappear.

At a prayer meeting in Ynysybwl a lighted candle floated over the heads of the people in the Zion Chapel. It was being carried by an angel who was shading it with a wing from a draught that was coming from an open window. The chapel cleaner, a woman who had loved nothing but good all her life, held her breath as the candle came near her, knowing that the slightest movement of air would have blown the candle out.

Way down in the infamous Great Western Colliery, William Hughes entered a manhole to avoid the coal trucks passing down the mine. He was standing there in the dust and drips when he sensed that the air was thick with all his curses of old and was oppressed by a great weight. Frightened, he prayed to God for His mercy and help and, as he prayed, he felt the fear lifting out of him, as if carried by an eagle, and straight out through the roof of the mine. Yet not only had his fear gone, his bitterness had gone also.

Overjoyed, he strode down past the pony stables and up to the working face. 'Raise your lamps if you believe in God,' he called out. This insistent scrape of the shovels and picks fell silent. 'Raise your lamps all of you that love the Lord.' One by one the lamps rose in the darkness until scores of them bobbed around like swarms of fireflies and the colliers began signing *All Hail the Power of Jesu's Name*, the sweet lilting power of the hymn echoing from working face to working face and from tunnel to tunnel.

In Wrexham, Ben Griffiths was walking home with his children's Christmas presents when a bearded man carrying a small dish approached him in a lane. 'Take this and eat,' the stranger said. After Ben had taken the bread and eaten it he was told: 'Now go and preach the gospel to every creature.'

Bookshops throughout Wales were complaining of a shortage of Bibles. Everywhere, except Cardiff, the police had become all but redundant and crime just stopped. Items stolen twenty years earlier were sent back and debts repaid – even those which had lapsed under the Statue of Limitations. Thirty-nine rugby clubs had closed down, with kits and season tickets burned. Those that continued playing had more players than spectators, while Noddfa Chapel in Neath reserved a class exclusively for ex-rugby players. There was often more rejoicing over the conversion of a rugby player than that of a drunkard.

Over half the public houses throughout rural Wales had now shut, with the other half verging on bankruptcy. Sir Marchant Williams, the stipendiary magistrate in Mountain Ash, had complained that, what with the lack of crime and the disappearance of drunkenness, there was nothing for him – or the prison – to do. As one waggish collier put it: 'Christ once turned water into wine, and, now, in my own house, he has changed beer into furniture.'

The whip curled and cracked in the air again and the horses snorted as the dray clattered through the yellow glow of the street lamps of Port Talbot. 'Ah ladies, I almost forgot – I have brought you all a small gift for Christmas,' Evan said, breaking the exhausted silence. He reached down to open his Gladstone bag and took out what looked like a bunch of sticks in the darkness. 'They are not much, but I hope you like them.'

He stood up and handed one to each of the ladies. 'They are pagan in origin, I am afraid.' He chuckled. 'They are love spoons which, many years ago, were carved by Celtic men to give to their future wives. You will see that they are all different. I had them made for you by a carpenter in Brecon.' He chuckled again. 'But I do hope that you do not think I am proposing to you all.'

Beth ran her fingers over hers. It was a most intricate and beautiful design, with hearts carved out of it and wooden rings dangling off the bottom. Priscilla kissed hers while Annie's gratitude so overwhelmed her she stood up and flung her arms around Evan shouting, 'Oh Mr Roberts you could marry me in the morning if you wanted.'

Back to Loughor for a well-earned rest, Dan wrote in his diary. *8s for the dray. Everyone tired. Newspapers talking of 60,000 converts so far. Merthyr Express says 200,000. Everywhere reports of the unaccountable are commonplace. The dove is coming home to roost. The old people are dreaming again of '59 and feeling its thrill.*

Chapter Fourteen

Late in the afternoon on Christmas Day the light was breaking up into darkness as Beth sat, stuffed to the brim with trifle and turkey, gazing into the parlour fire. Elaborate embroidered greeting cards trooped across the mantelpiece; on the other side of the fire her Dada was peeling chestnuts. Her brother Billy was snoring beneath a handkerchief on one of the brown leather chairs, his soft snores making the handkerchief flutter.

She stood up and walked over to the window to look out at the garden. The newspapers had forecast heavy snow, but only a few of the tiniest flakes were bouncing around in the breeze above the bushes. A group of tits were foraging among the roots of the hedge, all chattering, excited, as if they had just found a treasure trove of peanuts. She turned away from the window and went over to the sideboard where, in pride of place, in between a carriage clock and an aspidistra, her goldfish was swimming around and around a large rock inside his tank. She smiled as she watched the fish circle so energetically, getting nowhere fast. The fish was clearly as daft as the man who had won it for her in the first place.

From out the kitchen came the anguished shrieks of two children being scrubbed in the zinc bath before bedtime. They were brother Billy's, who had come down with his wife Jean from London for Christmas. Jean eventually emerged looking exhausted. 'Those two are going to be the death of me,' she told Beth. 'All those presents they've got and you know what they're interested in?'

'Not that old rag doll again?'

'The very same. That doll's got no nose, no ears, one button eye and they fight over it every year.'

Beth took Jean's arm and they both sat down near the fire. Her Mam came in carrying a tray of tea and mince pies; the smell, heavy with the torment of Tantalus, woke Billy straight away. Billy would have broken arms for his Mam's mince pies and, with the sleep still in his eyes, reached out and took two. 'Children gone up the wooden hill, have they?' he asked between munches.

'Go up and you'll find out, won't you?' his wife replied, clearly unimpressed by his parental enthusiasm.

'There's one thing I don't understand, Beth,' her Dada said as Mam poured the tea. 'This Annie Davies girl. It's her we read about in the newspapers all the time. Does that mean she's the leader of the singers, or what?'

'Not really.' Beth was accustomed to her Dada's persistent questions about the Revival and tried to answer as best she could, even if they were all becoming a bit repetitive. 'We all have a part to play, that's all. There's no question of anyone being the leader as such – not even Mr Roberts. Any of us can take the lead in the singing if we want.'

Others were also finding all this constant talk of the Revival a bit tedious too, Beth saw clearly when, as if at some prearranged signal, Billy and her Mam went off to the kitchen together without even finishing their tea. She guessed the two of them were having a quiet tipple in there. She liked her drop of sherry at Christmas, did her Mam, while Billy would have been happy to shave in the stuff. On the other hand, not only had her Dada given up all strong drinking since the start of the Revival he had even renounced his beloved pipe, too.

'You're going to Cardiff in the New Year, are you?' It was her Dad, at his interrogations again.

'Nothing's been planned yet.'

After twenty minutes of so of desultory questioning Billy came back into the parlour and Beth saw immediately that he had been drinking. He had that stupid smile on his face and his eyes were slightly bloodshot. She knew our Billy. She resented that deep; resented them out there in the kitchen enjoying themselves, with the rest of them, the pious and converted, in front of the hearth talking about the Revival.

Her Mam had increasingly distanced herself from Beth as the Revival continued, while her Dada had come closer and closer. In the process, her parents had become further and further apart too. It was all pointless and silly. Evan had taught that faith should heal a family – not break it in two.

Her Mam came in with yet another pot of tea and Beth detected no sign of drink on her though, there again, that woman was one of the world's experts at disguise. She kept her emotions dusted and locked away. She was careful to take shelter from the slightest breeze of controversy while her inner self was guarded in a treble-locked vault of privacy, and only occasionally had Beth sensed the dark trout of passion which had once risen in the pools of those sad brown eyes.

Her Dada was peeling yet more chestnuts, humming happy and clearly wallowing in the music of his family, when Billy and Mam went off to the kitchen together again. Beth felt a bright green flame of jealousy shoot inside her. She wanted an easy confidential relationship with her Mam, too. She wanted to be out in the kitchen with them. And she liked a drop of sherry at Christmas as well.

Her Dada's new abstinence, Beth had learned, had also caused another rift. Jenko had been the family doctor for as long as there had been a Williams family, but now he had been banned from the house on account of his 'alcoholic atheism'; all ailments, in future, were to be taken to the new doctor in town.

'We don't want people like him in this house. He doesn't know anything anyway.' Beth regretted that, since Jenko had helped her a great deal in the past – certainly far beyond the normal call of a family doctor's duties – and her Mam had also been very fond of him. She had never said anything, but Beth had always noticed how she always went quiet for ages after she had seen him. Jenko was a total shambles, it was true, but her Mam frequently said that there was always something rather beautiful about men who were a shambles. She was a bit of a lost cause herself, was her Mam.

There was en eruption of riotous laughter in the kitchen and her Dada put down his knife and went to find out what was going on. Beth and Jean exchanged alarmed glances since, from the angry rasp of her Dada's voice, it was more than clear that he had discovered what was going on.

'People should live and let live,' Billy shouted back. 'Christmas is never Christmas without a drink.'

'Nothing's anything to you without a drink, is it? At least show some respect for Beth's new work.'

Beth bit her lip hard and looked down at the carpet. Oh no. Not that. Anything but that.

'I'm not a boy any more. I'm a man. I can do what I want.'

'In your house maybe. But not in mine.'

Her Mam put her head around the parlour door. 'I'm going for a lie-down,' she said to the girls. 'It's been a long day and I'm tired out.'

'Goodnight, Mam.' Beth's heart went out to her. There she was, the frightened rabbit running for the safety and darkness of the burrow again.

'See what you've done now,' a voice boomed down the hall. 'Upset your mother again.'

'Me! She was happy enough until you came out here and started all that fuss.'

'Always the same you were. Self, self, self. Ever since you were a boy it was the same.'

Beth was furious with the pair of them, tearing apart this, the greatest day of the year, with their ugly raised voices and wounding insults, which they were continuing to stick into one another like knives. But that was men for you, wasn't it? They would never understand that anyone else had a point of view. They understood everything and were never ever wrong about anything. She went upstairs to find that her Mam was already in bed. She had got in that fast she could not have had time to take her clothes off, so perhaps she *had* drunk one too many.

'Are you all right, Mam?' Beth asked, sitting down on the side of the bed.

'Oh, just tired, you know. It's been such a long day and I certainly don't want to listen to those two row again. I've heard them rowing once too often.'

She did look very tired. Beth leaned across the bed and kissed that small porcelain face; those tight spare features. She smoothed her hand over the grey curls. 'Are you sure you're all right? You don't look your best.'

'Just tired. Christmas is always very tiring, particularly with Billy's children. Your Dad and me are old now. Can't cope, see?'

Beth continued smoothing her curls and, just for a second, she thought she saw a flash of devilry in her Mam's eyes. 'Tell me now,' she said, turning her head over on the pillow so she did not have to look at Beth. 'Have you seen anything of that Michael Evans? The cockle picker.'

'Who?' Beth asked trying to sound calm, but felt the colour rise in her neck, immediate. Her Mam had never mentioned him before.

'You know. The cockle picker with the strange eyes.'

'Oh I haven't seen him for ages,' she said vague. 'Why do you ask?'

Her Mam's words had come as a considerable jolt to her; almost like someone holding up a mirror to her secret thoughts. Only last week Beth had written a friendly letter to Michael, giving him all the latest news and asking why he had not come to talk to her when he had come to see Dan.

'Well the age is over. You're meeting him in the square tomorrow afternoon. Don't mind, do you?'

'What? What have you been saying?' And what was Michael up to getting at her through her Mam?

'I arranged it. Saw him a few days ago I did, and wanted to tell you but was waiting for a private moment. I was talking to him about you and he said you had just written him a letter. I know what it takes for you to write anyone a letter, so I thought you'd like to go for a walk with him when you came home. He's nice-looking and very kind. Your could do with someone like that.'

'You wouldn't be . . . '

160

'He brought me a puff ball, you know. The biggest puff ball I've ever seen, it was.'

'A what? You wouldn't be . . . '

'He was out selling cockles and I met him in the street. We got to chatting and I was saying you could never get a puff ball anywhere. The next day he comes over with the biggest puff ball I've ever seen. It's a fungus you cut into slices and fry like steak. Your father loved it, too. He's a lovely shambles, that boy. Could be good for you.'

'You wouldn't be match-making, would you, Mam?'

'No.' There was little firmness in that 'no'. She gave a slight cough. 'But I do know you like him. Mothers always know these things.'

'Mothers like *you* do.'

'I just want to see you happy, Beth. You're not, are you?'

'Course I'm happy. I've got the work now.'

'I don't think you're happy. I wonder about this Revival. I worry about what it's doing all the time.'

'You're a strange woman, Mam, but I do love you.' She leaned across and smoothed her Mam's cheeks again. 'Like me to make you a nice cup of tea, would you?'

'Mmm. Funny time to go to bed, isn't it? It was the drink I suppose. Drink always makes me tired.' Her hand came out from beneath the bedclothes and caught Beth's wrist so hard it hurt. 'You shouldn't have done it, Beth. You should have kept it. They all bullied you. Everyone bullied you but there's nights I still lie here and cry for it.'

'What are you talking about now, Mam?'

'You know well enough.'

'What?'

'Baby Rhion. You shouldn't have let your baby go. No mother should ever let her baby go.'

She kept hold of Beth's wrist; they were both silent for a moment.

'You'll never have first-born now, Beth. We could have stood up against the chapel together. You needn't have married that man, either. He was only an oaf, he was. It was bigotry that took your baby off you and now there's bigotry everywhere. Everywhere I turn there's bigotry.'

She turned to look up at Beth, her old eyes bloodshot with tears. 'I'm sorry. I shouldn't have said anything. Billy did give me a drink and I enjoyed it. But I shouldn't have said anything about your baby. That lovely baby. I'm sorry.'

'Don't you worry now. It would be good for me to talk about it. Neither of you ever mention it, but it would be good for me to talk about it. It's with me all the time, Mam. Every second of every hour of every day. We'll talk about it, if you want.'

'It doesn't matter.'

'Mam. Let's talk.'

'It doesn't matter now. The baby's gone.'

'That baby's never left me for a second, Mam. There's not an hour when I don't hold her in my arms.'

There was a cough and Beth turned to see her Dada standing framed in the bedroom doorway. 'I've brought you both some tea,' he said.

* * *

That night a cruel wind came sweeping in over the estuary, cutting the darkness into the thinnest slices and all but splintering the bare branches off the trees. So freezing and bleak it was, so full of the most vicious sadism, it even drove the wild horses off the marsh, sending them roaming the streets of Loughor in large, snorting groups.

But the horses were driven out everywhere they went – driven out from the fenced yard of the Lewis Arms by the publican; driven away from behind the rugby stand; even rousing Sergeant Jenkins, the redundant long arm of the law in the town, to drive them away from the shelter of the long privet hedge near the police station.

Sometimes the horses merely stopped in the middle of the road, all facing one another at odd angles, sheltering behind one another's bodies, the long hot plumes of their breath flaring like dragons' fire. Even then, engaged in this harmless act of self-protection, they were harassed by people who came running out of their homes with sticks and stones. Even though it was Christmas Day, even though there were the sounds of the Revival in the land, all those quiet snorts and tiny whinnies in the darkness made people fearful for their allotments, since those wild horses went really wild if they so much as sniffed a single cabbage.

Except for this lonely, harassed band of horses nothing else moved in the darkness. Everyone was indoors, as snug as those bugs in their rugs, in the bosom of their families; here and there the melodic sounds of a fireside *Noson Lawen*.

Out on the marsh there were just the calls of the curlews, hooting to one another in their puzzlement at the absence of the horses. Even the Moriah Chapel was silent for the first time that winter, the wind whistling soft against the windows as it slipped around and around the severe square shape, like some thief of the night trying to find a way to break in.

That morning had seen he greatest service in living memory in the

Moriah. Evan Roberts had not spoken – though he had been present – yet every pew had been packed with a congregation who had all been restored to one another with a religious idea whose time had come. They had hugged and kissed each other afterwards and, on the way back to Island House, Hannah Roberts had described the service as just bubbling with love.

Tonight, though, there was no outcry in the chapel – just the silent clamour of the bank of wild winter flowers arranged around the pulpit. The children of the Sunday School had gone out and gathered whole armfuls of mistletoe, holly, catkin, ivy and dock, which had been put together so skilful, it looked as if someone had gone out and stolen a whole hedgerow and brought it back on huge carts.

A single gas lamp hissed yellow through the black leaves of this hedgerow. Down in the middle of the empty polished pews, Evan was kneeling, his eyes closed and his fingers locked together as his thoughts sought and danced in the mysteries of the Holy Spirit. Tonight, on this Christmas Day, he was praying and looking for guidance and help for the future of the Revival.

His eyes flickered open and he looked around at the rows of pews, the bank of tangled winter flowers. He could hear his own breathing. He could hear the distant whinny of the wild horses. He could hear the ticking of the chapel clock marking away the hours to itself. He clenched his hands together, tight, and closed his eyes again.

His imagination created a pool full with the holy waters of goodness and love. He was baptising each of the ladies in this pool, stripping them of all taint of sin, giving them new heart for the next stage of the work, driving out old curses with new blessings.

He greeted each of them with a holy kiss as they waded up to him: Lavinia then Pat, Priscilla, Maggie and his great new treasure, Annie. Then came his beloved Beth, smiling and holding out her arms to him, her bosom shivering beneath her white blouse. His feelings for her were open and deep. He still cared more for her than any of the others. Her mystery beguiled him. Joy and sorrow ran, tantalising, together in her. Sometimes, when he looked into her eyes, he saw the triumph and failure of his nation.

His nation. Oh, his lost and wandering people! On this day of days he prayed that his people would come together as one again and descend into his purifying pool of goodness and love. The industry of the south was pulling the land further and further away from its true rural heart and he prayed that the people of Wales would come together as one in God; that they would, like the children of Israel, be led to the promised land of freedom, truth and unity; that they would find the strength to resist this coming hurricane of destruction and keep hope and love alive for the world.

Oh Lord, create a mighty new gathering and put yourself as king in its midst. Learn to love God, my people, so that he may always be with you, yes even unto the end of the world.

His fingers were interlocked, vice-like, when there was an eruption of warmth inside him, followed by the loud sound of a drip on the pew in front of him. *Plop.*

His eyes opened, startled. The clock was still ticking to itself. The wind was still whistling, soft, at the windows. The hedgerow was still tangled with yellow light. *Plop.*

He looked upwards, direct into the incandescent eye of yet another vision. Suspended in the chapel air he saw a slightly trembling hand. A nail had been driven into the wrist with the blood seeping out, red and warm, around the nail. Another drop fell slow – oh so slow – as slow as a feather drifting downwards in a breeze. *Plop.* It fell into the small puddle of blood on the pew, rising up again briefly to make a tiny red lighthouse. He reached forward and placed the tip of his finger into the puddle.

* * *

Boxing Day came strutting in, sunny but still cold, glittering to the eye but with a heart of pure ice. Everywhere the young bounded around hoar-frosted corners, carrying or dragging or whistling or riding whatever Father Christmas had so thoughtfully dropped down their chimney pots.

Iron hoops went whirling past small wooden horses mounted on wheels. Penny whistles competed with tin drums. Teddy bears, still fragrant with the smell of the shop, were introduced to moon-faced china dolls whose huge eyelashes closed with a click when their heads were bent backwards. Some brought out their music boxes – with those tiny ballerinas destined to pirouette for eternity – to play the tinkling standards for their friends.

The not-so-young were out promenading in their newest garments – their fur mufflers, silk scarves, those laced shin-high boots smelling of virgin, polished leather. The really lucky ones were wobbling along the roads on glittering new bicycles, usually managing a few frantic rings of their bells before riding into a suicidal wobble and falling off.

But Santa seemed to work in the most mysterious ways his carpentry to perform, since he had dropped a sledge down young Tony Hughes' chimney yet, since there was no sign of snow, Tony Hughes was pulling the sledge around the streets, dispirited, wondering if Santa knew something that no one else did.

'What's all this going on with my Mam, then?' asked Beth, giving Michael a nudge in the side as they both walked together out of the town.

'I just happened to bump into her. She's a nice woman.'

'Mm. Isn't she? Well, you made a big impression. I never knew puff balls were the way to a woman's heart.'

'What's the way to your heart, girl?'

'Don't mind that. Now, have you heard someone has gone and sawn down the rugby posts over in the field? They've just vanished. Dada told me this morning. He says it's the best Christmas present he's ever had. The town can't play their Boxing Day match against Llanelli.'

'What a load of nonsense all this is,' he snorted. 'What's wrong with rugby, anyway? They're even going around now saying that every rugby player must remember that he's kicking around the head of John the Baptist. We haven't had a decent game since the Revival started – all the opposition has gone to the chapel. This religion is making everyone daft in the brain.'

'You're still against it all, then? Michael, you just wouldn't believe the way people's lives have been changed. Hopeless cases transformed overnight.'

'You fancy taking to the hills?'

'If you like. Funny, but I've always liked going for a walk on Boxing Day, seeing all the children out playing with their new toys. What did Father Christmas bring you?'

He knocked the top of his head with his knuckles. 'Well, I've got six hangovers in here for a start.'

'It really is time you began staying out of those pubs, you know. One day I'll show you what drink does for your belly. Just put a lump of raw liver into a glass of gin and see what happens. It dissolves into nothing at all. That's what happening inside you.'

They followed the path next to the marsh and joined another which took them up over the crags which stood guard over the estuary. She was beginning to feel slightly ill at ease; she could see that he was not his usual talkative self.

'It was some poet,' he said, finally, 'who reckoned that valley sheep were fatter but mountain sheep were sweeter.'

'What poet was that?'

'Can't remember or, come to think of it, it might be the other way round. The valley sheep are sweeter . . . oh forget it.' He picked up a stone and threw it down a gulley. They both stopped to listen as it bounced and pinged its way down the rocks.

Further along they sat on a large rock and looked out over the sun-burnished sands and the black dots of the wild horses. 'Tell me then,' she said, 'what have you been up to since I saw you last?'

'Not much. I still work the sands when the mood takes me, but not much of anything else.'

'Not feeling too well?' she asked, soft.

'Not very clever at all, I'm afraid. Just feel fit for the graveyard most of the time.'

'Oh dear we *are* in a mess, aren't we?'

He stared ahead, holding his legs together and resting his chin on his knees. She was sad to see him like this. He was like some mountain spring when normal, his mind flinging out all kinds of stories and ideas.

He sighed. 'Have you ever been in the grip of a hopeless passion?'

She shook her head. She had not.

'I'm in one now,' he said, craning his head over his knees and looking down on to the rocks below. 'I keep waiting for it to go away. I keep on hoping that it will go away. Sometimes I think it has gone away. Then it gets worse.'

She shifted around on the hard rock, almost sorry that she had come. If she was somewhere at the centre of this hopeless passion – and that might not be too far from the truth – then what had promised to be a nice walk was going to get all fraught again.

'Some days I feel I've been thrown into a room with ten corners and eighteen ceilings,' he continued, miserable. 'Then, when I think I've pulled myself together, it all reaches up and shakes me by the ears again and the twitches start.'

'Twitches?'

'They're like mad maggots running around under my skin. You ever had them?'

She would have laughed out loud if she had not seen that he was being deadly serious. Only someone as daft as him could have got in such a state. Mad maggots indeed. 'Can't say that I have,' she said turning her head away, careful in case she did not manage to keep a straight face.

'I never know when they're going to start next. If it's not the twitches it's bits of me falling asleep or else my heart is racing. I had something like it after my father died. Palpitations, they are, but they were never as bad as this. There it goes. I've got one of those maggots running around inside my kneecap. It's my shoulders that get them the worst. Just by here. I get this feeling that I've got leprosy in one shoulder, then it moves over to the other side or starts crawling down my back. The other day this leg went clean asleep. Just wouldn't move at all. Then there's this lump that keeps swelling behind my ear and, when it goes awry, it starts growing on top of my head. Sometimes my lips go stiff and if it's not that . . .'

'Michael, you really must go and see a doctor.' She did not find it funny any longer. The cause was probably emotional but the effects were bad enough. She had never come across anything like it working in the hospital. They all suffered from normal illnesses in there.

'I went to see Jenko the other week.'

'What did he say?'

'He said it was some sort of emotional disorder. It ran in the family, he said. He also said that a lot of the Welsh troops had it in the Crimea. He told them to eat lots of apples.'

'What good was that?'

'You tell me. Old Jenko knows nothing. I went to him with an infection in my throat once. He asked if I had ever had it before. When I said I had he said well you've got it again.'

'So what's the cause? Everything has to have a cause.'

'You know, girl, it shows no sign of an end – nor a middle – nor a beginning, come to that.'

'You're not being very clear, Michael. Let's walk some more.'

'Well, girl. I've got this love for you and it's about killing me. That's about as straight as I can put it.'

She stood up, unwilling to continue the conversation. 'I thought we had sorted all this out. Let's walk, shall we?'

'No, sit down.'

'My feet are cold, Michael. They only get warm when I walk.'

'Damn your feet. Sit down. I just want to have it out with you and *then* you can go. I won't bother you again – if that's what you're worried about – but I do want a few answers.' There was a cold anger in his voice and she sat back down with him on the rock. The day had become very grey indeed.

'I can't love you, Michael. I just can't. I'm sorry, but there it is. There seems absolutely no point in talking about it any more.'

'You're in love with someone else. Is that it?'

'Don't be silly.'

'Well where is your life going? Are you going around singing for Evan Roberts for the rest of your life? Is that what you want do to?'

Her nostrils flared slight. 'If necessary. Yes, I will. He's become my life now and, strange though it may seem to you, he's where I want to be.'

'You're in love with him, are you?'

'Don't be so silly. I'm a new woman now. I've found my life's work – God's work. Oh, you can smile, but that's all I want to do. Look, Michael, I'm sorry if it's me who is causing you all these problems. I'm really very sorry indeed. But I'm changed now. Get that into your head, will you? Come to terms with that and, perhaps, you'll come to terms with these . . . mad maggots of yours.'

He stood up and sat back down again. 'I think you've thrown yourself into this religion business because you're escaping from something,' he said, quiet.

'Nonsense.'

'The more I think about it the more sense it makes. Tell me what it is, will you?'

'There's nothing to tell.'

'I don't believe you. I know as sure as there's a nose on my face you haven't told me the truth about anything. Jenko said there was something.'

'What did he say?' The question was as sharp as a wet flannel whipped across the cheek.

'He said nothing. Nothing at all. But I got the feeling there was something.'

'That big mouth.' She stood up feeling very cold and almost bilious. 'I want to walk. I feel faint.'

There was a noise behind them. They both went silent as a man led a horse past them. When the man had gone she looked down at Michael, who was crying. She stooped down and took out a handkerchief to dry his eyes.

'I told you I was in a mess,' he said.

She swallowed. She had so much wanted to talk to her Mam about it all last night. Her Dada had clearly heard their conversation, too. But not only did her Dada not want to talk about it, he did not even recognise that it had ever happened. She had wished often enough for someone with whom to talk about it. She swallowed hard again. 'There's something I'd better tell you,' she said.

He stood up and held her shoulders with both hands. 'I'm all ears, girl.'

But she did not speak for a full minute. He could see that she was finding it difficult. 'I can't Michael. I just can't. It's too shameful.'

'But you *are* going to tell me, aren't you?'

'My shoulders. You're hurting my shoulders.'

'I deserve to know. I've got a right.'

She looked up into his eyes and, with everything crumbling and choking insider her, kissed him on the lips. She wriggled around trying to get him to put his arms around her. He held on to her shoulders. 'Have you ever had a good shaking?'

'Stop bullying me, will you?'

'I will. I'll shake you until your teeth fall out.'

Her mouth opened and closed but nothing resembling words came out.

'You what? Tell me, won't you? What are you trying to say?'

'I've had a baby.' Her whole body began trembling and she thought that she was going to swoon, hardly able to believe the words had actually left her lips.

'You've had a what?'

She held him around the waist, put her head up against his jacket and just cried. She should not have said it. If only she could just die; if only she could just be carried away by the wind.

Now it was his turn to look at the fat blobs of her tears slipping down her flushed cheeks. He gave her the handkerchief back. 'Have a good blow on this. A good big blow. That's better.'

'I think we'd better sit down again.'

They sat down on the rock and he put his arms around her as she continued sniffing. After a few minutes he asked her to tell him about it.

'I had a baby. That's all there is to it really.' She blew her nose again. 'No one ever found about it and you must promise to say nothing. You promise?'

'Promise.'

'I couldn't get rid of it – I'd heard of women dying after trying to do it so I couldn't do that. I wouldn't marry the man. So, when I started to get fat, I went to Cardiff and had the baby. She's there now.'

'Someone must have known about it.'

'My parents. The man. And Dr. Jenkins. He arranged it all.'

'Jenko did?'

'Yes. I was afraid he had told you all about it when you mentioned him. You know what a big mouth he's got.'

'He didn't say anything. I was just guessing.'

'Jenko and Mam really stood by me. They took me to Cardiff, where the baby was fostered, then I went back to London to train as a nurse. Now I'm back.'

'So now we know all.'

'Now you know.'

She was already beginning to feel better now that she had told someone. It had been like lancing a long-festering boil. She put her head on his shoulder, feeling almost drained. He kept his arm around her; though silent, she could tell that he had not been shocked by her shameful story. He prodded her with a question now and then and she found it surprising easy to tell all, even though she had long since considered it unfit for human ears.

She began reliving her story while she was sitting down, continued it while they were walking along the cliff together – and then she would not have stopped talking even if he had wanted her to.

'At first I didn't tell the father, but had to tell him in the end because I was sure that Mam knew. She had known all along, as it turned out, but decided to say nothing until I did. The man thought the answer was simple and wanted to marry me. He was rich and they always get their way, the rich do. He kept calling over and begging me to marry him but, by then, I was so revolted by him I could hardly look him in the face.

'I had to tell my parents in the end and that was the worst part. Dada just sat slumped in his chair and cried. I will always remember that. But Mam didn't seem upset at all. She said she would stand by me whatever I decided to do. The man pleaded with them to make me marry him and, while Dada went on and on and on about it, I refused flat since I was sure that I no longer loved him. Then the man told his parents and they came over to the house as well and there was the biggest fuss. They were fond of me, too, and promised to buy us a farm of our own if we got married. We could even have a sea cruise together to get around awkward questions about dates. Just come home with the baby, you understand. But I was obdurate. Funny word that. Obdurate.'

'Go on.'

'There's not a lot else to tell. I put my foot down and said that I was not going to be like every other girl on the Gower. Only the posh, it's said, ever get married if the girl is not pregnant. Oh I would marry one day – but for love. Mam supported me to the hilt during it all. She even once said that was prepared to leave Dada to go away with me if I wanted her to. She said she would do anything to keep the baby. But I couldn't allow her to leave Dada just for my mistakes.'

'So how did Jenko come into it?'

'Well, for a month it was all tears and tantrums with that man refusing to go away and Dada beating his chest. I suppose I would have married him in the end if it hadn't been for Mam. It was Jenko who came up with the solution. He said he knew a couple in Cardiff who had always wanted a baby. I could go to the woman's house, have the baby and leave it with the woman. The understanding was that I would never see the baby again. The woman didn't want to appear cruel, just protecting her interests, I suppose. I went to stay with the woman in Cardiff when the time came. Baby Rhion was born on 1 March, 1900. At five minutes past five in the afternoon. The family was poor but I was sure the woman would be a good mother. "Now go home and forget anything ever happened," she said. Forget it ever happened! How can you forget something like that? For the past four years I have missed that baby every single day. Letting her go was the most foolish thing I've ever done. I can't love again, see? It was all true what you said to me about being cold and it hurt.'

'I couldn't have known.'

'Of course you couldn't but, after drifting around for so long, I've found the right kind of work at last.'

'Are you sure it's not the right kind of guilt?'

'Maybe. Maybe I do see the work as a penance, but it's a penance I enjoy and my life has been given a purpose which it didn't have before.'

The twilight was a symphony of black on grey: the soft sunshine dipping out of the gunmetal sky, picking out the black silhouette of the town's rooftops, the grey smoke drifting up out of the chimney pots, the black wheel of the pit sitting motionless and they grey cold river sliding, silent, down to the deep dark sea.

'I'm very cold now,' Beth said. 'Very cold.'

'Better get back to the fire then,' Michael said before kissing her on the lips.

She responded with a warm and tearful fervour, holding his head tight with both hands and kissing her way around his nose, his cheeks and lips. 'Much better than the fire, this is,' she said.

'Will I see you soon?'

She shook her head. 'We're off travelling around Mid and North Wales.' She was busy kissing him again. 'I'll write and tell you where we are. And if you turn up anywhere and just talk to Dan I'll give you a good bash.'

'I'm terrified.'

'Just be patient, will you? I have to continue this work now but be patient. What with your mad maggots and my past we could make a fine couple.'

'The very finest, girl.'

Chapter Fifteen

The Revival continued sweeping the land and, by the beginning of the New Year, fifty-two rugby clubs had closed down. Nevertheless isolated pockets of the resistance still existed and, on the Gower, the village of Pen-clawdd was in the very vanguard of dissent.

Indeed, Pen-clawdd's rugby club even prospered during those chill days and at 7.30 on a freezing January morning a record number of thirty-five members of the Pen-clawdd Rugby Club's Social, Cultural and Recreational Society gathered at nearby Gowerton Station for their annual outing.

The society was founded in 1886 for the purpose – it said the articles of association – of supporting the Welsh rugby team in its annual battle against England. The second purpose of the society – not mentioned in the articles, but evident to everyone in the village – was to get as drunk as wheels in the process.

Already, even at such an unholy hour, they were drinking on the platform; the crates for the journey piled high next to the ticket office. It promised to be the kind of event when the players were not so much carried home at the end of the day, as carried to the game before the kick-off. Such was their confidence in a famous Welsh win some of them had been celebrating for nearly two weeks now. All carried black-edged mourning cards to be passed out to any unfortunate English supporters: 'In memory of England who fell asleep at the Arms Park . . . '

Some of the forwards were already on their fourth bottle of the morning, belching sonorous, rubbing beer into the folds of their bellies, looking as if they wanted to set fire to a cat, or breakfast on a dog and a plate of stewed bullets. They hurled the empty beer bottles into the allotment on the other side of the railway line.

Michael would not have missed this day for anything. Beth had been gone for weeks and, despite a few letters of promising warmth, his maggots and rigor mortis were still playing him up. This day out was the best antidote he knew for human misery – unless some terrible accident occurred and England won, in which unlikely event everyone would be miserable to the point of suicide.

Michael was sitting on a beer crate, drinking with little Marnie Prees and discussing the great discussion which would go on throughout the day and much of the night too: the great and glorious game of rugby. When it came to the game and who should play what where for Wales there were no doubts for every single man in the land was an expert, with more letters after his name than a chiropodist. Every onlooker was a brilliant and shrewd analyst, knowledgeable in every facet of the game and far, far wiser than the selectors, who knew nothing whatsoever.

'You see, Marnie, that Jack Strand-Jones is just Llanelli rubbish. Whoever heard of a full-back who runs sideways like a crab? Doesn't seem to know how to run in a straight line at all. A full-back has got to have vision – he's got to see the whole pattern of the game – even before the kick-off.

'Now if they'd called in that Swansea boy . . . '

Gimpy Davies – as honorary treasurer for the society – circulated efficiently, marking his card and giving each member ten shillings' beer money. He was a humpback, one leg a good four inches shorter than the other, who had never been out of Pen-clawdd, let alone set foot on a rugby pitch, but who was entrusted with collecting the eightpenny sub each Friday night in the pub for this day of days. He enjoyed being involved with the boys, even if he was never allowed to travel with them.

Everyone agreed that Gimpy made an excellent treasurer, since there was a time-honoured tradition in Wales for honorary treasurers to run off with the funds the day before the outing – often with the honorary secretary's wife. But Gimpy, being Gimpy, was unable to run anywhere with anything.

The train was already overflowing with red-scarved drunks when it pulled in from Milford. Cheers went up as the crates were passed into the compartments, a few scuffles breaking out when hands, other than those who had paid their subs, tried to steal a few bottles.

'Give my love to the Arms Park, boys!' Gimpy shouted when they were all on. 'And don't forget the last train leaves Cardiff at ten past ten tonight sharp.'

'We'll be on it, Gimpy boy. Have no fear of that.'

Gimpy laughed the laugh of a raving maniac who had just been told he was going to become a Member of Parliament. He knew as well as everyone else that no one had caught the ten past ten the last couple of times the society had gone to Cardiff. Come to that, only three had got to the match at all one year. Last year, after the outing at Twickenham, three of their best players spent a month in prison after some small fuss in Trafalgar Square. One player had never been heard of again. Gimpy was actually quite pleased he was not allowed to go with the team.

With the train gone Gimpy was still chortling when, in the growing silence, he heard distant cries coming from the direction of the allotment. He limped to the edge of the platform to peer over and discover that Dai Llewelyn, Pen-clawdd's most fearsome prop forward, had somehow clambered into the carriage and managed to fall out of the door on the other side again, tumbling down the embankment into several lines of cabbages and sprouts.

'A fine bloody start that is,' he was muttering, hauling himself up out of the broken cabbages.

* * *

As the train rattled and shook its way down the track to Cardiff, Michael handed out more bottles. He enjoyed this small task which, in the event of any fighting erupting, meant that he was always the best protected. It also made him one of the boys – even if he never actually went about the place looking as though he wanted to eat a donkey sandwich or tear someone into lots of bits.

'You just couldn't get a better pair of half-backs than those Dancing Dicks though. What a joy they are. When did you ever see two men running ten ways at the same time? It must be like chasing a pair of revolving doors, it must. Reverse passes, scissors, dummies – the world will never see the likes of those two again. They should build chapels to them, not that Evan Roberts. What do you think Evan Roberts knows about the wheeling scrum as a counter move? I'll tell you. Bugger all, that's what. Bugger all.'

Michael passed more bottles out. Further belches were belched as they gazed downwards, hands clamped on one knee, self-satisfied in the completeness of their rugby wisdom.

'Now that Gwyn Nicholls is a lump of granite in defence, he is, and forked lighting in attack – a most unusual combination if you ask me.'

The train pulled into Bridgend and Michael wiped some beer off his mouth with the back of his hand. He wondered where Beth was now, who she was with and what she was singing. Some days he felt happy that they were getting on well and on others she gnawed away at him and he just wanted to be with her. Somehow, being in the midst of this laughter, beer-sodden groups was making him feel worse and he was just opening another bottle to console himself when his leg went as dead as a railway sleeper. 'Aaaaaaargh!' he yelled. 'Aaaaaaargh!'

'What's up, boy?'

'My leg's gone, *mun*. Stiff as a board it is.'

'Cramp,' said Marnie Prees, belting the leg on the kneecap with his bottle. 'Young, fit boy like you shouldn't have cramp.'

'Give it a good shake, will you?' Michael told Marnie. 'It sometimes goes away with a good shake.'

Two of them began shaking and pulling his leg around while the others watched with grave interest.

'All right, all right. Don't shake the thing off.'

'Which muscle is it?'

'It's all over my leg.'

'You don't get cramp all over your leg.'

'I do. Just shake it, *mun*. Steady now. Aaaaaaaaah! It's lifting it is.'

He could feel fantastic relief flooding into his leg just as it floods into the whole body when a preacher announces that he is coming to the end of a five hour sermon.

'You'd better get to see a doctor about that,' said Handel Morgan. 'What use is a centre whose legs go dead?'

'I went to a doctor,' Michael said, taking a reviving swig from his bottle. 'He told me to eat lots of apples.'

'What doctor was that?'

'Old Jenko over in Loughor.'

'Jenko!' The outbreak of laughter all but stopped the train.

'My father called in Jenko once,' said Handel. 'He had some kind of twitch in his leg as well, but when Jenko came falling in through the door – drunk with a broken leg and arm – the shock was so great my father's leg got better straight away and he hasn't seen a doctor since.'

* * *

At Cardiff General Station the group spilled out of the train, a flying wedge that went scything through the singing passions and sizzling shunts of the crowds assembled from all over the country for the big game. Bedragoned flags fluttered above the heads of the copper-ladlers, colliers, tin-platers, seamen, clerks and shippers. Many were carrying fat leeks with some, flush out of leeks, waving strings of onions about since onions, at least, had the same violent smell, redolent of a dead and dying enemy.

The cavernous gloomy bars – built by Brains Brewery as a tribute to a nation's insatiable and monumental thirst – were as packed as sardines in tins, the air a smoke-laden, beer scented fug as overflowing pints slopped this way and that – sometimes even down throats. Outside the bars there was slightly more air to breathe in Queen Street and St. Mary Street, where singing Welshmen, celebrating in advance, swung, ape-like, on lamp posts as ragged urchins begged for pennies, sold matches or stood around the glowing chestnut braziers on each corner to keep warm. Men were wading across the River Taff in the hope of climbing into the Arms Park without paying. Policemen stayed well back as drunks ricocheted along the cobbles of Quay Street.

The Pen-clawdd flying wedge flew into The Albert where Marnie, first to the bar, began passing back a frothing series of pints of the famous dark. In the far corner they then got down to some serious drinking and returned yet again to The Discussion:

'That Gwyn Nicholls could play fifteen Englishers all on his own, he could. You know, I've got a real fancy we're up for the Triple Crown this year. The All Blacks next season, too. I'm not at all sure we're up to them.'

'Course we are, mun – if only we can get rid of that . . . '

When kick-off time approached Michael was three parts gone as they formed yet another flying wedge straight to the ground, where they each paid a shilling at the wooden barrier and shouldered their way into the ground itself.

Michael knew of nothing quite like those early moments when he stood with his countrymen in this enormous theatre where a dramatic people were preparing to set up a series of genuine and passionate responses to a great struggle. Huge spasms of emotion rolled around and around the crowd; hymns burst out from different sections of the bob bank, duelling with one another under stands which were themselves shaking with the steady thunder of stamping, impatient feet.

The Pen-clawdd lads were so off their chumps with excitement they could barely speak. Even a fully qualified atheist like Michael could see, as he stood there, feeling this tribal electricity pulsing through his blood, how close rugby was to the chapel at the heart of the Welsh revelation; how both pulpit and goal post formed a focus for the same profound expressions of a tribe's view of itself as following a path of crusading fire.

Antagonistic though he was to the work of Evan Roberts he saw that the chapel's insights into the freedom of poverty and the rugby world's absolute insistence on amateurism reflected the same purity of values. The chapel talk of brotherhood and equality before the Cross, and Welsh rugby's classlessness and sacrifice of the solo dash for team effort, voiced the same instinct for democracy. When 40,000 choristers in this ground, the largest massed choir in the world, lifted their voices – as they were doing now – and sang William Williams' *Guide Me O Thou Great Jehovah* it was a massed heartfelt prayer that they might all be fed with the bread of heaven: an incredible number of points.

There had been a crucial oversight when the Bible had been written, aye. Moses had lost that important tablet when he had come tripping down the slopes of Sinai – the one that decreed that, in future, Wales should always win at rugby – preferably by eighty points to three. *You can give them three, Oh Lord.* When a player put on the scarlet jersey it was his sacred duty to uphold the honour of his land and, if necessary, shed his last drop of blood in the cause. Out of his death would rise the gift of eternal Welsh gratitude. The opening of each season marked the start of the dark and difficult quest for the Holy Grail of the Triple Crown.

The chapel-goer and the rugby fanatic never publicly accepted that there was any sense in which they were both going out together, of course, but at their most vigorous, they both celebrated the same belly-churning fervour; the same glorious vision of the ultimate triumph; the same mass ecstasy of a singing communion of souls as that present here now, this Saturday afternoon. Great eruptions of emotion were shunting up and down the terraces; hymns fluting and soaring out of thousands of throats and billions of goose pimples chasing one another from one body to the next, like a giant epidemic of marauding measles.

When kick-off time came some of the Pen-clawdd boys felt so anxious they set about relieving themselves, with Michael and others dancing around trying to avoid getting their trousers wet and warm. Well, Michael thought, that's one thing they don't do in the chapel.

Seagulls wheeled up high in the dull cloudy sky, their excellent view matched only by that of the Press and selectors who sat on a trestle table next to the touchline. The National Anthem was sung, the Welsh captain won the toss – the Lord really *was* looking on Wales with favour that winter – the whistle blew and for the next hour and twenty minutes the scarlet warriors of Wales put the white-shirted Sassenachs of England through the mangle, slow.

Fantastic, it was. All the Pen-clawdd boys just kept weeping and laughing with an almost certifiable dementia. Michael was transported straight to heaven; such feelings of jubilation sweeping up and down his body his rigor mortis didn't have a hope of attacking him.

Right from the kick-off the Welsh set up base camp on the English twenty-five and the giant Welsh forwards mauled and spoiled every English move. Fearless in the rucks, they were, and ready to castrate bulls with their teeth in the scrums. Steadier and tighter than a Roman phalanx the Welsh forwards kept driving forward, the steam rising off their backs as they sent out a steady flow of clean passes to the Welsh backs, who romped this way and that, faster and nippier than greyhounds with boiling hormones.

The chief Welsh executioners were the two outside halves – Richard Owen and Richard Jones, the legendary Dancing Dicks – who sliced and chopped the English defence into tiny diced cubes, dashing one way and another with now-you-see-now-you-don't runs, catching the ball with either hand or even their shoulder blades, leaving the English leaden-footed, heartbroken and very sorry indeed that they had ever given up hockey and so much as seen a rugby ball in the first place.

Throughout the game Michael and the boys kept doing little jigs of joy and hugging one another as the sweet carnage continued. Michael was so overcome by one try he kissed Howard Morgan hard on the lips – making Howard the first man he had ever kissed with any real passion. Joy affected people in different ways; Marnie just kept vomiting, noisy, while others sang until their vocal cords were no better than a battered bit of string. *Feeeeeeed me 'til I waaaaaaaant no more.*

Even on the odd occasions when the English got the ball they could do nothing with it, still less penetrate the Welsh defence, since the selectors had sensibly got rid of that Llanelli rubbish, Jack Strand-Jones, at fullback and brought in George Davies from Cardiff in his place. Davies had the presence and effect of a brick wall, converting two of the Welsh tries as well. Other scorers were Teddy Morgan, Rhys Gabe, Harry Watkins, Arthur Harding and Richard 'Dancing Dick' Jones, who gave their nation tries which still live and burn in the Welsh memory like some fearsome sin.

Come the final whistle the English captain went up to the Welsh goal line to see what it looked like.

The final score was Wales 25, England nil and, after the last whistle, as huge cataracts of relieved urine cascaded down and out of the stands, the exhilaration was even more unconfined and buoyant than on that momentous day when they relieved Mafeking. Joy poured out of the ground, mounted the backs of telegram wires, slapped itself on handbills and posters, was carried by cart and by bicycle, was shouted and echoed down valleys until it all came together in a great tidal wave which rolled straight across Wales until it collapsed into the Atlantic.

Michael was carried in a rolling, singing crush out of the ground, across the road and swept into the corner of a bar in the Queen's Vaults. Hoarse and very thirsty, everyone kept hugging one another and drinking any pint or whisky that seemed to be standing around available, as if some great mythic river of alcohol had burst over their heads, sudden. Some stood discussing and analysing the moves of the game in the lilting accents of West Wales or the hard, harsh vowels of Cardiff, others were singing *Sospan Fach, Bill Bailey* and *Boys of the Old Brigade* – one song after another or even, if you like, all at the same time. If they could not remember the words and were drifting, comatose, towards the floor they would always sing soft into their beer: *Feeeeeeeeeeed me 'til I waaaaaaaaaaant no more.*

Many songs – and even more drinks – later everything had gone hazy and Michael was reasonably sure that there was fighting going on all around him. He had no objection to that except that someone – a Sassenach probably . . . tried to steal his drink in the fray. Right out of his hand! He punched someone or something, went rolling one way with a massive explosion of pain in his left ear, before reeling backwards, retreating from yet another explosion in his nose.

Next thing he knew, there were three men kicking him with one sitting on his chest. Hah now, he thought to himself, quiet. Hah now, I've got them all where I want them.

All around him he heard the eruptions of tumbling tables and the bright shattering of breaking glass. Suddenly, over the other side of the bar, he spotted what appeared to be a row of Cardiff policemen, individuals famous throughout the ports of the world for their wonderful sense of humour and loving tenderness.

* * *

Michael came around, some four hours later, in a cell in Cardiff police station. Others were lying around, bleeding and groaning: some were still discussing the game with one another through the bars.

He tried to move but could not; his rigor mortis – or something even deadlier – had got him down his side. 'I've got this girl who keeps making bits of me go dead,' he told a man slumped in the corner of the cell. 'Ever heard of anything like that, have you?'

There was a distant scream of someone being tenderised by a policeman's truncheon. The man in the corner of the cell looked up, his eyes bruised black and nose still running red like a pair of taps. 'My Mam is going to make bits of me go dead when she finds out about this,' he wailed. 'My Mam will bloody kill me for this.'

Michael groaned deep in his pain again. Those parts of his body that were not giving him pain were still drunk. 'One minute it's that leg, then it's this leg. My back will be going soon and I'm that fed up with it all I wish they'd keep me in here forever. How'd I get in here anyway?'

'Anyone in here know the score?'

'Twenty-five bloody points to bloody nil that's what the score was.'

'And let's face it, boys,' said a tousle-haired lad in the cell opposite when the cheering had stopped. 'Let's face it now. England were bloody lucky to get the nil!'

Chapter Sixteen

Beth could feel the air getting thinner as the narrow-gauge Ffestiniog train toiled up the grey and brown rubbled slopes, its broad-bellied boiler exploding with power as it drove the steam into the small piston-boxes. Puffs of black smoke were belching out of the tiny green chimney, the wooden seats uncomfortable to sit on as the train carried the whole party up the sheer slate slopes.

Over on the horizon were the rocked, snow-capped peaks of the Snowdon range, full with their majesty as they crouched the length of the sky, with the stone cottages of the farmers and the polished tarns dotted over the foothills like travellers journeying on a slow pilgrimage.

Evan and the ladies were all crowded together in the small carriage, admiring the view. Beth found herself wishing that Michael was with her, so she could take his hand and share the beauty of the place. Any view was always better when shared with someone you were fond of. She could barely believe that she had met someone like Michael; someone who still seemed to want her, despite all that had happened. She had simply believed that no one like him existed.

As it was, things were getting better with Evan who, ever since Annie's arrival, had been a picture of sunny charm and affability. On occasion, they exchanged their secret sign and Evan always turned to Beth if he just wanted to talk about nothing in particular. Beth guessed that Evan was a bit shy of Annie, who could certainly be something of a livewire when she tried.

'You know, Beth,' Annie said. 'I only came to that meeting in Pontycymmer because I heard that Evan was off his head but, since then, it's been me that's been off my head and I glory in every minute of it.'

It turned out that Annie was having great problems with her father who, on learning that she was going to join the Revival, locked himself in his garden shed. 'Just sat in the dark on the seed boxes like some rogue mushroom,' Annie said in that merry way of hers.

'Even when Dan went over there he still wouldn't come out. Mad as a march hare, he is, when he gets going. He didn't mind Maggie going – in fact he offered to pack her bags as long as she took all her shawls with her. The problem is I've been taking lessons over in the Dowlais with that

Harry Evans, the voice trainer. Anyway, Harry tells Dada that I will become a lead singer in Covent Garden for certain – if not Milan. I didn't believe him for a moment but Dad is batty about the opera and was pleased as Punch about all this. All week he was walking about with this stupid smile on his face. Mam says he was smiling in his sleep, picturing me up there on the stage at the Coliseum. He even got his tails cleaned ready for the first night. But now he's convinced I've gone and ruined it all.

'But daft! You know what he's devoted his life to? Teaching his dog to count. I ask you. As it stands Ludwig – that's the dog's name – has got to four but the beast is sure to die before he gets to six. He's called Ludwig because Dad loves Beethoven. Every year on Beethoven's birthday Dad and his dog go out to the pubs of Maesteg and they both get roaring drunk. You've seen nothing until you've seen Dad and his daft dog staggering up the garden drive after celebrating Beethoven's birthday. The last time I spoke to him he was threatening to come along to one of our meetings with his dog. I can't tell you what a disaster that would be.'

'Particularly if it was Beethoven's birthday,' Maggie added with a sigh. She did speak now and then.

The train came to the end of the line with long explosive hisses of its brakes. Evan got out first, to help down the ladies one by one before they held up the hems of their dresses, as they stepped over the muddy, wet scree to emerge on top of Dinorwic slate quarry.

Everyone went silent as they stared down into the staggering grey grandeur of the place – the 2,000 foot high work face pocked and terraced by a century of quarrying; the slashed rocks cut sheer by saws and drills, the gaping black galleries burrowed into the sides of the cliffs, the giant yellow gantries, still for the moment, resembling monstrous stick insects with broken necks.

'It's just like a big grey cathedral,' said Beth looking up and around her, like a small child on her first visit to London. Indeed the sheer overwhelming size of the valley – about a mile deep and two miles long – made her feel nervous – as did the stories they had heard of its troubles.

Evan was striding down the track followed by Dan, the ladies and four members of the Press, when a whistle blew, bringing the rockmen and splitters out from their toils in the galleries to look down at the visitors. Word went from gallery to gallery and, by the time the group had reached the bottom of the valley, there were perhaps a thousand men all looking down on them – the rockmen, splitters, badrockmen and labourers, all just standing there holding their mallets, crowbars and chisels.

182

We might just be the first Christians thrown to the lions, Beth thought, looking up at all the men. The men might prove to be as cruel and indifferent as those Romans, quietly standing there in their helmets, moleskin jackets and baggy corduroy trousers. They would surely laugh or, even worse, throw rocks down on them.

'Sing *Great God of Countless Wonders*,' Evan asked, as he climbed up on an upturned slate wagon to address the men.

Beth stepped forward, looking at the others, worried. What possible point could there be to singing here she could not imagine, but sing they did and a miracle happened. The quarry was an acoustic marvel, picking up every note, amplifying it and carrying it along its entire length. They had never known anything like it, the words and melody twisting around and rising upwards like clouds being shunted around by the thermals of Calvary.

'I have come here to tell you that is time for all this bitterness to come to an end,' Evan said when the ladies had finished singing, his words carrying along the grey jagged slash of the valley with the authority of thunder. 'Enough bones have been broken. There has been enough trouble with the police. There has been too much wild talk about blacklegs and traitors. The time has come for brother to love brother. The time has come for the love of God to bring you all together.'

Just then Annie moved near Evan and began singing as he spoke. She had done this once before and now, without so much as a second's rehearsal, they were off duelling again, neither of them looking at one another, the one giving way to the other at key moments.

'Never doubt that you can build a new Jerusalem, my beloved men. But remember too that you will build nothing on bitterness. Nothing at all. You will build nothing on division and hate. Your foundations will be as sand.'

Annie continued her singing, her shadow-haunted voice surging down the valley in magnificent eddies. Beth watched it all, careful, not jealous in the slightest at the way Annie seemed to be moving her to one side. Between the two of them they were offering a shimmering vision of the coming apocalypse – all set out with a bare and beautiful passion. The sheer scale of both their sensitive personalities was terrifying: here, surely, was a partnership that really had been contracted in heaven.

'I'm not here to tell you which union to join but I am telling you to give up this fighting. No union on earth is worth that. Let the love of God enfold you and keep you. Remember that the son of man gave his very life for the love of you. Not for some union, but for you alone. Unions come from man but the risen one comes from God and God alone. There was not an ounce of hatred in him – not an ounce – and it is to him that you must now look in the time of your strife.'

'God bless you, Evan Roberts,' a voice called down from one of the galleries.

'May God bless all of you,' Evan called back.

Annie's voice took up the duel again, the ladies moving to support her now as workman after workman lifted their hands or tools in salute . . . three, four, five . . . eleven, twelve, thirteen . . . hundreds now saluting the group with hooters going off and great shouts cannoning down the valley.

When they reached the top of the track Evan turned to Dan and asked, 'Are we all staying under the same roof tonight in Bethesda?'

'It's tricky,' Dan replied. 'There aren't enough houses up here to take us all in.'

'I want us always to be together as we travel about, Dan. There must be no breaking up of the group now. The fellowship of prayer. That's what we all need. Tell them that I insist that we all stay together.'

He turned and smiled at Beth, reaching out and putting his arm around her. 'Remember that now, Dan. I insist.'

* * *

Visit to Dinorwic acclaimed by everyone a great success, Dan wrote in his diary. *All newspapers are agog with the great service at Dinorwic. But I'm worried about Annie and so, I think, is Evan on the quiet. She is turning the Revival into show business. She came, at first, as our saviour but may well turn out to be our ruin.*

Quarry now producing about 982 tons a day. Slate going on housing boom in the Midlands. Good for workmen to have their own homes at last.

Dinorwic been badly affected by three-year fight between owners and workmen over pay. The Independent Labour Party has been organising there. Three lockouts already this year, a quarryman said. Owners brought in own workforce from Liverpool, leading to fights.

Evan blames socialism, saying it's nothing but love of money. But the ILP has already doubled the men's pay at Dinorwic to 3s. 9d. a shift – not much set against £736,000 profits made there last year. The time has come for socialism now. Keir Hardie making a lot of noise and winning support in the valleys. In an odd way the Revival is preparing the ground. Evan is giving the men a new apocalyptic vision which they are going to express – politically. Independent Labour Party's newsletter says Tommy Evans has started another new group in Pontypridd with thirty-four members turning up to the first meeting.

184

Hardie is a Christian, of course. He too talks of the priesthood of all mankind.

* * *

The Revival had known some very noisy moments but the renewed publicity after the MIRACLE AT DINOWRIC – as the Press called it – began to make life all but impossible for the evangelical group. They returned to the valleys of South Wales, again travelling from one freezing mining town to the next, while confronting the most hysterical crowds ever.

Visitors were now journeying from all parts of the world to hear the 'wonder preacher' and his 'new amazing singer'. The police had to set up crush barriers around the chapels and even the Taibach wailers returned – much to Annie's amusement, since she was forever mimicking their weird wails. W.T. Stead also returned after a long absence, ransacking every dusty corner of his adjectival attic to describe Annie's voice: 'There is now no need for an organ in these meetings,' he wrote in the *Daily Chronicle*. 'In the thousand sorrowing voices is an organ of its own – all rejoicing in the sacred psalmody of their native hills. But even if all these voices were mute there is now one woman's voice in the meeting which could halt an army. This small woman has the voice of a nightingale and the face of Bouguerau's Madonna. Her singing is reminiscent of Christ's suffering in the garden. Her song depicts the triumphant progress of Christ and the rout of his enemies. Her name is Annie Davies and her voice will sweep the world.'

One day Stead even added further to the general madness by turning up and parading about the place in a prison uniform.

'What's the matter with him?' Beth asked Dan. 'Usually he's just boasting about everything, but now he's got that silly uniform on, with arrows all over it, and – even with Annie teasing him – he still won't say what it's all about.'

'Oh, he's getting old now,' Dan said. 'He's had some tremendous fights in his time but they've taken it out of him.'

'What fights were those?'

'He exposed a number of scandals when he was editor of the *Pall Mall Gazette*. There was the Dilke divorce and things to do with the Navy and slum clearance, as I remember. But it was his exposure of child prostitution that made his name. Back in 1885 it was. He bought a young girl for £5 and exposed the people selling her.'

'Oh did he now? That's interesting. What happened after that?'

'There was a trial at the Old Bailey and he was sent to prison for six months. That's why he dresses up in convict uniform now and then. Some sort of defiance, it is. But he never wore convict uniform in prison – but don't let him hear you telling anyone that. He was in Holloway as a first-class misdemeanant – even had his family visiting him there. But you won't say anything, will you?'

'How do *you* know then – if it's all so secret?'

'It's not a secret. But you've got to leave a tired old man his illusions. That's all he's got left now and he's got a right to them. All that publicity and the trial were too much for him.'

The hysterical crowds and constant publicity began exhausting and irritating Evan. He could see no holiness wherever he looked, just curiosity. He could sense no prayer – just a lot of empty noise. He was faced with what Dan had called show business. He began resenting Annie and what she had done to the work, going cold whenever she came near him and increasingly relying on Beth to comfort him. He also began shunning Stead altogether.

Beth could not understand any of it; Evan's growing reliance on her least of all. They were all in Treherbert one night and it was Beth's turn to wash up the dishes after the evening meal.

'Ah there you are, Beth,' Evan said, opening the door and coming into the kitchen. 'I was wondering where you had got to. I thought you'd vanished off the face of the earth.'

'Just washing the dishes, Evan.'

'Let me help you then.'

'Don't be silly, Evan. Go and put your feet up. It will be a tiring meeting tonight.'

'Come on now.' He grabbed the dishcloth out of Beth's hand and a tug-of-war ensued between them – the one snatching it away and the other snatching it back. Evan won in the end and held up the cloth, triumphant.

'Right. Where do I start then?'

'When was the last time you washed a dish, Evan?'

'Just show me where you put them, will you? I want to know everything you know.'

'That's not much,' Beth replied. 'You could write what I know on the back of a spanner.'

'Serious now, Beth. I want us both to spend more time together. We sing together in the meetings so we should wash dishes together. I can relax with you. I like your calm.'

'Look, Evan. Give me that cloth back, will you? What if I went and told all those reporters that the great Evan Roberts was washing dishes?'

'Tell them. See if I care. Washing the dishes is as important a part of the fabric of life as praise or prayer. They go on here, do they? Good. See. I'm getting the hang of it already. If we are going to do this work we must live together, pray together and wash dishes together. And in future, when we meet, we must always greet one another with a holy kiss.'

Beth lifted a saucepan up out of the soapy water, slow. She did not look up and neither did she say anything.

* * *

The Jerusalem Chapel in Treherbert was packed full that night. After Evan took off his topcoat, he sat on a chair behind the lectern and prayed. Despite frequent pleas from the congregation his private prayer lasted a full half hour.

'People have come to see the man and not the master,' a voice shouted.

Evan rose to his feet, his face pale and trembling at the jibe. 'One might think you have come from the North Pole but, even if you had just passed Calvary, you would still be colder than you are. You have been expecting me to rise for some time but I could not. There are three spirits in this meeting – the spirit of God, the spirit of man and the spirit of evil.'

He stood looking around him, understanding that he had lost his congregation and there would be no conversions tonight. His fist pounded the pulpit in anger. 'There is too much curiosity with you. You have just come to see what you have read about in the newspapers. When did you last pray? When did you last thank God for the food you eat?'

He continued scanning the surly, faintly scared faces. 'But what can I do? What can any of us do?' His oratorical imagination had sunk completely and it was because of these increasingly lengthy silences that the Press would soon come to dub him The Silent Evangelist. Even when Annie tried to break up the mood with a hymn he told her to stop. He put his topcoat back on again. 'This meeting is at an end. We must all go now. Pray, my people. Pray for yourselves and your lost souls. And remember that the Lord said that he would send the fire next time.'

The ladies followed him, uncertain, as he charged out of the chapel, only to find him waiting for them out in the road. He then marched off, waving people away as the ladies scuttled along behind him. Beth was sick with the anxiety of it all. Oh Michael, where are you? Why don't you take me out into the peace and quiet of your sands? Here all was lament

187

and disturbance and she'd had enough.

'The Ides of March, Evan Roberts,' a reedy voice shrieked out of the darkness. Beth turned. Oh no! It was that old man with black spectacles again. 'Beware the Ides of March for then you all fall. You and all your harlots, Evan Roberts. All of you fall in March.'

Evan stopped and turned around, visibly frightened by the old man's words. 'Take no notice of him,' Beth said holding onto his arm. 'He's been around before, has that one. If I'm not mistaken it was the same man who tried to twist my arm off once. Mad as a hatter he is.'

'You never told me about that, Beth. You should always tell me when anyone tries to injure you. If they injure you then they injure me also.' He put his arm around her and they all moved off up the road again. 'I just do not know what I would do without all you ladies. You are my only comfort in these evil times.'

'Everything all right, Evan?' Annie had moved up on Evan's other side. 'You don't want to get upset by that old fool.'

'You be sure to tell me about any injury at all, you hear, Beth? I just don't know what I'd do without you. Sometimes I get frightened you will all betray me just as the Lord was betrayed.'

'Don't talk such nonsense.'

Beth pretended that one of her laces had come undone and stooped down, leaving Annie to walk on up the street with Evan. She was playing around with her laces, wishing that Michael was around, when Evan came back. 'Where's Dan?' he barked. 'Go and get Dan.'

Alarmed by the unfamiliar shrillness of his tone the two ladies turned as if on marching drill. It was Priscilla who said, 'I'll find him' and hurried off in the direction of the chapel.

Small groups of people were standing on the pavements watching Evan as he strode round and round in the middle of the road in small tight circles, waving his arms about, furious. 'How can I preach when there is so much unbelief? That chapel was full of sin. Where's Dan? Idle curiosity. That is all we're getting in the meetings now – not the faithful or the searchers but the merely curious. I refuse to expose you ladies to . . .'

'You wanted me, Evan?' It was Dan.

'Where are we all staying tonight?' It was more of a shout than a question. 'I want to have a private meeting just with us. We must talk things out.'

'I told you this afternoon, Evan. I explained then. We're all in separate houses tonight.'

'Separate houses!'

'There was nothing else to be done. I tried but failed. You're with the minister and the ladies are scattered all over the town.'

'All over the town! We are all going home then. Right now. I told you. I said this place is run by the children of Satan. I have told you again and again, Dan. I need to have the ladies near me. I want them near me all the time. Not some of the time, Dan. *All* of the time.'

'It couldn't be helped, Evan. I told the deacons and they said they would try. There is a hotel in the town but it's booked full.'

'Booked full!' He choked on the words as if having heart seizure. 'Booked full!' He began circling around again, his hand slapping against his cheek hard. 'Booked full by the brewers no doubt. It is those vermin who need to be burned out of the land. Big money. It's the big money of the brewers that's behind all this. They are all out to get us. And Whitehall too. Those politicians would love to stop the Revival. Now they are trying to keep my ladies away from me. They know my ladies are my only protection, so the politicians and brewers have got together to try and split us up. Can we get back to Loughor tonight?'

'Impossible, Evan. Not at this time of night.'

'The chapel, then. We will all sleep together in the chapel. No. We will not. Not in that house of devils. A plague of boils on that house, a plague of boils and a swarm of . . . '

'Come on now, Evan.' Beth stepped forward and took one of his gesticulating hands. 'You're getting overwrought. Let me take you to the minister's house.'

'I do not want to go to his house. I want to stay with you.'

'We'll fix something, Evan,' Beth said.

His anger went away as sudden as it had arrived and Beth led him away up the road as meek as a lamb, leaving the rest of the ladies looking at one another, worried.

* * *

Yet the next day, Evan was his former self again, a picture of confident chirpiness with his tension gone. He even suggested, as they travelled the Bedwas road, that they should all go to a Music Hall one day, if only to see the nature of the frivolity they were fighting. Beth knew it was one of his little jokes but, in truth, she would have loved to have gone to a Music Hall, if only to hear the sound of laughter again.

However, such levity was to become exceptional now. Throughout the whole of January the meetings lost their lustre, with Evan indulging in longer and longer silences in the pulpit. The Press, including Stead, again lost interest in the Silent Evangelist and drifted away. Only Annie sometimes managed to salvage a meeting with a well-judged solo.

Beth felt oppressed by her role as Evan's main support, but responded dutifully, seeing no way out of it. She succoured him as she might have a patient in hospital, bringing him tea, learning when to praise him, when to stay away from him and how to judge his mercurial moods.

Her other main problem that winter was her cold feet, which seemed to get even colder when she got into bed. She resorted to trying the old trick of telling herself that her feet were not cold at all ten times, but that did not work either. It all might have been just about bearable if there had been some sunshine, but instead there were always those driving, chilly winds and, if it was not raining, falls of snow followed by slush. You just could not appreciate the gleaming white beauty of snow on the valleys when you were ankle-deep in the slush, with your feet as cold as a pair of ice-lollies.

Harsh winters were a bit like being pregnant, she decided. You started to believe that they were never going to come to an end. It was, they were told in the newspaper, the worst winter for years.

One night in Cilfynydd she sat down in her room after the service was over and wrote Michael a letter. The letter was the longest she had ever written and, in it, she told him of her fears for Evan and how, sometimes, she feared for herself too. She also explained that she was having doubts – yes, doubts – about the work and she wondered if she would be able to last out much longer. She told him that she missed him bad, but was careful to underline that she did not want him to come to any of the services. She had to sort her own way through all this, on her own, in her own time.

On the first night of February they had all been booked into the Bridge Hotel in Pontypridd. On the walk back there, after yet another lack-lustre meeting, Priscilla told Beth that she sometimes thought that converting people needed all the hard work of pulling out a foal that was lying backwards. She had attended one such birth; it had lasted nearly all night and, what with all the hot water that had to be carried in, she had never felt so tired. 'I'd like to live on a farm when all this is over,' she added. 'Lambing time is best.'

'Do you think it will ever be over?' Beth asked. 'The work, I mean.'

'Well it can't last for ever, can it? You know, Evan has started to look so tired. Have you noticed the lines on his face? There's a great strain in that face. I only wish he'd sleep more.'

'He always says he doesn't need sleep.'

They stopped at a chip shop and, although not hungry herself, Beth waited inside for Priscilla to get hers, turning away and smirking as

Priscilla bullied the owner into getting the chips right. 'None of that mushy stuff now, you hear?'

A child with a runny nose and wide appealing eyes was standing in the corner of the shop beneath the counter. 'Bit late for you, little lad,' Beth said to him. He stuffed his thumb into his mouth and turned his back on her. The heels on his shoes were scuffed flat and there were cuts and dirt where there should have been socks. She felt a distinct urge to pick him up and carry him back to the hotel for a good feed and wash. She often felt such urges when she saw street urchins and had to fight hard to control them.

'Have you noticed how Dan never complains about anything?' Beth said as they walked up the road, the picture of the little mite's face still in her mind. 'He has all that organising to do and has to run all over the place to try and get us all together in one house for the night. But never do you hear him complain.'

'He believes in the work,' Priscilla said, holding a chip up to her mouth.

'Mmm. I do wonder about that sometimes.'

'Dan! He's as solid as a rock. Do you believe in the work, Beth? I do sometimes look at you and wonder. I don't know. It often seems your mind is a million miles away.'

Beth picked out a chip for herself and took a bite out of it. 'Truth to tell, Scill, I'm worried. It's Annie really. I'm pretty sure Evan blames her for what's gone wrong. She turned us round and, in the end, we got lost. Annie can be terribly funny but strong characters always upset things. There was a nurse like Annie in our hospital. She never seemed to do anything, but her personality was so big she got the whole of the ward revolving around her. We're not even a group any more. That's what Annie has done for us.'

'Are you going to finish that chip or wave it around in the air all night?'

* * *

When they arrived back at the Bridge Hotel they found Evan and the rest of the ladies already seated in the foyer, taking a late cup of tea together. Beth saw that he was overcome with fatigue and clearly in need of a long rest; the strain of the work had taken away the lovely laugh lines from around his mouth. His legs were straight out in front of him and resting on their heels and his eyes were staring blank – at nothing.

A maid cleared away the teacups and they sat waiting for Evan to say the final evening prayer before retiring to their rooms. But he still just gazed straight ahead, as if in a trance. Priscilla coughed to remind him that they were all still there and Lavinia glared at her in reproof. Annie just sat quite still, back erect and her palms resting on her lap. Maggie was crocheting yet another shawl, while Lavinia and Pat just looked at Evan, as ever ready to move at his slightest whim. Now Beth too began to cough. She was beginning to resent the imperious manner in which Evan was treating them.

Evan reached down to the floor next to his chair and picked up a newspaper. He opened it and glanced at the headlines. 'War, death, disaster,' he complained out loud. 'War, death, disaster,' he repeated, leaning forward and spreading the opened newspaper out on the floor in front of him. Beth gave Priscilla an anxious glance as he knelt down on the newspaper as if it was an Eastern prayer mat, head bowed and forehead touching the ground. Maggie even stopped her crocheting.

He remained in prayer for a full five minutes, then stood up and sat back on the chair again. His eyes were closed and tears were streaming down his cheeks. Beth moved behind him and put both her hands on his shoulders, kneading them, soothing.

'There is so much suffering in the world,' he said, taking hold of one of Beth's wrists. 'There is so much suffering everywhere and I am the universal axis of pain. So much suffering and so little that can be done about it. Wars on the earth and weeping in the heavens. That's why there is so much rain. It's God grieving for the sins of his children.'

He rubbed his cheek against the side of Beth's arm. 'God has chosen me to shoulder this burden in the same way that Jesus took the full force of human sin when he was on the cross . . . '

He began sobbing again, hands still clutching Beth's wrists and eyes open as he ran his wet parted lips up and down the length of her forearm. Something inside Beth turned over and she looked away covering her disgust.

* * *

The next day was cold and the wind blew hard as they travelled across the valley to Hirwaun. None of them referred to the strange episode of the previous night, though Beth watched Evan carefully, ever the nurse keeping an eye on a patient who had suffered a relapse. Once again he had shrugged off his strange manner and was affability itself.

This good humour vanished immediate he mounted the pulpit that night. There was an obstacle in the meeting, he complained. There were wolves in the sheep's clothing who were trying to put an obstacle in his way. After requesting a hymn he retired from view.

When the hymn had finished he returned and said that two people in the congregation were not at peace with one another. 'What can be done? Pray. Make peace my friends. I am as sure that you are here as I am that I am standing in this pulpit. Oh bend them, Oh Lord. Oh speak to them.' He was sobbing as he put on his topcoat. 'This service should be guided by love. I must go out.'

There was an outbreak of loud prayer and protest when a man shouted, 'I know who they are, and chapel officials too.'

'It is between brothers,' Evan said, buttoning his coat. 'It is too painful. How can the Holy Spirit work when this is going on between brothers? If you are honest you will rise and say so. God wishes you to rise and say so. If you do not there is a terrible time waiting for you. Are you here tonight?'

'I don't know,' said the same voice in the congregation.

'It is between natural brothers. God will not accept praise from us until all this is cleared up.'

A short silence followed when a man on the deacon's seat – *sêt fawr* – rose. 'It is true, Evan Roberts. I have fallen out with my brother but now forgive him.'

Another man stood up. 'That is correct. We have not spoken to one another for ten years but I accept his forgiveness and now forgive him myself.'

They both walked over to one another, smiling and holding out their arms wide, and fell into an embrace.

'That's the way,' Evan shouted. 'The Holy Spirit is with us. Now let's have a real meeting. We will begin with *Great God of Countless Wonders*.'

The hymn was sung with sweet, gusting rapture and Beth had an attack of the shivers of old, singing in a way she had not sung for some time. In that one hymn the whole thrust and meaning of the Revival returned. Annie was her former driving, dominant self too, leading the ladies to ever greater heights which were met, both in range and power, by the congregation.

They sang the hymn again and again until, in a lull, a woman lifted her arms and spoke in a spout of tongues. Evan lashed out in tongues and, quite soon, the whole building was vibrating with crescendos of glossolalia.

* * *

The next night in a packed meeting in Treherbert the Holy Spirit seemed to be working with power again. The ladies were singing *Hark the Glad Sound* when the words just vanished out of Beth's mouth. She had spotted Michael sitting in the second row of pews from the front, examining his fingernails. The second row! Oh no. Embarrassment throttled her stiff. How could he do that?

Evan stopped the hymn. 'It makes all the difference in the world to be at the foot and under the foot of The Cross. But as sure as I am in this pulpit there is someone here mocking and that is the reason why I shall stop this meeting now. May I make an appeal to you who mock? Why come here and attack our character? Why not stay at home or in the tavern rather than come here to take away our character? All we have is our character. We are all the poor sons of miners here. We have no land. We have no money. We have no large homes. Yet we are proud of our religious character so why come here and mock it?'

Beth swallowed. The chapel may have been packed but, as far as she was concerned, there were only three people there that night – Evan, Michael and herself. It was a triangle and, although she had no explanation for it, she was certain that she was at its apex and there was a sense in which both Evan and Michael were competing for her favours.

She looked back at one and forward at the other. If Evan was referring to Michael he was not looking at him. If Michael was aware that he was upsetting Evan he was not showing it. Oh foof! She wished the dais would open up and swallow her.

Evan closed his eyes in silent prayer and, after some five minutes, the congregation struck up *Railroad to Glory* but he stopped them with a wave of his arms. 'No, no, no. Where is the one who smiled, if not laughed, when the young ladies were singing? No. It does not help if you sing *Railroad to Glory*. It will *not* be acceptable. We have to deal with this person who has come to break our character. But what a foolish, what a mad thing it is for a creature to rise up against The Creator . . . as blindly mad and utterly foolish as if a man were to go and throw himself in front of an express train in order to stop it.'

Beth could not bring herself to look at either of them. The faces of the congregation were bewildered and even sullen at Evan's arraignment. He began talking again and punching the pulpit and Annie stood up to sing, almost as if making an effort to save him from his mounting bad temper. The rest of the ladies joined in, hesitant, and this time, Evan gave way, but, no sooner had the hymn finished, he was full of dark accusation again.

'In the region of lost souls all will be lost. Remember the Lord's promise of the fire the next time. But I have a message. It is a terrible message – so terrible that I can hardly open my lips to utter it. There . . . there is a lost soul here. There is someone here who has been wilfully disobedient to the promptings of the Holy Spirit. Oh forgive, Lord. Forgive.' He strode down from the pulpit and walked halfway up the aisle where he sunk down on one knee and raised a hand. 'Oh dear. Oh dear. It is too late. This soul has gone beyond redemption. Too late, too late, too late.'

Many in the congregation began wailing openly as others also slumped to their knees. 'Forgive us, dear Jesus.'

'Praise you, Lord.'

'All too late,' Evan called out in his grief. 'Oh ye dark clouds permit a life-giving shower to fall.'

The prayers became louder. 'I have told you. It is too late for prayer. Even now the ashes of the lost soul are being scattered over the face of hell.'

Beth looked at Michael again. He was still sitting there expressionless, arms folded and head cocked to one side as if listening to a very boring lecture. Why was he trying to humiliate her in this way? He caught her look and winked. She felt quite faint. She would. She would kill him when she got her hands on him.

Evan hurried back to the pulpit and tried to speak but the words were garbled and turned into soft croaks. When he stopped croaking he tried to speak again, but failed. He chopped at the side of his neck with his hand. Suddenly his whole body stiffened and spread-eagled over the pulpit, convulsed. Screams came from the congregation when his mouth began to froth with bloodstained saliva. His fingers were quivering. The eyes were wide open and bulging, as if in deep terror at what they were beholding.

Chapter Seventeen

Jenko flung open his bedroom curtains and screwed up his eyes as the bright glare of the sunshine bored into the barren bleakness of his hangover. The winter had taken a day off at last, and a gang of starlings were staging their annual general meeting on the window ledge. On the other side of the road he saw that Gladys Ellis was busy stoning her doorstep. She spent most of her life stoning that doorstep and, judging by the skinniness of both the woman and her doorstep, they did not have much longer to go.

Why, his housekeeper wanted to know as he played with his egg at the breakfast table, did he insist on wearing the same pair of dirty socks when he had a whole drawer full of clean ones? When was he going to change his shirt? Why didn't he do this? Why didn't he do that? He humphed and mumbled but said nothing coherent. Whenever she opened her mouth he was careful to keep his closed: living with her would have been useless to the point of tuberculosis, without a sense of strategy.

When she got going she was as mindless and noisy as those starlings on his window ledge; in fact, he reflected, he far preferred it when she was praying all the time. God had to listen to her lunatic ravings then. He would go and visit Michael that morning, he decided. He could stand no more of this woman.

As he strolled through the town he saw that the sun had brought the women out on to the garden walls, where they were luxuriating deep in gossip. He always used to wonder what they spoke about until the time he listened in. As far as he could see, they just repeated, with different inflexions and random degrees of venom, what the other speaker had said. 'Getting better is he?' 'He's getting better.' 'Fancy that. Him getting better like that.' 'I told you he was getting better.' 'When did they say he was getting better then?' 'Started getting better last week.' 'Go on with you. Fancy him getting better like that.'

He brought his morning newspaper and browsed through it as he walked along the marsh road. The same old rubbish. A Cardiff man had printed a new pamphlet 'How to tell the time by the stars to the fifth of a second every night for ever and ever'. Only a tosser from Cardiff could have come up with something like that.

There was so much rain in the streets of London the horses were having to learn how to swim. Get away. Arthur Balfour had pushed through the second reading of the Licensing Bill. Poor old Arthur. The poor man's poor man. He was about as lost a cause as this King Berty of ours. As a prime minister he had spent his days paddling around in pools of philosophic doubt, but had finally blocked up the leaks in his mind to defend the Licensing Bill. That was going to cost him the chapel vote for sure, though Jenko had a clear feeling in his water that the chapel was on the run at last, since there was a report here that Evan Roberts had been having convulsions. Jenko snorted with derision when he read it. They were saying that it was the work of the Holy Spirit, but he knew better. This convulsion was the clear work of a bash on the head he had once treated Evan for, following an explosion down the pit. Well at least the storm clouds were massing and the Revival would not be lasting much longer. Now the convulsions were coming regular, the Revival would probably not last days, let alone weeks or years. They come faster and faster once they start. And you don't stop them with a cup of cold water drunk from the other side of the cup with your fingers in your ears, like the hiccups. There was a paragraph in the report that said the congregations were suffering from convulsions too. That was consistent anyway. Not for nothing did those wise old birds, the Romans, have a law which stated that if anyone should be seized by a convulsion during a meeting of the Comitia then the assembly was dissolved immediately. Convulsions, as the Romans saw, were a matter of temperament and propagated by sympathy.

He folded up his newspaper and put it under his arm. As if there wasn't enough madness about the place nearly a quarter of patients in Denbigh asylum were now religious cases, someone had told him.

The sun was still pounding down on his hat and even making a few dribbles of sweat fall down the inside of his leg when got to Pen-clawdd. There, on the seafront, he passed a large pinafored woman who was adding considerable lustre to her day by knocking the stuffing out of a little urchin. When she had stopped trying to twist his ear off she caught him with a fair old right hook and, not content with that, proceeded to stamp on one of his bare feet.

Jenko had long noted that they were good at incest and violence in Pen-clawdd. It must have had something to do with a crowd of Italians who once settled here. Mediterranean men had a most interesting range of perversions, in his experience, and little brightened their lives so much as giving their spouses a good hammering. He'd visited Naples once and all the locals did was fight morning, noon and night: even the babies were at it. It vastly improved their sex life, he suspected but, whatever the reason, there were many men in Pen-clawdd who took quite a dizzy pleasure in slamming their fists into their wives' mouths – especially after closing time on Friday nights when the cobbled streets were alive to the sounds of screams, slaps and breaking bones.

In their turn the wives took it out on the children and the children took it out on the cats. Being a cat in Pen-clawdd really was a fate worse than death.

A small woman, who would have even beaten his housekeeper in an ugliness contest, was standing in her doorway next to Michael's cottage.

'The slugs are prancing again,' she babbled. 'I told him next door. I told him to come in and see to them but all he wants to do is stay out on the sands all the time. There's slugs, snails, worms. All of them are dancing, they are, and making a terrible racket and he won't do nothing about them he won't. Not a thing. How can you sleep with all that eh?'

'Try earplugs.'

'Madder than him you are. Where can I get earplugs from?' She looked up and down the road before scuttling towards him as if about to impart a deep secret. 'He's training those cockles of his now. He's trying to get them to ambush me in bed. Got to lock my bedroom door every night, I have.'

'Must go,' Jenko said, hurrying to push open Michael's door and walk inside. It's little wonder Michael wanted to stay out on the sands if his neighbours were all as barmy as that. Jenko would have moved the house out on to the sands as well – and lived upstairs when the tide came in.

The living room was deserted but there was something different and almost wrong with the place. He had remembered it as being dusty with the curtains always drawn; the flagstones littered with dirty clothes and cockleshells; the smell of cat piss everywhere and a gang of goslings nestling in the coal scuttle. But the curtains had been taken down, the cleaned windows were revealing unexpected views and the furniture polished, mirror-like. There was no sign of a single lame animal – or their smells – and he walked out into the kitchen, where a woman with her back to him was boiling curtains on the stove. So he had gone and got himself a woman at last, had he? Jenko cleared his throat and the woman turned around.

She was not a tall woman but she made up for her lack of height with a large billowing bosom – pneumatic miracles in themselves – and big, full hips. Her hair was a wild barbed-wire mountain of red curls and, as she looked at him, a wicked smirk was breaking up her face and showing a slightly gummy set of teeth. Even with her wart and the splaying crow's feet around her eyes, he could see that the girl had lost none of her old magic.

'Well, look what the cat's dragged in,' he said. 'Megan Williams. Megan the Measles is back.'

'Jenko,' she squealed. 'It's sexy old Jenko.' She not so much walked as bounded at him, flinging her arms around his neck with her nose sniffing around his face in the style of a dog weighing up a possible mate. He just stood stock still, speechless for a change.

'So how are you, you old rascal? Still as sexy as ever I see. Oooh, I could rip your clothes off right here I could. Here and now.'

He continued staring ahead and she continued sniffing him, so he stuck out his tongue and gave her a whopping wet lick right up over her chin, along her nose and across her forehead.

'*Ach y fi,*' she said, stepping back and wiping off the trail of saliva with the palm of her hand. 'You're not supposed to do that, you dummy. You're supposed to sniff me back. That's the way you play it. I don't want all your germs.'

'There's nothing at all wrong with my germs. They've been brought up proper, have my germs. It's those other men you kiss you want to watch out for. Did you know there's two million microbes exchanged in every kiss? Did you know that, girl?'

'Can't get over it. Sexy and clever too. Come here. Let's have a good cuddle.'

'Well think of those microbes next time you go kissing the boys,' he said, stepping sideways as she tried to grab him again. 'Think not of the kiss or the stirring of the loins, but all those millions of microbes running and jumping about.'

'That was always your trouble,' she said, cornering him and getting her arms around his neck again, but keeping her head tilted well back for fear of receiving yet another lick. 'There's no romance in that black old soul of yours. When normal men tremble with passion you just think of microbes.'

She jammed her crutch against his leg hard, as her hand moved down and stroked his belly in small circles. 'When did you last feel the flames in there then?'

'Every time I have a stiff drink. And don't poke fun at my belly. Cost me a lot of money, that did.'

'Jenko, you could have me free any time.' She was about to start sniffing him again but was driven off by his protruding tongue.

'If you want to do something useful you can get me a drink,' he said, taking her arms off his shoulders and backing into the living room. 'So when did you turn up?'

'We've got tea.'

'Never touch the stuff. Got anything stronger, have you?'

'I'll have a look.'

'When did you turn up?'

'Yesterday. Day before yesterday actually. I've had some trouble with my husband so I thought I'd come home and look after brother Michael for a bit. He always needs looking after, that one. This place was a regular pigsty. I'll have a look for your drink.'

He took off his cape and sat down on an armchair. She hadn't changed at all. That one never would. She had a quality – rare and coveted in women – and that was pure sex, which she exploited ruthless. They used to call her Measles since almost any man foolish enough to expose himself to her voracious sexuality in bed fell in love with it and her. She took away all resistance and her terrifying skill in ripping open hearts had passed into the folklore of the Gower. Bill Pryce, the local butcher, never went near another woman after she had finished with him, and this house did well for meat while that was going on. He still got drunk every time he saw Michael.

Then that Tudwal Jones rained so many red roses on the house while *that* affair was going on, it was generally assumed that he had gone bankrupt because of it. She usually managed to dig out the ones with money but they were soon given their marching orders when it was all gone. Much like her father, all she ever left behind her was emotional debris and it had to be said that she enjoyed every wreck and every wounding, almost as if, in reality, she hated men and was waging a one-woman war of revenge.

It was rumoured that all the women in the village went on a celebratory outing to the Mumbles the day she finally got married and went off to Asia with some luckless rubber planter. Jenko had no way of telling what they would make of her return, since Megan spelt trouble. A thoroughbred Scorpio, she was war-like and quick to draw blood, viewing life not as something to be lived from day to day but to be waged as a military campaign, and never so happy as when hatching plots which involved a definite advantage to herself. Jenko liked her a lot.

'I can do you a small drop of brandy,' she said, walking into the living room and holding up a bottle containing an extremely small drop of brandy.

'That'll do,' he grunted. 'Don't suppose you've had time to make any of those scones of yours, have you?' Apart from her knee-trembling body he also remembered that she was an extremely good cook, scones and cockle pie being her great specialities.

'Jenko, you know I'd do anything for you,' she said, putting the brandy down on the table and crawling on her hands and knees towards him. 'Just a word. Just a sign and I'll climb Everest backwards for you, swim the Atlantic underwater.'

'I'll settle for that drop of brandy.'

'Men!' she said, crawling between his knees and showering little kisses on his folded hands. There was a whiff of musk in those massing red curls of hers and there was also a whiff of activity in his own hormone factory. There was still plenty of lead left in his pencil. If an ugly woman had behaved in this way she would have been clapped into irons in a wink but, somehow, this one always seemed to get away with it.

'Give us that drop of brandy, will you?'

'Men! You offer them your love, your body, your very life and what do they ask for?' She prodded him between his legs and began warbling to his fly buttons. 'A bloody drop of brandy,' she whispered soft. 'Isn't there anything in this old worm then? Eh? Any life there at all?'

He could feel his old worm inflating and, just then, Michael walked into the room, holding a sack in his hand. It was not what was going on but what *seemed* to be going on that worried Jenko. His black eyes bulged out like chapel coat pegs as he looked at Michael and down at Megan's head between his knees. He held out his hands wide in mock innocence and, although he had long thought he was actually incapable of it, blushed. 'Can't you do anything about this woman?' he blustered. 'I've been here for five minutes and she's trying to get my pants off already.'

'Put him down, Meg, will you? He's an old man.'

She stood up, smoothing her dress down with her hands, her lips pouting as she raked her fingers through her curls. 'I like old men,' she said, turning and giving Jenko the eye. 'Old men know what they're doing. Experience, see?'

'She's getting worse, not better,' Michael said. 'The baker called this morning and she all but ate him on the doorstep. You're a menace to the peace, girl. Go and make us a cup of tea.'

'He wants that drop of brandy.'

'Well, give it to him, then.'

She winked at Jenko and flounced out into the kitchen where all was clatter and bang.

'I don't know where she gets all her energy from,' Jenko said. 'With her everything is one long rampage.'

'Oh I know that one,' Michael said sitting down. 'She'll go charging around for a week then she'll collapse and go to bed for a week. Nothing by halves with her.'

Jenko noticed that he was still holding on to the sack and that there was a lot of movement inside it.

'She's been home for a couple of days,' Michael continued. 'All my animals have been shut out into the yard – even the cats. She's got everything cleaned and dusted – she was even dusting me this morning and everything is in the wash. She would organise the eggs inside my chickens if she got a chance. She says she's come back to look after me but, at this rate, I'm going to be dead with it all. Even the horse is sulking and the cats are too afraid to come in the house for their food.'

'You know I can't stand dirt,' she shouted from the kitchen. 'Nor all those animals of yours.'

'Those cats have got to come back indoors. It's too cold for them out in the shed.'

'Not in this house they're not. I'm not having them doing their dirties all over the floor.'

Michael looked at Jenko. 'See what I mean? One minute it's that peaceable and now I'm living with a hurricane.'

'What brings her back here?'

'She got fed up with her husband she says. Says he kept grinding his teeth in bed.'

'Mmm. So busy grinding his teeth he wasn't grinding her, no doubt.'

The clatter in the kitchen stopped and she walked back into the living room doorway, one hand on her hip and the other on the door. 'Jenko, he didn't have a good one in him. It got so bad I was falling asleep in the middle of it. I'd been fed up with him for ages and one morning I woke and just sat up in bed watching him snoring and grinding his teeth. All his hair fell out last year as well and, what with his piggish drinking habits and his friends who didn't have a good one between the lot of them, I asked myself what was I doing living with a bald, drunken pig who grinds his teeth in bed all the time. So I said to myself, I said "Meg girl this is no life for you. Get on home and look after your brother for a bit". So, boy, here I be and here I'm staying.'

She returned to the kitchen where all was clatter again. 'It's the cats I feel sorry for,' said Michael. 'They can't put up with her bullying ways. Meg's only happy when she's bullying someone. It's no wonder her husband's hair fell out.'

'What have you got in that sack?' Jenko asked, noticing the

movements again. 'You're not keeping your cats in there are you? Planning on drowning them to put them out of their misery like?'

'I've made myself a bit of money this morning. I've been planning this one for a bit. About a month ago I dumped a bag of offal in a rock crater which only appears twice in the spring tides – then and today.' He opened the neck of the sack and peered down into it. 'This lot feed on offal and, glory be, they were all stranded in the crater this morning.'

'All what were stranded?'

His eyes sparkled mischievous. 'All these, Jenko.'

Jenko smelled naughtiness immediate but was hardly prepared for what happened next. Michael took the bottom of the sack, stood up, began shaking it out over the flagstones and down they tumbled – a shining, smelling, leaping bundle of crabs and lobsters, all still wet with the sea and another with slivers of ragwort and seaweed hanging off them; the lobsters looking around with whiskers waving and claws dying for something to nip and the crabs zooming everywhere; a few disappearing under the chair and one even beginning to climb up Michael's trousers. A few eels and a couple of flatfish were also bouncing up and down in the mess, while the crabs kept on dashing to corners to find a place to hide.

'For God's sake, man,' Jenko said, climbing up on his armchair. 'For God's sake. Put them away.'

'Meg, Meg,' Michael shouted as he danced around among them. 'They've all escaped. What do I do, girl? What do I do?'

She walked back into the room, held the top of her curls with both hands and screamed blue murder.

'Don't just stand there yelling. Do something. They've all escaped.'

'Yaaaaaaaah!'

'Do something, girl.'

She jumped up on the table. 'Yaaaaaaaaaah!'

'Look there's one in the grate.'

She jumped off the table, ran out into the kitchen and came back brandishing a large broom. 'You lot are going out into the garden with the rest of them.' Michael began picking them up and dropping them into his sack but she was whooshing them out into the yard in clawing bundles. 'Out, out, out. Out of this house.'

'Watch it now girl. That big red crab is worth threepence to me. You'll be breaking him.'

'It's your head I'll be breaking if you mess up my floor again.'

'Look. You've broken one of its beautiful claws. Crabs have got feelings, too, you know. Poor little dab. Getting your claw broken like that.'

'Out, out, out.'

'Do you think,' Jenko asked final, still standing on the armchair. 'Do you think we could go down to the tavern and have a little drink? It should be open by now.'

* * *

Jenko's hands only stopped shaking after his second pint down in the Pen-clawdd tavern, and it was only when Megan went over to the bar to flirt with a few of the local boys that Michael said that he had found out all about Beth. Jenko said nothing.

'I went to one of the services again the other night,' Michael went on. 'It was bad enough before but now it's beyond. I didn't speak to her but the girl looks so fed up. I'm sure she doesn't know what to do next. Jenko, I just wish there was something *I* could do. I've got myself a new plan. Selling cockles at Revival meetings. What do you think? I know it sounds a bit mad but . . . '

'A bit mad! Whoever heard of selling cockles at Revival meetings? All that lot want is the Holy Ghost – not your cockles.'

'I've got to be near her, Jenko. Sometimes I go and see that Dan Roberts – he's a good socialist, you know – but this plan gives me an excuse to be around all the time – and make some money while I'm at it.'

'You've been out on the sands too long. The wind's blown away what's left of your brain.'

'I've got to be near her.'

'You're a fool, that's what you are.' His tone was serious. 'In matters of women you know nothing. No one ever got anyone by hanging around and being *near* her. So much piffle, that is. You've got to become an object of the love and not the lover. Have you asked Megan what she thinks about it all?'

'Yes and I'm afraid she told me.'

'Megan can be loud and even vulgar but there was never a greater warrior in the sex war. She'd know what to do with Beth. Just look at her now. She'd have all those boys at the bar crawling around on all fours if she wanted to.'

Michael sipped his pint, saying: 'The trouble with Beth is she's not some young kid working in a match factory or even an ordinary woman. She's a complicated woman who's had a baby so all the normal rules don't apply. I know how to tantalise a woman, make them jealous, play up the old wounds – all of our family have been good at that but, with Beth, nothing applies. She's gone off the boil. Doesn't know what to do with herself. Doesn't trust her feelings. I couldn't even start telling you what the baby has done for her. She told me once she gets scared that people can tell she's had a baby just by looking into her eyes!'

It was Jenko's turn to be silent. He lit a cigarette, coughing a tiny storm of smoke and ash over the table. 'You know what that girl's got?' he said after a bit.

'What's that?'

'Courage. More courage than the whole British army. When I was first called to see her the nipples had swollen up and the baby already on the move. *Everyone* around here gets married in that condition but not Beth Williams. "Never," she said. "I'll never marry that man." She not only said it, she also meant it which, again, is unusual to say the least in this part of the world. I went through the options with her and they were all nastier than the one before. I knew an abortionist in Swansea but wouldn't have trusted a pregnant marsh pony with that Polish butcher, and she really would have been safer going straight to the knacker's yard.'

He finished his pint and had another good cough over his cigarette. 'I could have given her some hickory-pickery pills for a miscarriage but the pregnancy was too far advanced for that to work. Her other option was even worse but common enough in the Gower. She could kill the baby straight after it was born by pushing two fingers down its throat. No one would ever be able to tell if the baby had just stopped breathing and, what is more, no one would care. As long as the bastard was got rid of everyone would have been as happy as the day is long – well the chapel would have been happy, which is the important thing. After I had gone through it all with her I thought she would go for marriage for certain but not that one. For a few weeks I was getting as desperate as her parents, waiting for her to relent, but she stood against all of us, defiant. In the end I took her to Cardiff. The rest, you say, you know.'

'Aye.'

'But don't go worrying about her joining Bobo's gang. It can't last, not now the convulsions have started. The only thing Bobo is going to get out of life now is a death certificate. The Revival is moving to a close.'

Megan carried over a tray of foaming pints, which she announced were all on the house. 'Don't let me stop you, Jenko,' she added rolling her eyes around in mock awe. 'It's always good to hear a man who knows something. All my drunken bald husband knew was how to fall over.'

Others joined the group; Jenko was much heartened to see that, just like the days of old, he had an audience who would lavish on him their attention and free pints. His audience were revival renegades too, only too happy to hear Jenko's ranting lambasting.

'When history comes to be written,' he pontificated, 'this Revival will be written of as the silliest. At least some of the other leaders had something to say, which is more than you can say about Bobo. This boy makes no sense at all. There's no doctrine, no system, no distinctive ideal. There is nothing of a colossal nature. Reason has been deposed and emotion handed its crown and sceptre. In the end this outbreak could well prove the final and noisy death rattle of non-conformity. That's what we're hearing now. The death rattle of the chapel.'

'Tell me something, Jenko,' said Megan leaning forward. 'Are you any good at spelling, are you?'

* * *

Late the following night Jenko was rolling home from the Lewis Arms in Loughor. He was feeling unusually cheerful: his housekeeper had taken off that morning for her annual two-week holiday with her sister in Milford. Two weeks without her and all those prayers was an unbelievably brightening prospect.

He was trundling homewards down the cobbled slope, humming and pondering on Herbert Spencer's latest riddle about Lord Acton when he passed the caped, silver-buttoned shape of the town policeman. Once he too had been a happy soul; now, after the Revival, he was morose to the point of toothache. There was simply nothing for him to do.

'Evening, Eddy,' Jenko said. 'Arrested any dead horses lately?'

'Very funny I don't think. Very funny indeed.'

The policeman continued his melancholy circuit and Jenko continued walking into a night, which began to spit with rain. If there was one thing worse than Loughor in the sunshine, he decided, it was Loughor in the rain. A worm of a place, it was, with a worm of a name and packed with wormy people. Even the sheep looked fed up with the town. He hated Loughor sheep. He always insisted on eating lamb chops in the wild hope of eating the bastard who kept knocking over his dustbin.

Careful to ensure that the policeman had gone, Jenko stopped under the yew tree for a quiet piss. At that time of night and at that distance from home he always stopped under that yew tree for a piss. It was the habit of a lifetime, just as others picked their noses or went to chapel on Sundays.

He opened his front door and his good humour evaporated when he saw a light in the kitchen and smelled cooking. So the old bag had not gone to Milford after all. But it was not like her to be cooking at this time of night – she was normally in bed studying Psalms. He opened the kitchen door to find that the table had been set for two; a bottle of wine stood in the middle. Homemade by the look of it, he decided, and quince by the smell of it. That was not the old bag's handiwork for definite: the only drug she was interested in was bicarbonate to make the tea taste stronger. There were various pots cooking on the range with the aroma of something beautiful baking gliding through the other smells. The sounds of splashes were coming out of the cold room and he opened the door, quiet, to behold a spectacle as awesome and impressive as a mighty punch on the nose.

There in his tub, washing herself in the sapphire foam was Megan, as naked as the day she was born but far, far sexier. Her shoulders and chin were sunk in the bubbling foam, her nipples riding about on the frothing tide like a pair of one-eyed jellyfish. 'Having fun, are you?' he asked.

'Hello, Jenko. Fed up, I was, so I though I'd come over and cook you a meal. You don't mind, do you? Me having the bath and all. Michael's bath is so small I get terrible cramps in it.'

He didn't mind in the slightest. She was not a young girl any longer – about thirty-eight now, he guessed – but, apart from her thick wrists, that was one big package of womanhood sitting there in his tub.

'Help yourself. And make sure to wash behind your ears.'

'Made you cockle pie, I have. Pinched the cockles out of Michael's boiler this morning. Pinched his wine too, come to that. I decided you could do with some feeding up. Looking a bit frayed to me you are. I'll be finished in a bit.'

He closed the door and took off his cape before sitting down and sampling the wine. It had the harshness of a slightly high-class vinegar but there was real bite in it, which sort of smacked against the inside of his left ear. When he'd finished the glass he poured out another. She came out of the cold room final with a towel wrapped around her, which revealed so much he did not know why she bothered with it at all.

'I like cooking and eating,' she said, ruffling his hair with her hand. 'That Michael won't eat anything. Just mopes about the place all the time. I got it out of him in the end. He told me all about the Beth girl. Sorry business, that. Made my knees go quite watery when he told me.'

'He told you all, did he?'

'Mmm. I think he did, anyway. Here, have another drink. Leave it now. I'll pour it for you. Men never know how to pour wine. You've got to hold the glass up like this, see? We ought to do something for Michael, you know. I don't like seeing my own brother like that.'

'We?'

'You know what I mean. Sort of interfere like. Nothing too obvious. Sort of subtle like . . . help things along a bit. Men who mope around after women are not men.'

'What do you suggest?'

'I've thought of a few things but let's eat first.'

Usually his housekeeper left him out a sandwich with curly corners for supper, if he was hungry he might expect cold bits of the leftovers from dinner. But Megan produced a steaming cockle pie out of the oven, followed by a plate of sprouts, boiled potatoes and a boat bubbling with thick, rich gravy. The very sight of it all made belly juices begin crumping like the sound of distant cannon and, lifting knife and fork, he tackled the banquet with greedy gusto. 'How did you know my housekeeper was going away?' he asked, his mouth full of pie.

'You told me yesterday in the pub. Going to Milford or somewhere, isn't she? I decided you needed fattening up in the right places. You do remember asking me to come over, don't you?'

'Of course.' He didn't remember inviting her anywhere. His memory must be falling apart by the second – whenever he sat and surveyed his life all he ever saw these days were great gaping holes inside even greater gaping holes.

He enjoyed watching her eat, though; she was as enthusiastic about that as she was about everything else. This one could turn cleaning her teeth into a triumphant opera. She still had dots of foam in her red wet curls with the eyes of her jellyfish half-peeping over the top of the towel. He wondered if . . . steady down now. Steady. She picked a stray cockle off her chin, popped it into her mouth and smiled at him through her chews.

'Do you ever leave it up to a man to decide what *he* wants?' he asked with genuine curiosity.

'Never. Men never know what they want. Never do. Have another drink. It'll help wash down the pie. Michael made it. He's good at wine but trouble is he keeps diving into it all the time. He says it's a poultice for all his pain. Stupid boy. Should have been a poet you know. There's too much feeling in him. He just can't control it. Poultice for pain. I ask you. It's a poultice for his brain he could do with.'

'I always tell him to drink more.'

'You would.' She refilled his glass. 'You know, Jenko, I've been asking some questions around the place about this Beth girl but no one seems to know much about her. I'd like to help Michael. You understand that, don't you?'

He shovelled in another slice of pie and now the quince began smacking against his right ear. It had the kick of a maddened pit pony. 'Sisters like to help brothers, I understand that. That's understandable enough. What's difficult about understanding that?'

'Jenko. You're getting drunk.'

'What've you put in this wine?' His vision swam.

'Oooooooh look! Your eyelids are sagging too. Come on now. And there was me thinking you were a drinker!'

The muscles in his face had indeed gone funny – as had other more distant parts – and, more by instinct than good judgement, he threw down the remainder of the quince. Now the drink smacked against the insides of both his ears alternately, just like a tennis ball. His neck gave way beneath the weight of his head, the table punched him on the forehead and the next second there was a lurching darkness and he woke up in bed naked, a glow of contentment in the pit of his belly, a cosmic daze in his brain – and being lectured.

'Well I didn't think much of that and that's a fact,' she was saying. 'Come on now, Jenko. You can't fade out now. I haven't had it for a month and I hear you can do it much better than that. I've heard what you've been doing to Mrs Gloria Edwards next door to the Post Office.'

Even in his deep, dark drunken disorder that remark set off a distant and corroded alarm bell. How did she know about that? If she knew about his doings with Gloria Edwards, five minutes after she had come home, then how many others knew too? Was there anything at all this one didn't know? He wondered idly if there was any more of that amazing quince left when she took him off for another boat ride around the lighthouse.

He gurgled and wondered where she had learned all these tricks. They only knew the missionary position around here but Megan seemed to have more positions than the Kama Sutra. He stiffened and seemed to levitate a good foot above the bed. Oh he hoped his bastard back wasn't going to go again. That had happened often enough whenever he got carried away in bed. One second bliss and the next – snap! – agony without end and nights sleeping on cold floorboards.

Superstition: that's what the Revival was all about, he decided as his neck was bent against the wooden bedhead and his left leg was hoisted high in the air. Superstition operates as effectively in religion as elsewhere. The Welsh mind has always been enchanted by the mysterious and the incomprehensible; it is always engaged by tales of the weird and wonderful. The fall of a star is always an augury of disaster; walking under a ladder entails the immediate loss of your pension; cows always fall on their knees on Christmas Eve. Start telling them about the fairies and the Welsh will sit patient forever.

He could only guess at what she was doing to him now in the darkness but, whatever it was, he had no objection whatsoever as he continued spinning around on the axis of something very warm, very wet and very nice indeed.

Superstition was, of course, the blood and fibre of the Welsh. Take a handful of tall stories, throw in a few big words like 'therefore' and 'marmalade'; stir in a few references to the occult and you'll always get them to swallow the lot in one big gulp. For the same reason it was almost impossible to understand Welsh history since legend and fact had become inseparably intertwined; there was just no way of finding out where facts stopped and the fictions began. It was no accident that one of the most famous Welshmen of them all, Iolo Morgannwg, was a notorious liar and legendary faker.

Now her hands had a vice-like purchase on his ears, her ankles around his neck too though he had absolutely no idea where the rest of her body had got to. His back was holding up well under the strain, however, and she seemed to be happy enough.

He had read in the newspaper that morning that Lord Onslow was bringing in a Bill to provide for the protection of under-sized flat fish. Oh was he now? Jenko bet the quality of his dinner wine was improved no end when he thought that one up. So now who was going to protect us from the oversized Lord Onslow? That's what he wanted to know.

He could feel the pressures building up behind the breaking dam as she stretched out flush with him, with Great Western Railway pistons shafting away in her hips. How long is the tail of Haley's Comet? Now there's a . . . there's a . . . .the dam broke all over the land and he was clean out of thoughts religious, thoughts cosmic and thoughts political. After the dam broke he sank ever so gentle towards his bed, like a leaf riding quiet on a soft summer breeze.

'Oooooh Jenko that was good,' she purred. 'I knew old men were better at it. I just knew it.'

Chapter Eighteen

The convulsion was Evan Roberts' most electrifying *coup de theatre*. After a month of languishing in moody silences and fractious accusations, the Revival's services became buoyant with possibility again, hundreds announcing their conversions nightly to the waving of thousands of handkerchiefs. The Press, sensing a dramatic end to a dramatic winter, returned in droves. Even the Taibach wailers seemed to gain renewed heart from the convulsions and, as their thin screechings rose around Evan's twitching, prostrate form, the Press gorged itself on the spectacle.

Stead came back again too, ruining Beth's supper one night by grabbing hold of her and the other ladies one by one. Thereafter he also played his part in fuelling the extravagances of the hour. 'There are regions of the intellect where infinity and transcendent glories and terrors cannot be represented under the forms of logical understanding,' he wrote in the *Daily Chronicle*. 'It is there that those who are taught of the Spirit see divine visions and receive revelations of the Lord. Many religious leaders had visions. Saint Paul had his blinding heavenly visions, his ecstasies, his gift of tongues. The Bernards, the Loyolas, the Luthers, the Foxes and the Wesleys had visions, heard voices, experienced rapt conditions, guiding impressions and openings. They all sprang from an exalted sensibility. But this mercurial Welshman, Evan Roberts, with his polemics, visions and convulsions is perhaps the greatest in a great and noble line.'

'Not a bad report that,' said Dan, riffling through the newspaper one night in a minister's house in the Dowlais. 'Pity Stead copied most of it out of a book.'

News was pouring in from all parts of Britain of how the Revival had spread over the border . . . an outbreak of Salvationist joy in Hull; overwhelming excitement in Bristol; packed churches in Motherwell. The Bishop of Rochester convened a hundred and fifty clergymen who sang *Revive Thy Work, O Lord*. In Gloucester, marching Christians were attacked by mobs from the taverns, and more than two thousand attended a service in Bradford. Further awakenings swept Ireland and the Isle of Man.

Dan had even received reports that the work was taking root in parts of North India and Tibet. Daily he found himself turning away all kinds of visitors wanting to see Evan – even, one morning, the famous explorer Sir Francis Younghusband.

With such fame flourishing hourly and invitations to visit piling up from every part of the globe Beth, for one, could never understand why it was necessary to cross and recross the valleys, bringing the good news to the already converted. Again and again, they had been told that they were going to Cardiff but no dates were ever fixed.

'I've told him we've got to take Cardiff,' Dan said to Beth over tea. 'I've told him that a great work in a great land simply cannot ignore her greatest city. But he keeps saying he's not ready for the place. He keeps saying that the Holy Spirit has warned him to stay away and how can you quarrel with that? We've got two ministers from Cardiff coming to visit him tomorrow, but I'm not sure he'll see them. I think he's a bit scared of the place.'

'Scared of what?'

'Your guess, my girl, is as good as mine. I think he's got some idea the city's a stronghold of socialism, and you know how he feels about that.'

The disappointment burned inside her deep as she looked out over the Dowlais to the dark flaming forest of the ironworks. She barely understood the strange utterances and high passions swirling all around her, but she knew all about the pain inside her; knew why she was so keen to go to Cardiff, even if wild horses would never have dragged it out of her mouth.

She wanted to go to Cardiff because she had given birth to baby Rhion there; she wanted to go to that city since, for three weeks, she had lain in bed in the mornings with that precious scrap of flesh lying on her bosom, listening to her soft breathing and feeling those tiny flailing legs. She wanted to go down to Pier Head where the ladies wore gorgeous bustles and carried parasols before setting off for a day trip on the paddle steamers. She wanted to see the dockland gulls again and walk past the high elegant houses of Bute Street, where she had once pushed Rhion in a pram. She wanted to go back there because she longed – no, *ached* – to see her daughter again.

The girl would be nearly five now and some nights, in the dark, Beth heard her call out. Whenever she looked into any child's face she felt the inner and overwhelming surge of motherhood. Would those spots on her left cheek be gone? Would those milky blue eyes have changed to her own brown? It was too early for her to have started school.

The sound of a hooter droned out of the ironworks and she turned away from the window, looking at Dan sitting at a desk writing his diary.

Just next to the fire grate Maggie was reading her Bible while Annie was brushing Priscilla's hair. Beth sighed soft. She often envied the ladies' sense of peace; the contentment that accompanied a living faith. She rarely seemed to feel any peace at all and, even if she did, there was always Michael churning it all up. Why hadn't he spoken to her when he came last?

She picked up a magazine and walked over to one of the armchairs, staring down vacant as she flicked over the pages. She had promised never to go near Rhion again, but if they *all* went to Cardiff surely there would be no harm done if she walked near Rhion's home and tried to catch a glimpse of her, would there? She need not have a guilty conscience if she went there as part of the work. The bond between mother and daughter was simple and undeniable. She saw that now. She had tried to forget. Oh, she had tried hard enough to forget . . . tried and failed.

She dropped the magazine on the floor by the side of the armchair and stared around her, choking back yet another sigh. Annie stopped brushing Priscilla's hair. 'There's hot water out on the stove,' she said to Beth. 'Take it up and wash your hair. It'll make you feel better.'

* * *

The next morning was diamond-bright with warm sunshine and blue sky as Beth walked with Priscilla across the cwm. Workers in flat caps and carrying snap tins were streaming to the ironworks. Huge yellow tongues of gorse were lapping across the brown bracken of the slopes. The seductive smell of a wood fire drifted across to them. 'Look at it all,' Beth exclaimed, unusually cheerful. 'On such days you could sing forever.'

When they both returned to their base they found that the front door of the manse was locked. Priscilla knocked but there was no reply, even though they heard the distinct sounds of excited voices inside. Beth could hear Evan's voice raging above all; she looked at Priscilla, but the latter shrugged her shoulders and knocked again.

The door banged open, final, and a white-faced Dan strode out past them and down the street. He was followed by Lavinia, who was urging him to come back. The two ladies stepped inside the house, hesitant, and Priscilla went into the parlour. Beth peeped into the back room to find Annie sitting at a dining table, her fingers pulling around her cheeks in deep distress. 'What's going on?' Beth asked.

Annie looked up but said nothing, her eyes bloodshot with weeping.

Pat and Maggie were talking together out in the garden and Beth was about to go and see them when Priscilla came into the room. 'There's been a big attack on Evan in the *Western Mail*. He's livid about it.'

'What kind of attack?'

'Don't know. He's torn up the newspaper and scattered it all over the place. He's like some mad fox in a chicken run, he is, muttering about treachery, knives and all kinds of things. I've never seen him so angry.'

'He called me a strumpet,' Annie wailed. 'How could he? A strumpet! Me?'

'He's just upset,' Beth said. 'Men always say things they don't believe when they're upset.'

'But how could he say that to me? A strumpet! I didn't write the article. Anyone would think it was my fault, the way he's going on.'

'How about me making us all a cup of tea,' Beth offered. Then Evan began shouting again. 'Those Judas reporters!' and 'the greatest criminal in the pulpit today!' drifted through the walls.

Beth opened the door to see Evan striding around the room, tearing up a newspaper and throwing it into the air like so much confetti. The room did indeed have the look of a chicken run after the murderous fox had run away. The chair had been tipped over and the tablecloth lay on the floor. His back was to her and he was still in a dressing gown.

'Newspapers. Cold vivisectors, that's all they are. Always noting the husk and ignoring the divine radium. The strongholds of the devil, that's all they are. The club of harlots come here telling lies . . . ' He had finished shredding the newspaper and began tearing up the pages of a magazine. 'If they are not exaggerating they are telling outright lies. Why do they persist in referring to the fact I never wear a watch? What's so important about that? The ferrets of the irrelevant . . . the bloodhounds of the world's evil, that's all . . . '

He flung the ragged remainder of the magazine into the grate. 'All this is going to stop. There will be no more reporters. Evan Roberts wants no personal following. Evan Roberts is going to keep himself in the background in the future.'

'Let's go out for a bit 'til he calms down,' Pricilla whispered to Beth. 'Let's go to the shop and get a newspaper. Better find out what all the fuss is about.' She closed the door, quiet. In his anger Evan had not noticed the intrusion.

All the *Western Mails* had gone that morning but the newsagent said they could read his, providing that he got it straight back. They both stayed in the shop, flicking through the pages, but could not find anything in the headlines. 'It could not have been *that* big an attack,' Beth said as she went back to page two to look again.

'It be in the letters,' said the newsagent. 'The letters. Shameful, I call it.'

Beth found the long letter difficult to take in all at once, especially as Priscilla kept sighing and oohing as she pulled it away from Beth's hands. The headline read: *Blasphemous Travesty of the Real Thing.*

Why, the writer asked, did Evan Roberts become so bad-tempered when things did not go as he wished? 'The holy fires have been burning brightly at my church in the Dowlais long before the evangelist's revival. We have had hundreds of converts here. But by threats, complaints, convulsions and incantations, which remind me of the prophets of Baal, Evan Roberts and his team have stoked up a false fire . . . I have never experienced such agony . . . the whole procedure is sacrilegious. Yet it is the mock revival, this exhibition, this froth, this vain trumpery, which the visitors see and the newspapers report. It is harmful to the true revival – very harmful.'

The writer continued for another five paragraphs, ending up with: 'The chief figure of this mock revival is Evan Roberts, whose language is inconsistent with the character of anyone except that of a person endowed with the attributes of a Divine Being. Are there now four persons in the Godhead and is Evan Roberts the fourth?'

The letter was signed by a Rev. Peter Price, B.A. (Oxford), Congregational Minister in the Dowlais. 'B.A. indeed,' Priscilla spat. 'Bachelor of Asses more like.'

They were both silent as they walked back along the curving road to the manse. Evan's sensitivity was wafer-thin at the best of times and he was immobilised for hours if a stranger looked at him the wrong way. How was he going to cope with this full-scale public attack on him? By withdrawing from the world? Had the end really come at last? She was surprised to find that she could ponder on the prospect with so much relief.

They walked gingerly into the house, finding no one in the back room or out in the garden. A tiny ripple of laughter came from the parlour so Priscilla knocked, soft, on the door and opened it.

'Priscilla. Where have you been?' Evan asked, in a pleasant, almost diffident voice. 'Where's Beth?'

'She's here with me.'

'Well come in both. Come in.' They stepped inside to find the other ladies all seated in a semi-circle around Evan. 'Take a seat, Beth. Why don't you sit down here, Priscilla?' He had a bright wide smile on his lips and there was no sign of the torn-up newspapers and magazines.

'I was just telling the other ladies,' he said waving a letter around in the air. 'I was just telling them that this morning I had . . . in the post this morning there was this letter.' He stretched out his legs and gave one of his soft chuckles. 'How nice it is to have a sunny day after all that rain. I always think that God is smiling when it is a sunny day. When there is thunder, God is playing skittles. When it is raining he has pulled his bathplug out and when it is snowing he is sending down armies of fairies.'

He stopped speaking and looked at the letter in his hand. 'In the post this morning I had this letter from a milliner in Cardiff. And do you know what he wants, this milliner from Cardiff?' He paused and held up his chin, looking around at the ladies like a teacher waiting for a reply – but there was none. 'Well this milliner from Cardiff is willing to give each of you ladies a free wardrobe of your own if he can use your names in advertising. I always suspected there was no trade lower than that of a milliner's. Who could ever trust a man who just deals in ladies' hats? So what do you think I wrote and told him?'

The ladies had no idea so he put his thumbs into the sides of his waistcoat and began chuckling again. 'Milliners.' He wiped a tear out of the corner of his eye with the tip of his forefinger.

'I wrote and told him that Evan Roberts regrets that Evan Roberts cannot take up the offer of this milliner from Cardiff. God will provide all the wardrobes we need and more. This is the work of the Holy Spirit and not a fashion parade. We have no need for the advertisements of the brewers or the filthy lucre of the milliners. It would not be so bad if this milliner did not come from Cardiff. Next they will be offering us free organs or trips to London.'

His chuckling had by now all but overwhelmed him even if the ladies found nothing to chuckle about, and just sat looking at him with faces as long and characterless as pokers.

'I wouldn't mind a trip to London,' Priscilla said, final, if only to try and break up the atmosphere with a bit of humour.

'You know I've always fancied singing up to Nelson in Trafalgar Square,' said Annie, trying to help. 'You think he'd hear me all the way up there?'

Evan took no notice of the banter and leaned down between his knees, to flick his shoelaces with the backs of his fingers. He was clearly winding himself up again. 'Did I tell you the minister here has taught the congregation a new hymn special for our visit here tonight? We had better . . . milliners. Hah. Now who in his right mind would want to be a milliner in Cardiff? A milliner in the Shanghai of Wales! Tonight, yes tonight we are going to have a great meeting. You mark my words. There is going to be a tornado of love in this meeting tonight. Don't read the newspapers but look to your own hearts. Don't listen to the milliners or those who would seek to stab me.' He stood up with the muscles in his face twitching as he shrieked at the ladies. 'Love there will be. A whirling tornado of love which will blow those newspapers back into the pit where they belong. Yes. There will be a sudden gale of destruction.'

He stormed out of the room, slamming the door behind him. The ladies all sat silent with Annie dabbing the corners of her eyes with her handkerchief. 'I'm so worried about him,' she whiffled. 'He just can't keep going like this. It's too much for any man.'

'I'll make us all a nice cup of tea,' said Maggie, putting down her crocheting.

* * *

There was a trickle of dark and evil savagery in the Tabernacle Chapel that night. It lurked in the large group of reporters, come to see how Evan was going to react to the infamous letter. It was in the Taibach-wailers, strolling around outside in silence, it was in the largely mute congregation inside, devoid of prayer and praise, come in the expectation of the end. But, most of all, this trickle of something evil was in the failing, flickering lights of the chapel lamps; so many were standing on the gas pipes the gas was only getting through intermittent, making faces indistinct and shadowy, as if in a bioscope.

Evan himself was a picture of a man under a huge burden as he stood up in the pulpit and looked around. Beth felt a slight shiver when she remembered the young erect man that she had first met. Now his shoulders were stooped, his eyes the dull colour of stone with the hair greying at the edges. The young laugh lines had gone too; his once fine features drawn and pinched with blackened bags under his eyes. A life of experience and torment had poured through that body in just one winter. Beth looked down at her own hands. She was so looking forward to the spring.

'There's too many people in this gallery,' a voice shouted. 'It's not safe.'

Evan said nothing for several moments. Then he called back with some of his old bite and fire: 'Are you a man or a worm? How can you worry about such a thing in the house of God? If all the pillars fell down at this second God would hold you all in his hand if he wanted. If . . . Remember your Bible. God hung the world on nothing. Love God. Trust in him and you will lose your wretched fear.'

He stopped speaking and scanned the faces, line by shadowy line. But even in the trembling darkness he saw only the unconverted and unconvinced. He shook his head in sadness.

Then one of the gas pipes broke and everything was engulfed in darkness.

'Gas, gas,' voice shouted. 'Escaping gas.'

'Be calm, be still,' Evan called out. 'This is the darkness that was on the face of the deep. This is the work of the Holy Spirit which is calling you out of the deep. Remember the glory that comes after the struggle through the darkness.'

Evan could hear scuffling, the beginnings of panic. Annie and Beth began singing *Diadem*, with the other ladies joining in, hesitant, but even all the ladies' voices could not hold out against the rising tide of fear, the spreading cries of warning.

'Stop the hymn,' Evan ordered. 'The battle is fierce. We must take care of our bodies. Break some windows. Break all the windows.'

One was smashed, then another; the crisp music of shattering glass erupted from every corner of the chapel. Storm lamps were brought in on poles, their lights breaking up the darkness in swinging yellow arcs. Some people left, groping their way to the chapel door. But the majority, soothed by Evan, gradually resumed their seats and in a minute or two were silent and intent once more.

'Very good,' said Evan, as a night wind whistled soft in the broken windowpanes. 'I would rather pay for all the damage myself than have the usefulness of this service impeded. The Holy Spirit is with us tonight, and mightily too.'

Annie took up *Thanks to Him* and, after she had sung the first verse alone, the rest of the ladies flung their voices into the many-layered harmonies with the congregation laying down a blazing groundswell. W.T. Stead reported that he had never heard such moving verses, with Evan standing ramrod erect and clapping them along in his natural domain of the pulpit as the hundreds of sorrowing voices cut through the swaying half-light.

Here is the saviour of the damned
A physician for the feeble ones
Here is one who loves to forgive
The sinners with their serious faults
Thanks to Him
For always remembering the dust of the earth.

218

'Are you ready then? Are you ready for the final days when God will fulfil His promise and pour out His spirit all over the earth? It will be a shower such as the world has never seen, with the spirit pouring over all flesh and all servants and all handmaidens. In those final days the old men shall dream dreams and the young men see visions. Are you ready for that? Will you be ready to deliver yourself to Jesus' two hands and compassionate heart? Oh, please be ready, since the final days of Armageddon, when the Devil will devastate the earth, are on us. Be ready for the great counter-attack in the blazing brilliance of the Second Coming.'

He bent forward and kissed the Bible placed on the lectern in front of him. 'Please be ready for, when He comes, the judgements will start and the wrath of the lamb will be great. Are you ready for that? Are you ready for those final days when powerful men will be reduced to tears? Those days when hearts of stone will be broken? Those glorious hours when hardened sceptics will be frightened into belief?

'But first Satan's back must be broken again, just as it was once broken on the Cross. First there must be the universal repentance of contrite hearts and only then will the flame of God, who will never abandon you or leave you desolate, burn the length of the earth. Be ready, my people. Do not get caught unawares. I beg you, down on my knees and with the pain of the world in my heart, please, oh please, be ready.'

The congregation rose up to meet him, hands outstretched. His speech stopped, started, choked and broke into a babble of tongues. He raised his arms out sideways with limp wrists, as if crucified, a loving smile on his lips as they poured out a steam of incomprehensible prayer and rapture. He spoke like this for nearly ten minutes in the eerie yellow half-light of the lanterns, the others in the chapel joining in on occasion. Then his hand began chopping at the side of his neck again and there were shrieks as his body convulsed, eyes rolling upwards and mouth foaming as he toppled sideways down the pulpit stairs.

Beth was the first to hurry to him, cradling him in her arms, pressing a handkerchief into his mouth to stop him biting on his tongue. His eyes began blinking rapid and he shook his head. 'Leave me be,' he said. 'I'm fine.'

He stood up unaided and walked back into the pulpit, holding up his arms victorious and smiling one of his flashing smiles. 'That was one of the hardest ordeals I have ever experienced,' he said. 'Further testimony to Christ's agony in the garden.'

Reporters had recorded every word and movement. The congregation roared its astonished adoration.

* * *

The next morning everyone, except Evan, travelled in two drays across the valley to Neath. No amount of questions – especially from an increasingly vexed Priscilla – would get Dan to reveal what was going on. All he would say was that Evan had been taken ahead of them and was now staying in the house of Mr and Mrs Ray Rhys in Godre'r Coed.

When they arrived at the large redbrick house, overlooking a mine on one side and a vaulting series of brown crags on the other, there was a policeman outside and it was already besieged by 'friends', autograph-hunters and well wishers. But even after the ladies had been ushered into the spacious parlour with its three huge aspidistras, still no one would tell them what had happened. It was Beth who felt most distraught amidst all this uncertainty, not even bothering to take her cloak off, just sitting next to the fire, sighing constant and tying knots in her handkerchief. She could hear people move up and down the hallway and, after half an hour, a burly man with a pince-nez perched on top of a large, ruddy, unravelling nose came into the room. 'My name is Dr. Melvyn Hughes,' he explained simply. 'I have examined Evan Roberts thoroughly and told him that he must rest. He is suffering from nervous prostration and, if he doesn't rest, then I have told him I cannot be responsible for the consequences. He has asked me to request you to stay here until he has decided what to do.'

By teatime there was still no word from Evan, so Beth wrapped up and walked out alone over the crags, stooping low as high winds drove a lively procession of clouds over the valleys. At the top of one cranny she stopped and looked down on a golden ferret eating the entrails of a dead sheep. There were tiny globules of blood on the ferret's whiskers as it tore and pulled at the fleshy, pink-veined intestines but, as it fed, it showed no concern that it was being watched, wiping its whiskers with a paw and looking up at Beth for a second before returning to its business and biting into yet another piece of intestine. She was curiously intrigued by the ferret's lack of alarm and wished Michael had been there. He knew all about those kind of things.

A smattering of cold rain curtailed her walk and she hurried back down the crags and through the swelling crowd outside the house to learn that two Free Church ministers from Cardiff had already visited Evan and gone away again. Evan had told them that he did not intend going to Cardiff after all. Beth was devastated. It was not that he was feeling unwell but the Holy Spirit had forbidden him to go, Priscilla reported. He had continued praying for guidance, but the Voice had insisted that the Cardiff mission would not be divinely favoured. He could not, he had always insisted, go anywhere or do anything without specific advice from the Voice. The minister had even begged him to send the ladies, but he had turned that idea down also. Beth mimed the two words 'turned down' in disbelief. He what?

She had to work very hard to conceal the bitterness that was clogging inside her when Evan finally did come down to the parlour. If anything he looked worse now than the night before, full of sleep, moving woodenly and taking an age to sit down in the armchair. He was wearing a dressing gown with carpet slippers on his feet. There were bright bruises on his ankle – from his convulsed fall from the pulpit, Beth guessed. His once-lovely hands were shaking, too.

'I was taking a wash from the bowl when the Voice told me not to go to Cardiff,' he said picking his words with great care. 'I felt a great pressure all over my body and went down on my knees to pray for the salvation of souls everywhere.' He did not look at anyone direct as he spoke, and stretched his body rigid on occasion as if relieving a pain.

'The Voice said that the faith of the people was being proved as much as my own. Did I not sustain thee during the months of this winter in the sight of the world? The Voice then told me that I must keep a seven-day silence here and see visions of the last things.' He paused and held up a hand to stifle a small cough.

'I have already apologised to my hosts Mr and Mrs Ray Rhys,' he continued. 'They have agreed to leave me alone here in the house. I want the rest of the ladies and Dan to return to their own homes for the next seven days. I just want my faithful nurse, Beth, to stay here with me for fellowship and help in the hour of my need.'

A blush flushed on Beth's neck and she gazed hard at the fringed damask on the mantelpiece as the other ladies glanced at her, curious. Annie, in particular, showed her disappointment at being sent home. For herself Beth would have given anything to have been sent away, but what could she say? She could not walk out on a man in the 'hour of his need', particularly with the eyes of the world looking on this redbrick house in Neath.

* * *

Much later that night everyone had left the house except Evan and Beth, who were both sitting on leather horsehair chairs next to a fire in the parlour. Beth just sat staring into the crackling fire, her manner still frozen with disappointment, hands folded together on her lap. Evan was reading Isaiah in the Bible.

Your heart was proud because of your beauty; you corrupted your wisdom for the sake of your splendour.

Evan put the Bible to one side and went down on his knees in front of the fire. He closed his eyes and held his fingers, prayerful, to his lips. 'Woe is me,' Evan called out as he reached out for Beth's hand. 'Oh dear Lord, help me in the time of my destruction.'

He took Beth's hand and cried out in the purest fear as an avenging angel hovered overhead. Blood was dripping from its talons and all that could be heard was the mighty swish of its wings.

Then, letting go of Beth's hand he plunged both of his hands into the glowing coals, taking out a large fiery lump and holding it to his lips.

'No, Evan, no,' Beth screamed out, reaching towards him with imploring hands. 'Don't do this, Evan.'

But the hot coal did not hurt or injure his hands or lips in any way. 'You see my guilt is gone and my sins are forgiven,' he said, quiet, as he held out the coal towards her like a chalice. 'How stands your guilt, my beloved Beth?'

They were back on a hill looking out when the light began turning into darkness and the darkness began turning into light. There was no heat in the sun and no glow in the moon. Just the sounds of rebellion echoed throughout the land when a great dark chariot began forming in the sky. It came moving fast, driven by thunder and bigger than a mountain range, a huge whip cracking overhead and flashes of lightning darting out of the wheels. The chariot sent out huge circles of noise all around it and the very earth shook as if shivering in constant earthquake.

Everywhere the people of the world cried out in their terror. They ran for the shelter of their caves and dug feverishly into the ground with their bare hands. But there was no escape from the judgement of the chariot; its shadow fell over the fleeing and the hidden and, as darkness fell thick, the anguished screams of the tortured people mingled with the cries of hyenas and jackals.

'Our sign, Beth. Hold out your hand and take God's hand. Lost is lost, Beth. Gone is gone. But God will save you, my beloved. Saved is saved, Beth. Reach out for his hand now.'

Then the shadow of the chariot fell over the face of the world. No one escaped. Babies were battered. Homes were looted. Wives were raped. Men had been stabbed and such as had been left behind were lying on beds of maggots and wishing that they were dead. Moles crawled over the fallen silver idols. Columns of black smoke drifted up out of mountains running with blood. Down in the streets there were ravens.

'You cannot sleep, Beth. Not now. It's these visions. They are acid in my brain.'

'You're hurting me, Evan.'

'Please, Beth. Not now. I'm scared, you see. I don't understand anything. This acid. ACID, Beth. This fire in my mind. Please help me.'

'Evan, you're hurting me. I can't breathe.'

'But Beth. The Lord will renew all in the new creation. You see.'

A Japanese fan was nailed to the wall. A black marble clock stood in the middle of the damask on the mantelpiece. Just next to the grate was a pipe rack.

And when the shadow of the chariot had passed away the sun grew warm again and there was a glow in the moon. The people were revived with a sense of justice and put crowns of flowers on one another's heads. Their prophets could see again, the deaf could hear and the lame leapt around like deer. The ravens flew away and there were abundant crops in the singing deserts.

I am what I am. Behold, I am with you now. I will keep you and bring you back to this land. I will dry all tears. My victory will be final.

Chapter Nineteen

It was a Wednesday, with the weather still brimming over with malice and slander, when Jenko picked up his newspaper at the shop and went down to the Lewis Arms for his morning surgery.

Evan Roberts was now in the sixth day of his seven-day silence, he read, which at least meant that Jenko did not have to spoil his first pint by reading yet another turgid report about some turgid meeting in some valley town where the sheep and chapelgoers all had about the same sized brains. Better still, wonder of wonders, the letters pages contained yet more attacks on the Revival and The Silent Evangelist.

The Bishop of St. David's had picked up a tiny ecclesiastical hammer. 'Our attitude should be one of sympathy, watchfulness and prayer . . . we must guard against irreverence . . . and that abuse of feeling known as sensationalism. Another wrote, 'Our protest is against the dogma of an endless punishment since it violates our conception of a God of love.'

He put down the newspaper. Apart from four card players in the far corner of the tap room the pub was completely empty. He sniffed with a small whiff of self-pity. There just wasn't anyone at all to drink with any longer – unless you enjoyed playing cards all day which he did not. Even Megan had not been back to give him another ride around the lighthouse and, for some reason, his patients were not being very patient with him either. All he got were footling complaints from footling people. He picked up his newspaper. Chamberlain was sounding off again. There was another one. His prophecies were mostly lies and half his facts were fictions.

He finished his pint and was up at the bar about to buy another, when Harri Webb walked in, a mournful midget of a man with a black goatee beard and shoulders just a little shapelier than those of a conger eel. When he was not in bed Harri spent most of his time ratting and was doubtless making a return visit with a ricked back. What a palaver. Jenko had tried everything short of a medieval torture rack and now suspected that something to do with not enjoying a day's work was at the bottom of Harri's complaint – not a feeble spine. Shunning work and mindless gossip were both well-loved traditions around here.

Jenko returned to his seat and Harri followed, handing over the obligatory pint. 'Same thing, Jenko,' he sighed.

'Still playing you up then, Harri boy?'

'Aye. Just can't seem to straighten myself out. Even ordered a wonky coffin I have 'cos I'll break in two for sure if they lay out my corpse straight.'

'Well, there's only one thing for it now, Harri.' Jenko paused for dramatic effect, taking a deep sip from his pint. 'We've tried all the conventional methods so now you're going to have to move around on all fours for a week.'

Harri's furry eyebrows disappeared up behind his cap. 'Go 'round on what for what?'

'Walk around on your hands and feet, keeping the knees stiff for an hour at a time – four times a day and once in the middle of the night. It's a new cure from Berlin. The Berlin four-footed cure. Marvellous results as well.'

'Jenko, I can hardly manage to sit down in the shithouse let alone walk around on all fours.'

'Well it's either that or your wonky coffin, Harri boy. Did you ever hear of prehistoric man suffering from a bad back? Well, did you?'

'No-o-o-o-o.'

'Did you ever hear of a caveman suffering from appendicitis or neuralgia or dropsy? You ever read anything about them suffering from any of these silly modern diseases?'

'Can't say I have.'

'And why do you think that is, Harri? Eh?'

'You're the doctor, Jenko.'

'Because they spent all their time on all fours, that's why. Try it out for a week and see what happens.'

'Couldn't you just give me a good bottle instead?'

'It'll work, Harri. Friskier than a newborn lamb you'll be at the end of it. Do wonders for the circulation, too.'

'I'll give it a try then. You want paying or will the pint be enough? These cures from Berlin must come expensive.'

'I'll settle for the pint for now. We'll talk about pay next week.'

There was another lull in the surgery and he managed to finish Harri's pint in peaceful reflection. He was bored silly with being a doctor, he had to admit, and some of his suggested cures were getting more flippant by the day. Only last week Keith James had come to his surgery with as rampant a collection of crabs as he had ever seen. He had warned him often enough about patronising those Swansea knocking shops.

'Very easy cure for this,' Jenko told him. 'You just get a bottle of gin and three cups of sand and then you rub sand and gin into the pubic hairs.'

'What use is that?'

'Well the crabs get drunk and stone one another to death.'

Keith did not think that was very funny at all and, come to that, he had not seen him since. As if he cared. His idea of a good general practice was to have one colossal rich patient who suffered periodic from 'flu. His treatment for 'flu was brutal, fast and one hundred per cent effective. Every 'flu germ within a mile radius died though, to be honest, it did not leave the patient with too much bounce either.

He looked up and something old and long forgotten stirred inside as a woman walked towards him with a pint in her hand. There was still real character in that exquisite face and these liquid brown eyes. The hair had gone into tight grey curls and there were wrinkles on her face but Mary Williams still had a serenity about her, still had that female something that reached out to the male.

'Hello Enoch,' she said, putting the pint down in front of him. 'I expect you could do with this.'

'Mary. How are you, woman? Sit down.'

He had once, when young, walked out with her and it was just possible that, because of her, he had spent the rest of his life having a love affair with alcohol. Seeing her marry another man had been one of the great disappointments of his life and even today, when all the passions had been largely spent, he could still not look at her without feeling that old stirring inside. With her cynicism would have been difficult; without her it became inevitable.

'I'm worried about my Beth,' she said. 'At my wits' end I am, Enoch. She's come back home and I was wondering if you would come over and have a look at her.'

He nodded. Apart from never addressing him as Jenko – which even the local children called him – she was unfailingly polite to the point of formality with him. She acted as if they had never so much as held hands all those years ago.

'What's the matter with her?' he asked.

'Come home she has and shut herself away in her bedroom. Just can't understand it. Came home two days ago and shut herself in. Her father even tried to drag her out but she wouldn't budge. You know what she's like when she decides she's not going to do something. Won't speak, won't eat. Oh Enoch, I don't know what to do. Just don't know.'

He patted her on the hand. 'She's left Bobo, has she?'

'She must have done. She was supposed to be with him in Neath but left sudden. Won't talk about anything. I thought . . . I hoped you might have a few suggestions. She's always liked you, Enoch. You helped her when others would have turned their backs. She might talk to you, might tell you what's wrong.'

'I'll have to see her.'

'When can you come?'

'What about him?' It was childish but, even after all these years, he could not bring himself to speak her husband's name.

'Well, amazing as it may seem, it was him who suggested that I get in touch with you. He couldn't do it himself but he's that worried . . . he . . . you know . . . after what he said to you as well. But it's not for him I'm asking. It's for me. And Beth.'

'Any clues what's the matter?'

'None. She's been in her bedroom for two days now. Not a word, not a smile, nothing. She's in a worse state than when she came back from Cardiff all that time ago and we all know that she suffered enough then. I hate seeing her suffer, Enoch. That girl's done nothing but suffer. She thought the chapel would help but it didn't, did it?'

'Anything to do with the old business would you say?'

'I just can't tell. I used to be able to talk to her about anything but, since Evan Roberts came along, we haven't been able to talk about anything important. You might understand what's happened, Enoch. You're not the greatest doctor in the world but you always had a good understanding. You will see her?'

'One condition.'

'What condition's that?'

'You'll let me buy you a stiff drink first. You seem in a worse mess than that messed up daughter of yours.'

'Doctor's orders is it?'

'Aye. You could call it that.'

* * *

Bert Williams was polite but not exactly delighted to see Jenko again, ushering him into the front parlour and making him take a seat while staying standing himself. Jenko had long noted that small men were always looking for such psychological advantages. Mary offered to make a pot of tea but Jenko held up his hands in horror. He believed that part of the chapel's success lay in the fact that they had put the word around that there was no tea to be had in hell.

'We thought you might be able to help Beth,' he said, stiff, addressing the wall. 'Her mother and me are sick with worry about her and, if there is anything you can do, then, of course, we are . . . ' The pomposity drained out of his voice and his tone changed. 'I'm sorry about what I said to you that day. These are changing times and we've all been too hasty in our judgements. You've always been a good friend to the family. It's nothing personal you see. It's just that you are an unconventional man and we are a conventional family. The conventional always have difficult understanding the unconventional, don't you think?'

Jenko shrugged his shoulders. 'I've my own conventions also,' he pointed out. 'It's just that they're different from others. But I'm not upset by what you said if that's what you're thinking.'

There was a momentary look of blankness on his face. 'Tell me one thing, Jenko. Do you think we should have allowed Beth to keep the baby?'

He shrugged again. 'You knew what I thought at the time. Nothing I've seen or heard since has suggested that I was wrong. Mothers need to keep their babies.'

'Mmm. I can see how a man like you would think like that.' There was no critical edge in his words. 'I have often thought that a man who never worries about what anyone else thinks is a blessed man indeed. But I do worry. There is always the chapel, you see, and had we allowed Beth to keep her baby, it would have meant moving from the area. We couldn't allow her to go on her own. I've got a good job at the colliery, the home here, the relatives. It would have been too great a wrench for everyone.'

Jenko steepled the fingertips of his left hand against those of his right. Why Mary had married this man became a greater mystery with every word he spoke. A flight into the respectable, perhaps? Women are forever falling in love with men who are difficult and dangerous but invariably end up marrying the merely reliable. They got the boredom they at heart wanted, he supposed. 'I had better go up and see Beth,' he said final.

'If there's anything you need you've only to . . . '

'I'll have to look at her first.'

* * *

He had little idea what he was going to say to the girl when he walked into the bedroom. After one look at her, he was not convinced that he should say anything at all. She appeared to be asleep so he sat down on the side of the bed. Her hair was thick with neglect and her hands curled up together on the pillow in front of her. The cheeks had hollowed out slightly too – through not eating, he guessed – but he could see from the faint tremors in her eyelashes that she was not asleep and decided to sit it out until she wanted to confront him.

He passed his hand over her eyes but, apart from a lot of flickering, they still did not open. He took her wrist and held it for a while. The pulse was down slightly and he felt around the side of the neck but found no glandular swelling. He sat back waiting for a little spark of old knowledge to come flashing up. It was a rare day indeed if you managed to make an accurate diagnosis on such obscure states of shock which all this listlessness suggested. He had seen enough of that in the Crimea, when men had come staggering back from the front hardly knowing the year let alone the time of day. The medical profession had no really effective antidotes for shock either, except for liberal doses of laudanum, the passage of time and a lot of rest. It was that wise old bird Hippocrates, wasn't it, who said that healing was as much a matter of time as opportunity? The real question here was what had brought on the shock?

She moved her head and looked up at him. There was no recognition in her eyes nor any mobility in her features, but she did continue to stare at him.

'I've come to have a chat with you,' he said. 'I'm told you're not feeling well. You want to talk about it?'

She swallowed but her silence was as stony as her stare. He rubbed the tip of his tongue around the front of his teeth wondering what you talk about with someone who does not want to talk. Her hand picked a strand of hair off her forehead and let it fall again. He remembered that her mother had the habit of doing that. 'What's the trouble, Beth?'

She shook her head and swallowed again. 'I don't know. It all seems . . . just don't know. Can't make any sense of anything. You ever feel like that, do you?'

'About three times a day. And that's before breakfast. What happened?'

'It's all so pointless. Everything's pointless. I just want to die.'

Coming from a girl so beautiful, her words were so shocking he wanted to roar with rage but said nothing. The Lord only knows he had heard people say things like that often enough and, in many cases, death would have been a merciful release. But from Beth, a woman with everything to live for, it was almost a criminal offence punishable by a good flogging. He decided to go for the raw nerve. 'Is any of this to do with Evan Roberts?'

She closed her eyes and gave a sort of stifled sob as she turned her body over. 'I'm tired now. I think I'd like to have a sleep.'

'Are you sure there's nothing you want to tell me? You *can* tell me. You know that.' She shook her head. 'Do you want me to call back again?'

She opened her eyes and looked along the length of the pillow, only to close them again. 'I don't know. If you like.'

'I'll call again soon.'

'Only if you like. It doesn't matter if you don't.'

That night Jenko was deep in gloom. He did not even bother to go to the Lewis Arms, electing instead to sit with a decanter of port in front of the fire. He could not shake off thoughts of Beth as he sat there, twiddling his thumbs and gazing into the glowing coals. Sometimes he came up with something if he worried about a problem long enough but, in this case, there was an almost total lack of information to worry about.

If she was in shock then something had shocked her and if Evan Roberts was at the bottom of it – which he was reasonably certain was the case – he could hardly go over to Neath, interrupt this deafening Seven-Day Silence and ask him out straight. Even if such an excursion were possible he would never get a decent answer: just a load of ranting mumbo-jumbo which would contain every species of rubbish except a decent answer. He sighed and refilled his glass. It was the way of the world these days. Muddle-headed prophets were multiplying everywhere like mayfly in permanent hatch.

The other possibility that kept coming to him was to call on the daft cockle-picker to see if he could come up with something. He had once watched Michael stir up a half-dead horse with his chuckling act so, if he could do that with a half-dead horse, what could he do with a merely silent girl?

But Beth's best bet, he decided, was to get on a train and get the hell out of it. Twice now she had broken down bad and, that being so, she clearly needed to get away from the pressures that reduced her to a crumpled paper bag with such ease. Most places had their own brands of hypocrisy and humbug but none quite so well cooked as around here. It took great strength of mind to stand against this ebbing tide of sense and flooding tide of madness.

His thoughts were still circling the issue when there was a knock on the door. That's all he needed. Halfway through a decanter of port and some sledgehammer about to have a baby or falling foul of the Grim

Reaper. He was busy trying to hide the decanter behind his armchair when his housekeeper showed in Megan and he was surprised at how happy he was to see her.

She took off her coat, explaining that she had been down to the tavern looking for him and had got worried when she found that his chair was empty. There was no particular reason for her visit though she fancied a drop of whatever it was he had in that decanter. Michael was being that irritable so she thought she would come over here. 'Those men in Penclawdd are so dull,' she moaned with real feeling.

'They are all dull around here, girl. There's more drips in this part of the world than there are in the Cheddar Gorge. Here, have some port.'

They sat and worked through the port decanter together, chatting about this and that. Jenko was careful not to mention Beth; did not even say that she had come home. The last time they had discussed Beth's problem Megan had come up with a variety of solutions, each more absurd than the last. Her most absurd suggestion was that Michael simply went over to her house and raped her.

'Women really like firm, violent action,' she claimed. Well you do at least, Jenko had thought.

But, tonight, there was no talk of Beth or Michael and he merely settled back, telling her things in the way that old men do. Yet, even as he spoke, she pleased him mighty, always making him laugh with her funny little quips, forever touching him and rubbing up against his knee like some affection-starved cat. He liked all that. His body might have gone to seed, with bits falling off everywhere, but it still responded to being brushed and touched.

Midnight came and went. The port decanter was long finished and, in the absence of anything else to drink, Megan blew out the lamp and soon had him gargling on a hot cup of carnal delight.

Later in the contented darkness she said, 'Beth's back home. Heard, have you?'

His toes curled up tight. He should have known better. This one ran a better intelligence operation than the British army. When he did not reply she elbowed him and said, 'She's home you know.'

'Oh is she?' he said vague.

'You know damn well she is, Jenko. The way I see it is that we've got to get her baby back for her.'

* * *

231

Beth left us in a mystery, Dan wrote in his diary. *She even left without taking her trunk. Evan refused to speak of her, even to tell us why she had gone. Priscilla left too so now the rest of us have been waiting on Evan. Sitting around and drinking tea. The average national consumption of tea is six pounds a year but we all must be drinking far more than that. Everyone misses Beth. Her departure is a symbol of impending change. We know that the end cannot be far away.*

The Taibach wailers came back this morning at 11.35 – ten of them they were – and just stood at the end of the garden looking up at the house. Can't seem to think of anything to wail about. But we can.

To make matter worse the Babylonish Stead turned up unexpectedly too, talking in his usual muddled and shapeless way. He wore yellow tweed trousers and a yellow cap, prompting Annie to say he looked like a daffodil. Evan would not see him so he insisted on speaking to me. I have never liked him. He tells too many lies. He also quotes from books like William James' Varieties of Religious Experience *and pretends the words are his own.*

This afternoon Stead went over to Merthyr to interview Keir Hardie, the colourful member for the unemployed. 'The House is still without a labour group but it is coming,' Hardie told Stead which he put in The Daily Chronicle. *'Like most prophets, Hardie is somewhat difficult to get on with,' Stead also wrote.*

There are 40,000 unemployed men in London and five million throughout the country, Hardie also told Stead. Hardie wants to set up a register for the unemployed, local distress centres, the expansion of public works, shortening of working hours and possible experiments in the colonies.

Chapter Twenty

Spring soon began bustling into the Gower with all the grandeur of a coronation procession, bejewelled with sunshine, trumpeting enthralling promises of warmth and ordering a hard, bitter winter to stand to one side.

Down on the edge of Peter Taylor's farm there was the first taste and smell of honeysuckle. Blackbirds were busy building their summer homes in the hedgerows. In the shade of their tangled roots, purple patches of crocus and yellow puffs of primrose grew shy. In the woods there were carpets of bluebells and the golden yellow trumpets of the daffodils stretched upwards in an avid embrace with the sun.

Out on the sands, a white haze hung in the cloudless sky as Michael worked a bank down near Llanrhidian. The life of the cockler had been tough indeed that winter. The high tides had swept away the cocklers' carts only the week before, while the freezing seas had so thinned out the cockle beds it was a rare tide indeed that yielded as much as one sack. Those starving oystercatchers did not help matters, either. This scarcity meant that the price of cockles was high, fetching up to three pence a pint in Swansea market. A few of the cocklers had thrown in their rakes and gone to look for work up in London.

Michael raked along the side of a line of air holes and thought of Beth. Had there been a moment that cruel winter when he had not? She was screwed right down inside him like a permanent bout of 'flu. Some days were worse than others but, even on the better days, she was there stealing his thoughts greedy and, when he dreamed, he always dreamed of her. All was flight, anxiety and confusion in his dreams though. When he woke, he could not get out on to the sands fast enough – even in freezing fog.

There was no escape from her on the sands, mind. He sometimes believed that the push of the wind against his back was the gentle insistent push of her hand and often caught himself gazing out over the marsh hoping that she would come walking towards him. Her spirit was everywhere on the sands and he remembered just about everything she had said – and where. He could never look at that ridge at the edge of the marsh without remembering that she had once sung on it or pan the patch of mud without seeing where she had slipped.

The cockles were meagre as usual and, after digging and raking for some two hours, he took a break. He sat on his cart eating bread and cheese and was only wondering how long it would be before he saw any of the usual summer bird visitors to the sands – those oyster catchers were always around – when a yellow wagtail called and proceeded to inspect his rake and sacks. He flicked a lump of bread towards the bird but either it was not hungry or had not seen the lump since it just wandered towards him and looked up, bold as brass, its head and chest a tiny blaze of yellow in the sunshine. He dropped another lump of bread, which it pecked at this time, occasionally picking it up and shaking it around before it flew away, final, as if alarmed. A minute later it returned with a mate and the pair stayed near him as he worked for a few more hours, until the tremendous surge of waders told of the turn of the tide. He was a little saddened when the wagtails flew away as well.

The tide yielded just over half a sack of cockles but, judging by the length of some of the long faces of the returning cocklers, they had not managed even that. At least, unlike most of them, he did not have a family to feed unless Megan counted as family. Not that she was any burden. Meat, fruit and vegetables had been arriving at the cottage in such mysterious quantities of late he half suspected that she was having an affair with the owner of Swansea market himself.

She was busy cooking in the kitchen and he was pouring the cockles into his boiler when Vera's head rose over the yard fence, her throat clearing in readiness for a cantata of complaint. 'What's the trouble now, Vera?' he asked, weary.

'That sister of yours has been stealing my cabbages again, she has.'

He sighed. 'How do you know?'

'Last night I had seven cabbages in that garden. Counted them I did with my two hands. Now look at them. Six. Cabbages don't walk, do they? I mean they don't grow legs and go for an afternoon stroll on their own, do they?'

'Just because one is missing it doesn't mean Meg took it. It's not logical.' He bit his lip after using that word. Whatever else Vera was strong on it was not logic – even if she knew the meaning of the word in the first place.

'I don't know about logical. I wouldn't know about all that, would I now? She's always stealing my cabbages that one. What with her stealing my cabbages and the slugs and snails prancing all over the place I haven't got much of a chance, have I? Eh? What chance have I got against all them?'

234

He called for Megan to come out into the yard and she stood at the kitchen door wiping her hands in her apron. 'Vera here,' he said, poking his thumb at the old crone. 'Vera here says you've been stealing her cabbages.'

'You'd better watch your lip you had, Mrs Owen,' Megan said tossing her red curls around and widening her eyes with much self-righteousness. 'Going around calling someone a thief. That's not very nice is it? You'll be having that Evan Roberts after you and where will you be then? Hell. That's where liars go.'

'Well, you have, haven't you?'

'Have what?'

'Been stealing my cabbages. They don't walk do they? I mean they haven't got legs.'

'I wouldn't want your smelly cabbages, Mrs Owen, even if they had six legs. They're full of slugs, your cabbages are. I wouldn't feed one of your cabbages to that horse and he'll eat anything. He wouldn't even eat one of your cabbages if it was wrapped in chocolate and he'd even *run* somewhere if there was chocolate around.'

Megan looked around to Michael for support but he had turned his back and poured the remainder of the cockles into the boiler. He knew she had been stealing the cabbages. She had been too calm in the teeth of the accusation and, as usual, was trying to wriggle out of it with a load of old banter. If she had not been stealing the cabbages she would have been over that fence and all but buried Vera in the cabbage patch of hers. He knew our Megan.

'How do you know they're full of slugs?' Vera cackled on. 'Been looking at them, have you?'

'I wouldn't look at your mouldy old cabbages for all the cockles in Wales.'

He dropped his empty sack on the ground and walked into the kitchen. Cabbage was indeed boiling on the stove and, come to think of it, they'd had quite a lot of it lately. He wished she wouldn't do that. The old girl almost had heart seizure worrying about her prancing slugs without having her cabbages stolen as well.

The row was still blazing away in the yard so he walked into the living room and sat down next to the fire. He really was beginning to wish that Megan would just go away again and leave him in peace with his animals. Everything had been quiet, if very dirty, before she had come back but now it was all either open argument or secret conspiracy. When she was not quarrelling with Vera about her cabbages she was feuding with the milkman about his short measures or plotting with

Jenko who had been calling over regular. Michael was sure there was something going on between those two but, quite what, he could not work out. Perhaps she was knocking him off to get free medicine and treatment for that rash on her leg which was upsetting her so much. He wouldn't put anything past her.

'Look Michael, these cats have got to stay outside in future.' Having disposed of Vera she was back in the living room and having a go at him. 'There were muddy paw marks all over the kitchen table this morning.'

'It's their home, too.'

'Not on the kitchen table it isn't. There's B coli germs in cats. Jenko told me.'

'Jenko believes there's germs in everything. Why don't you leave the cats alone? There's no harm in them. *And* they've been here longer than you.'

The barb sunk home and she poked her tongue out at him before retreating to the kitchen. Men were supposed to do as they were told, in her book, and never answer back. She should have been a queen bee in a hive, he decided. It was a job she would have adored, what with the total obeisance bees always show their queen.

'I just can't stand having them on the table that's all,' she shouted from the kitchen. 'All they do is lie around the house all day. Cats should be out hunting and shagging. All these do is snore all night and eat all day. They're too lazy for any sex.'

'Not everyone is as mad about sex as you are. There are some who can live without it.'

'Who? Name me one person. What nonsense you talk sometimes. Sex is what we're built for – all the rest is propaganda.'

That was pure Megan, that remark. She held it as an absolute article of faith that the only acts of any importance in the world took place between the sheets. Michael's greatest mistake had been to tell her one night all about Beth and since then Megan had positively overflowed with Machiavellian plots and plans to put it all right. It was not too long ago that she had even woken him up *in the middle of the night*, sitting on the side of his bed and jabbering some nonsense about powdered rhinoceros tusk. It appeared that the Chinese used the powder to get their women on heat and she seemed reasonably certain she could get her husband to send the odd tusk or two over.

'He'd probably think it was for you,' Michael said.

'He'd know better,' she snorted, her nostrils flaring with mock huffiness. 'I don't need any powder to get *me* going.'

'Yes. There is that. Look Meg, just forget about it will you?'

Lately she had forgotten about it and that again was pure Megan. The range of her interest in anything rarely lasted for more than a few days largely, he suspected, because she was too interested in herself. But what he could not understand was who was stoking her fire these days. There was no obvious suitor and she always said that she got headaches if she did not have it at least once a day.

'Your food's ready,' she called out.

He sat down at the kitchen table and saw immediate, by the way that she was banging the pots and pans around, that he had upset her. He decided not to hold out the olive branch just yet. 'Why don't you leave poor old Vera's cabbages alone?' he asked.

No reply but plenty of banging and crashing.

'She'd probably let you have a few free if you asked her nice. I planted them in the first place so there's no need to steal them, is there? It gets her blood pressure up.'

'Oh shut up, will you? Just shut up.' She slammed his food down on the table so hard it chipped the plate.

'I like eating off broken plates,' he remarked.

'Good. Well I've done something to please you then, haven't I?'

She flounced into the living room and slammed the kitchen door behind her. When that one got her rag out she was always wandering about the place looking for doors to slam. He took a bite out of the meat pie and, sure enough, the front door opened and closed. She had probably gone down to the tavern to sulk. The meat pie was delicious – as was the cabbage – and he wondered if she had got her claws into that poor butcher again. There was a time the butcher had it so bad he kept turning up daily with buckets of liver and lambs' hearts so, instead of cockling out on the sands, their father organised a sort of meat stall, selling off the meat to the other cocklers cheap.

His forehead furrowed when he heard the sound of whispering voices coming from the living room. So she had not gone out at all. Someone had come to see her and now they were both locked in some feverish conspiracy. 'But you've got to tell him,' he heard her shout above the hissing whispers. 'He's got a right to know.'

He stood up and opened the door to find Jenko sitting on an armchair, his flabby features unusually gloomy and his tongue unusually still.

'Go on. Tell him,' Megan said nodding at Michael.

'Tell me what?'

'If you don't tell him I will.'

'Just what's going on here?'

Jenko stared at the wall and narrowed his eyes. 'It's about your Beth,' he said.

Perhaps it was the unexpected mention of her name – the public echo of a secret thought that was always on his mind – or perhaps it was the sudden funereal way he spoke of it, but his imagination was seized by the fear of a terrible disaster and he slumped down on a chair as if punched hard.

'There's no need to worry,' Jenko added, alarmed by his reaction. 'Beth *is* ill but she'll be all right.'

'What's the matter with her? Where is she?'

'Home. She's been there for a while and in some kind of shock.'

'Why didn't you tell . . . '

'I had reasons, Michael. Good reasons. She's suffering from some kind of trauma. She's left Evan Roberts and is showing a bad recurrence of all those old symptoms she had after losing her baby. It's all a rotten bloody mess.'

'There's no treatment for it then?'

'None that I know of and none that anyone else knows of either. The family wants her to go away somewhere and, as for herself, she doesn't know what she wants.'

'What do *you* think we should do?' Michael asked.

'The child, Jenko,' Megan broke in. 'Tell him about the child.'

Michael looked at her, dark. So that was why she had not been prying into his emotional life lately: a certain sign – he should have guessed but had not – that she was prying into it elsewhere.

'What's all this about the child?'

Jenko moved his jaw around but still did not take his eyes off the wall. 'Your sister has known for some time that Beth was home but I made her promise not to tell you until we could see if Beth was going to recover.'

Michael glared at Megan and then back at Jenko: so that's what they had been plotting about.

'Anyway, the other day your sister came up with an idea,' Jenko went on. 'I've thought about it hard and we may be clutching at straws and there are many who say I've made that my life's speciality but . . . '

'Stop beating about the bush, will you?'

He blew out a long stream of air and began studying the ceiling. 'Well your sister's idea is that we should all go down to Cardiff and bring back Beth's daughter. Or rather *try* and bring her back.'

Michael stood up and sat back down again. 'What good would that do?'

Jenko lifted both palms in the air. 'Don't say anything for just a moment. Just shut your gob and give your arse a chance. I've worn my brain out turning it all over. Just listen, will you? First it is possible we can get the girl back. I've put some money to one side and, down in Cardiff, money doesn't just talk, it shouts its head off. I know where the girl is and the parents – the foster parents – are not that well off. The real question is what good, if any, would bringing her back do for Beth?'

'I think it would do a lot of good,' said Megan.

'Be quiet, you,' Michael said to her sharp. 'If you want to do something useful go and feed the horse. Go on, Jenko.'

'Well, if we brought her back here it might bring Beth out of her shell and force her to come to terms with herself and with you. You see, she feels a lot for you. I know that. She's also still grieving for her baby. She told me that this morning. She said she missed her baby all the time, regretted letting the girl go when she did. She also, as a matter of happy fact, wants nothing more to do with the chapel so bringing back the girl might be the best resolution to everything. You included.'

'You make it all sound easy enough.'

'It is easy, Michael,' said Megan.

'Keep out of this Meg, will you? What are the drawbacks?'

Jenko smoothed his belly around with his hand and still would not look at Michael direct. 'Lots. It's anything but easy. As a matter of long-standing principle I have always believed that you cannot tamper with the emotions. People either feel certain things or they do not and, in my experience, no amount of interference can manufacture feelings and attitudes if they do not exist. But you see I think, no I *believe*, that these feelings do exist and what we need is some form of catalyst to bring them out. The child might be the catalyst.'

'You make her sound like one of your pills. You still haven't explained the drawbacks.'

'Well there are lots, aren't there? We're not dealing with some stupid woman who does as she's told. She's a private woman with a streak of the wildest obstinacy. She would hate to think that she was being used or manipulated. Also the physical presence of the girl might serve to reinforce Beth's guilt that she had in the first place, let alone abandoned it. There's thin ice everywhere – but you're an intelligent man. Tell me what you think.'

'Why not just ask her out straight?'

He shook his head. 'She'll just say no. She promised never to go near the baby again and that one keeps her promises. But, if we get the child to come and live here, she might just accept it all as a job done.'

'Might.'

'Might. It is a sort of answer but whether she'll see it that way is

239

anyone's guess.'

'Would it help if I went over and spoke to her?'

'What about?'

Michael shrugged his shoulders. 'Oh, things. I could test the water with my elbow. Help make my own mind perhaps. Do you think that would be a good idea?'

'Yes. Yes I do. It's worth a try for certain. There's nothing else left.'

* * *

It was early afternoon, sleepy with heat and midges, when Michael pulled on the doorbell and dismay decanted inside him as he came face to face with Beth's father. 'It's you, is it?' he asked.

'I'm afraid so.'

'What do you want?'

'I heard Beth was home.'

'Who told you that?'

'I was wondering if I could speak to her.'

'She's ill. Can't see anyone.'

'Please, Mr Williams. I must talk to her. It's very urgent.'

'What's urgent?'

'Just let me speak to her, will you? Only for a few minutes. I won't upset her.'

'I've told you once. She's ill. Will you please go away?'

Michael nodded. 'All right, but can I see her when she's well?'

'That's up to her, isn't it? At the moment it's up to me and I'm telling you she's ill.'

'Look, Mr Williams, it's difficult to explain the importance of it all but I really must speak to Beth.'

'Do you have difficulty understanding English? She's ill.'

'Well, at least ask if she'll see me.'

He closed the door and seemed to have been gone for an hour though it was only a minute or so before he opened it again. He shook his head. 'I'm sorry. She really is very ill and seems to be sleeping now.'

'Can I come back over later?'

'I'm asking you to believe that it's gone beyond everything.' The belligerence had gone out of his words now and Michael saw a lot of pained confusion in his eyes. He had not shaved that day either. 'There's no helping Beth now,' he continued. 'But she's our daughter and we'll look after her come what may. It looks as if there's nothing anyone can do for her.'

Michael turned away, sharp, alarm flooding up inside him. He walked out over the crags at the back of Pen-clawdd, following a path along the scree towards Hermon Chapel. Down below him there were the stone cottages and grey slate roofs where the people lived out their lives. That was Evie Evans' cottage and all Evie ever worried about was his garden in general and the size and health of his tomatoes in particular. Just over the road lived Stan Pritchard, whose idea of heaven was to go out into the woods with his ferret. Betty Powell was taking in her washing as a pony and trap went clattering past.

He shielded his eyes from the low-slung glare of the sun. He too had once been happy in those streets and wanted to be so again as a part of the community with a family to fend for and a woman to love. But, for the woman he really did love, there was nothing anyone could do for her. There was nothing *he* could do for the girl he loved. Or was there?

Chapter Twenty-one

'Welcome to the lavatory of Britain,' Jenko muttered from beneath his cavernous hat as the three of them walked out of Cardiff General Station. 'What you see before you is God's most spectacular mistake and the sooner we get out of this place the happier I, for one, will be.'

After the placid pace of the Gower the energy and bustle of Cardiff that day was breathless. Everywhere there were opposing tides of movement with men in collarless shirts and flat caps, stumpy women in lace shawls and carrying baskets, speeding delivery carts and clattering trams packed full with people.

Here a ragged match seller, there a boy struggling with a bag full of *Western Mails* almost as big as himself and, from across the road, the tinkling sounds of Salvation Army tambourines.

Bute Street, Jenko had explained on the train journey down, was just over a mile of tall Victorian houses where bankers and merchant shippers trundled around in hansom cabs during the week and listened to a German brass band in Loudoun Square on Sundays. In the heaving filth of Cardiff, Bute Street was its one posh and refreshing oasis, and baby Rhion had been placed with foster parents in Loudoun Square, which was halfway down Bute Street itself and just off it.

But no sooner had they walked the five hundred yards from the station to the beginning of Bute Street and passed under the railway bridge than they saw that, in the few short years since Jenko had last been there, the booming coal industry and the expanding docks had changed all that, complete.

What had once been a home of elegance and gracious living had become a Hell's Acre; a flourishing slum teeming with rag pickers, maimed miners, skittle sharks, ticket-of-leave men and child beggars. Chinese sat on steps in the billowing steam of their laundries. Arab tribesmen were playing pitch and toss with ruffians from Los Angeles, while groups of brawny Irish stood outside the doors of the pubs, glass in hands, and stared at the trio and Megan in particular whose daring lace blouse, which exposed more than it concealed, actually made a few of them take an involuntary step forward.

A mangy dog was sniffing around the heels of a sailor long gone mad and, straight through these milling hordes, walked a tall African man, naked from the waist up and carrying a plank on his head. An Arab was wheeling a sheet of corrugated iron on a bicycle and, over on the opposite gutters, five children were playing marbles. Even the bumptious Megan seemed taken aback by it all and slipped her arm into Michael's after a West Indian, with a wondrous collection of completely rotten teeth, actually placed himself in front of her and leered down her cleavage.

More vivid than the people were the smells – a spiralling collection of laundry, spices, stale beer and cassavas all bound together by a heavy hoop of dereliction and decay. The noises were the savage sounds of industrial hammers, blaring hooters and loud whining music from the Orient. The air tasted like nothing on this earth – or the next.

'It's even worse than Bombay,' Jenko said amidst much fluttering of his handkerchief. 'Even a Bombay beggar would get up out of his gutter and demand a deportation order out of all this stink.'

The romping smells and dull colours of a slum were intensified by a light spring sunshine which bounced off the walls and pavements, and they only had a break from the cloying soup of the air when they stopped on an iron bridge which straddled a canal. Here a light breeze was sprinting down over the water from somewhere fresh and unsullied by what the Press had begun to call Tiger Bay.

'It's the story of my life,' Jenko said as they leaned on the iron parapet and watched a string of coal barges being pulled down the canal by horses or, in one case, by the bargee's own muscle power. 'Did I ever tell you that the first time I saw a desert it was raining and covered with grass? I went to the Antarctic once on a ship and it was so hot we had to keep swallowing salt tablets by the ton. I've missed so many boats I could have started my own navy. At least I now understand why Bobo always refused to come to Cardiff. He'd be lucky to find a doubter here, let alone a convert.'

'What's happened to him anyway?' Michael asked, leaning forward to peer down at the stacked coal in the hold of a barge passing beneath them. 'Haven't heard anything about him at all after his great silence.'

'Gone soft in the head, I heard. All those convulsions must have dislocated his brain. The word is he just stood up one night and said he'd had enough.'

'He'd had enough!'

'Aye. Announced he was returning to a life of prayer. Hope he stays in it, that's all I can say. That one's going to have an awful lot of explaining to do when he faces Saint Peter at the pearly gates.'

'What about you, Jenko?'

'What about me?'

'How are you going to explain your wicked ways to Saint Peter? I bet you didn't even go to Sunday School, did you?'

'Once. When I was ten. But they just made me hold a fat Bible over my head all afternoon. Said I was talking too much.'

'You talking too much!' Megan laughed as she ruffled her hand around the back of Jenko's neck. 'Jenko, you're the quietest man I know.'

His hat nodded up and down in agreement. 'That's true, that. Shy, modest, speaks only when spoken to. One of life's barge horses, reliable and strong, like one of those down there.'

'What if they've moved away somewhere?' asked Michael. 'I'd move fast enough if I was living in all this.'

'How much money did you bring with you, Jenko?' asked Megan.

'Enough.'

Megan slipped her arm into Jenko's and Michael followed on behind. There was something going on between those two for definite. The old doctor had even tidied himself up lately – or she had tidied him up – and there was an unfamiliar shine on his shoes, an unknown crease in his trousers. He even seemed to have lost his gravy-stained tie.

Michael looked around at this flourishing slum and felt angry about what he saw. Here they were in the richest country in the world and these poor people had barely enough food to eat. Well, the new Independent Labour Party was soon going to put an end to that, and no mistake. Men like Keir Hardie were going to act positive about this theft of people's labour, while all the chapel could do was shiver in its sins and pray to a dead God. Yes, it was now but a matter of organisation and the men were going to wrest back their rights. The colliers were striking again that week in Merthyr and Ynysybwl.

'What if they just tell us to go away?' Michael asked.

'Stop fretting, boy,' Jenko said. 'Let's take it as it comes, shall we?'

They passed Moosa Omar Outfitters and the Adelphi pub before turning into Loudoun Square which, far from being a home for the great and gracious, was a vast pile of tenement blocks laced together by washing lines with frozen avalanches of rubbish flowing out of the doorways, people of various colours standing around in dispirited groups and a gang of children busy kicking in one another's teeth on a patch of mud in the middle of the square.

'So what happened to that German brass band you were telling us all about?' Michael asked.

Jenko looked around him and lifted his hands, amazed. 'It's a plot, I

244

tell you. Probably started by Evan Roberts and the chapel. Not so long ago you could have brought your favourite aunt down here. Now it's not even fit for your horse.'

'My horse wouldn't come down here, that's for sure.'

They found No.14 and Jenko told the other two to wait on the pavement as he walked up the steps inside. 'I'm coming with you,' Michael said.

'Me too,' Megan chimed in.

Jenko walked on in and Michael turned back to her. 'There's no need for you to come in,' he said.

'I'm not staying out here on my own. This place is worse than Hong Kong and I thought that was bad enough. The lizards out there were so big they wore climbing boots, they did.'

'You know, girl, you're even beginning to talk like Jenko.'

'He's a lovely talker though.'

'What's going on between you two?'

She gave a lip-curling sardonic smile, which could have meant anything. They both went into the hallway where prostrate bodies and strident smells immediately overcame Megan's fear of being left out in the square on her own, since she skipped straight back out through the door again. Michael followed Jenko's shoes up the stairs to the landing where he had to step over a large body lying in a puddle of dried vomit. 'Certain you've got the right place, are you?' Michael asked.

'I'm not certain of anything any longer,' Jenko said, walking along the landing, knocking on a door and opening it without waiting for a reply. Inside there was a row of stump beds with dirty feet sticking out at all angles and, on one bed, a woman, with a face as white as alabaster, was groaning loud. The smell, Michael guessed, was a mixture of rotten potatoes, salted fish and body sweat though, the more you sniffed it, the more you found in it. Urine for certain and even pears. The big toe on one of the sleeping man's feet had turned bright purple.

'Hey you,' Jenko shouted at an old man sitting on the floor, his back against the wall and a brown bottle between his legs. 'We're looking for Mrs Jesse Lewis. Used to live here. Mrs Jesse Lewis.'

The old man looked up and said quite a few words but, although a few could be understood in isolation, they made no sense at all strung together.

'I expect he's asking for a drink,' Jenko decided. 'We all want a drink,' he shouted back at the old man. 'Where is Mrs Jesse Lewis?'

The old man began to gibber again and the woman with the alabaster face cried out with a startling ferocity. 'Cholera I can do without,' Jenko said turning around. 'Come on. There's cholera bugs in here bigger than Alsatian dogs, all ready to rip you apart.'

'Hadn't you better look at her?'

'Out. All that old dear can look forward to is a deep planting.'

The body in the vomit had disappeared when they walked back along the landing while a woman, with her hair tied up in a scarf and a cigarette dangling from her mouth, opened a door, looked at them and slammed it shut again. Jenko knocked on it but they both left double quick when something shattered loud against the door inside.

Once back out in the square Jenko rubbed the flat of his hand around one eye weary. 'Jesse Lewis was a decent lady. She wouldn't live in that. It's clear she's moved.'

'Where's your crystal ball?'

'We'll just have to ask around. This bunch here are the butty gangs working shifts to dig the new docks. When that bunch get up the next bunch go in to sleep. I can't see the point of asking *them* anything. I'll try a few of the neighbours and then it'll have to be the police.'

'There's just one thing I can't understand about all this,' Michael said to Megan when Jenko had left them and walked into the next house. 'Why is he putting himself out so much?'

'Perhaps it's to help Beth?'

'Perhaps. And perhaps it's something to do with you.'

'Me? Why me?'

'You haven't been . . . have you . . . you know . . . '

'Michael. How could you think such a thing? He's old enough to be my father.'

'I can't see that's got anything to do with it. Not where you're concerned anyway. Nothing you'd do would surprise me. You could come home with King Edward himself and that wouldn't surprise me. Now what . . . '

She nodded towards Jenko as he emerged from the house, again dusting his nose with his handkerchief. 'There's so many packed in there they've even got orange boxes for the kids to sleep in. Even the lavatory is blocked up for more sleeping space.'

'What do they use for a lavatory then?' asked Megan.

The three of them all turned and looked up at the house.

'One another's orange boxes maybe?' Jenko suggested.

'Maybe one another's pockets,' Megan added.

'You and your jokes,' Michael said, angry. 'You just wait until we get ourselves organised. Those Chartist riots will be as nothing when we start clearing up this lot.'

A child with his trousers held to his vest with a pin stood in front of them holding out his hand.

'So what do we do now?' Michael asked, looking away.

'The police station. The police know everyone in an area like this. I bet there's so many burglars living down here they work shifts to avoid forming jams under the bridge.'

They followed a cobbled alley back up to Bute Street. Megan wanted to stop and watch a group of Chinese who were so engrossed in a game of mahjong they did not even notice they had attracted spectators.

'My kind of people, the Chinese,' Jenko mused as they began walking again. 'All they ever worry about is their belly and what hangs from it. No religious problems with them. No sooner do they get off the gangplank than they all become lapsed Buddhists and begin chasing the girls or else gambling morning, noon and night.'

'I knew a Chinese man once,' said Megan.

A short silence followed then Jenko asked, 'Well, what about him?'

'Nothing about him. I just knew him. Does there have to be anything about him?'

'Well it's a bit like announcing you had some bread and jam yesterday. So what?'

'So what yourself. So what nothing. We don't all have to make long speeches every time we open our mouths, do we?'

They continued bickering all along Bute Street until they had to cross the road to avoid a gang of squabbling prostitutes who were jostling around the pavement and making such wild threats it reminded Michael of the first rugby match of the season between Pen-clawdd and Loughor. One was whirling a handbag around in the air with all the force of a demolition ball.

Megan and Michael waited outside the police station as Jenko went in. A seagull dipped low over the street, wings fluttering as it cawed angry, before breaking away to glide over the outlying warehouses. 'You've let him have his way with you, haven't you?' Michael asked her and knew the answer immediately when she fluttered her eyelashes, mock bashful.

'I just think he's so funny. I'm fed up with young oafs with no brains so I thought I'd try something different and took him to bed.'

'*You* took *him* to bed?'

'That's right – and you know another thing? He may have bits falling off him, as he's always saying, and he may drink too much but he's really good at it. You know what the Chinese say? It takes a long time for the kettle to boil and, oh, does he boil when he boils. You don't mind, do you?'

247

'Me? Why should I mind? It's your body, girl. You do what you like with it.'

A breeze was blowing a newspaper down the pavement towards them. So it was true. At least he now saw why Jenko was in such a good humour and being so helpful. When you get the information all kinds of things fall into place. The newspaper stood on its edges before making a slow, hesitant somersault.

'We've got an address,' Jenko said emerging from the police station, exultant. 'Dudley Street. Over in Rat Island, as it's known. We can cut through the docks.'

The dockland itself, a huge patchwork of glittering water and brown busy cranes, was a relief from the foetid stink of Bute Street but there was no less bustle on the wharves: the winch men yelling themselves hoarse as the huge iron grabs sent landslips of coal thundering down into the holds, blackened dockers whistling instructions from ship to shore, small puffing billies pushing lines of trucks along the intricate criss-crossings of the rails. There were grain ships from San Francisco; rusty tramps from Africa and some five men – working in the rigging of a windjammer – practically staged a riot in mid-air when they saw Megan flouncing past. She loved every wave and catcall while her two companions had to walk away from her when she began blowing them kisses back.

'Come on, Salome,' Jenko said. 'You'll be getting whipped at the mast the way you're going on.'

'Ooooh Jenko. Do you think they'll use *real* leather whips?'

Michael could not help laughing at her. No matter what the circumstances she just kept bubbling like a shaken bottle of pop and, what with Jenko's stream of bad jokes as well, it was almost impossible to get serious about anything. They stopped to read a notice on one of the telegraph poles.

See the Convict Ship *Success.*
Amazing chains. Huge holds. Accommodation for 800.
Berthed at Hill's Dry Dock.

'Only some old Wykehamist wit in Whitehall would call a convict ship *Success*,' said Jenko. 'I bet they had a good laugh in the Reform Club the night he told them about that.'

Dudley Street was a small row of grey terraced houses. As they walked towards No.23, the butterflies were back in Michael's belly again. Jenko knocked on the door and walked into a short hallway where a tree branch lay in the dust next to an old pram. Again he knocked on the door of the living room and walked straight inside without waiting for an answer. Michael supposed that it was his life as a visiting doctor that enabled him to do that.

'Mrs Jesse Lewis, isn't it?' he heard Jenko say. 'You may remember me. Jenkins. Dr. Enoch Jenkins. I've brought some people to see you.'

The curtains in the room were drawn, with a small coal fire smouldering in the grate. In one corner the head of a dog was poking out from beneath a half-collapsed sofa, chewing on another branch, while a small woman with grey hair was sitting on a chair next to the fire, a shawl around her shoulders and a small baby in her arms. There was apprehension, if not fear, in her old face as her visitors followed one another into the darkened room and she kept on pushing up her elbows – as if the baby was slipping out of her arms and she was trying to effect a better hold on it.

'Keeping well then, are we?' Jenko asked, sitting down opposite her. 'These are two of my friends. Michael and Megan.'

'Pleased to meet you,' Mrs Lewis said, barely glancing at them standing just inside the door.

'You've moved from your last address we see. Overcrowded, was it?'

'We had to.' She lifted the baby up again and frowned as if in the greatest discomfort. 'They made us they did.'

'A new baby as well.'

'Two now. Three in fact. We had another two years ago.'

'Times difficult are they, Mrs Lewis?'

'Ted had it difficult in the docks. The Irish, it was. They took over all the labour. Undercut everyone. The men asked for a halfpenny a ton and the Irish offered to do it for a farthing. Ted was a foreman as well, but he lost that too. Just the Irish there is now. And the blacks.'

'You do remember me then, Mrs Lewis?'

'You brought Rhion here, didn't you? Yes. I remember.' She became even more ill-at-ease now, kept looking up at the clock as if she had to go somewhere at any second. The clock had stopped.

'How is Rhion?'

'She's all right. Rhion's all right.'

'Can we see her?'

'She . . . she's out playing. Spends a lot of time with a friend up the road.'

'She's well then?'

'Well yes. Well enough anyway. As well as any of us are.'

Jenko pushed out his lower jaw and, after a few moments, said, 'Mrs Lewis. What would it take for you to let us have Rhion back?'

Michael winced at the directness of the question and looked at Megan.

'Take?' Have her back?' I don't understand.'

'I'll try and make it clearer then, Mrs Lewis. Rhion's natural mother is missing her baby . . . '

'Beth, wasn't it?' Yes. A lovely girl she was too.'

'You see, Mrs Lewis, Beth has been missing her baby almost every day since she left her with you. She believes that she has made a terrible mistake and the loss of her child has caused her untold problems – to her health and mind. She hasn't eaten a full meal in nearly five years, Mrs Lewis. She keeps losing weight something terrible and, on some days, can't even speak for her grief. Not to put too fine a point on it we have come here because we fear that it is only a matter of months, if not days, before Beth dies of a broken heart.'

Michael had to take his hat off to Jenko for that little speech. He had all but burst into tears himself and even Megan was sniffing as she took hold of his hand.

Mrs Lewis looked down at her own baby and held it closer to her. 'Can you really die of a broken heart?' she asked.

'It's as easy as dying of a broken neck, Mrs Lewis. Is there anything we can talk about? Any way we can come to some kind of arrangement, which would suit you, Rhion and her mother? We would, of course, see to it that she had the very best of everything and you would always be able to see her whenever you wanted.'

'I don't know. You'll have to ask Ted. He makes all the decisions around here.'

Michael felt Megan squeeze his hand and, for the first time since the plan had been mooted, a flame of hope flickered inside him. At least it had not been the blanket refusal he had feared all along. But there was a problem here. He just could not understand Mrs Lewis. She had given in too easy. In all her movements and words she seemed a woman surrounded and defeated. There was a dullness in her responses and a curious lack of anger or even any real curiosity at the way strangers had walked into her house and asked if they could take away her eldest child. It just was not natural and certainly did not accord with the lively picture Beth had once painted of Mrs Lewis.

Perhaps life in a slum really did devastate the personality, he thought. The socialists had got it right when they spoke of how poverty destroyed human dignity, how it took away the very character of man. At the very least Rhion would be far better off out of all this. She would be far better off almost anywhere but here. He looked back into the hallway wondering where she was.

'What time do you expect your husband back, Mrs Lewis?' Jenko asked.

'He's not long left and shouldn't be back much before ten. Can you come back then?'

'Working is he?'

'No. I said. I said he wasn't working.'

'The pub is it?' She nodded. 'What pub would that be, Mrs Lewis?'

'Rothesay Castle. On the other side of the dock in Maria Street.'

Megan stepped forward and touched Jenko on the shoulder. 'Why don't you two go over there and I'll sit with Mrs Lewis?'

'You don't mind if I stay here do you, Mrs Lewis?' Megan said sitting down. 'I've been on my feet all day and they're killing me they are.'

'I've got to go out soon.'

'Oh that's better. Let's have a rest for a minute and I'll make us both a cup of tea.'

Mrs Lewis looked around her, unhappy, almost as if she felt a trick which she could not quite see through was being played on her.

'What's the name of your dog, Mrs Lewis?' Megan asked as she looked up at the two men and jerked her head towards the door. 'You two had better get going. Had the dog long have you, Mrs Lewis?'

'Right, boy,' Jenko said standing up. 'Let's get over to the Rothesay Castle and do some business over a pint. I like doing business over a pint. Gets my tongue flapping, a few beers do.'

'So what do you make of it all?' Michael asked as they walked back through the docks, stopping at a level crossing to let a coal train clank past in front of them.

'Couldn't be better. Just couldn't be better. It's funny how women who foster a child usually end up having a stream of their own. Fostering must do wonders for the old baby-making equipment. They're living in poverty. Mr Lewis is out of work and on the drink. Remember, they were given money to take the girl in the first place so it was no great act of love on their side.'

'I didn't know that. Why wasn't I told that?'

'Perhaps because you didn't ask but, in answer to your first question, I don't see any great difficulty.'

'How much are you going to offer him?'

'Well I've got a hundred guineas to play with but don't expect to pay anything like that. We'll take it as it comes.'

A thickening dusk was moving in over the dockland by the time they got to the Rothesay Castle. The taproom was throbbing with seamen of several races, the stink of mulled wine, big-breasted strumpets and whinnying craters of laughter. Just inside the door a man standing hand on hip and the other raised limp, in the general shape of a teapot, blew a kiss at Michael. Two children were sitting together under a table though it was the radiant ugliness of most of the drinkers that was the most impressive. There were men with bad teeth, eye-patches and more than a few with harelips. A woman with phossy jaw sat next to a piano and, just under a gilt scroll mirror sat a brawny sailor rippling the folds of his hairy belly in front of an old black man smoking a silver pipe.

All were cackling with equal measures of happiness and drink, giving off such an aura of electrifying jubilation that Michael felt an intruder into another world; a world where people preferred their atheism hot and warm; a world where religion and politics were strictly for those who could afford it. Not for nothing was the pub known locally as The Bucket of Blood.

'My kind of pub this,' Jenko winked as they threaded their way through the throng. 'Villains make my kidneys tinkle.'

When they got to the bar Jenko asked the bar man if he knew a Ted Lewis. 'Over there,' he said pointing at a table in the far corner where a man was sitting alone in front of half a pint. He was a small man with work hands and, even though he had not shaved, there was a certain character in his features as he sat surveying his drink like a melancholy parrot.

'Ted Lewis, isn't it?' Jenko said, putting down a pint in front of him. 'I've bought you a drink.'

'Why?' he asked as they both sat down on either side of him. 'Now why should you be buying me a drink?'

'Because you've got something we want.'

'Ho, now. That does make a change.' He lifted up the pint and let it hover just an inch from his nose. 'What's that then?'

'We've just called at your house and been talking with your wife,' Jenko amplified.

He put down the glass. 'I told Hutchings I would pay him next week. I told him. I told him I'd pay next week.'

'It's nothing to do with your debts, Mr Lewis. In fact we might be able to help you with your debts.' Lewis picked up his glass and he poured the beer down his throat. 'As I said, you've got something we want.'

'Haven't I seen you somewhere before?' Lewis asked Jenko.

'You have indeed.'

'Oh, wait a minute now. Aren't you some kind of doctor?'

'You've got a good memory, Mr Lewis.'

'That's it. I knew there was something about you. Didn't you have something to do with my Rhion?'

My Rhion. His use of the word *my* almost made Michael vomit. He could not even pick up his own pint of beer, convinced that he would indeed vomit if he drank it.

'It's about your Rhion that we've come to see you, Mr Lewis,' Jenko said. 'Now I don't want to waste your time – or ours – so I'll tell you straight why we've come. Rhion's mother wants her back.'

'Oh does she then? Does she?' The corners of his mouth curled into a wry smile and he picked up his glass to finish his pint, wiping his mouth with the back of his hand before putting the empty glass back down onto the table. He was clearly deliberating, though quite what was on his mind was difficult to tell. 'Oh does she then?' he repeated.

'She does.'

'Well, she can't have her. She's my eldest girl, that. I love her dear and wouldn't part with her now. Not for a million pounds I wouldn't.'

'Let's just chew it over a bit, shall we?' said Jenko. 'Let's have a few drinks and chew it over. We're both men of the world – I could see that, as soon as I saw you, all that time ago. Now the facts of the matter are that her natural mother . . . '

Michael stood up and walked straight out of the pub. He should have seen that it would all come to this. There were no miracles on offer in the market that day. You just don't go around buying other people's children – no, not even in these bad times you don't. He stood outside in the street watching a dog widdle against a wall, now turning around to sniff at the damp triangular patch. Above the outlying warehouses was the luminous red glow of East Moors copper works.

Sorry Beth, my love. We tried and we failed. You'll just have to work it out another way. The difficult ends of life can never be tied up into one tidy knot. Life did not operate like that – life was bruising, usually disappointing and forever tangled.

But it was evident that no such sense of defeat had overcome Jenko. A good ten minutes later, the darkness had settled around the copper works' sunset and he had still not come out, doubtless deciding to make the best of a bad job and get drunk instead. He was about to go back into the pub and haul Jenko out when he heard Megan's voice.

'Michael. I've brought someone to see you.'

He turned and saw Megan standing there hand in hand with a child. Shivering slightly he went down on one knee, putting the ends of his fingers under the child's jaw and moving her head around into the light of the pub. She pulled her head away from his touch but, even in the half-light, he would have recognised those eyes anywhere, the particular shape of the cheekbones. So this was the tiny scrap on whom so many tears had been shed and so many lives had been wrecked. But the general appearance was that of a street urchin; her clothes ragged, the hair dirty and badly cut. He put his palm against her ribs and she shrugged it off.

'There's more meat on a butcher's bike,' he said. 'This girl's starving.'

'You've got it. And she wasn't down the street playing with a friend. She was upstairs locked in a room.'

'What?'

'She was locked in her room. Mrs Lewis broke down and cried after you left. She told me that her husband hates this little one and would I please take her away. She's locked away all the time and given leftovers – if anything at all. He knocks her around too. She *begged* me to take her away.'

He stood up with everything crumbling inside. 'Stay there. I'll get Jenko.' He walked back into the pub to find Jenko with a pint to his lips and eyes swivelling towards Lewis who was speaking.

'Better get out here a second,' Michael said.

'We're getting somewhere,' Jenko replied. 'Give us time will you?'

'Out now. There's something I want you to see.' Michael turned to leave and turned again. 'You stay there,' he told Lewis. 'We'll be back to have a word with you.'

Once outside Michael pointed at Rhion and Jenko crouched down in front of her, taking hold of her wrist and lifting her eyelid with a thumb. 'So this is little Rhion,' he said, smoothing the side of her chin and peering at her neck. 'Poor little mite. Those are bruises there. I wonder how many more we'll find on her?'

'Mrs Lewis told me that he beats her, particularly when he comes home from the pub,' said Megan. 'He says he never wanted her in the first place. He says it was the girl that brought him all his bad luck. Everything was fine until she came, he said. Mrs Lewis begged me to take the girl away for her own good, Jenko. *Begged* me.'

'The black enamelled bastard,' Jenko spat. 'And I've been in there slinging drinks down him and listening to him telling me how much he cares for the girl. Well let's go back and talk to him again.'

Jenko swept through the crowded taproom with all the verve of a galleon under full sail. His tongue all but jumped out of his mouth when he started on Lewis. 'You were given a sacred duty to look after that child!' he bellowed. 'The police are going to be very interested in you locking up a child like that!'

Lewis frowned and moved around in his seat, uncomfortable, as others in the bar came over to see what the fuss was all about.

'This snivelling maggot,' Jenko continued turning to them while pointing his finger at Lewis. 'This thing that moves lower than a worm was given money to look after a baby. And what does he do? He keeps the little mite locked up and starved. He knocks her around and treats her worse than a rat. Well, Lewis, you've pissed on your chips proper now.'

'I've got two little girls,' said a barrel-chested seaman. 'How about I give him a little smack?'

'Go on, Harry. Give him a little smack from me too.'

'You're going to pay dear for this!' Jenko boomed on. 'When a woman trusts her blood to a man and he locks it up and starves it and beats it there's payments to be made.' Jenko turned again to address the gathering crowd. Michael had long believed that, had Jenko ever decided to become a preacher, he would have been the world's greatest – him on the crucifixion and there would not have been a dry eye in the chapel.

'The mother of the baby is grieving for her child but he won't part with it. The mother is in danger of dying of a broken heart and this vermin would prefer to lock up the child and beat it silly rather than let her return to her mother's arms.'

'Just say the word, mister, an' I'll tear 'is ears off,' said the seaman, raising his original offer of a little smack. He looked big, dumb and very drunk and Michael did not doubt he would do it either.

'Go on, Harry. Tear 'is ears off.'

'Chop 'is balls off,' advised another.

Lewis stood up, seeing a menacing circle form around him. 'I was going to let the girl go,' he said, holding up his elbows, ready to ward off any punches that might come scything in his direction. 'I didn't want the girl from the beginning. Does nothing but grizzle all the time, she does. The mother can have her back. I only agreed to look after her for a while anyway.' He nodded towards the door. 'Let's talk outside.'

The seaman lurched against Michael and he was leaving the taproom. 'You want me to give 'im that little smack?'

'Not just yet. Later maybe.'

'Just say, that's all. I've got girls of my own an' I'll pull 'is legs off, I will.'

Lewis was standing on the pavement, hands in pockets, his back to Megan, Jenko and the child. 'All right you can take her,' he said without looking around. 'I never wanted her.'

'We'll take her now,' Michael said. 'We don't want you hurting her again, do we?'

'Take her, I said. But I want compensation. Five years I've looked after that child. That's got to be worth something.'

'How about a broken jaw?' Michael offered.

'I'll tell you what you will get Lewis,' said Jenko. 'You'll get five guineas and five seconds to run for it. Otherwise this boy will break your back. Won't you, boy?'

'Just give me the money,' Lewis said holding out his hand and moving away from Michael. 'I said you could have her.'

As Jenko paid him off Michael delivered a hefty boot straight into Lewis' leg making him tumble sideways and scattering his coins over the road.

Jenko grabbed Michael's arm. 'Steady now. We've got what we came for.'

'You'll all go to prison for this,' Lewis shouted at them as he picked up his coins. 'You'll all be sorry about this.'

Michael made towards Lewis again but he scampered away into the blazing copper-furnaced night.

Chapter Twenty-two

Michael was sitting by the fire whittling a doll, Rhion standing at the window looking out into the grey morning dotted with baggy black clouds possibly stuffed with yet more snow. There had already been one snow fall that morning, a thin white blanket still lying on the ground. The winter was clinging on to the land, tenacious.

One of the cats came dashing into the room sudden, closely followed by the other. The year's first bluebottles had hatched which, if nothing else, had given the cats something to chase. Now they were both hurdling around the room in pursuit of yet another luckless fly. There were times when the chicken joined in these chases, too.

Rhion turned and watched the cats scamper around and around the chairs. Pitch, the tortoiseshell, was quite stupid and slow-witted, only managing to catch a fly the one time when she sat on one by accident. But Toss, the Siamese, was expert at catching them even in flight and indeed soon caught this one, sitting down with eyes half-closed and neck bent towards the floor as she chomped on the live fly which was still buzzing noisy in her mouth.

It was then that Rhion walked towards Pitch and picked her up by the forelegs. Oddly enough Pitch, who was as aggressive as she was stupid, did not object to this rough handling. She allowed Rhion to cart her around and around the room for a couple of minutes until she tired of it and, with a mewl and a wriggle, jumped out of her hands. Rhion watched the cat race out of the room and returned to look out of the window again.

It was the first time she had shown any interest in anything in the three days she had been in the cottage. She had refused to eat or even speak and, most of the time, just sat around the place lifeless, moving only when taken by the hand and led. She did not laugh or cry, appeared neither happy nor sad and Michael found this dreadful lack of animation worrying. Sometimes he tried to tantalise her with funny faces and old broken toys, but all to no avail.

It was Jenko who had suggested that they leave it for a week or so before telling Beth. She was still recovering from her illness and Jenko was afraid that any kind of surprise might set her back. He also wanted the child to settle down and let the bruises heal lest Beth should see the evidence of the child's ill-treatment. Michael had readily agreed to this, particularly as he was sick with nerves when he envisaged the moment when he would have to face her and tell all.

'You what?' he could just hear her shouting livid with rage. 'You've done what?'

They had decided to keep the girl inside the cottage to prevent news of her existence taking flight on many tongues and getting carried over to Loughor. The few tradesmen that had called and seen her were told that she was a distant cousin come to stay after her mother had died.

He put the knife and wood down into the grate and walked out into the kitchen where Megan was busy cooking. 'That one is going to love this meal,' she was saying with theatrical conviction as she joggled some diced beef around in a frying pan. 'Tried everything, I have, but she's going to wolf all this down in one go.'

'I'll believe it when I see it,' he said and walked out into the yard to look out over the estuary. Today was the first day of May and people all over the Gower gathered in the streets at the dawn of this day and sang its welcome with all the young girls, by custom, washing their faces in the May dew. But there had been no welcome this year since, apart from just a few days of sun, hard cold winds were still sweeping in over the sea, humping great sacks of rain on their backs. Then the rain had turned to snow.

The fishermen had reported that the seasonal shoal of sparling fish had not yet arrived either, while down at Llanrhidian a school of hungry otters had come down stream and out on to the marsh to forage for crabs. It was a winter without end, aye.

Even as he stood there in the yard he saw a large white snowflake riding on the wind. It was being chased by another and yet another, all cavorting and dancing drunken. One landed and dribbled cold down the side of his nose; others dissolved in his hair and slid over his scalp. The flakes were so fat they were settling again and already the cocklers were moving in off the sands and returning to the village with their blankets wrapped around their shoulders. In normal times he enjoyed the mysterious, faintly magical snow but times had been far from normal. This winter had been much like being put through the mangle slow and he ached for sight of the sun again.

His horse was pawing at the floor of his shed and he went in to give him a bit of a chuckle to cheer him up when he heard the noise of scraping coming from the next garden. He peered over the fence to see that Vera had two coats on and was shovelling like mad. 'A waste of time just yet,' he pointed out. 'Why don't you wait until there's something to shovel?'

'I'm not going to get stuck in here like in '96. Three days I was stuck then. Three solid days. You remember that, do you?'

He remembered it well. They had three days of peace and quiet as Vera accepted food sent in on a fishing line out of the top bedroom window and her husband snored right through it, just as he had snored right through life. He left her to it and was going back inside when her snow-fluttered head rose over the fence. 'Three solid days I was stuck in that house there. Three whole days and no one bothered to even come and dig me out.'

'You had a husband then, Vera.'

'Asleep all the time, wasn't he? All he was ever good at was sleeping.'

'Well times are different now, Vera. I wouldn't see you stuck in a snowdrift.'

'Yes you would. You'd love it if I was stuck in a snowdrift.' There was plenty of sarcastic emphasis on the word 'love'. 'That sister of yours would anyway. Love to see me buried in a snowdrift she would. She'd steal *all* my cabbages then.'

He doubted if Megan would burrow through a snowdrift just to steal a cabbage but kept his doubts to himself and was opening the back door when his horse ran across the yard – ran! – and tried to barge his way into the warmth of the kitchen. 'Afraid of the snow, then, are we?' Michael asked, grabbing the mane and pulling him back to the shed. 'Your days of flopping in front of the fire are over, mate. Even the cats have trouble getting in. Now get back in there or I'll punch you where it hurts.'

He slid the bolt on the stable door and walked into the kitchen to find Megan in a quiet fury, her face white, the lips tight and curled down at the edges. 'What's the matter?'

'That girl,' she muttered, flinging a saucepan into the skin. 'She's not normal. Diced beef and cabbage I gave her. She just sat looking at it so I put a spoonful in her mouth. She gave it one chew and let it all fall out. I even went all the way over to Bracchi's for ice cream this morning. When did a little girl not like ice cream? Might as well have not wasted my time.'

'She wouldn't eat the ice cream?'

'Wouldn't even look at it. I ended up eating it myself. And, in case you're interested, she can speak. She can say "No" but I doubt very much if she can say "Yes".'

He went into the living room where Rhion was standing at the

259

window, her small hands on the sill, looking out into the snow. 'Not hungry again, eh?' he asked.

She turned and glanced up at him with her large brown eyes before looking out of the window again. 'You fancy a walk in the snow do you?' No response. Worse than her mother this one. 'We can go out for a walk if you like.'

He sat down next to the fire and warmed his hands. It would have helped if the two of them could have just talked but, compared to her, even his dumb horse was a brilliant talker.

Megan came in and put a cup of tea in his hand. 'When are you going to tell Beth?' she said, sighing.

He blew on the tea, the knots in his belly tightening up again. 'Perhaps tomorrow. Perhaps next week. Jenko's going to see her. I'll see what he has to say.'

'The sooner the better I'd say. People don't last long if they don't eat. Aren't you worried?'

'You have a way of asking the daftest questions. 'Course I'm worried.'

'There's no need to raise your voice, is there?'

'Well it stands to reason, doesn't it?'

'You don't need to get abusive about it.'

Rhion was taking sly glances at them and moving slow away from them along the window, almost as if she was aware that she was at the centre of the acrimony and, in consequence, was soon going to get a cuff on the ear. Michael sighed when he noticed what she was doing. It was just possible that she was merely unwilling to be bullied by Megan, he thought. If she was anything like her mother she was unbullyable – if there was such a word.

'I'm trying my best, you know,' Megan moaned on. 'I've tried everything I could.'

'Let it be. I think I've got a way of making her eat. I can usually manage a small donkey after a day out on the sands so I'll taker her out there with me tomorrow. You'd like that, wouldn't you, Rhion? Going out with the horse as well.'

She acted as if she had not heard him and touched the inside of the window with her fingertips, as if trying to move the snowflakes which were melting and dribbling on the outside.

Later that afternoon the snow stopped. He was whittling the doll again when Jenko called, bleating about the weather and the arthritis in his left knee; the way his feet were but blocks of ice and wondering why Scott had ever bothered going to the North Pole when the Gower had to be a good ten degrees colder and a far greater challenge than that damned Northern place which just messed up all your compasses. And all those complaints before he had even sat down.

Megan pulled off his boots and put them to warm in the grate before fussing about him as if he was a new baby in the house. He seemed to like it all too, accepting her mothering with meek nods and slight lifts of the hand.

'Have you eaten?' she asked when he had finished final complaining about the weather.

'Had a liquid lunch.'

'Liquid lunches are no good for you. I'll cook you something.'

'Any of the brandy left, is there?'

'Food first. Brandy later. I just can't understand how you got as fat as you did. You've got to eat, you know. That girl's going to get no bigger than a button if she doesn't eat.'

'How is she?'

'The same,' Michael said. 'Won't drink. Won't talk. Won't do anything.'

He looked over at Rhion who was sitting on a chair quiet, head bowed and studying her knee. He took out his pocket watch, looked at it and put it back before getting up to look into her eyes, hold her wrist and feel parts of her neck and shoulders. She took the examination with sullen good grace.

'There's something wrong here,' Jenko said after a while.

'Are you telling us?'

'Well something wrong and yet not wrong,' he added. 'You see the bruises are healing up fine. There was a very bad one on the arm but that's all gone. She's not gaining any weight but doesn't seem to be losing any either. Yet you say she's not drinking, let alone eating?'

'She wouldn't even touch her ice cream,' said Megan. It was still rankling with her.

'Don't understand it. Just can't understand it.' He returned to his chair, shaking his head. 'If you stop eating you just waste away. It's as simple as that.'

'*You* haven't wasted away, have you?' Megan asked.

'I drink. There's goodness in the drink but, unless the girl has got a secret hoard of booze, she's rewriting the laws of biology. She's not ailing in any real way. Perhaps food really is bad for you. I always suspected it was.'

The three of them stared down at the floor like three workmen gazing into a newly completed hole. 'I went to see Beth this morning,' said Jenko at last.

'Oh aye,' said Michael, getting ready to jump into the hole.

'She's improved a lot, but I think you had better get over there this afternoon. As soon as possible.'

'Why's that?'

He locked his black baleful eyes on Michael. 'I'm not sure how to put this.'

'That's not like you, Jenko.'

He fluttered his fingers around in the air. 'She's planning on going to Australia.'

'Planning on going where?' asked Megan.

'Down under. I never thought anyone in their right mind would want to go to Australia but she's gone and booked to sail out of Cardiff next week.'

Michael studied his right hand. He had cut one of his fingers while whittling the wood and there were rough abrasions from his shovel. He turned it over and back again as if looking for any further dirt after a wash. Outside the snow had turned into rain and was pouring down steady, hissing on the roof and tinkling into one of the overflowing butts in the yard. There was a thinner drip coming from the kitchen. 'Well, that's that then,' he said after a long pause.

'What do you mean, that's that?' Megan asked, almost choking on her own question.

'It sounds plain enough to me.' The notes in his voice creaked. 'That's that. Beth goes to Australia and I keep the little girl here. That's that.'

'But you've got to tell her, Michael. You've got to get over there and at least tell her. Tell him, Jenko. He's got to go over there and at least tell her, hasn't he?'

Jenko nodded. 'We've come too far now. She's got to be told what we've done. She can still go to Australia, if that's what she wants, but she has the right to know.'

'As you say.' Michael pointed to Rhion. 'Shall I take her with me?'

'No. It would look too much like the blackmail that it is. Just go and tell her what you've done. Don't go expecting her to fall into your arms . . .'

'I'm not *that* stupid.'

'Well just keep it in mind. She might even get angry but tell her anyway. If you go there this afternoon you'll find her parents out. They're going to Swansea.' He rubbed his eyes. 'I really do need a brandy now, Meg,' he added, an unfamiliar tiredness in his voice.

'I think we all need a brandy,' Megan replied.

And so, wet with the rain and his heart racing, he was back on the dreaded doorstep of that house again; just standing there with hands in pockets and wondering what his reception was going to be this time. A kick or a kiss? It would not have surprised him if he was kicked and then kissed. Nothing to do with that family would have surprised him. Not for nothing did they live in Crazy Town. They had always said that *his* family was one of the oddest around here, too. The Williams lot just *looked* normal. Ah well. In for a penny . . . He pulled on the bell.

Beth answered the door, her face so pale and drawn he was unsure if it was indeed her for a second. But she actually smiled and appeared glad to see him. The prism revolved again. 'Hello girl,' he said. 'Are you in?'

'Michael. How lovely to see you. I was about to write you a note. Of course I'm in. Come inside.'

He took off his cap and walked into the hallway, glancing up the stairs and out into the kitchen.

'Mama and Dada have gone out,' she said, as if sensing the cause of his anxiety. 'Come in here, will you? Sit there. There's more cushions there and it's nearer the fire. You're wet through.' She sat opposite him, brushing her hair off her forehead, though not saying anything and just gazing at him with a moue of a smile on her lips.

Her warmth enfolded and cheered him immediately. He was genuinely glad that she seemed to have improved, even if it now made it more difficult for him to say what he had come to say. He folded and unfolded his cap as if unsure what to do with it.

'Do you want to hang it up?' she asked.

'It's all right. It'll be all right.' He looked up a the cornices on the ceiling. 'First day of spring as well. You don't expect snow in the spring. I got the shock of my life when I saw that snow this morning.'

'You're still out on the sands then? I often look over there and think of you.' He began turning his cap inside out. 'Dada told me you called over the other day. I'm sorry I didn't see you. I've been very ill you know. But I'm feeling a lot better now. How's that silly horse of yours?'

'What happened? What made you ill?'

'Who's to say? All my puff seemed to go out of me. Perhaps it was those meetings or what but, some mornings, I was just waking up and finding tears running down my cheeks. Nothing made any sense in all the commotion. A few of the other ladies were affected like that too. I got to . . . then there was the silence with Mr Roberts. He was even worse affected than us in the end and there was that . . . that night . . . ' She paused and bit her lip, looking down at the floor. 'Oh well, it's all over now.'

'What happened to Roberts?'

'I'm not sure. There's reports in the papers he's living with some people in Leicester. He may have come home, of course, but I've heard nothing. His state is not too surprising I suppose. Over the past months he must have said more words than most people speak in a lifetime.' She laughed with a hint of that old effervescence that had once beguiled him so much.

'You mentioned that night. What happened?'

'Oh Michael, let's not talk about it anymore. I just want to put it all behind me. How are you keeping? Tell me everything about what you've been doing.'

'I . . . ' He was about to form his lips around the dreaded confession but, somehow, it did not seem to want to take shape in his mouth. What right did he have to take her happiness away from her? 'I'm still working the sands. I could be better but I've been far worse. But tell me about you. What are you going to do now?'

'Well, I've got some good news for a change.' He braced himself since he already knew the nature of her good news but still did not want to hear it. 'I've decided to start another life and go to Australia. Isn't that wonderful, Michael?'

'Wonderful.' He put down his cap on the seat next to him and folded his arms. 'Wonderful. I'm very pleased for you.'

'I've an aunt living near Melbourne. She's got a small farm outside the city. She and her husband, that is. Sheep, cattle, that kind of thing. I thought I'd work there for a while before deciding what to do. It's a land of great opportunity, Michael. Aren't you pleased?'

'I'd be more pleased if you told me that you were about to cut my right hand off.'

'Oh dear.' She looked so crestfallen at that remark he wished that he had not made it. 'Oh dear me,' she sighed again. 'It couldn't have worked, Michael. I am very fond of you *cariad* but we were both overtaken by circumstances. The circumstances were too much for us.'

'Circumstances can be changed. Love can change circumstances. I could have given you what you needed but now you're running again.'

She gazed at the fire for a few moments before clearing her throat and speaking with slow and almost surgical care. 'I need a new start after all the fuss this winter. I owe it to myself to try a new start. Since I made the decision I've been happier than I've been for a long time. There's been too much of my past around here. Just the very thought of being on that ship makes me happy with excitement. It's costing eighteen guineas. One way, that is. I even dreamed that I was already on the ship last night. Oh

Michael, can you imagine it . . . '

He knew that he had been beaten even before she began speaking. He had always believed that a love affair does not evaporate overnight – it falls apart bit by bit, corroded by accident and – what had she called them? – circumstances. Something told him that they were now both watching the last big bit fall away, that there was no longer any point in hurling himself against the cliff of her obduracy like so many breaking waves. If he loved her at all then this love meant that he had to let her go and discover whatever it was she was looking for herself. There was no advantage to her in digging up her past now.

The decision, made there and then, was surprisingly easy to make. He could look after Rhion easy enough. The girl would be some consolation for the loss of her mother; a part of her that he would always have.

'How long will the voyage last?' he asked.

'Well two months for definite. Possibly longer.'

'Depends on the tides and winds I suppose.'

'Mmmm. And the cargoes. They warn you there's always liable to be a change of orders to do with the cargoes and the only thing they do guarantee is that you'll get there, somehow and at some time, in the end.'

He picked up his cap again. Perhaps they would both get there in the end. At least conclusions were now in sight – even if they weren't exactly the conclusions he had hoped for.

'When are you sailing?'

'Out of Cardiff next week. May the ninth.'

There was another silence. That ship, that ship. After dreaming for so long of taking sea journeys himself it was surprising that he did not even want to get on that ship with her. There was Rhion to think of now.

'Well look after yourself, girl,' he said standing up. 'The French say, I think, *bon voyage*. Try and send me a letter, will you?'

'Of course. But do you have to go just yet?'

'I'd better. It's getting late.' Getting late! When had he ever left her of his own accord? He suspected that it was something to do with fear of blurting out his little secret. She also stood up and moved so close to him he could feel her breath on his face.

'Would you do just one thing for me?' she asked.

'Just say it.'

'Take the goldfish and look after him for me. It's Dada. He's not terribly fond of changing the water.'

'All right. At least you'll have to write to me now – even if only to find how the fish is doing.'

'It's a deal my love.'

Her use of the word 'love' made something inside him jump like a startled frog and he lifted that eternally rogue lock of hair off her forehead and put it back into place. Her composure was all of a jumble too, and she looked close to tears as they stood together in the doorway.

'I'm still not convinced about all this seaweed,' he said, nodding down at the tank in his hands. 'I told you before. Goldfish don't get on with seaweed.'

'He's been getting on with it all right so far but take it out if you want,' she said. 'Dada's friend said it wouldn't hurt it. He knows about fish.'

Her parting kiss had real warmth and even fire in it and only ended when he got a bit carried away and slopped a fair bit of the goldfish's water over her dress. Even the goldfish was against them, he decided.

Rain speckled on his face as he walked back to Pen-clawdd but he was far from ripped apart, almost relieved. The end had been clean and, just for once, he was walking away from her home with his dignity intact. All that rotating rigor mortis had been getting on his nerves as well and those mad maggots had all but driven him crazy too.

He took a deep breath as the goldfish's water slopped against the arms of his jacket. Soon the summer sun would be warming them again and, although he did not have Beth, he did have her baby – and her goldfish. It was all, as they say, far better than a kick in the head.

The steam was all but coming out of Megan's ears when he confessed to her that he had not told Beth. 'Let's get this straight shall we?' she asked. 'You go over there to tell her you've got her baby. You don't tell her you've got her baby and you come back here with her goldfish.'

'That's right,' he said knocking the tank's wall with a knuckle. 'Pretty, isn't he? Horace he's called.'

'Haven't you got enough animals around here?'

'Horace isn't an animal in case you hadn't noticed. He's a fish. Aren't you, eh? A pretty little fish who just swims around and around.'

'Waifs and strays. That's all you're interested in.'

'Aye and there's plenty of us around, aren't there?' he asked looking straight at her. 'And some of us stray more than others.'

'What do you mean by that?'

'Come and look at the fish,' he said to Rhion who had been sitting through it all without so much as a murmur. He walked over to take her hand and was extremely sorry to see her lift her arm to protect her head when he came near.

'See? The girl's terrified,' said Megan. 'She needs a mother around. I can't look after her.'

'Can't or don't want?'

'She needs a mother, Michael. *Her* own mother.'

'Look. I'll get out a blackboard and do it in signs if you want. Beth is going to start a new life. Rhion is staying here with me. When the girl grows up she can start a new life if she wants.'

'It all sounds mad to me.'

'Mad it may be, but that's the way I want it.'

'I suppose I'll have to stay then.'

'Oh not the suffering martyr act. It doesn't suit you, Meg. You don't *have* to do anything. You never have done and you're not likely to start now.'

'But she's not eating.'

'She'll eat. I'll get her eating. I've got ways. She's going to be my partner out on the sands, aren't you? As of tomorrow consider yourself apprenticed.'

'I've had enough of all this,' Megan said, putting on her coat.

'Where are you going?' he asked, worried that she might be going over to tell Beth herself. Megan had made interference one of her life's great specialities.'

'I'm going to find Jenko and get as drunk as a skittle. Doubtless he'll have something to say about all this.'

'Doubtless. But you make sure he says them to me and not to Beth.'

'You lot. What with you and that girl and that goldfish . . . and all these bloody animals. You're all going to be the death of me.'

The next day fluffy dandelion seeds were parachuting on the breezes and the wild horses were scattered over the sun-splashed marsh when Michael took Rhion for her first outing down on the sands. She sat on the cart and kept looking around her, frightened by all that high, wide space, as he scouted around for signs of cockles. But, after a while, she just sat there peaceable in an old coat of Megan's – about ten sizes too big for her – hands nowhere to be seen and feet dangling out from beneath the coat's hem.

He began collecting a variety of shells, taking them over to her and spreading them out on the cart. One was the long thin shell of a razor fish and he explained to her that, in olden days, men used to split them down the middle and actually use them to shave their faces.

She was hardly intrigued but neither was she indifferent so he gained confidence that he would win her over in the end. He had decided that he was going to talk to her and tell her things, whether she liked it or not. Soon she would hear all the stories of the marsh and sands – the ones his father had once told him – and, who knows? she might just come to love the place as he did. That would be a great help to any girl. The marsh and sands were the best place he knew to grow wild.

He began working while stealing glances at her. At one stage she did play with the shells, but stopped when she saw she was being watched. Sometimes, he fancied, her face intensified into the absolute image of Beth. It was uncanny – the long-lashed eyes, the high cheekbones and the slight obstinate jut of the jaw. How long did obstinacy stay obstinate? He just did not know. The wind blew the girl's hair around as she looked over at the sea and up at the birds diving and wheeling all around them. That sulky private dignity was Beth again.

Later she jumped off the cart when his back was turned and searched for some shells of her own. He could have sworn she was even having a word with them but, when she saw she was being watched again, she stood up with a haughty lift of her head and waddled away like some over-sized bat that had forgotten how to fly in that huge coat. He would have to get her some proper clothes when he next went to Swansea market.

He worked well, striking a rich patch, and had almost filled a sack of cockles when a noisy bleeping swarm of oystercatchers came swooping over their heads. A second fluttering, gabbling cloud of the birds rose from the other side of the marsh, banking high before diving to join those already circling above them. Their white bellies flashed as if on fire as they turned against the sunlight; Rhion was so alarmed by their sudden whooping pandemonium she ran to take shelter under the cart.

'Don't worry girl,' he said, deciding to pack up and return home. 'They're just getting ready to go back to Norway. Tonight they'll all be gone leaving the warblers and waders to have the sands to themselves.'

It was a strain staying out on the sands on the day the oystercatchers left – no matter how well the cockles were coming up – since they bustled around and around, calling to one another deep in hysterical excitement at the prospect of a long flight. It was the kind of shrill music that people went mad by. He always felt that much better when they went away. He got used to their monotonous calls as winter progressed but, when they had gone, there was a more satisfying and musical silence out on the sands. The waders only really sang at the turns of the tide and the rest of the day was quiet apart from the odd call of the gulls and the wind whistling soft in the sands.

His horse ambled back slightly faster than he had ambled out and

Michael wondered if Jenko and Megan were going to leave his decision on Rhion unchallenged. He doubted it and returned to the cottage, fully expecting to find them there, but the place was empty. 'Well, baby, it looks as if it's just you and me now,' he said to her, putting some bread, cheese and cold ham pie on the kitchen table in front of her. After a day on the sands he was confident that she would wolf down the lot but she just took one look at it, stood up and walked into the living room. He bit his lower lip. Was he doing the right thing? He was not sure. Perhaps he might have to tell Beth after all. In any event, he still had another week to go before she sailed.

Come the dusk he washed Rhion with a damp flannel, pulled one of his shirts over her head and took her upstairs to bed. She just lay there with her eyes wide open so he began making up a long and complicated story about fighting men with long hair who invaded a deep green valley to capture children and turn them into slaves. He was struggling to work out a happy ending when her eyes closed – whether through the call of sleep or sheer boredom he could not tell – and he kissed her on the forehead, blowing out the oil lamp and staying there for a few minutes listening to her being.

When he went downstairs he banked up the fire. Outside the wind had stopped humming and the night was very still.

* * *

The next morning he awoke at cockcrow and made a pot of tea, taking up two cups for Megan and Rhion. The girl just frowned at hers, as if it was laced with arsenic. From the unrumpled bed in Megan's room, he saw that she had not come home again. He wondered if she had moved out without even saying goodbye but, checking under her bed, he saw that her bag was still there.

Back down in the living room he had to evict the cats who were busy harassing the goldfish and, when they were ejected into the yard, the chicken began harassing them. The chicken was the only creature the cats had any respect for and, when she got moving, she pecked lumps out of them and they cried like babies having hatpins stuck in them. He sat down at the kitchen table with defeat grabbing him like a tight-fitting vest. All he needed was to find his horse in a bad temper and he would go back to bed himself. Discipline. That's what this lot needed. If they were not fighting amongst themselves they were refusing to eat and sulking or else trying to kill his goldfish and, if not that, out on the tiles all night misbehaving. It was all like living in an eisteddfod of lunatics.

Much more of this and he would trade in the whole lot for one well-behaved hedgehog.

He finished his tea and poured out another cup; his imagination busy constructing an elaborate regime of terror. There would be a guillotine in the yard and thumbscrews on the wall. A stretching rack for those who refused to work and red hot pokers for those who refused to eat. He was trying to work out where to locate the ducking stool when Megan walked in, her eyes puffy and red through lack of sleep and all her curls somehow pushed to one side of her head. A double-locked chastity belt with spikes all round it for her. She sat down at the table and all the muscles in her face seemed to have gone funny. A poet might have called it a well-sexed look though, there again, he might not.

'It's good to see someone's been out enjoying themselves,' he said, pouring her a cup of tea.

'Enjoying myself!' Her hands were shaking so much she could hardly hold the cup steady. 'He's not a man, he's a machine. He's after it all the time. For a man who's spent all his life gazing into the working end of a bottle of beer I don't know how he does it. He's going to wear me away.' She held the cup to her lips with both hands and chuckled. 'Not a bad way to go though.'

'Well who would have believed it?'

'Believed what?'

'Jenko performing like that. Must be something they put in at the brewery. Are you going to move in with him, are you?'

'I've been thinking of it. Oh think of the scandal. They'll be able to gossip themselves silly for a year on that one. Trouble is I just don't want to leave you alone with the little one.'

'I've told you. We'll manage. Anyway I'd prefer to live with her on my own. What did Jenko say about me keeping her?'

'Oh, he was drunk when I told him. He didn't seem concerned in the slightest and muttered some rubbish about man having control over his destiny. You know how he gets.' She sipped her tea. 'Is Rhion eating yet?'

'No.'

'You should have told her mother, you know. I'm still convinced of that. Mothers have ways with their own.'

He picked up a teaspoon and played with it. 'Maybe. But I'll give Rhion a week and, if she's not eating by then, I might just tell Beth.'

She stared at him hard. 'It's too late Michael. She's gone. Beth's gone.'

He shook his head. 'No she's not. She's got another week to go. She told me.'

'Michael she's gone. Jenko only heard himself this morning. It seems

270

she told everyone – even her parents – that she was going in another week because she wanted to leave without any fuss. She left home last night and is due to sail out of Cardiff this morning. Her mother came to see Jenko first thing today. That's why I left early. He wanted to talk to her alone.'

A cold hand turned around inside him. 'That's Beth. She would swim the Atlantic to avoid any fuss.' He stood up.

'We could catch the midday train to Cardiff, Michael. We might still find her.'

'No. It's done now. Let her be.' He walked out into the yard and gazed out over the estuary, where the blaze of sunshine on the full, still tide made him shade his eyes. So the end had really come at last. I'll always be there behind you, girl – always be right there behind you. If you chase the winds long enough you might find it. He put his hands on the fence and Megan came and stood next to him, putting an arm around his waist and a head on his shoulder. 'You're not going to start fretting again, are you?' she asked.

'Never felt better.'

'Do you want me to stay here with you?'

He shook his head and tears flew out of his eyes. He supposed that he had always secretly hoped that she would still come; that there was still a chance. He took out a handkerchief and blew his nose. 'I really would prefer to be on my own, Meg. Just call over now and then would you? You know. Cook us a meal now and then.'

'Of course. I'll come at the end of every tide – and make sure Jenko keeps an eye on the girl too. Send a message over to Loughor if you want anything. Anything at all.' She squeezed his arm and kissed him on the side of the neck.

'Go away will you. You're making me worse.'

He remained standing at the fence and only moved when he saw that the tide was turning. Rhion all but jumped out of bed when he shouted at her. 'Come on you. There's work to be done. You're going to get bed blisters if you stay there much longer.'

She neither helped nor hindered him as he dressed her and just kept looking into his eyes. When he had finished dressing her she lifted a finger and pointed at his face. 'Crying,' she said with a frown.

So she could speak. Even in his tears a strange burst of happiness exploded inside him. So she did know some words: so she did understand the English language. She seemed concerned about him too. It was all some kind of start, to be sure.

'I'm crying because you won't eat, you sledgehammer.' He patted her backside. 'Now get down those stairs.'

She walked towards the door, obedient, but stopped and turned back to look at him. 'Crying? Why crying?'

Her words, her very first words, made him cry even more, the tears running copious down his hot cheeks. The problem was he was not at all sure why he was crying. 'Get down those stairs, will you?'

That night he was holding Beth tight on the prow of the ship as it rode up over the waves then came down hard on the bows. Silver flying fish broke away from the ship as the salt spray rained against their faces. He was woken by the noise of a high wind rattling the slates in the cottage's roof.

He fell into a light sleep again when there was a knock on the door and Evan Roberts came into the bedroom wanting to borrow a cup of sugar. Evan sat down on the bed as Michael poured a torrent of abuse on him for what he had done. Later Evan was asking if he could borrow the horse when Michael was again woken by the wind. He lay looking up into the darkness, realising that he had to go to the lavatory. Offensive though the night was, there was no way of putting it off.

He lit the oil lamp and was halfway down the stairs when he stopped still. Even in that high wind he knew all the noises of his home; the soft sudden thumps of cats jumping off ledges; the stairs which creaked when stepped on; the way the wind made the front door rattle. But tonight there was a strange and alien noise in the cottage.

He entered the living room and held up the lamp; the goldfish was moving around in his tank. There was the movement of tins or cutlery or something and he crossed the room to open the kitchen door.

Rhion's face turned up into the yellow glare of the lamp; a lump of bread in one hand and her cheeks puffed up with food. Her eyes widened in fright and she coughed out the food, squealing with a trapped animal's fear as she scuttled straight past him with her head well down, bolting across the living room and straight up the stairs. She moved so fast he did not have time to move, let alone think.

He put the lamp down on the table and examined the remains of her meal. There was bread, a piece of pie and some nibbled bits of cheese. Oh no. The poor little slum rat. It was evident that she had learned long ago that food should always be stolen in the dark of the night. It was also clear that she tidied everything away after she had finished eating. He went out to the lavatory in the yard and the relief was abundant in more senses than one. So that's why she had not been losing weight. His chuckles were curiously amplified by the small wooden shed as he gave way to a lot of pleased sighs and dreams.

Later he went up to the little slum rat's room, finding her buried under her bed clothes and doubtless anticipating a few hefty belts. He made sufficient noise to ensure that she knew he was there and sat on the side of her bed rubbing his hand up and down her trembling back. 'Only badgers eat by the light of the moon, but it doesn't matter,' he whispered. 'You can be a badger if you want. Just feed when you like, girl. It doesn't matter a bit.'

There was a very broad smile on his face when he lay back on his own bed. He was now sure that he was not going to have the trouble with her that he'd had with her mother. He would get the badger under control. She could always eat like that if she wanted as well – at least it would save him the trouble of cooking food and washing up the dishes afterwards. If nothing else, he would have to make sure that there was enough food about the cottage to get stolen in the first place.

Outside the wind was still howling, demented.

Meeting in Princes Road Chapel, Liverpool, Dan wrote in his diary. *It was crowded when Evan walked in at 7 p.m. but he said nothing until 8.30 p.m. when he walked out again.*

In Sun Hall he complained that he was being hypnotised by a member of the congregation and walked out. The Revival is at an end.

Chapter Twenty-three

The deckhand dragged her trunk into a small dark hutch and Beth stood waiting for him to lead her to her cabin. They just looked at one another, blank. Well?

'This is your cabin, ma'am.'

She could hardly believe it as she stepped inside the small black hole and peered around. There was a bunk barely the width of a bookshelf, a drawer underneath it – for her clothing she supposed – and a corner shelf holding a basin and jug of water. Everything was dusty and, even worse, quite smelly; the cabin was down below the water line beneath the capstan on the aft deck. Two months in this!

She sat on the bunk and undid the collar of her blouse for more air. Oh foof! Distant noises of coal being poured into the hold were echoing down through the ship, the *Penarth Endeavour*, a steamship registered in Cardiff. They even had sides of meat hanging out on the deck, and all those sailors leering at her had done nothing to allay her dark forebodings either. She had forgotten that a ship was worked by sailors.

A sudden clanking noise made her jump. It was the capstan just above her head, occasionally freewheeling on its gears as it took the strain of the ship's mooring rope, chuckling loud like chained ghosts about to start the night shift of a haunting. The clanking stopped again, giving way to the despairing creaks in the bulkhead and the gentle sloshing down in the bilges. It was all the strangest symphony of odd noises: *crank, cackle, crank, slosh, slush, groan, gluck, slosh, gack.*

She began sweating so much she had to undo her bodice also. Breathing was about as difficult as chewing a bit of tough meat and the smell of oil was so strong she could actually taste it in her mouth. At least the air would freshen up when they sailed, she supposed, at seven o'clock on the next morning tide. The only thing that had cheered her up that afternoon had been seeing a minister of the cloth evidently taking the same voyage. She had retained something of her trust in God and, but for a short prayer for strength, would have got off there and then. There were also, she had been relieved to see, two other ladies making the voyage.

She took off her dress and lay back on her bunk, her lungs still fighting for breath. The capstan clanked again. She could have gone up on the deck to take some fresh air, of course, but she had resolved to stay in her cabin until the ship had sailed. The blunt truth was that the ship was so close to her Rhion's home in Loudoun Square she was scared that she might do something silly; that after all this she might mess everything up again. She was sure now that God wanted her to go away; sure that He wanted her to start life anew so she was going to stay put, right here, until the ship was safely out in the Bristol Channel. *Crank, cackle, slosh, slush.*

But how the dockland had changed since she had been here last. Travelling in the dray down Bute Street she had been surprised and even alarmed by all those black and brown faces. All those lovely houses had changed into ugly pubs and noisy Chinese laundries. One mad man had even jumped on the running board of the dray. She prayed that Rhion was all right in all that mess. She would never have left the girl to grow up in anything like that; she would never have abandoned her in the beginning if she had known the way the place was going to turn out.

She tossed and turned to the noise of the capstan and shed a torrent of tears. She wept for Rhion, for Evan, for Michael, for her parents, but most of all for Rhion until, unable to bear the suffocating heat and the rising burden of her own misery any longer, she put on her dress and climbed up on deck where a fresh night wind was blowing in over the calm waters of Bute East Dock. She held her hair up in a knot, letting the breeze dry up the sweat on her face. Her eyes had gone puffy with tears.

Over on the other side of the dock was the tiny white corrugated Norwegian Church, Norske Sjonamskirke, sitting like a forgotten doll's house next to the Thisbe Mission Ship. A few lonely drunks staggered across the wharves to their own ships, past the windjammers, clippers and new steamships – all tied up together like rows of upturned insects, black on bright grey, in the moonlight. All around her stood a forest of black, broken-necked cranes and, just visible on the horizon, she could see the rooftops of the houses of Loudoun Square.

She crossed the aft deck and stood, hands on rails, looking out over the Bristol Channel. It was down there on Pier Head she had walked Rhion in the pram, her mouth round and open in her first smile and tiny arms flailing like a fighter unable to hit anything. Urchins had dived off the end of the pier to retrieve pennies thrown by the promenaders on Sundays. Parasoled ladies walked up and down, some stopping to bill and coo over her baby. *Her* baby. She leaned forward as if punched and felt she was about to be sick into the coal-black waters. The capstan clanked and cackled behind her.

The tide was full and she noticed a man rowing a skiff out into the channel. A low drone rose into the still night as the tiny flash of a paddle steamer appeared at the channel's mouth. The steamer's golden lights glittered and glinted like a rising pile of jewels as the great revolving paddles pounded and squished towards the pontoon. A forward deckhand threw a rope to the man in the skiff, who missed it and checked himself as he nearly fell into the dock. The captain leaned over his bridge and roundly cussed the man in the skiff. The crowds on the decks cheered wild when the man in the skiff cursed the captain. The deckhand threw the line again, successfully this time, and soon the swishing steamer was being winched up against the bobbing pontoon with the passengers, many drunk after a day out in Weston-Super-Mare, tumbling down the gangplank.

Beth watched the last of them leave and, when all the steamer's lights were doused, she returned back to her bunk where she wound up her fretwork clock and lay back on her bunk, falling into a fitful sleep threaded with bad dreams.

When she awoke it was nine o'clock. She could feel no movement in the ship. She dressed quick and went up on deck where the purser, surrounded by a group of passengers, was explaining that there had been a change of orders and they would be here for another two days.

Beth stood on the outskirts of the complaining group as the purser continued to explain the paramount demands of cargo and the way even passengers were secondary to cargo orders from head office. Maybe it was meant to be like this. If the ship had sailed when it was supposed to, then that would have been that. As it was, it must be a sign from God that she should go and see . . .

Loudoun Square was in a shocking state when she got there, every coloured skin in the world milling about her and those cholera hovels with pitiful ragged mites everywhere. And No.14 . . . good Lord what had happened here? She lifted the hem of her skirt up out of the rubbish on the doorstep and peered down the abject hallway where a man lay spread-eagled, as if dead. She turned away immediately with relief bubbling up inside her – the Lewises were a respectable couple who must have moved somewhere else, thank goodness. At least that was an end to it and she could sail with a peaceable mind. She had checked and found that life was all right for them. Or was it?

Well that was that, she decided as she hurried back down through the throbbing energy of Bute Street. She had promised that she would never return to see Rhion, and now she could keep the promise if only because she did not know where the Lewises were any longer. That was fine, wasn't it? Things were always simpler when you didn't know anything.

She stopped on a corner to watch a group of Moslem children pouring out of the Cairo Café, laughing delirious among themselves while chanting and singing the good news of *Eide Mombarik*. They had gathered around a man carrying a huge green and golden flag who, with a long whinnying yodel, began running off down the pavement pursued by a stream of children, white robes flowing in the sunshine, until they all reached the small mosque on the corner of Peel Street where the adults greeted them with yet more chants of joy.

Beth was sharing in their festive happiness when a group of men shouldered their way past her, arguing fierce. She caught a glimpse of a familiar face among them. Older, yes, scruffier too, poorer for certain but that was Ted Lewis and no mistake. After pacing around for a few seconds she plucked up enough courage to rush after them into the Rothesay Castle.

'Excuse me, Mr Lewis,' she said touching him on the arm at the bar. 'You do remember me don't you? Beth. Beth Williams.'

His reaction quite shattered her. 'What in hell's going on now?' he screamed at her and backing away, as if she was about to attack him. Everyone in the bar turned and looked at them in silence. 'Aren't you lot ever satisfied? You came and took the girl back. What more do you want from me? Blood?'

Beth stared at him, incredulous. Then she fainted.

Michael had returned from a successful day working the tide. He was unloading his cockles and pouring them into his Dutch boiler, with Rhion standing near the horse in her oversized overcoat. Then Vera's head appeared over the fence.

'Michael Evans, Michael Evans,' she shouted, bobbing up and down with excitement and holding a small egg between her thumb and forefinger. 'Look at this then. What about this? The tortoise has laid an egg, she has.'

The old crone was cackling so much you would have sworn that she had laid it herself. 'Congratulations,' he said without much enthusiasm.

'Laid it on the path, she did. Do you believe that? Right there on the path. It's a miracle your cats didn't get it. Or that thieving sister of yours. What do you do with it?'

'How'd you mean?'

'Well how do I hatch it? Do I take it to bed with me or what?'

'Put it in a box of sand and leave it out in the sun.'

'I can't do that. You can't leave anything out in the sun these days. The slugs would get it – or your cats – or that damned chicken of yours. They'd just eat it, wouldn't they? I mean that's what you'd expect from them, wouldn't you? I mean . . . '

He noticed that Rhion, comforting thumb in mouth was circling away from Vera as she spoke. He could see how the old battle-axe could be quite terrifying to little girls and he was very pleased when the girl came and stood behind him, her hand holding the bottom of his jacket as Vera continued slandering his animals.

'Got a new tortoise of your own I see,' Vera said, nodding at Rhion. 'Where'd she hatch out then?'

'She came in a box of sand. That's what you need for that tortoise egg. Plenty of sun and sand and less of the old nose.'

He unloaded the rest of his cockles and lit a fire under the boiler. He was sitting on a bench watching his chicken chase a fly around the yard when Megan came into the kitchen behind him and dumped a bag of groceries on the table.

'Jenko wants to know if he can tell Beth's mother what we've done,' she yelled out of the window. 'He says she'll keep it quiet. What do you think?' –

'Ooooh uuuuummmm.' He was as abstracted as the wind.

'Anything wrong with you, is there?'

'Just thinking about something. It was hot out on those sands today. Drifting heat hazes everywhere, there were.'

'Did you hear what I said about Beth's mother?'

'Mmm. The answer's no. I don't want anyone knowing. No one. That sun though. Hot it was.'

'She *is* her grandmother. She might be able to help.'

'I don't need any help,' he said sharp. 'Tell Jenko no.'

Out in the yard Rhion was facing his horse, who was standing with his head lowered and snorting some sort of secret snort language at her. 'I'll teach you how to ride him one day,' he said. 'He'd like to have someone really tiny riding him, wouldn't you? Not very keen on heavy loads, are you?'

He tapped her on the shoulder and pointed at the kitchen door. 'Come on, badger. Time for bed. Bed.' She stuck her thumb into her mouth and walked into the kitchen. 'I'll be down after putting her to bed,' he told Megan, who was slicing a beetroot.

'Don't you put her in the tub?'

'She'll get one a week like the rest of us. On Sundays.'

'What about food? Is she eating?'

'She's eating. But she steals it in the middle of the night. Don't you badger?'

'Well, well.'

He put the girl to bed. Later, after Megan had gone, he was sitting at the table in the kitchen reading the latest copy of *The Miner*. It described itself as a journal for underground workers but he liked the reports on the troubles overground: the way the miners were organising for a sliding scale of wages, arbitration courts and regulations of outputs. Strike after strike was drawing blood. The socialists were on the march at last.

He was turning over a page when the front door opened and Beth walked in. He let his paper fall to the floor and understood at that moment what it was like to be struck dumb.

'I've been down to Cardiff to get on that ship,' she said cold. 'I've been told you've got Rhion here.'

He nodded. 'You'd better sit down,' he said.

She sat down on a chair opposite him, her arms folded like a teacher waiting to hear a very good excuse for some very bad behaviour. No, she didn't want a cup of tea, thank you. No, this chair was perfectly comfortable. When it was evident she would have to ask him direct, her question was sharp and very much to the point. 'Why did you do it, Michael?'

His shoulders shrugged around as if he was on his horse going over bumpy land. He had long been expecting that question but had thought of nothing by way of a convincing reply. 'I thought it might help you,' he said final. 'We knew that you were still missing her . . . '

'We?'

'Jenko and Megan and me.'

'Oh did you now? Did you put an advert in the *Swansea Evening Post*, did you? Is there anyone else who doesn't know now?'

'No one knows anything. We . . . we just thought that bringing back the child would help you. It was as simple as that.'

'Help *you*, do you mean? Oh Michael, it's the worst thing I've ever heard. Why didn't you ask me first? Did you really think I'd come to you because you had Rhion? Did you really think that? I thought you had brains as well.'

'I didn't know what I thought. Jenko decided it might be a good idea – for you, not me – and I was still full of doubts even when we went down to Cardiff. But when we found that Rhion was being treated like an animal we just felt that anywhere was better than where she was.'

'Treated like an animal? I don't understand.'

'The girl was starving and beaten by that Lewis. Meg found her in the house locked upstairs. She had to come with us after that.'

'How is she now?'

'She's getting better. She wouldn't eat at first but I've only just discovered she was stealing food here in the middle of the night. I call her the badger.'

Beth closed her eyes and took in a long breath through her nose. 'Just how bad can everything get? Just how bad?'

'How did you find out she was here? I wanted to tell you the day I came over but couldn't.'

'The ship had been delayed a few days. There was some change of cargo so I thought I'd go and see Rhion for the last time. I knew I shouldn't have but I just couldn't help myself. I couldn't find the house but I bumped into Lewis in the street. He refused to speak to tell me what had happened at first.'

'Jenko and me had fun and games with him. He's a crafty devil is that Lewis.'

'I'm sure he is. I got so wild with worry I even gave him money in the end. Even then he wouldn't say much but he did say that two men and woman had come and taken her away. He was vague about who – a bit scared, I thought – but, from what he did say, I guessed it was you. It sounded the kind of thing you'd do. I must say it didn't even occur to me that Jenko was involved but it's all clear enough now.' Her voice trailed away. 'Why, oh why, didn't you tell me you had her?'

'I tried but, when I saw you wanted to make a new start, I just couldn't.'

'So what are you going to do now?'

'I'm going to look after her. She's a likeable girl and does as she's told – not like some around here. We'll manage. Don't worry about us.'

'Well, you've given me a bit of a fright and I wasn't sure what to do. But, if you're sure you can manage, I will go. The ship sails tomorrow night.'

'You do what you want. Don't worry about us.' He was astonished at his own calm; one of the cats climbed on to his lap. 'The girl will manage fine. I'll look after her as if she was my own. She gets on well with the cats too, even seems to like the old goldfish. Just stands there watching him for hours.'

'You've taken out the seaweed, I see.'

'Mmmm. I was never convinced about that. But don't worry about the girl. You'll just have to trust me.'

'I do.'

'You'll want to see her, I suppose?'

'Yes. I'd like to very much.'

He lit a bullrush candle and took it up to the bedroom. Rhion was fast asleep, her thumb in her mouth. Beth sat on the side of the bed and pulled the sheet down a little. 'Who cut her hair?' she whispered.

'Megan.'

'It's terrible. There's ridges everywhere.'

'It was the scissors. They're not very sharp.'

'But she's eating, you say?'

'Well not . . . ' Rhion stirred and turned over, exchanging thumbs in the process.

'Will you leave us for a while?' Beth asked.

'Of course. But, if she wakes up, she might get scared seeing you. You'd better give me a shout if that happens.'

He tip-toed out of the room and walked down the stairs to sit next to the fire. He wondered what would happen if Rhion did wake up; if there was any way a child could recognise her own mother. He wondered what was moving through Beth's veins. He even still nursed a faint hope that the child would make her want to stay after all. But, there again, he had known Beth long enough to understand that she was not moved through her emotions; that, however strong the emotion, she always managed to control it with her mind. It was only wild dreamers like him, with no control over their feelings, who usually ended up in mad messes.

But he did not believe that he was in a mad mess now. It had a certain jumble about it that appealed to him; after all, he could still have a woman and even get one to come and live with him if he ever found the need.

* * *

Beth sat in the hazy dancing light of the bullrush candle for more than half an hour gazing down at her baby. Nothing moved inside her as she sat in silent communion with the child's being, holding her hands as if in prayer as she listened to the soft breaths of the flesh and blood that was her own flesh and blood. This was hers too.

When she came down she smiled at Michael and he fell in love with her all over again. He saw that she had again gone through one of her startling transformations of mood – now the complete and full woman, the replete mother. He wanted to take her in his arms and hold her tight forever. Indeed he got up to do that but walked straight past her and out into the kitchen.

'I'm sure you could do with a cup of tea now,' he called out.

'Oooh yes. I wouldn't mind a sandwich or something as well.'

'I don't know what we've got. Some cheese, I think. Plenty of cockles, of course.'

'A plate of them would do fine. I've been so worried I haven't eaten for ages.'

'You're worse than that daughter of yours, you are. A real daft pair if you ask me. Why don't you hang up your cloak behind the door?'

He put the kettle on the stove and she came out and sat at the kitchen table. 'What are you going to do then? Did you think any more about buying a farm?'

'Well, you can still get land cheap in the Black Mountains, I hear. But there's no hurry. I'm happy enough here for a bit. I couldn't leave this place now and anyway there's no schools in the Black Mountains. Rhion has to go to school.'

'Ah yes, school.'

'She fits in well here, you know.' He was even getting a bit cocky now. 'They're all misfits in this house – and it's good for children to grow up with animals. It teaches them how to care for life. I think Pitch will be having kittens soon and the badger will like that. I've never known a child who does not like kittens. There's some salad around here somewhere. Meg made some salad.'

'Oh I'm not that hungry. Don't bother. Really.'

'You've got to eat. There's plenty of cockles.'

'The tea will be fine. Really.'

He poured the boiling water into the teapot and stirred it with a fork. She was quite flustered and he could never remember her being like this.

'You don't have to go,' he said picking his words, careful, as he poured the tea. 'I'm not expecting you to change your mind but I do want you to know that you can stay if you want. And, if it doesn't work out in Australia, you can come back here any time you want. Any time.'

She blew on her tea to cool it. 'I like sitting in kitchens,' she said. 'The warmth, the smell of food, the cosiness. Better than sitting in vast parlours any day or that ship. You should see my cabin. Even your chicken would turn up its nose at it. Smelly and dirty. *Ach y fi.*'

'You don't have to go.'

She sighed. 'I know. But I've got to clear my mind, you know. One way or another the Revival went bad for me. I just think I need to get away and breathe some different air.'

'What happened? You never said what happened.'

She bit her lip ruminative and sipped her tea. 'It doesn't matter now. It's all done with now.'

'You can tell me.'

'No. It's all over and done with.'

There was the finality of a judge's sentence in her words. He saw that it was pointless to argue. She reached out and gripped his arm. 'I would love to stay here with you both. But I must go away and forget. Believe me, there's an awful lot to forget. For someone who has always believed in a quiet life I haven't done too well.'

'No. You haven't done very well at all. Perhaps you'll find what you're looking for in Australia.'

'Perhaps.' She let her hand drop and lowered her head. 'But I doubt it.'

He patted her shoulder and kissed the top of her head. 'Come on, girl. You must be worn out. You can take Megan's bed. When do you have to get back to Cardiff?'

'Midday. I'll be on time if I get there by then.'

* * *

He could not sleep at all when he got into bed. He just lay there, staring up at a shaft of moonlight which sliced across the bedroom, the dust hanging fine in the startling purity of its glow. He blew into the air, soft, causing the dust to buck around as if disturbed by a gale. It settled down slow and he blew again. He thought of the Revival and how it had blown people around like that; of how Evan Roberts had caused small storms, followed by yet more small storms.

It still did not make sense to him that Beth, a girl of massive and independent will, had got herself caught up in these storms. But, there again, she was often not what she liked to appear; there was much that was broken inside her – perhaps forever. Doubtless she would find the same set of problems in Australia as she had found here – with beauty like that, he decided, she would always find problems. He blew the dust again. So there they were – under one roof, all in separate beds, all orphans of small storms.

He was dozing off when his bedroom door opened. 'I can't sleep,' Beth whispered without coming inside. 'Are you asleep?'

'Not yet.'

'Do you think I could get in with you?'

'There's room for two.' His heart went lurching down his body and he turned his face to the window and moved over as she climbed in next to him. He was not going to upset her by getting provocative – the memory of that day when she had gone mad in the cave was still vivid with him. When she had settled down he turned on to his back and looked up at the ceiling. 'I've been lying here blowing that dust around,' he said.

'Can I try?'

'If you like.'

She blew upwards. 'You're doing it far too hard. Just give it a soft blow and it looks like a storm in slow motion. Let it settle first and I'll show you.'

They were both looking up waiting for the dust to settle when he jumped as her naked side brushed up against his. 'Did you put on that nightgown I showed you?'

'No.'

'You know what you're doing, do you?'

'No.'

'Has anyone ever told you that you're as unpredictable as a hand of cards?'

'No.'

'Hands that keep on changing mysterious after the bet has been made. That's the way you are.'

She sighed as if deep in exasperation. 'Look Michael it's our last night together. Don't think I haven't thought about all this because I've thought of nothing else since I got into your sister's bed. I've decided I want to give you something for what you've done. What you've done for me and Rhion. I've got nothing to give except my body. It's best gift I've got, so please will . . . '

'But what?'

'Please shut up and accept it, will you?'

'But look . . . '

'Shush. Just shut up. I want to do this for you because I'm grateful. That's all.'

He took it slow from the off, slipping his arm under her neck and pouring gentle kisses on her cheeks, nose and lips. The moon lit up her open, curious eyes as she worked her arms around his back and pulled him over on top or her, returning his kisses now but making them firmer and longer, closing her eyes in the weeping fusion, the mute gulps of a mounting passion and hands moving over warm flesh.

'Are you sure you know what you're doing girl? It's not too late to stop.'

'Don't worry, *cariad*. I wouldn't do it if I didn't love you.'

Her words lit such flames in him they could have burned down the cottage. 'I love you too, girl. I'll always love you, I will. Always.'

In the silent clash of hips he rode up and down into her, barely daring to take a deep breath, for fear he would lose what he had and held, until, with a soft whimper, the whole of his being was poured into her in a gentle bucking flood. They did not stop after that either and rode out the rest of the night together – breaking on the anvil of a passion that destroyed – discharge following discharge with him unable to stop and her whispering, urgent and repeated, 'love you, love you, love you' into his ear.

They finally lay back, sweating and exhausted, with the dawn breaking over the marsh, and he told her that no man could ever have been given a greater gift.

'Some of the greatest gifts are the easiest to give,' she said, holding him tight.

Chill mists streaked the dawn as he lit the fires and went out to clear the horse's shed. He was already beginning to miss her and, after such a night of surrender, was even worried by her reaction – fearing that she might somehow once again decide that he had taken advantage of her.

When Beth woke she turned to see that Michael had gone downstairs. She felt heavy, warm and replete, gazing at the wall while a part of him dribbled hot out of her. She put her hand on the juices and rubbed them around inside her leg. The feeling was so strong and complete she did not feel so much as a flicker of the old guilts that had once torn her apart. Sated bubbles hung in her bosom. There was a warm smile inside her like a pregnancy. She was a woman again and happy – urgently happy.

She got up and flung her cloak over her before first looking into Rhion's room, gazing down at the sleeping child as she stroked the side of her neck with her hand. Then she went down, finding Michael at the sink filling up a bucket with water from the tap. She walked up behind him, resting her head against his broad shoulders. 'What do you want for breakfast?' she asked.

'We can always fry up some cockles and have them on toast.'

'Fine. I'll get the tea and toast ready. What about Rhion?'

'I let the badger get up when she feels like it.'

'Shall I go up and wake her?'

'Leave her be for a bit. She gets cross when she hasn't had enough sleep.'

The water was brimming over the top of the bucket and trickling down the sides into the sink. He reached out and turned the tap off before banging it with his hand and turning it on again. The sink also began to fill up with tea leaves eddying around in the water.

'What time is the tide?' she asked. 'Are you going to work it today?'

'Might as well. Keeps me occupied and I don't want to upset the badger. She likes it out there, too.'

'So you'll both be ready for a meal at about six then?'

The paint on the wall was crumbling and flaking. Now the sink was overflowing, running over the cracked porcelain ledge and down around their feet. He swallowed the hugest swallow. 'Are you saying that you're not going after all?'

'Well I have been telling you I love you all night in case you've forgotten.'

'What about Australia?'

'Who wants to go to Australia?'

'What about your things on the ship?'

'Who wants things? They'll send them back sometime. If I went away you'd only get yourself another woman.'

'No, I wouldn't.'

'Yes, you would. I'm not going to let anyone else look after you two.'

By now the water was flowing across the kitchen floor and out onto the ash path in the yard. But still Michael did not turn it off, merely stood there, staring at the flaking wall, almost as if he was afraid of turning around and finding that he was in a dream. 'You'd better know something straight off,' he said.

'What's that?'

'I snore in bed. My feet smell terrible. Neither do I take many baths.'

'Do what you like. If taking baths makes you unhappy don't take them.'

He turned around and they kissed. 'Shall we go back to bed for a bit then?' he suggested.

'If you like.' She stuck a wet kiss on the tip of his nose. 'Anything you like. I'm just giving in, I am. As of now I've given in.'

They woke a few hours later when Rhion came into the bedroom, still in her nightdress. She prodded him on the shoulder. 'Mungry,' she said, giving him another prod. 'Mungry.'

'Women,' he muttered rolling over. 'Badger, meet your mother. She's doing all the cooking from now on.'

'No she's not,' he was told, accompanied by a sharp dig with the elbow. 'We're going to do everything together. If I'm at the stove I want you there too.'

'But I can't cook.'

'Well you'll have to learn then, won't you? Anyway there's things I want from the shop. Hello, badger.'

Rhion stuck her thumb in her mouth for a ruminative suck and frowned as she looked at her mother.

'Come and give your Mam a kiss then,' said Beth, reaching out to try and grab her. Rhion saw her hands coming and darted straight out of the room. 'A fine welcome that is,' she said as they dressed.

'Give her time. She's scared of you pet.'

'I do understand that. I do understand some things it might surprise you to know.'

He was walking down the stairs when he saw that the tap was still running, flooding out the kitchen and much of the backyard.

'Forgot to turn the tap off, didn't we?' Vera cackled, her hands on the fence. 'You'd forget your head if it wasn't stuck on your shoulders. That father of yours was always doing that. He never knew what time of day it was either.'

Beth came out into the yard to see what all the talk was about. 'I left the tap on,' he told her pointing at the pools. 'While you're out here you'd better meet Vera. Vera, this is Beth. She's going to be living here from now on. Beth – Vera.'

'I'm very pleased to meet you Vera,' said Beth.

'Getting married then are you?' the old crone asked after a few seconds. Michael winced. Vera's knack of saying the wrong thing at the wrong time was nothing less than wonderful.

'That's right,' Beth said taking a few steps towards her. 'You'll be coming to the wedding I hope.'

'Don't know about that. I'd have to get a new hat, I would. You've got to get a new hat for a wedding, haven't you?'

'I'll take you down to Swansea one day. I've got to buy some new things so perhaps we can go together? They've got some lovely hats in Johnston's. Suit you as well.'

'Lovely hats cost lovely money. Money doesn't grow on trees does it?'

'They're not very expensive. Pennies that's all. Pennies. I'll lend you some money if you're short.'

Vera's mouth opened and closed, vexed in the face of this small and unfamiliar wind of charm and generosity coming out of Michael's backyard. 'Would you like some cabbages, would you, Beth? I've got more than I can use out here.'

'That would be nice. We could do with a cabbage or two, couldn't we, Michael?'

'Come over and see what you want. There's some parsnips here as well. Like parsnips, do you?'

Michael had listened to this exchange with his mouth sagging in disbelief. It was a dream, it was. He never did make the tide that day nor, come to that, did he make the next tide – or the one after that.

Chapter Twenty-four

That week the summer burst forth over the estuary and everywhere the very earth sang songs of renewal. Bees were out and busying themselves with their mysterious tasks with pollen. Hedgehogs roamed the lanes and gnats tumbled about under the shade of trees. Lilac branches hung heavy with fragrant blooms as frogs leapt about in watercress streams. Every twilight was aflutter with vibrant whistles and returned swallows.

Down near Broadoak colliery two squirrels were making repeated attacks on Angharad Rees' cherry trees. Covered in paper bags and old socks the cherry branches were, but still those squirrels got those tiny luscious red balls and ran away with them, leaving Angharad jumping up and down with anger.

On such a Friday afternoon, full with summer, Michael and Beth were sitting on the cart, with Rhion jammed in between them, as the laggard horse ambled his way slow along a lane towards a picnic on the sand dunes of Llangennith.

'Cockleshells,' he said.

'What about them?' she asked.

'I've always thought that anyone who can think of something to do with cockleshells could make himself an awful lot of money.'

'What kind of thing?'

'I don't know. That's what I'm thinking about. As it is, they're just used for foundation work or for the drainage for houses. Wasted, they are.'

Beth put her arm around Rhion and, when she shrugged it off, she just put it straight back again. 'What about cockleshell necklaces?' she suggested. 'But they're not pretty enough for that, are they?'

'Maybe not. Some sort of ornament perhaps? You could make small ships out of the cockleshells.'

'*You* could.'

'Serious now. We could start a business together and take a stall in Swansea market.'

'What's this, then? Dream of the day, is it?'

'I enjoy dreams.'

Rhion climbed on to his lap and, just as she was settling down, Beth picked her straight up and placed her down on hers. 'Why don't you start dreaming of university?' she asked. 'You passed all the exams once, didn't you?'

'Well we can't now, can we? Not with the badger here.'

'Of course we can. I could always get a job to help out. Work behind a bar or something.'

'You behind a bar! That I would like to see.'

'Why not? I could build up my muscles pulling all those pints.'

'Whatever do you want muscles for?'

'To knock all those daft dreams out of your fat head. Wouldn't we, badger? Knock some sense into him.'

'It's this horse that needs something knocked into him.'

The horse had been following the twists and turns down the lane leading to the dunes but was now moving so slow they were all but going backwards. Evidently, he was in a fit of depression at having to pull three people *and* a cart. His ears had not pricked up all morning either.

'Poor little dab,' said Beth, giving Rhion a kiss on top of her head. 'There's not much go about him, is there?'

'He has his moments, to be fair. I did get him to gallop about six months ago and he did kick a dog not so long back, but these days he's got so he won't even move his legs apart when he's having a piss.'

'Look. I don't want you using bad words in front of the badger,' said Beth holding her hands over Rhion's ears. 'You didn't hear that, did you, little one?'

'Come on now, Lightning,' said Michael standing up on one leg and kicking him with the other. 'Let's have some action, shall we?'

With that the horse stopped altogether and lurched his head sideways to graze on a patch of dandelions on the bank.

'Do you think we'll get home?' Beth asked.

'We'll get home all right,' Michael said, climbing off the cart and leading him down to the dunes. 'This one likes going home. It's going out he doesn't like. Do you, eh? Your idea of heaven is to be lying in your shed all day having your back scratched and munching hay.'

They left the horse with the cart and crossed the dunes to the beach where the breakers were coming in high and proud, as the gulls circled above the ghostly spray. 'I hope this university you've been thinking about is on the sea,' said Michael, lying back on the beach. 'I don't ever want to spend a day not seeing the sea.'

Rhion wandered away from them and Beth followed in her wake. He sat up and watched the two of them moving across the sand together, with Beth picking up shells and showing them to Rhion, who looked at them with the gravest suspicion before turning her back and walking away. Later Beth lifted up the child and whirled her around – a manhandling which Rhion accepted sullen before walking away again, glancing back to see if Beth was behind her again. Rhion ran and screeched, but was soon caught again and given another good tossing.

He lay back on the sand. Everything – but everything – was perfect. When Megan had called the night before they had told her of their decision, and she just cried and went away again. Jenko had sent flowers and Vera had sent cabbages. In front of the fire he had read Browning's love poems to Elizabeth out loud and, later, in bed, their bodies had told one another fiery stories of turbulence and passion. It was all as if some radiant butterfly had just emerged from the chrysalis; even more radiant and caring than the one he had loved at first, boundlessly affectionate and even insisting that she and Rhion go with him to the forge when he had to fix his boiler – 'in case he got lonely'.

There was no sign of any of the old anxieties or confusions; no talk of Evan Roberts or the chapel; nothing of any seriousness about anything. With her not raising any big issues he was damned certain he would not either. It was almost as if one long hard winter had disappeared like some distant nightmare.

Beth came running over to him, out of breath. 'Michael, come quick. There's something I want you to see down on the shore.'

She went running back down to the sea, stopping only to scoop Rhion up under her arm. He jumped up and ran too. Was it a washed-up body or something? Nothing could be less likely. A huge shoal of fat, pink starfish had been stranded on the sand by the ebbing tide. There were hundreds of them lying around in the pools and on the rocks like chopped-off hands. He picked one up and its fleshy tentacles windmilled around slow as he held it in front of Rhion, her eyes widening slightly in alarm as she took a few steps backwards.

'They eat all along there,' he said. 'See all those little tongues? They just wander around in the sea and suck up anything that takes their fancy. All along there.' He took another step towards Rhion and she took another step back. 'This starfish is called Fred. All starfish have different names so that their mother can tell one from another.'

The girl wrinkled up her nose and looked up at her mother.

'Don't believe a word of it,' said Beth. 'He's just talking rubbish as usual.'

'No, I'm not. It's true, that is. When a mother starfish has a baby starfish she gives them all different names. What are you laughing at?

Those are all the girls over there. This one's called Phyllis and that one's Doris. She's Violet and I forget what the other one's called. All these names go back to the time when starfish were all either called Peter or Catherine. Stop laughing will you? When the mother wanted one of them to come over, to see if they'd washed proper, she called out one name or another but all but got run over in the crush so it was decided, at a grand council of mother starfish, to give each one a different name.'

'I don't think,' Beth said. 'I can't say that I've ever, in my whole life, heard a bigger load of rubbish.'

'Are you calling me a liar?'

She folded her arms and stuck out her jaw, defiant.

'Yes. Yes I am. You're the biggest liar that . . . that ever walked on two legs.'

'You know, I hope, what happens to people who go around calling other people liars?'

'What's that?'

He turned his head slow and nodded at the sea. 'They get washed in salt water.'

'You wouldn't dare.'

'Wouldn't dare, would I? Well what am I then?'

She glanced back behind her over the empty sands and back at him. 'Michael Evans you're the biggest lia . . . ' The rest of the word turned into a shriek and Beth dashed away, her arms flailing around, with him after her in a flash. It took just five strides for him to catch her and lead her into the bubbling curling waves. 'What am I then?'

'Liar, liar, liar.'

'Your last chance now. What am I?'

'Liar, liar, liar.'

That was it. He pulled her arm and she pulled back. He pulled again and, losing his balance, was caught by a wave and they both tumbled over on their sides in the hissing foam.

'Liar, liar, liar.'

'Come on then,' he said lifting her up and dragging her out deeper into the waves. 'I hope you're a good swimmer.'

'Michael. I can't swim a stroke.'

They were up to their waists in water and wrestling together when she kissed him hard and they both sank out of sight like a pair of drowning porpoises. They floated up on the prow of the next wave, still kissing with him dribbling salt water over her, when his legs were caught in the undertow and over they bundled again. Curious gulls dipped and cawed over their heads.

He stood up finally and, looking back at Rhion, let go of Beth. The girl was standing where they had left her on the beach, but she now had her hands up against her eyes, crying. They both ran to her and Beth picked her up, but she reached out her small arms for Michael.

'It was only fun,' Michael said taking her. 'Just a joke. Come on. Let me show you.'

Beth put her arm around his shoulders as they walked knee-deep into the waves with Rhion's arms so tight around his neck they would have strangled him if they had been bigger. 'See? There's nothing to be scared of.'

They walked a little further out but had to wade back to the beach when she began crying again. 'Poor thing's scared of her own shadow,' Beth said, taking her and giving her a big hug.

'Me next,' he said.

'You'll get a good clip across the ear if you're not careful. Poor little badger. That monster scared you, didn't he?'

Their clothes dried as they ate their food. Later, on the journey back home, Michael pointed at a tree. It had a very thin trunk and just one bent branch with three leaves on it, the whole lot sagging helpless in the breeze as if wondering if it should fall over and die and be done with it.

'Look at the shape of that tree. Reminds me of this horse here.'

Beth thought the tree was hilarious. 'It looks just how I feel when I get out of bed most mornings,' she said.

'Tree, tree,' Rhion said, suddenly.

'She'll be talking in sentences soon,' Michael said.

'Well it'll make a change from listening to him all day long won't it, badger?'

'Tree, tree.'

For the remaining few miles every tree was met with the greeting 'Tree, tree' with all three of them chanting the words together.

'You know, cariad,' Beth said at one stage, putting her head on his shoulder. 'If I had a tail I'd go around wagging it all day long.'

The fragrances of the day lifted at Pen-clawdd, however, since standing outside the cottage, was her father looking as happy as if he had just swallowed five pounds of raw onions.

'I'll see to him,' Beth said climbing down off the cart. 'You take the badger and horse around the back.'

The father stared cold at Michael as he went by and, once in the yard, Michael lurked around the kitchen door, holding Rhion by the hand and trying to overhear what was being said but only catching the odd angry word. He was frightened that the father was going to destroy what they had together; that he would bring all the old problems running back again. After a while his fright got too much for him and he was about to go inside when he heard the front door slam. He found a melancholy Beth sitting on a chair in the living room. She looked up at Michael and gave a long sigh.

'He says I'm no longer a daughter of his. He says the very least I could have done was gone away somewhere else to save him the shame of it all.'

'Thinking of himself again.'

She looked at him, sharp, telling him that she could criticise her father but not Michael. Even in her distress she still had this bright flame of loyalty.

'He says Mam is upset about it all, too. I don't believe that. All Mam ever wanted was for me to be happy. It seems even Evan Roberts called over the other day, asking about me.'

Michael sat down sensing that the war drums were being beaten – that the Red Indians were muttering over the hill, whooping and ready for the attack. He smoothed Rhion's hair. 'Shall we run then?'

Beth looked at him, blank, when, with immaculate timing, Rhion tottered over to her and actually climbed on to her lap. Beth cheered up immediately and kissed the girl on the cheek.

'What then?' he asked again.

'What what?'

'Shall we run from them?'

'Foof! I'm not running anywhere. They can all go and jump into the lake. Can't they, badger? They can all go and boil their heads. We'll face them all, won't we, baby? We might even invite them all to our wedding.'

'That's another matter,' Michael said, lifting his forefinger and prodding it towards her. 'You were telling Vera about our wedding and I thought you were just joking. Now you're telling the badger. What about me? Yes. Me. Marriages take two, you know. Don't I get any say in all this?'

'Say anything you like. You usually do. I've never known anyone talk so much. You're worse than that Jenko when you get going.'

'Well I always grew up to believe that it was the man who did all the proposing. That was the way I was brought up. But there you are going around telling Vera and the badger and the horse, for all I know, that you're getting married. What about me?'

'I'm not sitting around here waiting for you to propose. I've been sharing your bed, in case you'd forgotten. We girls have got to have some standards, haven't we, badger?'

'Men have got standards too, you know. I've got more standards than you've ever heard of. I've got standards they haven't ever heard of in the Bible.'

'Oh you're just being silly now,' she said, an amused smile on her face and her hand smoothing one of Rhion's legs. 'When did you ever read the Bible anyway?'

'Girl, you'd be surprised at what I read.'

'Look, if you're so keen on proposing why don't you propose? We two women can't hang around forever, you know. We want to be honourable members of the community. Go on. Propose.'

'Oh well . . . ummmm . . . how does it go? Haven't had much practice at all this. Um . . . Beth Williams will . . . '

'Hold on. Down on your knees. *I* always grew up to believe that a man went down on his knees when he was proposing. That's better. And where's the ring? We like diamonds, don't we, badger? Big diamonds. But, just this once, we'll settle for a curtain ring.'

Michael sighed and, muttering something along the lines of how men could always change their mind, got up and tore a ring off one of the curtains. He went back down on his knees again, holding the ring in his fingers. 'Beth Williams I don't have . . . '

'Look stop messing about and get on with it, will you? We haven't got all day, you know. Me and the badger want a cup of tea.'

'Wouldn't all this be better at sunset or with some wine or something?'

'Are you going to kneel there all day gabbling or what?'

'Beth Williams, will you marry me?'

'Well, badger, what do you think? Do we want him?' Rhion was busy sucking her thumb and did not seem to think much of the proposal at all. Beth turned back to Michael. 'Tell me, oh kind sir, what prospects have you got?'

'Who's gabbling now? Come on, girl. My knees are hurting.'

'Well me and the badger say the answer's yes – providing you promise to make the tea every morning.'

'I promise.'

'The both of us, mind.'

'It's all true. You really are the biggest bully.'

'No good having second thoughts now, kind sir. You've asked and the answer's yes, yes, yes. Breach of promise that would be if he tried to get out of it now, wouldn't it be, badger? We could have his house off him and his horse too – though, on second thoughts, he could keep the horse and we'd just have the house here.'

'We're not married yet and there you are talking about taking my house off me. Hang on. Do we have to marry in the chapel?'

'Well you can't get married in a pub, can you?'

'Oh I don't know. We could always get married out on the sands. Get some daft minister to marry us at sunset. The gulls could be the choirboys and the wild horses could be the ushers with the guests carrying lighted torches and . . . '

'You're being silly again now,' she interrupted. 'Look, give me that ring, will you, then go and make us a cup of tea. We're both as dry as a bone.'

Travelled up to visit Evan in his new temporary home in Leicester, Dan wrote in his diary. *Bought him a new pair of shoes in Bon Marché for 1s 9p. There was a Sikh wearing a turban sitting in the same carriage as us. Everyone stared at him but said nothing. It seemed strange that we were fraternal brothers. Hardie has been talking a lot about the possibility of the workers of the world coming together for united action. The Socialist Party of America now has 40,000 members.*

The home of Mr and Mrs Jesse Penn-Lewis was one of those smart suburban jobs but I was surprised by the child servant who answered the door. Might be one of those partial exemption scholars the Fabians were always making a fuss about – goes to school but can work 27½ hours a week.

Evan seemed in good spirits and pleased with his new shoes. Had lunch of boiled bacon, cabbage, potatoes, currant and suet pudding. I told him that I had joined the Labour Party again but he did not object, as I had feared, even seemed pleased when I told him of the 'new theologians' in the valley like Rev. R.J. Campbell who were marrying the idea of social justice with the Immanence of God. I also told him how Hardie had said that socialism was woven from the same loom as Isiah; that Jesus was, after all, the son of a working class carpenter and that, when Wycliffe was inveighing against the usurers, he was merely showing himself to be an early socialist.

Yes, but can your socialism hold together the family? was all Evan asked.

He said he was sorry he had left the work so abrupt, but he had not been feeling well. He even said he was planning to come back to Loughor soon and start work on the Revival again. But he will not. He is an old man sucked dry. His face is desert-craggy. His articulation faulty. Even as he outlined some of his new plans he broke off to complain about his wart and the difficulty of getting

Robin starch for his shirts. I told him we still have £875 3s in gifts.

Caught the 6.35 p.m. train back from Leicester. Read of the new work of the Workers' Educational Association in the Labour Leader. It's good that the workers are taking education seriously. Such as the WEA and the ILP will lead the people against privilege and poverty. Half the income of Britain is earned by one ninth of the population. Half the national capital belongs to one seventh of the population. That is the reason for poverty. Socialism is the enemy of poverty and poverty is the enemy of socialism.

New winds are blowing hard. Socialism is feeding on the underbelly of this society with its country homes, champagne, weekends in Marienbad, colonialist wars against the Boers, speculation in South African diamonds and Australian gold. There are 20,000 Chinese working in slavery in the Rand mines. That is what we socialists must stop. And we must stop it now.

Chapter Twenty-five

Returned swallows or no, it was that summer which should have been sued for breach of promise since the next day was as cold as a dead haddock, with fat clouds sweeping in over the Channel, glooming dark and threatening to soak all and sundry at any second.

The three of them had gone on a cart down to Swansea to buy some new clothes for Rhion and, on the return journey, it bucketed down. 'Oh rain, rain go away,' sang Beth, putting her cloak around Rhion. 'Come again another day.' She was very worried about the little one who, for several days now, had developed a dry cough with a slight croup in it.

However, she did not seem too bad today. Quite soon they were all soaking wet, but it hardly mattered with Michael so full of himself these days – he even sang 'Lily of Laguna' to the rain, difficult though it was holding the notes with raindrops driving into his mouth. The toll-keeper at Waunarlwydd was so astonished by this outbreak of song in the rain he let them go through free.

'That's the first time he's done that,' Michael said.

'Maybe it's the first time he's heard you sing. You've not got a bad voice. It's not good but not bad. I'd give it E for effort.'

When they got back to the cottage Beth whisked Rhion straight up the stairs to get her changed. 'We must get the badger some warmer clothes,' she said when she came down. 'Those were all summer things we bought her today. I'm that worried about that cough. It's gone on too long. I've put her to bed.'

'I don't suppose you fancy putting me to bed?' he asked as he knelt in the grate, trying to get some life into the fire.

'Don't you ever think of anything else?'

'How about a cup of tea, then?'

'All right. But you finish the fire.'

Later she took a cup of tea up to Rhion. He was washing his hands when she came down again. 'The badger's not at all well. Come up and look.'

The girl was lying on her bed, occasionally turning her face down into her pillow and coughing into it. 'It's just a cold,' he said, pulling her blankets up around her shoulders. 'All children get colds. I used to get one a week when I was young.'

'I just wish she'd eat more, that's all. She won't have the strength to fight colds if she doesn't eat more. Do you think we should call Jenko?'

'He doesn't know anything. He told me once that most of his cures were bluff. Just keep the girl warm and she'll be all right in the morning. Colds don't take hold if they're nipped in the bud.'

'I wish I could be as sure as you. That cough is beginning to sound awful.'

'Leave it for now. I'll get Jenko in the morning if it gets any worse. Not much point getting him now because he's probably drunk. The best time to get him is before the pubs open.'

'If you think so. But I'll sit here for a while. You go on down. I'll stay here.'

He went downstairs and counted what money they had left after the day's shopping. It was precious little. On his own, he usually made enough to eat well, with a few surplus pennies for a few surplus pints of beer, but there were the three of them now and he had been thinking of trying to raise a loan for a small trawler. There was real money to be made in mackerel and hake. Some trawlers, he heard, could make as much as two pounds a day if they caught a good shoal. The problem with making real money was, as usual, having to lay out real money in the first place. Tch!

He decided not to have his tea until Beth came down again. But after a quarter of an hour she still had not come. He hoped that she was not going to make too much of a meal of being a mother; that after all those years of guilt and neglect, she was not going to smother the girl with excessive love. He had seen that happen in a few families around here and, for some reason, the children did not flourish proper in it – they became spoiled, awkward, always holding their hands out. Not that Rhion was anything like that. She wanted nothing and demanded even less.

When Beth did come down she sat on the flagstones between his legs and gazed into the fire. 'I'm worried. I'm so worried I'd like Jenko to come and have a look at her.'

'She's only got a cold. Children always get colds.'

'I'm not sure it is just a cold. She's running a high temperature and is short of breath. She's getting a bit blue around the lips too. It could be a bad cold, but I want another opinion.

'What could it be if it's not a cold?'

'I'm going back up to sit with her.'

'Drink your tea first. Might be a bit stewed now.'

'I'll take it up and have it there.'

Her face was drawn with anxiety as she poured out the tea and, somehow, she transmitted it to him. After all, she had been a nurse. She knew about illness and was not given to sudden alarms. He went up the stairs after her. The child was coughing hoarse and there were beads of sweat on her forehead. When she was not coughing her nostrils were flaring and collapsing with the difficulty of breathing.

'Shall I go and get Jenko now?' he asked.

'Yes. Get Megan too and be as quick as you can.'

Beth was standing in the doorway of the cottage, anxious, when Michael returned with Jenko and Megan on his cart. 'Come quick will you, Jenko?' she said, ushering him up the stairs.

Michael picked up one of the cats and sat with Megan in the kitchen. 'Serious, is it?' Megan asked. 'It sounds serious.'

'The little one has got a heavy cold. It's the mother thing, I suppose. You'll remember our mother used to suffer worse than us when we had something wrong.'

'She did too. Even if I had a cut leg she'd be there suffering worse than me. What with her and our father it's a wonder we weren't dafter than we are.'

The cat was purring loud and rubbing her head around his sleeve.

'They're back in fouling up the place, are they?' Megan asked, her lip curling up at the corner in open distaste.

'Aye. Beth likes them well enough. But we don't see much of the chicken after you threw it out. It got proper rejected and won't come in at all now.'

'Well I did some good then. Animals should be out of doors. That's what I like about Jenko. He hates animals too. He says . . . '

Jenko came into the kitchen and there was something about his manner which made Michael hold on to the cat tight. He looked at Megan and then at Michael. His features were cold and still, his whole face a pen and ink sketch in atrabilious thunder.

'Bad is it?' Michael asked.

'It's worse than bad. Rhion's got pneumonia.'

'More serious than a cold, then?' Michael asked, standing up to go upstairs.

'Much more serious than that. Sit down. Her chest has swollen up and there's laboured breathing. I haven't told Beth yet, but she's a nurse. She knows these things. I'm sure she knows.' He turned his back on Michael. 'The long and the short of it is I don't think the girl will recover.'

Michael laughed out loud. 'You are joking, aren't you?'

'Would that I were. With an adult there is some kind of chance, but with a child like her, none.'

'But it was just a cold, wasn't it?'

'Pneumonia is a virus, not a cold. We've no cure – none at all. The girl is as weak as a kitten already. She's not been eating proper and now there's no fight in her body.'

He put the cat down and watched it walk out into the yard, where it rolled over on the ash path, head awry as it gave its back a good rubbing. A sparrow flew on to the back wall and the cat sat up and moved into a crouching position, body low and shoulder-bones high as she took one slow step after another towards the wall – only stopping and sitting down again when the bird flew away.

'You heard what I said, did you?'

Michael nodded. 'I heard. How long?'

'Two days at the most. There's not time even for leeches. The lack of oxygen leads to brain failure. We can keep her sponged and give her the odd steam inhalation, but that's all.'

The cat was licking her paw and rubbing it over her snout; another sparrow flew on to the wall and it began stalking again. The afternoon sunshine had brought out the flies, too. The kitchen tap was dripping loud and it really was time he put in a new washer. He looked at Megan when the muscles in his face began twitching and he had to hold them still with both hands. Jenko caught him by the wrist with a grip that was quite painful.

'If you're going to go to pieces then you've got just one minute to do so. You can sit there in the corner for just one minute and go to pieces but then your time is up. You hear? It's Beth you've got to look after now. If she means anything at all to you you've got to keep on top of it.'

'He's right,' Megan said. 'Beth will need you now.'

'Well?' Jenko asked.

'Well what?' Michael said rubbing his wrist.

'Are you going to pieces or not?'

'I'll try and fight it.'

'Well, just for once in your life, do that. And stay afloat.'

'I'll go up to her. What shall I say?'

'There's nothing to say. She'll know. I'll go back and get some laudanum. I'll come back over first thing in the morning, but it might even be too late by then, of course.'

Too late by then? Just what was the man saying? Michael kept swallowing, feverish – as if choking on some invisible food – before going up to sit next to Beth in the bedroom. The window was open with a brisk sea wind flapping the curtains around. 'You want me to get you something warm?' he asked, seeing the goose pimples on Beth's arms.

'It doesn't matter.'

The little one's breathing was still very laboured, with her nostrils inflating sudden like a balloon before collapsing flat. Her cheeks were quite white too and, when she coughed, her eyes opened and there was the most frightened panic in them as her lungs stretched and cried for more air. Beth sponged the sweat off her forehead and, in between the deeper struggles for breath, the badger lay exhausted with her eyes blinking, rapid, without focusing on anything.

'Shall I make you a cup of tea?' he asked.

'It doesn't matter.'

He went into their bedroom to find a shawl which he put around Beth's shoulders. Dusk had fallen now with a brisk south-easterly whipping in over the sands, making the bedroom curtains flap so much he had to tie them up into knots. Rhion fell into a short fitful sleep and they both sat there, silent, looking down at her. A ragged little scrap so inexperienced in the world, he thought – yet so familiar with its pain. He studied the tiny blue tracery of veins on the side of her forehead; the hands, so small and helpless; the hair that grew so abundant, all that exquisite engineering by nature: and all for this. This!

After some ten minutes she was woken by her own croaking cough and the panicking struggle for breath began again. Beth sat holding her hand as the girl wept, soft, with the misery of it all. Occasionally the girl coughed up some sputum with a pink strain of blood in it.

An hour or so later Rhion's breath became very shallow and her fists clenched and unclenched, before she made a tiny thin sigh and closed her eyes again. Beth took her in her arms and kissed her head. 'Peace at last, my baby,' she said and lay the girl down on the bed, smoothing the damp hair off her face. Then she kissed her again and covered her face with the sheet.

Nothing was said as they walked down the stairs and sat down at the kitchen table. Beth just kept staring down at the flagstones; her shoulder slumped in total and abject defeat. He boiled the kettle and made tea but it was left untouched. Only once did they catch one another's look, but he could not make out what was in her eyes. They were cold, alien to feelings.

They stayed in the kitchen until dawn and a stream of thoughts and images followed one another through his mind like unconnected dreams.

He remembered the day of the train crash and the time when he had first heard Beth's voice. 'How are the cockles this year?' she had asked.

He recalled seeing the first meeting of the Revival and once, when a child, receiving a mighty hammering in this very kitchen for stealing a loaf of bread out of the bakery. He thought of lots of things but whenever his mind came face to face with Rhion's death and its consequences he could not think of it in any coherent way at all. He could not even bring himself to believe that the child had died. She had just gone to sleep for a while; taken a rest after being in great pain.

It had been the same when his mother had died. Even when he saw her lying in her coffin on the morning of her funeral he had still refused to accept it. He had just stood there, staring at the sleeping face, waiting for her to breathe; wanting her just to get up and give one of those sleepy smiles she always had when she woke. Even when the muffled bell of Hermon chapel was being struck and the mourners were standing around, caps in hand and handkerchiefs to eyes, as his mother was being lowered into that awful damp hole with its brown and grey layers of clay, he *still* refused to believe that she had died. While the others were throwing handfuls of damp earth on to the coffin he had the strong, almost violent, urge to leap down into the earth with her and tear off the lid of the coffin to make sure that there had not been some terrible mistake.

He wiped the tears away with the sides of his hands as he thought of that day. So there was death in the cottage again and with it, the same numb, if human, refusal to look at it square in the eyes.

He cut bread to make toast but burned it and tossed the slices into a bucket. So that damned God had delivered another of his sudden and savage hammer blows . . . *Steady now, boy. You've got to stay afloat.*

Beth had not so much as moved, let alone spoken, all night and when dawn broke into a huge grey umbrella with white streaks, the cockerels in the village crowed and a strange black cat with a white chest sat on the kitchen sill and stared in at them with large fiery diamond eyes.

Beth stood up final and walked into the living room, coming back into the kitchen and putting on her cloak. She opened the kitchen door and stood there, waiting for him. He picked his jacket off the back of the chair and they both walked out through the village and past the wild horses on the marsh, stopping only to watch an otter in one of the pools, diving again and again down into the waving weeds in search of food.

Out on the sands, flocks of gulls were sitting in the manner of silent sentinels next to the mirrored pools. The air was perfectly still and cold. A faint, almost ironic, ship's hooter sounded through the slumbering sea mists. Beth's hair appeared oddly untidy and, when she did look at him, she said, 'It's not going to be very good for drying clothes today.'

'There'll be other days,' he said, taking her hand.

They walked the full length of the sands until the flowing tide forced them to cut back into Llanrhidian. The villagers were already up and about their business. In one of the grey stone houses a woman was shouting at her children and the sign of the Dolphin pub had come off one of its hinges. They still kept the stocks on the village green and, next to the stocks, sheep with their young were grazing on the grass. The two of them took the high road back to Pen-clawdd and, by the time they got there, the tide was as full as a summer harvest and lapping up against the sea-front walls. Its vast surface was as smooth and still as it was silent.

The front door of the cottage was open and they found Megan in the living room, weeping inconsolable. Beth took one look at her and walked straight out through the kitchen and into the yard where she stood gazing out over the sea. For himself Michael did not know what to do – or who to try and comfort – so he put the kettle on. He was pouring out the tea when Jenko walked into the kitchen and gave him one of those small pats on the back that are the common currency of funerals. It was his touch that made Michael cry out loud for the first time. All the night he had managed to stay afloat, until Jenko had laid a hand on him, and now globs of silent tears were being pumped up out of him by the hiccuping sobs inside.

'What time did it happen?' Jenko asked.

'I'm not sure. About three.'

'How is Beth?'

'She's all right.'

'You're all right, are you?'

'I'm fine.'

'I had brought some laudanum for the girl but the two of you had better take it instead for a few days, until everything is sorted out. Leave it all to me. I'll arrange the funeral.'

The funeral! The death that always leaves you bleeding and the funeral that pours salt over the wounds. Oh, he did not want to go to another funeral. Not the rack of all that grief all over again.

'Have you thought of the funeral at all?' Jenko asked. 'I might be able to arrange some sort of Christian burial – if that's what Beth wants – but it will be difficult. You know how blind and bigoted the chapels are about . . . you know how they are about . . . '

'Bastards you mean?'

'Yes.'

He rubbed the hams of his hands hard into his tears. 'You'd better ask Beth what she wants. It's all up to her. I think she's taking it better than me.'

Michael watched Jenko walk out into the yard to stand next to Beth. A whirling shaft of sunshine broke through the grey clouds and passed over them as they both faced the sea. Beth pointed at something and began talking. Jenko was nodding as she spoke at some length. Her reactions were as unpredictable as ever and now she was speaking with the quiet business-like determination of a farmer wanting to get the best price for his cattle.

He wondered if she had decided to leave him after all. But it didn't worry him. He loved her and, within that love, she could do whatever and go wherever she wanted.

Jenko finally walked back inside. 'I've got a job for you,' he told Michael. 'I want you to get out your cart and gather all the wood you can find. At low tide I want you to build a pyre down on the sands. I'm going back to Loughor to tell Beth's mother – Beth wants her told – and I'll arrange for a coffin while I'm there. Beth doesn't want any more problems with the chapel. She doesn't want any more problems with anyone and wants the child cremated on the sands today.'

'Today?'

'Today. Apart from a chapel funeral – which is out of the question anyway – there aren't many other choices, unless it's to bury the girl in some quiet backyard. Beth says you would probably prefer it her way, too. Out on the sands, I mean.'

Beth came into the room and stood behind Jenko. When Michael looked at her she closed her eyes and nodded.

'We'll have to move fast then,' Michael said tapping his forehead with a knuckle. 'The tide is full now so we've – what? – five hours to gather wood and set it up on the sands, which will give it about three hours to burn before it's washed away. I can get the wood and there's plenty of driftwood on the sands, but the question is can you get some kind of coffin within four hours?'

'I'll get something. We'll keep it unadorned and take it down under the wood on the cart. No point advertising anything.'

'Any form of service at all?' Michael asked.

'No,' Beth said. 'I just want the child burned.'

Hearing such words in her mouth was a shock and he wondered if he knew her at all. Even more astonishing was the calm efficiency with which all this was being executed but, if that's the way she wanted it . . .

He rode the cart down to the wood near Crofty and waded into the tangled brambles and ferns, looking for dead branches. He pulled them out with such ferocity that soon there were bloody cuts and gashes all over his hands and arms. It was as if he were trying to extract some primeval revenge on the branches since, if any refused to budge, they were ripped out of the surrounding foliage with a terrifying vigour and broken over his knee like so many necks.

His torn shirt was as one with his skin as he gasped for breath and looked around for the more concealed branches, leaping into the brutish blackberry brambles and tearing out yet another yellowing bald limb. The dead to burn the dead. He was in such a rage he would have torn up a tree by its roots had it dared to stand in his way as he – the maddened bull – continued ripping and pulling at the branches for some two hours, until he had far more dead wood than he could put on the cart.

When he rode back to the village he had mellowed and burned off something very nasty; he almost felt as if he had left something murderous behind him in the wood.

Megan told him that Jenko had already returned and was upstairs with the coffin. Beth was sitting and staring into the fire, hands on lap and as calm as she had been all morning. Her head turned towards Michael. 'You've cut your hands,' she said. 'I'd give them a good wash if I were you.'

'Are you all right?'

She looked back at the fire without replying and Jenko came down the stairs, his shirt sleeves rolled up. 'The job's done,' he announced to no one in particular. 'Does anyone want to have a last look at Rhion before I nail the box up?'

Michael shook his head and Beth remained quite still. 'I'll remember her as she was,' she said.

The staccato crack of the nails being hammered in was the worst sound. The banging seemed to go on forever, echoing down through all the rooms in the tiny cottage, making the floor vibrate and the window panes shake. Beth forced the side of her fist into her mouth and closed her eyes. Megan began crying again. Michael walked out into the yard and held himself. At least it would soon be over. There would be none of the elaborate and protracted rites of a proper funeral. There was that – if precious little else.

That afternoon they followed the ebbing tide as it moved out at walking pace. The grey sky had broken into filamenting cirrus clouds – promising fine weather to come – with the sea breezes whipping flashing shadows across the marsh and the grazing wild horses. A grey foal ran towards them, only to be chased away by its mother.

Michael was leading his own horse on foot, Beth walking next to him and, just behind, Megan, Jenko and Mrs Williams. The cart creaked and tilted, anxious, beneath its vast pile of dead branches as it followed a different route to the rest of the cocklers; a rutted muddy track which would take them down to a shingle bank, just opposite Crofty, where there would be no nosey-parker eyes.

When they reached the bank the white skeletons of tiny white crabs were caught in the odd clumps of grass while the receding tide was draining out of the cockleshells and shingle in many thousands of exploding bubbles, turning them over and over in a long laughing hiss.

The coffin was of a plain white wood, surprising light as Michael took it out from beneath the great awry vulture's nest of piled wood. He put it down on the bank and, sensing that they were all waiting for him to get on with it, made a base of thick branches before placing the coffin on it and piling up the wood on top.

When he had finished building the pyre Jenko took a can of paraffin and slopped it all over the wood. 'Bodies need a lot of burning,' he whispered to Michael. 'We'll be needing some more driftwood.'

'There's a lot trapped in one of those gullies over there.'

They both clambered over the bank, leaving the three women standing motionless next to the pyre – almost in silent disbelief at the drama unfolding all around them – and each returning with a large armful of white, sea-bleached driftwood. Michael had wondered if anyone was going to say anything by way of prayer but no one moved.

Jenko nodded. 'Light it.'

The first match was blown out by the wind but Michael managed to light a paraffin-soaked rag with the second and pushed it under the base of the pyre. The wood ignited immediate, the blast of the heat catching his cheeks with such a force he had to take a few steps backwards. He went down on one knee.

The roaring flames bent and waved in the breeze, making the branches crack and fall over on one another. The heat was intense and screamed with its own internal urgency as the fiery sparks flashed and danced in the air like cavorting demons. There was another groan as the branches collapsed in on themselves and on to the coffin. He put on some more driftwood, thankful that they had taken the precaution of amassing more, since otherwise the coffin might have been exposed before it had been fully burned.

The breeze changed direction and Michael moved around the fire, away from the full squall of the sparks and smoke. Beth did not move, however, and neither did her mother. Both stood arm in arm, with sootied faces, as they watched the furious flames destroy a part of their own blood. Megan could not even look at the fire; Jenko just stood stock still, hat in hands, the waving red of the flames flickering in the blackness of his eyes, as silent and unhappy as the prophet who, after years of repeated and unheeded warnings, was seeing all his prophecies come true.

The fire began to smoke thick and Michael piled on more driftwood before going back down on one knee again. Out of the corner of his eye he saw a hand letting some sand trickle down on the cinders. It was Beth's last tribute to her daughter and, dusting her hands against one another, she turned and walked away. Her head was bowed as she left and the breeze made her cloak billow all around her. He watched her leave as the branches groaned in on themselves again. He had first met her not far from this very spot. Better allow her the privacy of her grief, he decided, and stay here to keep watch on the fire until the tide had turned and washed it away.

'You can all go if you want,' he said. 'I'll stop and keep an eye on the fire.'

'What about Beth?' asked Megan.

'She needs to grieve on her own. She'll come back when she's ready.' He stood up and walked towards Mrs Williams, holding out his hand which she took with both of hers, 'I'm very sorry about all of this,' he said.

'Not nearly as sorry as me. Give her lots of babies, Michael. That's all she wants now.'

'She can have twenty babies if she wants.'

'There was only one she ever wanted,' Jenko said. 'And she's lying in those ashes there. Come on, Mary. We'll walk back. Meg?'

They walked back over the marsh and Michael stayed with the horse. There was no sign of Beth. He gathered up yet more driftwood and built up the fire until the furnacing charcoal was so deep and thick it sent a long column of black smoke rising and curling over the sands. He only left when the tide had come right up to it, the frothing tongue of the sea hissing into the heat, lifting up pieces of dead black wood and making them revolve. Soon the shingle bank would be washed clean and back to normal. Lucky shingle bank.

The cottage was packed with its own emptiness when he returned. He washed up the dishes for something to do. He would accept whatever Beth said, he decided; there would be no quarrel. He finished the dishes, then cleaned out the horse's shed, picking up a wire brush and giving him a brisk grooming. The horse liked that and his muscles vibrated with a nervous contentment as the brush picked up tiny bundles of brown and grey hairs. When he had finished he walked away and the horse came after him, nudging him in the back, wanting to be brushed again. He so much valued the loyalty of animals – it was those humans who kept changing as regular as the tide. Where had she gone? There'll be no quarrel, girl, just come home and say what you're going to do. He stood still in the yard, looking down at the brush in his hand.

'I've got some cabbages for your Beth, I have.'

He did not need to look up to know that it was Vera.

'If you send her around I've got some nice onions for her as well. Where is she?'

'I wish I knew,' he said so soft she could not hear him. 'I just wish I knew.'

He walked back into the cottage and the emptiness of the place washed over him again – all the laughter and love of the last few days shattered in just one night. Tch! If Beth did decide she was going away again then he would also leave this cottage and the area for certain. Not one of his daily dreams this time – hard intention that was. These rooms would be haunted forever by Beth's laughter and Rhion's quiet presence.

Even as he sat there next to the firegrate his mood became so brittle and intense he could actually hear Beth's laughter out in the kitchen. He could actually see Rhion trying to slide out of the room unnoticed when the zinc tub was produced for her bath. There was a bump in the kitchen and he was sure it was the badger stumbling into something. She was always doing that – always moving around the place backwards and not looking where she was going. Oh, come in here, Rhion girl. There's a lot of stories I haven't started to tell you yet. Come here now and sit on my knee. I'll tell the one about the man who loved a woman so much he became a monk after she died. He lived in a cave, he did, and every morning for the rest of his life he woke up shouting out her name.

'You're not filling her up with all those daft stories again, are you?'

'There's nothing daft about my stories. All my stories are true.'

'Absolute rubbish all of them. Why don't you start teaching her to read or do her sums or something useful like that?'

'What for? Waste of time that would be wouldn't it, badger? Fire the imagination first – that's what you've got to do. See? She agrees with me as well.'

'Don't you go listening to him now, badger. You'll end up as daft as he is, you will.'

The goldfish swam around and around. There was another bump out in the kitchen and he walked out to catch one of the cats trying to get into the food cupboard. The cat ran straight out into the yard when she saw him, leaving his hand swiping at the air. Oh Beth, isn't it time you came home now? You've been gone for more than five hours and I'm getting so cold with it all. There'll be no argument. He returned to the living room and sat down again, shivering with cold spells that kept getting colder. There was the distant slamming of a door in the terrace and another burble of voices. He did not heed their words.

'Vera is back out there again with that tortoise egg of hers.'

'Oh aye. What does she want now?'

'She says she doesn't believe you about the sun and sand to hatch it. She says the slugs will dance on it. She says she thinks she should take it to bed with her. Keep it warm and safe under her pillow.'

'Oh go and tell her to take it to bed then. Doesn't matter, does it? Then come back and take me to bed. I'm getting that cold with all this. Can't take any more punishment. I want to be warm and safe too.'

* * *

The dark came and still she had not returned. He decided to go out and search for her, wandering the deserted Pen-clawdd streets and even looking into the tavern – not expecting to find her in there – but looking anyway, perhaps because that was where he had always run when beset by troubles. The heads of the regulars in the tap room turned towards him but nothing was said. There were some polite greetings but he guessed that the story of the fire on the sands had been stretched by many tongues, ending up as some evil rite of crazed witches.

He left the tavern and hurried past the forge. There was the silhouette of Betty Powell undressing behind her bedroom curtains and the sound of his footsteps on the cobbles. He turned and took the road to Loughor, the full moon glaring down on him like a destructive curse. The night was empty of everything but deep foreboding.

Perhaps she had gone to seek Jenko's advice; perhaps she had gone home to her mother; perhaps she had done a lot of things but, whatever it was, the spirit of the night caught hold of him and he broke into a run, leaping a wire fence and scattering a flock of sheep as he cut a few hundred yards off the bend in the road to Loughor.

He ran straight into the Lewis Arms to find Jenko and Megan both as drunk as a pair of butcher's boots. But there was no pleasure in their drinking. Jenko was trying to find his mouth with a cigarette while Megan was sitting with her arm around him, her eyes bloodshot and rheumy through far too many drinks and tears. Their table was covered with empty glasses and, when he sat down, they did not, at first, recognise him.

'Michael. I'll have a pint,' Jenko said final, his body swaying dangerous as he tried to get his cigarette into his mouth again. 'Just one for me and get one for yourself if you like.'

'Beth. Have you seen her at all? Have you seen her?'

'Have I seen her? Why should I have seen her? Have you seen her?'

He left the pub and went down to the square where he turned and turned again before noticing the policeman standing in the glow of the lamplight. 'Do you know Beth Williams?' Michael asked.

'I do.'

'Have you seen her anywhere around? Anywhere around tonight?'

'She's gone to Australia I heard. Went more than a week ago, she did.'

He ran down the hill to Emlyn House and pulled on the bell. Mrs Williams opened the door immediate, almost as if expecting someone. 'I'm worried about Beth,' he said. 'Have you seen her tonight?'

'She hasn't been here, Michael. But come in, will you. There's matters we want to talk about with you.'

'Not now.'

He ran back up the garden path, deciding to return to Pen-clawdd. But he was no longer the runner he used to be and, just near the castle, he had to stop to catch his breath. His body had got quite exhausted with everything over the last day or two and only the conviction that something terrible had gone wrong kept him going at all.

It was while standing with his hand on the iron rail outside the castle that he had a thought which was as likely as it was alarming. Had the girl gone and made a vain escape back to the chapel? Had she seen that infernal place as a way out of it all again? He sprinted across the road and up a lane to see that there was indeed a light on inside Moriah Chapel.

He pushed on the oak front doors, but found them locked. He vaulted over the tombstones along the side of the chapel, shinned up the same drainpipe perched on which he had once witnessed the start of the Revival and looked down at the rows of empty pews inside. It was difficult making out anything with just that one dim, flickering gas light but he did spot a blurred shadow of a figure sitting alone and praying in the front pew. Oh Beth, girl. Not this way again. Any way but this way again.

He dropped back down on to the soft earth of the graveyard and hurried around to the rear vestry, opening the side door and following the short corridor which came out next to the pulpit. The door burst open with a crack and the head of the praying figure jerked upright.

'Beth? It's time to come home, girl. We all need you back home.'

He walked around the front of the dais and reeled as if punched. It was not his Beth at all. It was Evan Roberts kneeling there, hands interlocked prayerful and his hazel eyes gazing up at Michael. His face was full of age and sleep. There was no youth or laughter left in the preacher any longer.

'Looking for Beth Williams are you, my son?' Even the voice had gone old, though there was still a certain dignity in it.

'You know full well I am. So what have you done with her now?' The words of his shrill accusation echoed around the empty chapel like trains over the horizon. 'What mischief have you done to her today?'

'I did mischief to no one. I went among the people and taught them about the ways of God and his angels. There was no mischief in my teaching.'

'Well your time is finished. You and yours. All finished for good.'

'There is much violence in your soul,' Evan said, standing up. 'You come here to a house of God talking of the vitriol and wormwood. But wait. I know you. I have seen you before. Oh yes. You were the one who came causing all the trouble in the meetings.'

'Me!' Michael was all but speechless. 'Me! Me causing all what trouble? You've caused enough trouble in one winter to last anyone ten lifetimes.'

'Yes. I know you now. One of the many agents of the devil sent to destroy the work and very mind of God. I know you all right. My name is disruption and I shall rule the world.'

Michael took a step forward, the fury of his hatred thickening dark in his chest. 'Finished. You and yours finished. Be certain the old order has gone forever. The unions. Socialism. Keir Hardie. They'll bring in the new now – start a new world they will – with real answers.'

'You understand nothing,' said Evan taking a few steps towards him, some of the old authority coming back into his voice. 'The socialists will just bring more greed and strikes, so they will. The unions will achieve nothing. Even now as I speak a great spirit of evil is rising up which will spread a cloak of darkness over the world that will last a century.' He stifled a cough with his hand. 'But the path of the Lord is reconciliation not division. Come here now, my son. Come, kneel and pray with me for the world.'

'Pray with you! Pray with you to a dead God. Oh no. Not me.'

Michael picked up a vase of flowers and hurled it the length of the chapel, spraying the plants over the pews before it shattered into hundreds of pieces against a gallery pillar.

'My name is disruption,' Evan said, quiet, looking back at where the vase had broken and then at Michael again. 'My name is disruption and violence and I will rule the world.'

Michael smacked his fist against a pew. 'That's what I've got to say to you and your dead God. Political surgery from now on – feed the hungry and clothe the poor by milking the rich. That's the socialist way. The Great Surgery is to come now. You and yours are all at an end.'

'No, no, no.' Evan raised an emblematic hand. His voice became harsh and destructive. 'I hear everyone talking of politics and socialism. Everywhere I travel they talk of this heresy as if it was something to do with the unfolding will of God. No. Their love of money is unknown to a holy God. Their talk of the priesthood of men is just a lie to further enslave us in this mystery of iniquity.'

The veins in Evan's cheeks throbbed bold. His eyes were wide and wild with the growing urgency of his words. 'All this foolish talk – all these false prophets are but the first messengers of the coming man of violence. Yes, he's coming now. You see him? I see him now, him and his dark angels all escaping from hell. Know he's coming. Tell the people. Tell them they are going to lose their families. They will be driven from their homes. They will cry out in their desolation because they will not be able to hold their babies in their arms.'

Evan strode down the aisle and mounted the pulpit, raising his arms and letting his hands dangle forward as if his wrists were nailed to the very air. 'I am telling you of this coming cruelty but I don't understand my visions. They have become acid in my brain. This acid . . . you see? My visions tell me that the hour has arrived. The time has come. The Holy Spirit tells me it will grow, and it will grow, and it will grow and it will grow. Millions will be stricken down by this man of violence who will bestride the world like a Colossus. He will arise on this coast and on yonder coast. He will arise in the north and arise in the south. Even the very elect of God will bend at his feet. He will come with all the powerful signs and miracles of the lie. It will be like a flood. And oh, my people, my poor tortured people . . . Weep now for your children and your children's children since the spirit of lawlessness will engulf the world.

'Oh my poor lost and fallen people . . . ' His mind was still boiling furious, his trembling hands now covering his face – unaware that Michael had long since left the chapel and was now running hard along the marsh road back to Pen-clawdd.

A carpet of slow-moving sea fog rolled in over his feet as he trotted down the road past the old oak tree where the owl hooted emptily into the moon-varnished night. He was very tired now, his running awkward, his mind dissolving under the strain of things. He stumbled and fell, something ripping inside his ankle and bursting into pain as he rolled over in the fog. He managed to stand up and hobble back to his cottage where, swollen ankle or not, the silence and desertion of the place again hit him with the force of a sand-filled sock.

He searched the bedrooms, calling out her name, before limping down into the yard and looking out over the estuary. A single black cloud moved across the glowering face of the full moon. His dementia was as big and full as the very night.

<blockquote>Beth!</blockquote>

<blockquote>Beth!</blockquote>

<blockquote>Beth!</blockquote>

<blockquote>Beth!</blockquote>

<blockquote>Beth!</blockquote>

It was while standing in the yard that a spear of intuition ripped deep down inside him, savage. The sands! She had once said: *If there's anywhere I'd really like to die it must be the sands. They must be the most beautiful and dangerous place in the world.*

Where else had she gone but back out on the sands to be with her baby?

He moved towards the horse's shed, stumbling forward on his swollen ankle. He stood up and fell again. The tide was turning now and he had to get out there fast. He all but pulled the horse's head off as he yanked him out of his slumbers. The horse yawned and tried to reverse deeper into the shed so Michael bit him on the neck. The horse whinnied, angry and tried to bite him back but, at least he was awake now and, just to make sure, Michael bit him again.

The second bite made him furious with aggression and, once through the yard gate, Michael wrapped both his hands in his mane, flung himself on and heeled him in the flanks hard. He broke into a gallop and, when he did slow down, with his head turning from side to side looking for a foot to bite, he was heeled hard again.

He galloped down the twisting slopes of the village of Crofty, past the inn and Mafeking House and out on to the marsh, taking the first pill so fast Michael had difficulty staying on. The horse jumped one of the gullies and all was sudden and disturbed movement since they were travelling through a large pack of resting wild horses. The night rumbled soft with effronted snorts as they jerked themselves up and began running away together, their hooves thundering quiet.

Michael heeled the horse again and soon they were following that path down to the shingle bank where the funeral pyre had flamed that morning.

The outlying tongues of the incoming tide had just reached the bank when he jumped off the horse, hopping down into the water, cupping his hands to his lips and calling out her name frantic.

Beth!

Beth!

Beth!

Beth!

He moved further out and the silent foaming tide was swirling around his legs and waist. There was a movement near by, but it was only his horse gone to stand in the sea to cool off after the long gallop. He waded deeper into the sea. With his ankle gone he was in danger of being caught by the marauding currents unless he left immediate. But he hardly cared as he called out her name again and again. There was a distant cry of a cormorant and the glow of the moon was ferocious.

Then he saw a large black bubble moving around in the water about ten feet away from him.

The tide was carrying it to him as, choking for breath, he half-swam and half-limped to meet it. He lifted it up and the sound of the water running off it was very loud. It was her cloak.

Even louder than the sound of the water running off the cloak was the sound of the night breeze hurrying in over the estuary. Even louder than the sound of the hurrying breeze was the savage weeping of his breaking heart.

He let the cloak fall back into the water. Beth. Oh Beth girl what have you gone and done?

The final thread had parted now. The night was untwining and full with the promise of a coming storm. Already huge ugly black clouds were piling up over the land in a Himalayan range of evil which only forked lightning would disperse. That which was once loved deep was lost forever. The die had been cast and the sand had finally trickled out of the hand. The shadow of all that was hateful was striding across the sea. The dark days of cold love and shrieking pain had begun.

Oh Beth, girl, just what have you gone and done?

Footnotes:

- Of the thirteen rugby championship titles of the Edwardian era Wales took six and tied one. Only Wales managed to beat the New Zealand All Blacks rugby side on their tour in 1905.

- W.T. Stead, the father of modern muck-raking journalism, died on the *SS Titanic* when it sank on its maiden voyage after colliding with an iceberg on 15 April, 1912.

- Keir Hardie, the member for the unemployed and founder of the Labour Party, represented Merthyr from 1900 until his death of pneumonia on 26 September, 1915. An unswerving apostle of world peace it was believed his spirit was broken by the juggernaut of world war. The first Labour Government was formed by his colleague Ramsay McDonald in 1924.

- At the end of the Revival the chapel was posted missing, presumed dead. Evan Roberts went into seclusion for the rest of his life, first staying in Leicester then, in 1932, moving to Cardiff where, a lone and solitary figure, he lived on charity until his death on 29 January, 1951, aged seventy-two. He was buried in Moriah Chapel, Loughor, where a granite monument was erected to him in 1953. The carving shows him at the age of twenty-six.